CW01625090

Forever Springtime

Wing Chun Legacy

Lori A. Levesque

ISBN: 0615684815

ISBN-13: 978-0615684819

DEDICATION

To Susan and Marty who have unconditionally stood by me for so many years while I weathered life's storms. And to Jeff, whose support and love has filled my once empty heart. Thank you all for your absolute friendship, heartfelt advice, therapeutic laughter, and so much more.

CHARACTERS

Kay Chen Smith	Teenage descendent of Wing Chun Legacy
Ng Mui Si Tai	Buddhist nun, founder of Wing Chun
Yim Wing Chun	First female of Wing Chun Legacy
Kai Chen Boussard	Chinese/French American descendant of Wing Chun Legacy
Vaden LeBlanc	French American Shipping Magnate
Ji-Kin Lau	Manchu warrior in Triad Secret Society
Prince Tuan	Nephew to Empress Dowager/Head of Triad Secret Society
Sebastian Madden	Vaden LeBlanc's best friend/Shipping Competitor
Caroline Pennington	Socialite
Tzu Hsi	Empress Dowager of China
Fung Do Duk	Triad Elder/Buddhist monk
Bak Mei	Triad Elder/Buddhist monk
Jee Sin	Triad Elder/Buddhist monk
Miu Hin	Triad Elder/Buddhist layman
Yim Yee	Father to Yim Wing Chun
Jianjun Lei	Gang member/bully
Fong-la	Laundry shop owner in America
Suzette Boussard-Minot	Aunt to Kai Chen/Sister to David Boussard
David & Ying Boussard	Parents to Kai Chen Boussard

PROLOGUE

"If ignorant both of your enemy and yourself, you are certain to be in peril."
— Sun Tzu, *The Art of War*

August, 2005
White Plains, New York

"I don't want to do this anymore! You can't make me," the seventeen year old teenager yelled vehemently at her mother.

Kay Chen Smith recklessly threw the razor-edged star clutched between her fingers across the room. Although the deadly weapon sped with amazing speed toward her mother, Liu Chen, she adeptly moved to her right a fraction as the object sailed passed her to embed into the rattan backing hanging on the wall. Glaring at her mother, Kay Chen watched as a finely arched dark eyebrow lifted to silently imply her disdain of her daughter's action. Her mother's angled oriental green eyes reflected the disappointment not voiced. Without a word Liu Chen nodded once and left the training hall, her regal countenance expressing obvious contempt.

A sob emanated from the hormone laden young girl who flung herself onto the polished wooden floor in frustration. She wanted to be normal. She yearned to hang out with her friends from school, to hold a part time job, to go to movies and on dates with cute boys, and to eat at McDonald's at least once a year! She wanted to enjoy her youth before it was gone and she had no memories…other than this all-consuming family obligation.

"Why must I do this? Why can't I have a life like the rest of my friends? I hate my life! I hate this family and their damned traditions!"

Her furious screams echoed throughout the Dein, or training hall, that was filled with various weapons and martial arts paraphernalia. Despair, anger, frustration, and some nameless sense of urgency consumed her. She did not understand why her entire life had revolved around her family of women being the keepers of this ridiculous martial art. So many people did martial arts these days. They competed in tournaments and exploited it in movies. They even went to the Olympics! There was no special significance to it all anymore. Why did she have to carry this supposed secret of Wing Chun? Although it was not a popular martial art in America it was still prevalent in Asia. Besides, why couldn't her two other sisters who were younger and more dedicated carry the tradition? They loved the daily training for hours. She hated it!

She glared at her reflected image in the mirrors covering one entire wall. Most people told her she was quite exotic and beautiful with her long dark brown hair hanging to her waist like a curtain, the subtle red highlights glowing as though on fire when the sun touched it. She stuck her tongue out at her reflection, hating the subtle oriental appearance to her eyes. There was not a blemish on her pale, almost alabaster white skin. Almond shaped large green eyes surrounded by indecently long, thick lashes reflected the frustration and anger within her mind and heart. Full, pouty red lips hid straight while teeth, thanks to the two years of braces her parents had forced upon her.

Bottled up fury suddenly exploded throughout her and she swiftly side-kicked at her reflection, her foot mere millimeters from the large sheet of glass on the wall. She controlled the kick and held it in place for several seconds before smacking the glass lightly with the ball of her foot as she bellowed out another yell of anger. When she kicked her foot was almost above the top of the mounted mirrors.

Kay Chen spun around with incredible speed and glared at her image with hatred. At almost five foot ten Kay was taller than most girls in school, a fact she hated. The one thing she did take pride in was her athletic, powerful, and conditioned body from years of physical training. Kay Chen did not worry about gaining weight or diets or other such typical teenage girl nonsense. Her martial arts training kept her as fit as an Olympic athlete and flexible as a cat. She stared at her extremely toned arms and legs, broad shoulders, and abdominal muscles a gym workout could never reproduce, and wondered how others viewed her physique. Maybe they considered her body boyishly athletic, or thought she was a lesbian? Ha! The thought almost made her smile for a moment. Unfortunately, she did not smile often enough. She hated being Kay Chen Smith. She wanted to be anyone but herself right now.

In the reflection of the mirror the shiny metal star she had so recklessly thrown near her mother's face glinted as though taunting her to do it again. Swiping at tears still on her face, Kay Chen walked over to the wooden wall covered with rattan backing. The rattan protected the wooden wall behind from the many martial arts instruments in the training hall which was located across the garden from the main house. She glared at the offensive star, her green eyes so much like her mother's as they continued to spill tears.

What was she thinking? She could have truly hurt her mother who had been nothing but good and kind to her throughout her life. What the hell was wrong with her? She knew this anger and frustration was stemming from her own desires but never had she done anything so heinous toward any of her family or anyone else. Watching the disappointment in her mother's green eyes hurt her more than any words she could have spoken. Her silence as she had walked away was worse than any punishment.

"Damn!" She yanked the star from the wall as a large section of rattan fell on top of her. Flinging the scratchy item off of herself with a frustrated yell she glanced up and gasped in surprise. Built into the wall where the rattan section had covered it was a cupboard with finely decorated doors. Ornate carvings of a snake and crane in battle were meticulously etched on each door with inlaid ivory forming each animal. Her shaking fingers reached out to trace the beautifully polished wooden and ivory carvings.

"What the-," her voice broke as she lightly tugged at one of the door handles. In the twelve years she had been training in their family Dein she had never known about this cupboard!

The door opened with no resistance as she felt a sudden rush of shame fill her mind and heart. As an honor student she had studied biology and chemistry. She understood the make up of her hormones that presently raged as a teenager. That, however, could not be blamed for her actions today. There was no excuse for her loss of self-control in thoughtlessly throwing a razor-edged metal star at her mother. Inside her a war raged for independence, the right to make her own choices, and the assertion of her own will. Yet, the dishonor she felt at her actions toward her patient and kind mother made her consider turning around to go apologize. As she turned slightly to do that very thing an image in the shadows of the cupboard caught her attention. In one corner was a small leather bound book. It was the only item in the large space, almost invisible in the shadows.

Her breath caught in her throat as she reached out to pick up the book. The leather was soft, worn and buttery to the touch from years of handling. The pages were yellowed and appeared very fragile and old. Chinese characters called logograms filled each page. As she carefully turned the pages without actually reading, she could see the changes, the differences in the logograms from different writers. Curiosity overcame her as she moved to a corner of the enormous room to sit down. Sliding her back against the wall she folded her legs beneath her and opened the cover.

"Wing Chun Legacy," she read aloud, recognizing the Chinese symbols then snorted with derision. She had no interest in the ancestral legacy of Wing Chun. Rubbing at the now drying tears on her cheeks, she sniffed.

"Stupid," she declared, but she wasn't sure if she meant the situation, the book or herself was stupid. Right now all three seemed pretty plausible. Kay Chen raised her arm to throw the book across the room as her anger surged again, but something infinitesimal stopped her. Bringing the book to rest upon her thighs she took a deep breath and sighed, releasing her resentment.

"Work smarter, not harder," her mother always said with a serene smile.

Maybe there was something in this book to show evidence to her mother that the legacy of their family no longer need continue? Perhaps this book held the answer to her current dilemma? Eager to find a way to relinquish the hold that Wing Chun seemed to have on her destiny she clenched her straight white teeth. Determined to change her current fate and the outcome of the women in their future lineage by using what she discovered in this book she turned the first delicate, weathered page and read…

Part I

Birth of Wing Chun

CHAPTER ONE

It is only one who is thoroughly acquainted with the evils of war that can thoroughly understand the profitable way of carrying it on.
-Sun Tzu, *The Art of War*

January 12, 1644
Forbidden City, China
Ming Dynasty

"My daughter, my blood, you make your father proud." The blowing wind and snow swept his words away like petals in the breeze on a beautiful spring day, but his words were loud enough for Ng Mui Si Tai to hear. Ice broke under the wheels of the carriage as it quickly transported the girl from the lavish Forbidden City, home to the Chinese Emperor.

The Ming general nodded in satisfaction as the carriage took his only child, Ng Mui, to the Sil Lum (Shaolin) temple noted for its religious and military arts scholars. His wife stood by his side, refusing to leave him or the Forbidden City even though she knew they both very well may die in the upcoming months. To send Ng Mui away was the right decision for many reasons. Many Ming generals and prominent Chinese families sent their sons to study rigorous military arts training from the warrior monks of the temple. Daughters sometimes attended the temple, but General Fai Chang Tai had it from authority of a Buddhist monk with mystical vision that his daughter was destined for greatness in this life and would somehow have influence over China's fate one day. And so he sent his only child to the Shaolin temple in Hunan Province to not only be protected from inevitable war, but to allow the monks and nuns of the temple to train his daughter in politics, warfare, increased martial arts training, and court decorum, which would prepare her for the emperor's government once the Chinese ruled again.

"Ng Mui". His wife's broken cry for their daughter tore at his heart. Placing his arm around her shoulders for comfort he helped escort her back inside the long hallway to their private quarters near the emperor within the Forbidden City.

The rebels, led by ex-soldier Li Zicheng, would soon overtake the Great Wall and overthrow Emperor Chongzhu. Beijing would fall and the Ming Dynasty would begin to collapse. General Fai Chang Tai's warning from the mysterious monk of the impending, predictable disaster did not seem conceivable, but he would not risk his only daughter's life when the monk proclaimed her future importance to China. Ng Mui, although quiet and humble, maintained a sharp mind, watchful gaze, and athletic prowess many men could not claim. Surely, Buddha honored him and his wife with such a daughter! What import she would make upon this changing country the general could not understand but he would do as the desperate monk had implored.

It would be the last time he ever saw his beloved daughter.

May 26, 1644
Forbidden City, China
New Qing Dynasty

"Quickly, we must leave," the general urged his wife during the advanced siege. He tightly held her hand as they ran through the once immaculate Forbidden City, walled cities within walled cities to protect the emperor. Many of the levels within each other now lay in ruin covered with rivers of blood, reeking of death from the bodies scattered about the citadel. Priceless art was destroyed. The emperor could not be found during the melee. Genera Fai Chang Tai now realized the implications of the monks foretelling. Ending was Emperor Chongzen's rule and the Ming Dynasty.

They ran across one area of the beautiful gardens with flowering trees and bushes, manicured lawns, and innately carved statures. Delicate lily pads in ponds with bright orange and white koi fish swimming seemed odd to the general as he noted the panic within the Forbidden City, yet there was serene calm within the clear water where the fish resided. His wife screamed as she stopped running, causing him to pause and turn her direction. The dead emperor's body swayed to and fro from a nearby tree, his eyes protruding from their sockets with his tongue thick and black in his mouth. His regal attire remained intact for all to note the Chinese ruler was slain. The general's finest warriors had not protected Emperor Chongzen.

"Ng Mui!"

"Ng Mui is safe within the Sil Lum temple. We are not safe," the general barked, pulling her faster as they ran across the garden to the next level within the citadel in their attempt to escape the Forbidden City. Suddenly, they were surrounded by Manchu soldiers. The general had no time to react even though he held his sword. As though in slow motion the gleam of a sword whizzed by his face. He felt the slight breeze from the tip of the blade as it actually sliced some of the coarse black hairs from his cheek. Glancing to his right he watched in agony and horror as his wife turned to look at him, mouth open as her head toppled to the ground and rolled to his boot. Blood spurted from her body as it fell limply to the ground. He knew her mind recognized the fact of her fate, her death, before the light of life left her beseeching eyes.

The general stared into the now blank and glazed eyes of his wife as he waited his death, for nothing mattered now. His beloved wife was dead. The inevitability of the moment remained, but relief filled him for he had done as the monk and fate had decreed. Ng Mui was safe within the haven of the Hunan Shaolin temple. Her destiny for their country was just beginning, even as his ended. Keeping his gaze transfixed on his wife's face he almost smiled.

Ng Mui has her mother's eyes, he thought with satisfaction. Then he felt it. For a moment it felt like the sting of a bee as the blade sliced through his neck as easy as butter. There was no real pain after the initial slice of the blade as his senses dulled, but he could no longer draw breath. Even as he felt his body shudder for a split second, his mind still could perceive he had been beheaded. He saw the ground rushing up to meet his wide open gaze as his head toppled from his body, and then there was nothing.

Rebellions lead by groups in the provinces arose and destroyed the Chinese administration. As predicted, Li Zicheng led the insurgent army causing the fall of Beijing. The Ming emperor was found hanging on a tree within the Forbidden City in the imperial garden with his general not far away. Upon word of his death the Manchu crossed the Great Wall, killing Li Zicheng now that he was of no use, and marking end of the Ming Dynasty. The Manchu Qing Dynasty would now rule.

1645
Fukien Province
Southern Sil Lum Temple

Ng Mui heard of the fall of the Forbidden City. China was now under Manchurian rule. Their country would be forever blemished and tainted with an evil it could not survive if the Manchu remained in power. Word of her parent's death came as no surprise. When her father sent her to the Sil Lum in Hunan Province she instinctively knew he was protecting her due to uprising of the Ching. The new Kangxi Emperor held power now within this new Qing Dynasty.

"One day," she predicted with a whispered breath to her dead parents as the group of students followed Buddhist monks and nuns through the rough terrain to the Sil Lum located in Fukien Province. It would be their new home hidden away from Manchu rule, for now.

"Yes, one day," a bitter voice ground out next to her, just loud enough for her ears only, as they marched along the mountain side.

Ng Mui turned to gaze at the man several years older than she who trudged along the new worn path the three hundred students and disciples were making. Fung Do Duk appeared to be a reasonable man with varied talents in the martial arts. Practicing with him in the Dein had been quite enlightening and painful. She enjoyed their sparring time together immensely as they were equally matched in physical skill and mental ability.

"I am sorry to hear of your parent's death. It would appear most of our families were killed during the siege," Fung Do Duk stated sadly , and then sighed heavily. "I have yet to consider my path now this new emperor is in rule. What good will military training do if we are lowly Chinese? We will never be allowed into the Manchu rule as soldiers or officials. Even you will be shunned as a Chinese woman. Not even fit to be concubine."

"I do not worry over such things. Change happens constantly. It is inevitable. We watch and we wait. We will know what our purpose is when the time is right." Ng Mui stated simply and adjusted the bag of meager belongings she carried over one shoulder as they continued their trek up the mountainside.

Fung Do Duk contemplated her words as they wearily trudged across the mountains until dark. Ng Mui was pretty enough for a girl and she did not talk much as most girls were apt to do. No, there was something intensely different about her that kept him alert. Her razor-sharp mind with a keenness for critical thinking gave him and other students much reflection. Although not very tall her body was more powerful, fast and agile than most male fighters he knew. Fung Do Duk knew the gift of wisdom was not bestowed upon many in life but it was clear Ng Mui had received many blessings. He could sense she was on the threshold of enlightenment this lifetime. *How profound*, he considered before reflecting on his own path to enlightenment as was the path of Buddhism.

It took five days, sunrise to sunset, to reach the Shaolin temple in Fukien Province. It was significantly larger than the Hunan temple. This elaborate temple housed over three thousand disciples. As a monk or nun it offered slightly more protection against the Manchu than being a simple student at the temple. Students were known to come from wealthy Chinese families and the Manchu wanted the extinction of any previous high officials, especially their children. The seclusion and secrecy of this temple was of grave importance to the future of the Ming Dynasty.

Upon arrival at the temple the Elderly Abbot addressed them with a serious tone, "Each student must decide whether or not to become a layman monk or laywoman nun. This consists of taking the five layman or laywoman's vows mandated to all disciples. Those vows include no stealing, killing, lying, sexual misconduct, or intoxication. To become a full monk or nun you will take three hundred sixty-four vows and shave your head. You must give up all worldly possessions. You will don the various colored robes denoting your station and level as Buddhist monk or nun. As layman or laywoman monks and nuns your heads remained unshaven.

"You will be taught, according to the wisdom of Buddha, to make your robes of "pure" cloth, which means cloth that no one wants. The types of "pure" cloth include that which had been chewed by rats or oxen, scorched by fire, soiled by childbirth or menstrual blood, or used as a shroud to wrap the dead before cremation. You will scavenge cloth from far away rubbish heaps and cremation grounds. If a part of the cloth is unusable it is to be trimmed away, and then the cloth to be used is washed. It is dyed by being boiled with vegetable pieces such as tubers, bark, flowers, leaves and spices like turmeric or saffron, which gave the cloth a yellow-orange color. These orange robes are considered your ceremonial and meditation robes. For daily toil and martial arts practice you will fashion a split skirt with robed jacket that is bound around the waist with cloth."

For the next several days the new laymen monks and laywomen nuns foraged for material to make their robes. It was a long and arduous process, but necessary for their spiritual journey in this chosen religious path. Once the ceremony was completed they began further training in their originally chosen path from the previous temple, whether it be martial arts, warfare strategy, government politics or whatever their personal calling.

Ng Mui, although quite a solitary figure in that she kept to herself, was befriended by Fong Do Duk and three other monks over the next year. Within the temple most of the monks and nuns trained in various forms of martial arts and use of weaponry. Even with thousands of disciples training in physical combat, Ng Mui stood out with her sharp sense of timing, intuitive ability to predict her opponent's next move, and her lightning fast blocks and strikes. The four monks who sought out Ng Mui were also outstanding in martial art ability and honed in on the one woman who gave them unique singular competition.

"What does the laywoman, Ng Mui, do in the mountains each day? She is stealthy and secretive," Bak Mei stated to his three other laymen brothers one day as they walked to the Dein for afternoon weapons training.

"I did not know of this, Bak Mei. Perhaps we should follow and discover what she hides?" Jee Sin considered aloud, his warrior mind already considering multiple strategies and outcomes. They paused, knowing the chastising and perhaps even punishment they would receive from the Elder monks if caught away from their practice.

"A laywoman nun should not be away from the temple unless on a mission," Miu Hin considered thoughtfully then shrugged as though it was of no consequence.

"Let us consider this path we contemplate more carefully, brothers," Fung Do Duk cautioned. "The Elders may be sending her off for meditation or other duties."

"Why send her off when those tasks can be accomplished within the temple area?" Bak Mei barked scornfully. "She is a simple nun of no consequence!"

Fung Do Duk laughed outright. "Ng Mui is of consequence, my brothers, and there is nothing simple about her."

"Then let us see what our sister begets, shall we?" Bak Mei challenged. The four layman monks moved swiftly from the Shaolin temple compound to find Ng Mui somewhere in the surrounding mountains. Over the next year they unsuccessfully attempted to follow her and to their frustration they could not discover where she went to each day, but it was obvious from her evolving fighting abilities that she was receiving private training from someone unknown to the temple.

"Ng Mui's stance is like a piece of bamboo, firm but flexible, rooted but yielding. It is a softness that I sense, more powerful than the tension and force we employ," Jee Sin observed aloud, carefully considering her actions as she easily defeated Bak Mei while sparring in the Dein.

The monks observed Bak Mei, the oldest of their group. He was of average height and looks, but very muscular and strong. His Leopard Kung Fu style was fast, deadly and ferocious, but he sometimes lacked finesse. Bak Mei was known as a lantern fire lighter with his ability to whip his legs and back joints to propel his body to twice his own height. He would do this incredible feat to light the Sil Lum temples high lantern fires on the walls. Bak Mei trusted that his singular skill would lead him to victory rather than forethought in strategy. It was this deficit he understood about himself, but did nothing to try to correct. Due to his upbringing of wealth and status of son to a member of the emperor's council it did not surprise the others at his arrogance.

It was Fung Do Duk, a tall, lanky young man with a closed expression most of the time as though deep in thought, who was the unspoken Elder leader. Jee Sin recognized that Fung Do Duk was quite proficient in the Dragon and Tiger fighting styles of Kung Fu from years spent training with his military father prior to the Shaolin temple. He was known for his powerful punching and firm stances, and Fung Do Duk was fearless and very aggressive. The use of his palm strikes and finger claws labeled him ferocious. Right now, Fung Do Duk considered Jee Sin's words.

"Yes, it would appear that Bak Mei is fatigued and Ng Mui is quite comfortable, even after several hours of training. Interesting," Fung Do Duk surmised as he watched Miu Hin approach the tiny nun to train.

Fung Do Duk and Jee Sin vigilantly watched Ng Mui.

"Ah! See how her limbs are drawn in to protect the central area of her body and also to maintain balance? Her hands do not move beyond the vertical circle of her center. See how she swings her arms in front with the hands crossed at the wrists? To reach outside this area, her footwork is used," Fung Do Duk stated with excitement and a sense of awe.

Both men studied Miu Hin who was over average height and build, but he was considered by all of the nuns the most handsome of the monks. His dark almond shaped eyes, straight white teeth and almost sinfully long eyelashes belied his temperamental tantrums at time. His lack of self-control was his cross to bear. His fighting style paralleled Bak Mei with Dragon and Tiger, although renowned for his boxing technique. It was his inner chi, so strong and potent, which allowed him to be one of the fiercest fighters amongst the disciples at Fukien Shaolin temple. The evidence of Miu Hin's frustration at struggling with the small nun at the moment showed in his flushed face and more powerful exertions.

"Yes, and notice her vertical straight punch. She will progress with that punch in rapid succession unless the first strike is ineffective. She then uses that time to reconsider her or her opponent's next move. Her range remains close for trapping where she then defeats the other fighter," Jee Shin noticed with obvious admiration at her battle strategy as Miu Hin was felled easily. "I wish to know more of this style she is implementing."

"As do I, brother." Fung Do Duk announced with avid interest. Turning to Jee Shin, he noted the man's rapt attention on Ng Mui, even as he studied his brother.

Fung Do Duk noted that Jee Shin sported a short and slender body. He was lithe and exceptionally fast with his hands. Although not considered attractive at all due to his protruding front teeth and a pock marked face from acne, of the five friends he was the most likeable and friendly. The good natured Jee Shin was always able to bring a smile or laugh to someone. His flair for using long fist techniques during fighting taught the other four friends to beware his hands during combat. He was known for battle strategy, in reading his opponents body language and facial expressions to anticipate movements, which gave him a unique edge in fighting. Although not from an exceptionally wealthy or important family, his father had been a favored merchant amongst the emperor. Many referred to Jee Sin as the 'Zen Master' and he was considered a powerful Shaolin monk warrior.

Fung Do Duk, the eldest in learning rank, recalled the day he suggested the five of them train diligently together but he was now unprepared for Ng Mui's evolving abilities and knowledge. This could either bring about discord amongst them or unite them with a greater purpose. The prudent path is to ensure the latter occurred if the Chinese were to overthrow the Manchu some day.

That evening with prayer to Buddha finished the five friends walked together in the gardens of the Shaolin temple.

"Ng Mui. We wish to know how you have acquired such evolving martial art skill. Will you share your knowledge with your brothers?" Fung Do Duk requested.

Ng Mui studied each man's face carefully, gauging their intent and how her admission may affect the future outcome of this temple and the disciples within. Sweeping an arm in the direction of one of the many separate temple gardens they proceeded to follow her.

"I wondered when you would ask." Ng Mui laughed softly, a rare sound from the reserved girl who had not yet reached her seventeenth year in this life.

Crossing a wooden bridge over an immaculately tended stream with lily pads and bright koi fish, the group settled in the temple garden and sat lotus style upon the soft green grass. A soft wind swept across the area, sending the heady scent of lavender from the nearby flowers and trees. Water from a fountain several yards away splashed quietly in the oncoming evening as the sun burned bright red to the west. Patiently, the men waited for the young girl to reflect upon what she would tell them.

"One day I walked into the mountains for meditation as requested by the Abbess of this temple," Ng Mui spoke clearly then dropped to a whisper. "On one occasion I encountered a battle between a snake and white crane along a stream. Their movements were profound, inspiring, but more so the strategy they employed. It gave me pause to consider many things. The snake, though possessing no limbs, was able to skillfully defend itself. The snake lured the crane into initiating the first move by coiling up its body while constantly moving its head. It was curious that the snake remained poised for the most opportune time to swiftly attack.

"The crane used the opposite tactic. Its frantic movements were to distract the snake while also waiting for the perfect moment to commence an attack. The crane jumped up and down and side-to-side to avoid the snake. Thus, it tried to bait the snake into initiating the first attack. Smacking the advancing snake aside with its wings the crane followed by attacking with its beak. It tried to lure the snake further within the range of its beak by dancing back. If the snake took the bait the crane would instantly lash out with one of its talons and then follow up with its beak. It was the one leg balance of the crane that held my fascination during this attack. That sense of balance fascinated me." Ng Mui paused thoughtfully as the men waited in eager anticipation for her to continue.

"This battle displayed unique strategy and technique. It was through the snake and white crane battle that Buddha spoke to me, telling me to apply strategy and techniques of the crane and snake into human combat. It is not simply the use of the specific motions of the two animals, although important and applicable, but rather the strategies I observed during the encounter. I have spent the past year working to de-emphasize size and strength, and instead use this snake-crane strategic superiority to defeat an opponent."

Jee Sin broke the pregnant silence by asking, "Who eventually won the fight, sister, the snake or the crane?"

"The snake won but was badly injured. I am certain within days the snake had also died from the crane's beak strikes," Ng Mui stated with a knowing smile.

The monks listened keenly as she told her tale, leaving them speechless for many minutes before Fung Do Duk spoke in revered tones, "Sister, it is truly Buddha's will that you have attained this enlightenment. We would be honored to be your students of the white crane-snake style."

The three other monks pressed their palms together with Fung Do Duk and bowed toward Ng Mui, who returned the respectful gesture. These five warriors would spend the next ten years in the Dein and become known as the Five Elders of Sil Lum, where major animal fighting arts were taught in the great fighting hall. Although Ng Mui studied different martial art styles, such as the Mui Fa Pai, or Dragon-Tiger system, it was her White Crane-Snake fighting system that grew with increasing popularity. She trained her brothers in the crane-snake art, but withheld deadly vital information and the true essence of the martial art, which she practiced meticulously on her own. In the end, they combined many elements of their different fighting animal styles to create the Five-Pattern Hung Kuen.

Alone, Ng Mui utilized the Muk Yang-Chong, or wooden dummy, to perfect the most deadly of techniques in harmony with the spiritual aspect of movement. She invented the Plum Flower Posts, three inch wooden posts driven into the ground at various heights to train balance and develop leg strength like the White Crane. She allowed the softness of the snake to be her guide in movement. It may be her destiny to assist her brothers and sisters of the temple in fighting skills to overthrow the Manchu regime when the time was right, but Buddha had also spoken to her during her vision regarding the sanctity for many elements of this art to be held in secrecy for only those pure of heart and worthy of such responsibility of knowledge.

During this time Ng Mui became a full nun, invoking over three hundred sixty-five vows and shaving her head bald. Now over twenty-five years old and in the peak of her physical ability, she and the other monks and nuns began to train large numbers of Ming loyalists to fight and use weaponry. They prepared for the uprising of the Chinese against Manchu rule. However, time was short and they did not have another ten years to develop the complete skills of their martial arts into so many loyalists.

Their combined arts were shortened and simplified to assist different body types, learning aptitude, and physical ability. Jee Sin's recognition of Zen battle strategy allowed maximum number of loyalists to be well-trained in a shorter amount of time. They wanted to return China to its previous freedom and prosperity. It would soon be time to overthrow the Qing and restore the Ming! The Qing suppressed those Chinese who practiced martial arts and weapon practice. Although the Qing guards had yet to discover their intent or location, Ng Mui intuitively discerned it simply a matter of time for there were always those ready to speak for the right price, or to believe they were saving their own life.

1673
Fukien Shaolin Temple
Qing Dynasty

"Find the nun, Ng Mui Si Tai, and bring her head to me!"

The Manchu general admired the beautifully tended front gardens of the Fukien Shaolin temple as his thousands of Imperial soldiers broke the peaceful serenity that surrounded the area. Their powerful mounts crushed delicate, rare flowers and saplings. The soldiers intentionally destroyed priceless statues and artifacts as the Ming loyalists, monks and nuns fought not only for their Chinese freedom, but for their lives. Over twenty thousand soldiers surrounded the once tranquil temple in order to achieve a goal, the death of one dangerous Buddhist nun. The Manchu general prepared for the daunting task of defeating the three thousand monks and nun, together with their trained loyalists, by employing his entire army to kill them.

The feats of the Five Elders of the Fukien Shaolin temple had spread throughout China and fueled the fire of rage inside the current Kangxi Emperor, but especially the tales of the Abbess Ng Mui Si Tai. Countless words of her magical martial arts ability filled the Forbidden City on a daily basis, as did controversy over the Shaolin temple disciples training Ming loyalists for an uprising against the Manchu. Fury over this insult by lowly Chinese peasants prompted the Kangxi Emperor to call his Imperial Guard to destroy all Buddhist temples and their disciples.

"I fear the devastation that will occur this day," the captain stated nervously to his general. "In the past monks and nuns were used for battle to destroy opposing forces. Who would believe that once over one hundred monks and nuns could defeat three thousand soldiers? And now, because one nun's ability to stir an uprising against the Kangxi Emperor-,"

The General's sharp bark of laughter cut him off. "You are quite mistaken, Captain. She knows more than you will ever understand. Religion and politics have always walked hand in hand. Unfortunately for this particular nun she has chosen the wrong path guided by her Buddha. Her head on a post should remind the Chinese that Manchu rule. The fall of many great Empire's have been due to women. It will not be the case this reign."

Both men gazed toward the temple. The bright orange robes of the monks and nuns stood out strikingly against the dark colors of the Manchu uniforms as battle ensued. Although his twenty thousand troops were winning, his admiration of the monks and nuns fighting abilities could not be suppressed. One monk or nun could easily fight five armed soldiers at once. The sharp cries of agony precluding death echoed throughout the once serene valley. Manchu soldiers were felled easily but the nuns and monks could not sustain this exhausting encounter for much longer. Many hours passed as they watched over half their Manchu army fall to the uncanny disciples of the temple. Yet in the end, the temple fell.

"Report!" the Captain's yell brought forward twelve Manchu soldiers.

"The temple and all inhabitants, but five, are destroyed."

"Five?"

"Four monks and the nun, Ng Mui, are gone," another admitted uneasily. He backed up his mount as fury passed over the General's face. "The Five Elders have safely escaped."

"I shall not rest until they are dead!" A deep roar of frustration from the General echoed throughout the area before he spun his horse around and sped away.

The Five Elders, cloaked in brown and carefully hidden nearby silently slipped away into the mountain side terrain. Word traveled quickly regarding the devastation of thousands of monasteries in various provinces. All suspected religious sanctuaries and their inhabitants within Manchu rule were destroyed. For nearly a year and a half the Five Elders trekked to the western mountains of China. Traveling independently, they disguised themselves as Taoist priests and a nun. The Buddhists were being slaughtered throughout China by the Kangxi Emperor in order to ensure the death of the Five Elders. Disguised as Taoists they were still free to enjoy religious immunity and rarely were questioned by Ching troops.

Ng Mui could not help but consider the irony of Taoism versus Buddhism. Instead of achieving enlightenment, the Taoist achieved balance, much like the White Crane standing on one leg. Instead of following Buddha, Taoism followed 'the way' and believed life is good, rather than believing desire leads to suffering. Although many Taoists did follow Buddha, the Five Elders carefully hid their Buddhism under a very strict Taoist façade.

Almost nine hundred miles northwest in China they eventually reunited at a temple on O-Mei Mountain in Sichuan Province. After witnessing the massacre at the Fukien temple there was heated debated amongst them as to the future path they must employ for a Ming Dynasty return to Beijing. It is at O-Mei temple they form the Triad, a secret society, to overthrow the Manchu government.

1675-1677
O-Mei Mountain Temple
Qing Dynasty

The Triad was conceived and thrived as a secret society of Ming loyalists, devoted to a future Chinese uprising against the Manchu sovereign. They were committed to fighting injustices. The four Elders and Ng Mui pledged all within the society to secrecy to ensure the purity of the Triad's essence and purpose. Caution ruled the Triad. The Elders were more selective in whom they allowed to join to preserve their honest intent and prevent another destruction as had occurred at the Fukien Shaolin temple. Their motto became one of 'Crush the Ching, and reestablish the Ming'.

"Have we not learned our lesson at the Shaolin Temple in Fukien Province? Must we stir another uprising to be defeated again?" Bak Mei's anger could not be contained as the Five Elders conferred together. Of the four men, only Miu Hin had not taken all vows to become a full monk and still carried a head full of dark hair. The other three men were full Buddhist monks. Ng Mui was Abbess at O-Mei and as they walked to the Dein the sun reflected off her bald head, along with her other three bald brothers.

Ng Mui remained strangely silent during the vehement argument between the four male Elders this day. The ongoing dispute revolved over how much political involvement the Triad should actually invest, and how many students should actually be taught to fight. Political involvement remained the main discord between the men. For weeks Ng Mui carefully listened and observed their interactions, words, body language, and lack of control. Bak Mei's arrogance and anger concerned her. Jee Sin's 'Zen Master' strategy acutely fueled the rage within Bak Mei. Her vision during meditation only weeks ago came to light as the men quarreled for hours. As the vision remained clear in her mind's eye, Ng Mui knew the coming events were inevitable. The similarity of her past revelation with the White Crane-Snake style was not lost on her as she observed the escalation between Bak Mei and Jee Sin.

Jee Sin was the White Crane and Bak Mei the snake.

"Your strategy is as faulty as your fighting ability," Bak Mei shouted as they entered the Dein and sat facing each other in a circle. His livid gaze traveled over Jee Sin in contempt. Complete silence filled the Dein as the other Elders intently listened and watched.

The smaller, usually peaceful and friendly Jee Sin suddenly leapt to his feet lithely to stand before the larger Bak Mei. "You cross the line with your verbal insult, brother. Your ignorance, arrogance, and insults will not be tolerated."

Bak Mei hissed between teeth much like the snake, "Then let this be settled in combat, *brother*." The slur of sarcasm was not lost on any of the Elders, especially Jee Sin who nodded in acceptance. "Whoever wins this match shall win deciding fate over the Triad's path."

"You do not totally comprehend the result of yours actions should you continue this path," Ng Mui warned the two men in a firm voice. Her words echoed in the Dein, yet neither Bak Mei nor Jee Sin listened to her, although Fung Do Duk's concerned gaze lit upon the nun. The expressionless countenance of Ng Mui belied the sorrow reflected in her eyes.

The two Elders moved to the training floor to begin their battle. The three other Elders watched in fascination and horror as Bak Mei moved first. His series of punches and kicks were outmaneuvered by Jee Sin who knew his brother's way of fighting as well as his own. Jee Sin effectively landed several blows to Bak Mei's face and body in a counter attack. This only infuriated Bak Mei more as he employed his tucked-in, crouched Leopard posture to defend himself against the swift and stealthy Jee Sin.

"Surely, they will not actually hurt each other," Miu Hin proclaimed in self-assurance but his voice quivered with uncertainty. Ng Mui felt his gaze turn to her for confirmation, but she remained stoic as she continued to watch the anticipated demise of the Five Elders.

Ng Mui's vision had not shown her exactly how the Five Elders disbanded, but she had seen herself alone on a road leading to a path of fulfillment and enlightenment. There was more to the remainder of her life than being an Abbess and forming the Triad. In understanding the deadly secrets she held regarding the White Crane-Snake application to martial arts, her vision included the passing of this secret to another student. The person she chose must be pure of heart to ensure its legacy. If the undisclosed information and skill she held fell into the hands of someone immoral it could forever change more than lives, or this country. It could change the future of many things. In evil hands this powerful martial art could destroy the future of humanity. Even as fleeting thoughts of this crossed her mind, Ng Mui watched in sorrow as events unfolded before her between Bak Mei and Jee Sin.

The intensity of their battle grew with Bak Mei becoming more lethal with his movements, parries, and blows. Jee Sin, although a strategist, was no physical match against Bak Mei who thirsted for only his own path for the Triad. The smaller Jee Sin was becoming increasingly weary and Bak Mei used this to his advantage. Sweeping Jee Sin's legs out from under him and knocking him onto the mat, Bak Mei pounced atop the man using a series of his trademark phoenix punches to his eyes.

The other Elders knew this strike to Jee Sin would be deadly as Bak Mei's standard fist with extending knuckle of the index finger slightly protruding focused on those vulnerable areas. They understood all the power behind the delivery of the punch focused on that one knuckle, which then twisted like a corkscrew motion to drill the strike deeper. Jee Sin cried out in agony as Bak Mei rose and threw his arms out wide in semblance of the phoenix rising in victory.

"No!"

Miu Hin ran to Jee Sin as Bak Mei glared at Ng Mui and Fung Do Duk, as though daring them to challenge him. Neither Elder said a word as they sat together, watching Miu Hin as he picked up their brother. They pointedly ignored Bak Mei. Bak Mei had disgraced himself not only as a monk, but as a Triad Elder. Tears streamed down Miu Hin's face as he carried the now blind and unconscious Jee Sin from the temple. Jee Sin's blood trailed across the training floor. His eyes were gone, pushed into his skull, and they knew the outcome would be fatal. Bak Mei's expression was one of power and defiance as he turned and strode from the defiled Dein.

"Sister-," Fung Do Duk began, but suddenly paused as he saw the sad realization crossing Ng Mui's face.

"Come, let us tend to our brother and prepare for his passing," Ng Mui whispered as she rose fluidly to her feet to follow Miu Hin.

Jee Sin's death three days later brought change to the O-Mei temple. The air was filled with a charged edginess as everyone skirted away from Bak Mei. They no longer wished to be associated with the monk who was now looked upon with dishonor and disapproval. Miu Hin's clear animosity of Bak Mei seemed to add to the temple's uncomfortable atmosphere. Fung Do Duk became reflective and silent, comparable to Ng Mui, at the change in events. Jee Sin's remains were burned and many prayers offered as was custom. Bak Mei did not attend. He had broken his vow of not killing. There was neither pardon nor reprieve for him.

The four remaining Elders met in the Dein two days after Jee Sin's ceremony. They sat lotus-style with their legs crossed beneath them, facing each other. Ng Mui and Fung Do Duk appeared calm with no expression on their faces. However, Bak Mei and Miu Hin glared at one another as though already in combat. Ng Mui could see the calculations each were making as they mentally and spiritually prepared for an encounter. Again, her mind clearly recalled the outcome of the previous altercation and anticipated another tragedy if the two men chose to challenge one another.

"You have disgraced this temple, your position as Elder, and insulted the Buddhist way as a full Buddhist monk. You have shamed the honor of the Triad and are banned from the O-Mei temple," Ng Mui declared calmly to Bak Mei. Her gaze never wavered from the man who barely held his anger in check.

Bak Mei glowered at the tiny nun. "You may be Abbess, but you do not comprehend the implications if you disband the remaining Elders. There will be no Triad."

"The Triad will remain, Bak Mei. Your action in killing Jee Sin predicted this outcome. You know this is what happens when you break a vow," Fung Do Duk stated simply as he gazed directly at Bak Mei.

"Bah! He should not have-," Bak Mei began to argue heatedly, but Miu Hin cut him off.

"No, Bak Mei, you should not have killed our brother. You are now outcast. Leave this temple with your meager belongings. If you speak of the Triad outside of this temple your life is forfeit." Miu Hin spoke the unspoken. The Triad had become quite selective and in divulging any information to their secret society was worthy of immediate death.

"You challenge me, brother?" Bak Mei spat at the man sitting across from him. "You have always been the weakest link of the Elders. What will you do if I speak of the Triad? What? Do you wish for yourself the same fate as your brother, Jee Sin?"

Ng Mui and Fung Do Duk knew Bak Mei had lost all reasoning. Hearing his irrational ranting he was now considered a serious threat to the Triad and all who were at the O-Mei temple. He was no longer a monk, had shamed himself before Buddha, and held no obligation to the Triad. Bak Mei knew too much. He was also a serious physical threat as had been demonstrated during his fight with Jee Sin. They could no longer trust the man they had known much of their lives.

Miu Hin reacted recklessly and emotionally at Bak Mei's words. Jumping to his feet he confronted his nemesis who had once been his brother in all things. "Stand and I shall show you the weakest link!"

Ng Mui and Fung Do Duk watched silently as the two men crossed to the training floor inside the vast Dein. Miu Hin was the one unshaved Elder who was not a full monk and stood out in striking comparison to Bak Mei's bald head. Although many considered Miu Hin handsome and athletic, he was no match against the powerful Bak Mei whose anger gave him a mystifying strength and frightening aggressive ability. Miu Hin and Bak Mei faced each other, both appearing confident and knowledgeable. The lightning fast hands of Miu Hin pummeled Bak Mei before he could defend himself as blood spurted from his nose. Righteous fury fueled Miu Hin as he attempted to apply the techniques Ng Mui so effortlessly used during practice. During this time other disciples of O-Mei temple began to filter into the Dein to sit lotus-style around the arena area where the two men fought to the death.

Bak Mei allowed Miu Hin to tire himself and then pounced on him, his anger propelling his body against the smaller man as they fell to the floor. For minutes they grappled for superior position, arms and legs twisting, punches tight and quick to vital areas before Bak Mei wrapped an arm around Miu Hin's neck. Using his palm he pushed against Miu Hin's cheek as his other hand gripped his jaw. The sharp sound of Miu Hin's neck snapping and Bak Mei's satisfied grunt filled the silent, now completely filled building. Bak Mei rose to his feet as he turned to the two remaining Elders.

His glance settled on Fung Do Duk who was already rising to his feet. Ng Mui did not move or say a word as her oldest friend moved silently toward Bak Mei. Although she knew she would be alone in the near future during her travel she did not know the outcome of all the other Elders. She had only known the Five Elders would be no more, yet the Triad would live on. Now, as the final two men faced each other with Miu Hin lying dead only several feet away, Ng Mui watched as fate wove its fabric before her eyes. Should Bak Mei defeat Fung Do Duk she knew he would turn on her. In this, she knew the outcome.

"Brother, surely you know you cannot defeat me," Bak Mei stated arrogantly to Fung Do Duk who simply shrugged. "So be it."

Bak Mei made the first move with his famed tiger claw movements, wanting to quickly end this fight between himself and Fung Do Duk. However, the wiser monk seemed to anticipate every move Bak Mei employed and easily evaded any strikes. Fung Do Duk countered with devastating hits to Bak Mei's ribs and kidneys. For over an hour the two men battled, their grunts and heavy breathing the only sound amongst one thousand disciples. Silence permeated the area as Fung Do Duk adroitly bypassed Bak Mei's powerful punches. Swaying to his right fluidly, Fung Do Duk instantly moved forward and with the heel of his left foot crushed Bak Mei's outer foot and ankle. The loud snapping of bone and Bak Mei's scream of pain as he fell to the floor was announcement that the fight was over. Fung Do Duk stared down at Bak Mei's compound fracture of his foot and knew he would be crippled.

Several monks came forward to carry the screaming Bak Mei from the training hall as Ng Mui and Fung Do Duk moved to help other monks tend to Miu Hin. Today was a sad loss, indeed. The Five Elders were no more. The Triad remained but it would be in leadership held by Fung Do Duk. Ng Mui would announce her departure after Miu Hin's funeral ceremony. She was not certain where Buddha would send her but her faith never faltered. Her path had been set the day her father sent her from the Forbidden City all those years ago.

"I did not wish to kill Bak Mei, simply teach him a lesson," Fung Do Duk admitted wearily.

"This I know, brother." Ng Mui offered a gentle smile to her long time friend. "Much will change at O-Mei temple. It is inevitable."

The change was unexpected. Bak Mei died from infection of his injuries several days later. Ng Mui saw it as the outcome Buddha had wanted and did not question the meaning behind it all. Fung Do Duk felt guilt at Bak Mei's death, although unintentional. A bell resounded at the temple, announcing all disciples to convene within the Dein. Minutes later the training hall was filled as the Abbess, Ng Mui, stood before them.

"It is Buddha's will that I am called to leave O-Mei to train other Triad followers," she stated simply. "Fung Do Duk will remain at O-Mei to train our brothers and sisters. What you have witnessed these past days is not the end of the Triad. It is simply the beginning of a new path for the Triad. We all have a calling in each life we live to finally achieve enlightenment. Fulfill your calling to the Triad."

Placing her palms together she bowed once toward the disciples who returned the respected gesture. As she walked from the Dein complete silence followed. The only sound heard was the soft breeze rustling the leaves of trees. There was no sound when Ng Mui moved. There was no imprint upon the dirt or grass where she crossed. She moved like a spirit amongst awkward, clumsy humans. She was, indeed, enlightened by Buddha. The Abbess would be truly missed at O-Mei but the disciples respected her words and vision, and they respected Fung Do Duk's natural leadership. They would follow her orders to their last breath and allow Fung Do Duk to lead them to Ming victory when the time was right.

CHAPTER TWO

In making tactical dispositions, the highest pitch you can attain is to conceal them.
- Sun Tzu, *The Art of War*

1700
Daliang Mountains
Yunnan Province

The Daliang Mountains between Yunnan and Sichuan provinces became Ng Mui's new home where she and many transplanted disciples built the Bok Hok Jee, or White Crane Temple. Mild seasons claimed the beautiful area, which housed impassable rivers that flowed through deep mountain gorges. Many lakes allowed the area to flourish with vegetation and lush flora uniquely specific to the area. The terrain made it possible for many farmers to harvest well throughout the year with rice, corn, barley, soybean, tea, and sugarcane. There was no beauty more pronounced than this region for the variety of flowers, blossoming trees, and plant life. There was no place more serene for Ng Mui to finalize this end to her life, for time rapidly spun its elemental factor at a dizzying pace.

Ng Mui's name was known throughout China as she was still eagerly sought by the Kangxi Emperor, even after these many years since the destruction of the Fukien Shaolin Temple. However, the reverence beheld to her by the Chinese loyalists protected her. No one would dare desecrate the life of the nun who diligently worked so hard reviving Chinese rule, nor violate the path of a soul touched by Buddha. Ng Mui's final path to enlightenment, the greatest honor a human could achieve in any life, was known to many. Her name would someday be legend.

Ng Mui enjoyed her weekly trip to see the merchant, Yim Yee. The three mile walks each way allowed her to stretch her legs, enjoy the scenery, and inhale the beauty of Yunnan Province. It also gave her time for deep reflection upon many things. She knew her time in this last life was at a turning point. Soon she would discover the one pure of heart who would inherit the blessing of her martial arts knowledge and skill given by Buddha.

Ng Mui watched Yim Yee and his wife as they constantly smiled at those who came to do business. He was a simple man, selling bean curd and tofu with his quiet wife. They had an exceptionally lovely daughter, Yim Wing Chun, a girl of fifteen whose flawless complexion and delicate features caught the attention of many men. Her demeanor led many to believe her shy, yet her athletic ability and fondness for Kung Fu remained her family's pride. Their happiest moment would be in one year when Yim Wing Chun married her betrothed, Leung Bok-Lao, a local merchant and anti-Qing revolutionist who had recently left on a long journey for supplies. Ng Mui took pleasure in hearing of their uncomplicated happiness each week. She constantly witnessed Yim Yee's generosity toward those less fortunate. And she observed with distress the attraction Yim Wing Chun's beauty provoked amongst other local men, as was clear this day.

"Yim Wing Chun, your betrothed should not leave you unattended. What kind of man is he to leave a beautiful girl alone? You deserve better, a man like me who will not leave you." A tall, muscular man hovered near Yim Wing Chun. He lecherous gaze traveled coarsely over Yim Wing Chun's slender, developing body. His intent could not be clearer.

"Leave me alone, Jianjun Lei," Yim Wing Chun stated softly, but firmly as she moved away from him.

Ng Mui surreptitiously watched the scene unfold before her as she stood near Yim Yee and his wife. Word of Jianjun Lei and his band of bullies were known all over Yunnan Province. They were ruthless and powerful, constantly harassing Yim Yee, his wife, and their daughter. Jianjun Lei relentlessly pursued Yim Wing Chun and had recently begun to threaten the merchant and his wife with retaliation if they did not allow him to wed their daughter, instead of Leung Bok-Lau. The warnings from Jianjun Lei became more pronounced with each visit.

"Do not walk away from me when I am speaking to you, Yim Wing Chun! You are becoming brazen and arrogant for such a lowly daughter of a merchant," Jianjun Lei snapped angrily as he attempted to grab her upper arm.

Ng Mui observed the young girl adeptly move away from the larger man. Yim Wing Chun's nimble agility and instinctive reflex made Ng Mui smile. The young girl stood in front of her parents as though to protect them. Yim Wing Chun's long dark hair lifted lightly in the breeze as Jianjun Lei sneered across the merchant stand.

"You will regret this, Yim Wing Chun. We will see who you turn to when all is taken from you and your betrothed is not here to help," he sneered darkly, his threat clear. Turning on his heel Jianjun Lei strode away from the family, his thugs following closely behind him.

"Bah! That man is trouble. All will calm down once Leung Bok-Lau returns. Jianjun Lei is fearful of him," Yim Yee chuckled but there was an uneasiness which belied his humor as he continued to stare at Jianjun Lei's departing back.

Ng Mui collected her items as she curiously watched Yim Wing Chun quietly assist her parents. The girl was an obedient daughter, calm and respectful with a ready smile for everyonc, yet there was a seriousness about her that spoke of a strong spirit and formidable will. Ng Mui sensed the pureness of this young woman. It gave her much consideration on her travel back to the White Crane Temple.

The following week Ng Mui returned to Yim Yee's mercantile to discover it closed. Instinctively she recognized that a tragedy had befallen the family. Although seventy-one years old, Ng Mui moved silently and quickly to the rear of the mercantile where the family resided. Their house was small and simple with one large room, housing screens strategically placed for privacy. The sound of soft crying clearly came from the rear of the home as she approached the entrance. Ng Mui peered inside to see Yim Wing Chun preparing her mother's body for cremation. Yim Yee sat in a corner, his face grim and tired. Yim Yee's wife was dead. The Abbess felt sorrow fill her heart.

"Ni hao, Yim Yee and Yim Wing Chun," Ng Mui greeted, announcing her presence. They leapt to their feet and upon recognizing the Abbess, bowed graciously before her.

"Abbess, we are honored with your presence," Yim Yee stated, his eyes red and his face pale from the loss of his wife.

"My sadness is deep at your loss. May I ask what happened?" Ng Mui knew Jianjun Lei somehow followed through on his threat and killed Yim Yee's wife, and sweet Yim Wing Chun's mother.

"She was in market yesterday when a masked attacker stabbed her in the back. I cannot help but believe this is Jianjun Lei's evil work," Yim Wing Chun stated brokenly as fresh tears coursed down her cheeks. "I should never have let her go alone."

"Daughter, do not blame yourself for this man's evil deed. Buddha will see that karma is just for Jianjun Lie," Yim Yee declared with clear faith. His glance met Ng Mui's. She nodded her head in agreement of his words.

"I would be honored to provide the blessing of your wife, Yim Yee, if you will allow?"

Yim Wing Chun turned back to preparing her mother but glanced at the Abbess who stood a few feet away. Their eyes met fleetingly, but in that moment Yim Wing Chun felt her life begin to shift. Their lives were interlocked, she and the Abbess, as yet she did not understand.

"We are the ones most honored, Abbess," Yim Yee spoke reverently to the woman who had become their friend. They heard the many stories of Ng Mui's mysterious martial arts from local merchants. Both were honored to have a great Abbess perform the ritual ceremonial blessing over their loved one.

The remainder of the day was spent finishing the preparations. Ng Mui's serene presence was calming, much like a soothing balm over a horrific burn. Her hands were knotted and worn from years of use, yet gentle as a delicate breeze on a balmy day as they helped Yim Wing Chun prepare the deceased woman. Friends and locals who knew the family came to pay their respects as the Abbess began the ceremony. Yim Yee and Yim Wing Chun maintained a sense of tranquility and composure during the cremation. Once inside the quaint home they appeared lost and uncertain.

"Abbess, Buddha has sent you to us as our blessing this day, and we thank you for all you have done. It is late. Please honor us with your presence for a meal and bed to rest in so that you are replenished for your travel back to the Shaolin temple tomorrow," Yim Yee offered almost desperately.

"I accept your kind offer, Yim Yee. Indeed, it has been a long day for you as well," Ng Mui offered knowingly as she accepted the soft cushion before the low table. Discreetly, she examined Yim Wing Chun's every moment as she prepared a meal of flavorful broth, rice, bean curd, tofu, and fresh vegetables.

Yim Wing Chun moved as fluidly was flowing water. There was no sudden jerking or abruptness to her movements. Her sense of balance as she deftly juggled several items was impressive as she stood on one leg to reach extremely high where a string of dried herbs hung. Her decisive and comfortable movements spoke of a great sense of 'chi', or energy connecting mind, body, and spirit. A sigh of contentment escaped from Ng Mui as she watched the young girl's wicked movements with the blade while chopping herbs and vegetables. It was clear the girl had been practicing Kung Fu with a finesse of a master at such a young age. Ng Mui knew she had most likely found who she wanted to teach the White Crane-Snake style of martial arts, the person who would keep the most deadly secrets that had never been shared with anyone. This girl simply needed to be untainted and pure of heart. It would be easy enough for Ng Mui to discover such truth.

1700
White Crane Temple
Yunnan Province

"The Abbess, Ng Mui! I must speak to her, please."

A girl's cry of desperation broke the silence at the entrance to the White Crane Temple. Many monks and nuns flocked around the disheveled young woman. Scratches marred her snowy white skin with deep bruises covering her arms and angry welts littering her wrists. Her torn clothing indicated she had struggled greatly as it hung with large ripped shreds of fabric. Falling to her knees, the young woman's body shook with emotion. A monk darted quickly away to find Ng Mui as nuns escorted the girl to a building to tend to her injuries. Within moments the Abbess entered the room where Yim Wing Chun sat upon a pallet on the floor.

"Sisters, thank you for tending Yim Wing Chun," the Abbess offered them a gracious bow of thanks and respect for their concern. The nuns replied with the same gesture before silently quitting the room. "Ni hao, child, are you seriously injured?"

"Ni hao, Abbess," Yim Wing Chun greeted Ng Mui. "I am simply hungry, sore and tired. I seek your help for my father, not for myself." She brushed tangled hair away from her face.

Ng Mui studied the young woman, noting her selfless words. Yim Wing Chun's only concern was for her father and not for herself. The trait of selflessness during adversity told the Abbess everything she wanted to know about the girl's character. "What help might I offer, child?"

"My father has been arrested, falsely accused of stealing. You know my father would never do such a terrible crime! Jianjun Lei has destroyed our family as he threatened. After my father was arrested his men came to my house. I tried to fight but there were too many of them. They kept me tied up for two days with no food or water to await Jianjun Lei's arrival. I was able to escape and came to you before he arrived," the girl stated as her voice began to break. Tears filled her eyes and threatened to spill but she rapidly blinked them away, attempting to remain strong.

"You will remain here. I will see to your father."

With those few words the Abbess smiled, touched Yim Wing Chun's face gently belying the power of her hands, and then left the room. Moments later the nuns returned. They helped her bathe, tended her wounds, and gave her the typical laywoman practice outfit of long split skirt with a top. A wide band was wrapped around the top to keep it closed and snug against her skin. She graciously accepted the meager meal of flavored broth and rice, but it was the iced cold refreshing water that she drank eagerly in large quantities. The nuns escorted her to a straw filled mat in one corner of the room where she finally lay down to rest for the first time in days.

By morning Ng Mui returned with Yim Yee. Neither discussed the events of his release, nor did Yim Wing Chun ask about them. Yim Yee embraced his daughter as tears streamed down their faces. Although her father was dirty and disheveled he was not injured. Several monks came to tend to him as the Abbess lightly touched Yim Wing Chun's arm.

"Feel free to explore the temple while your father and I rest. There is much to discuss."

Yim Wing Chun bowed respectfully to the Abbess then looked around the Shaolin temple grounds with immense curiosity. Flowering trees with pink, white and purple blossoms littered the grounds, their fragrance blending with the heady scent of the various flowers planted strategically around ponds, near wooden bridges and along stone walkways. One building held several monks and nuns who cooked most of the meals for all disciples each day. Many buildings were housing for the disciples to rest. As she passed the occasional disciple she automatically bowed in reverence and respect with the gesture returned. The temple grounds held an air of mystery and magic, a peace and calm that belied the power held within its compound. The religious sanctuary itself was now empty, but sounds of metal clanging and grunts could be heard coming from the largest structure located farthest away from the entrance.

Following the noise, Yim Wing Chun found herself at the entrance to their Dein, or training hall. Inside monks and nuns practiced various forms of Kung Fu that she recognized; Choy Gar, Lee Gar, and Mok Gar that focused on boxing technique and speed, Dei Saat Kun ground fighting, and White Tiger Kung Fu. Amazed at the sight of hundreds of disciples assertively practicing their arts, some with weapons such as butterfly swords, long wooden staffs, tonfas, and sai, Yim Wing Chun hesitated at the entrance.

"Come," a voice urged lightly as a nun approached her. Yim Wing Chun followed the young nun and sat beside her near the edge of one area of the practice area. "You know Kung Fu?"

"I practice Hakka Kuen Kung Fu," Yim Wing Chun stated, feeling humbled as she observed the skill, speed, and knowledge of the monks and nuns inside the Dein. Although she had been performing martial arts most of her life she had never seen such remarkable talent.

"Shì de, Hakka Kuen is a good basis," the nun approved, and then added, "but there is so much more."

"Shì de," Yim Wing Chun agreed. She avidly watched the incredible feats of the monks and nuns who could move almost faster than her vision could take in. They jumped and leaped to incredible heights. Their skill was profound and impactful with the weapons they employed in practice against each other. For hours Yim Wing Chun assessed movements of footwork, handwork, joint manipulations, strike placement, pressure points, momentum and leverage. An intangible force gripped her heart as she suddenly realized all of this called to her soul. She wanted to learn.

"Come, Yim Wing Chun. Let us have a meal with your father and talk," Ng Mui's voice startled the young woman who jumped to her feet in surprise and bowed automatically.

They quit the Dein and joined Yim Yee in a small room near the kitchen where they obtained a bowl of rice, flavored vegetables and a fish broth. They sat at the low table barely a foot off the floor, gave a prayer of thanks to Buddha, and ate in relative silence as they enjoyed the meal. Once finished, Ng Mui glanced from Yim Yee to Yim Wing Chun with an odd expression, almost one of finality.

"I am getting old and my time in this final life will come to pass soon enough, yet there is one mission given to me by Buddha I must fulfill before leaving this earthly plane," Ng Mui stated as her gaze pointedly alighted upon Yim Wing Chun. "I have seen into your heart and it is pure and selfless. Knowing this I wish to teach you, to pass on my knowledge from Buddha. It is with most grave consideration that you must decide upon this task, child. It will not be easy to hold this gift for many will try to take it from you. Many will kill for this knowledge."

"I owe you for my father's life, for your goodness during my mother's death, and for your kindness to us all. I am beholden to you, Abbess," Yim Wing Chun stated with tears of thanks in her eyes.

"No, Yim Wing Chun, you are not beholden. You must freely accept this responsibility. It is a deliverance and a curse. In the hands of one so selfless and good it is a blessing, opening up a world of spiritual enlightenment that results in a powerful physical manifestation. And yet, this blessing carries with it a power that many wish for themselves. In this, comes the burden of maintaining its purity. The burden of this responsibility carries a curse for you will forever be sought after once it is known you hold the secret". Ng Mui rose fluidly to her feet holding her meager bowl and walking staff, belying her advancing age. "You have the qualities I have been seeking in the one I wish to bestow this knowledge and skill, this secret. Think carefully before accepting child, for it will forever change your life and affect the lives of those around you."

Ng Mui left the room. Father and daughter looked at each other, speechless for a few moments. "I do not comprehend this gift she wishes to share with me, but it must be Buddha's will to have brought us to this path with the Abbess. It is my destiny."

"Shì de, daughter, it is Buddha's will," Yim Yee agreed.

"Shì de," Yim Wing Chun whispered the affirmation as she collected their bowls to return to the kitchen. One who truly believed never questioned Buddha's will. She and the Abbess were together at these crossroads in their lives for a reason. She did not know what the secret was or what was expected of her, but she was ready.

This was her destiny.

Several months later
Yunnan Province

Yim Wing Chun proved to be the perfect student.

Ng Mui could not have chosen any person more worthy of her secrets concerning the White Crane-Snake style. The young woman reminded her of herself when she had been her age; full of unquenchable energy, patient, focused, and driven with a natural athletic ability and martial arts sense that were truly blessings from Buddha. Yim Wing Chun relentlessly practiced from sunrise to deep in the night, learning the Plum Flower Posts of varying heights to defy the rules of balance while working with various weapons. She worked as though possessed in learning every single weapon inside the Dein until they had become an extension of her body, as familiar as breathing. Her incredible aptitude for the five patterned Hung Kuen in mimicking the various fighting animals impressed Ng Mui. But it was Yim Wing Chun's speed and fluidness with the Muk Yan Jong, or wooden dummy, that truly surprised the older nun. She effectively blocked the extending arms of the wooden dummy at lightning speed with her hands, forearms, feet, legs and knees.

Yim Wing Chun was ready. The secrets of certain deadly strikes and lethal manipulations had been taught to her. Ng Mui knew the humble girl's sense of honor would preserve and protect this information from those who would exploit it for their own reward or evil manipulations. She had observed Yim Wing Chun practice fighting eight Buddhist monks in the Dein. Her movements were like softly flowing water and as silent as a petal on the wind. Each strike placement was so precise and exact that it was the only strike needed to stop her opponent. Yes, Yim Wing Chun was ready. Only one issue remained.

Jianjun Lei.

"Tài hǎo le," Ng Mui approved. "Spiritual daughter of mine, we are finished."

Yim Wing Chun spun around effortlessly in the air with a butterfly sword in each hand. The curved lethal blades sliced downward as she landed silently on nimble feet. Strands of her long, inky black hair lay against her snowy white skin. Her sloped, almost black eyes held a calm that gave Ng Mui satisfaction in knowing she had chosen the right person to pass this skill and knowledge.

"You must challenge Jianjun Lei to a public fight. Once openly shamed he will no longer bother you. It is your time to marry your betrothed who has stayed with your father these many months".

Ng Mui saw her aged visage reflected on the blade of one butterfly sword. Once youth had been hers with no wrinkles on her face, but this body, this shell of humanity was winding down. Her spirit was complete and prepared for the final path of enlightenment. Her quest upon this earthly plane would soon be ended.

"You must keep this secret to pass to your daughter someday, and she her daughter, and so on. But not just any daughter should keep this burden. Only the daughter most worthy, selfless, and pure of heart should be considered, Yim Wing Chun, even if she is not of your blood. Pledge to me and to Buddha your acceptance of this vision, Buddha's will."

Gently the young woman placed the swords on the training floor and bowed deeply before the nun. Tears shone brightly in her eyes. "I pledge to you and to Buddha to maintain the White Crane-Snake secrets you have taught me, Abbess, and to only consider a daughter most worthy."

"Tài hǎo le," the woman sighed deeply with satisfaction, "Tài hǎo le. Come. Let us prepare to leave the temple. Your young man has been waiting these many months for you with your father, and both will be eager to see you."

The Abbes told Yim Wing Chun to keep the simple training outfit of banded top and split skirt she had trained in for these many months to continue her practice in private. She packed it away in her tied bundle with other meager belongings. Wearing a simple black dress to return to town and pulling her thick black hair up in a tied scarf wrapped around her head, she and Ng Mui began the trek back to her father's house. They traveled in comfortable silence along the lush and beautiful road.

Ng Mui, although completely satisfied she had fulfilled Buddha's will in choosing and training the young woman, she would be leaving her with a sense of bittersweet sadness. She had become quite fond of the quiet and unassuming Yim Wing Chun whose humility and kindness had earned great respect amongst the Shaolin temple disciples. Yim Wing Chun would have made an excellent nun, and perhaps in another life she had been one or would be in the next life? Her patience in learning and deference shown to all had solidified Ng Mui's choice of this deadly knowledge. She could almost hear Buddha telling her it was time to reach enlightenment, to finally end this life with no further rebirths or lessons to learn, to be at peace.

They arrived at Yim Yee's home late that evening to an elated reception. Yim Wing Chun's betrothed, Leung Bok Lau, had never questioned her training at the White Crane Temple. As a Ming loyalist who knew of Ng Mui's repute he had silently accepted there was a reason for Yim Wing Chun's training. This knowledge gave Ng Mui great satisfaction that he would never question or attempt to obtain his wife's secret legacy.

After a meager meal, they rested for the night to prepare for when Yim Wing Chun would challenge Jianjun Lei in public. They did not have to wait long. Within days his band of ruthless thugs had reported to Jianjun Lei that Yim Wing Chun had returned to town. Even though Jianjun Lei knew Leung Bok Lau was staying with her family, it spurred him further to try to claim the woman for his own before she married the merchant.

Yim Yee and Leung Bok Lau waited at the merchant stall holding tofu and bean curd, both anxious for this to end. They were not worried for Yim Wing Chun. If Ng Mui had trained the young woman then there was no question as to the outcome. Ng Mui stood at the north end of the road, leaning heavily on her staff, watching the expected events unfold. Her gaze settled on Yim Wing Chun who stood in the middle of the road as Jianjun Lei stomped toward her. Ng Mui knew the girl well after spending so much time with her training. Yim Wing Chun appeared quite calm and relaxed but therein was part of the secret. As the 'Zen Master' Jee Sin, once stated regarding battle, "*The success of each battle is mainly in the preparation.*"

"Yim Wing Chun, you will be mine!" Jianjun Lei's bellow of rage echoed throughout the small market. Vendors and patrons paused, their gazes following the large man's form marching toward the tiny woman who waited calmly in the middle of the road. As he neared her, her voice rang clearly in the market for all to hear her words.

"Jianjun Lei, I challenge you to a fight. If you win I will marry you. If I win you will leave me and my family alone".

Jianjun Lei's expression of anger changed instantly to humor as he laughed heartily. His gaze traveled over her with instant disregard. It was clear he considered her challenge a joke and did not take her serious. Crossing his arms across his chest he leaned forward and said softly so that only she could hear, "You will pay for this challenge. I will make you suffer greatly."

"Do you accept the terms of my challenge, Jianjun Lei?"

Jianjun Lei's face suffused with a redness that expressed his fury at her calm demeanor. His fists clenched and his breathing increased as he allowed his temper to build. "I accept your challenge, Yim Wing Chun. It will be your own fault when you are seriously injured or crippled, but either way, you will be mine".

The nod of her head was the only action she made as she waited for his first strike.

Ng Mui watched as Jianjun Lei stood taller, uncrossed his arms and drew in a deep breath as his gaze narrowed on her face. He gave no warning, but the skilled Yim Wing Chun expertly watched him telegraph his movements before he made them. His gaze darted to her feet as his body shifted. Suddenly he crouched low and immediately swept his leg out to knock her off her feet. Before his leg could reach her ankles, Yim Wing Chun stomped down on his knee as he extended his leg. The resounding crack of a bone breaking and his subsequent scream of pain was announcement that the fight was over.

"Get her!" Jianjun Lei's six other gang members came into the street at once, while he rolled on the ground and clutched his dislocated knee.

Ng Mui's expression never changed as she serenely observed Yim Wing Chun defend herself against six attackers, two with knives. Deftly, the young woman moved to a clear portion of the road with more room. Two attackers came within striking distance. She gracefully sidestepped one attacker, grabbed his wrist with one hand and shoved her other hand against his elbow, dislocating it. Immediately, she pushed him away and used the backward momentum to spin around and strike the other man with a series of punches to his face from her centerline so fast that he was unconscious before he hit the ground.

A roar of fury resounded from the other four men who charged her at once. Yim Wing Chun focused on the two men with the knives as she remembered Ng Mui's teaching.

'Always remove opponents with known weapons first, then those with unknown weapons, with the understanding that all opponents are weapons in and of themselves'.

As a knife was thrust toward her, Yim Wing Chun used her crossed wrist block to stop the attack. Rotating her hands, she captured his wrist, stepped forward and redirected the knife into his chest. Without pause, she softly moved to her left and right, like the snake, fluid and graceful as her feet lightly danced upon the dirt road leaving no footprints. The man with the other knife fruitlessly attempted to stab her but she was too fast and anticipated each strike. As he swung his arm wide to change the direction of his blows, she stepped into him and swept his feet out from behind. The man fell backward as she dropped to her knee, breaking his elbow and sweeping the knife from his hand.

Instantly, she spun around in a crouched position. With the blade held lightly in her hand, she thrust it several times into the man who advanced on her before without hesitation. Using his forward falling momentum, she lifted and tossed him over her shoulder. The last man smiled as he pulled a knife out. They circled each other, stepping over the lifeless bodies littering the ground. As he stepped closer, Yim Wing Chun snapped her wrist and the knife she held flew through the air, embedding deeply into his right eye. He made no sound as he fell to the ground limply.

The market area was silent as all eyes traveled from Yim Wing Chun to Ng Mui then back to Yim Wing Chun. This story would be told repeatedly for centuries. Yim Wing Chun had been a pupil of the famous Buddhist nun, Ng Mui. Even as the implications began to manifest within the people of the market, Yim Wing Chun bowed humbly before the Abbess who returned the gesture. Although the nun's face appeared expressionless, it was Yim Wing Chun who saw the love in the older woman's eyes before she used her staff to turn around and begin her trek back to the White Crane Temple.

Ng Mui's destiny was ending. Yim Wing Chun's legacy was just beginning.

Part II

Legacy of Wing Chun

CHAPTER THREE

If you know the enemy and know yourself, your victory will not stand in doubt; if you know Heaven and know Earth, you may make your victory complete.
- Sun Tzu, *The Art of War*

1895
Forbidden City
China

It was a period in Asian history when a Manchu woman ruled China. It was the only time a woman ruled China. So began the fall of a powerful civilization established for many centuries once ruled only by men. Wrought with greed, power and political manipulations within the Imperial family, and religious conversion among the Chinese, their society faltered. British and German soldiers invaded their coasts, raping their women and land. Merchants claimed unique goods and artifacts for monetary gain. Protestant and Catholic religions wreaked havoc among Buddhists and Taoists. Mutli-racial children born in and out of wedlock became a common occurrence and social dilemma.

The Chinese were uprising against the Manchu government who had ruled with an iron fist for so many centuries. The Triad, a secret society once established by the Five Elders as an honorable element to assist in the rise of the Ming Dynasty, was now filled with illegal opium drug trade with foreign merchants, gang warfare for their own personal power and monetary gain, and other illegal activities. This was a dangerous and ruthless time that would forever change the country, its inhabitants, Asian and world history. It was a time known as the Boxer Rebellion.

Fifteen girls were ushered into the Throne Hall of the Empress Dowager Tzu Hsi, who regally awaited them on the raised Dias. The

Empress was perched upon her throne ornately decorated with mother-of-pearl, forming the shapes of writhing dragons. Eunuchs surrounded the Dragon Throne. Their long-skirted, belted uniforms hid their shame and denoted their ranks.

The Empress was an intimidating and beautiful woman with manipulative black eyes wisely assessing each girl critically. As per Manchu custom she and the prospective concubines wore their straight black hair drawn back from their forehead and fastened in a bun. Where the girls wore a square headdress with a tassel hanging, she wore an elaborate crown indicating her ultimate position of authority. Tzu Hsi was known for being shrewd, determined, and ruthless. Having once been a concubine who now ruled a country, she was quite astute at reading others and of verifying their true unvoiced intent simply by listening and watching. Not to mention the many secret spies she employed to watch those she deemed potential threats.

The vast Throne Hall regaled splendidly furnished glowing lanterns and bright, lethal looking dragon symbols considered sacred emblems of the semi-divine, semi-human Son of Heaven Buddhist religion. Along one curtained wall stood a long table filled with delicacies and abundant dishes to tempt any palate. The Forbidden City housed a citadel with high purple walls, three artificial lakes surrounded by flowering trees and shrubs that barred to the grounds to all but the privileged.

Ji-Kin Lau and fourteen other girls had been handpicked by the Empress Dowager. This day two girls would be chosen as concubine to her son, Kuang Hsu, Emperor. Racial purity could never be contaminated, with Manchu officials forbidden to take Chinese wives or concubines. Although her son, the Tongzhi Emperor, sojourned as official leader of China, he was actually only a figurehead dominated by Tzu Hsi, who ruled with ultimate fervor and control. He was of age, seventeen, to rule but the Empress had no intention of relinquishing he power and kept her son busy with opium and women. The Tongzhi Emperor could not beget an heir due to a genital defect, thus this slight predicament ensured Tzu Hsi's position and power as Empress. If her son were to die there were three Princes' in line to the throne, which she could also easily manipulate.

As the girls entered the Throne Hall they bowed deeply before the Empress and young Emperor before kneeling to prostrate themselves upon the floor before them. When the signal was given several minutes later, the group of young girls rose and proceeded to the long table where they seated themselves. Ji-Kin Lau felt the Empress' gaze upon her, critically observing for decorum and beauty. A future adversary or opponent needed to be studied carefully and kept at bay, but also the two concubines chosen for the Emperor must be presentable and easily controlled.

Ji-Kin Lau gracefully carried herself across the room, remaining poised and serene, as the Empress studied each girl with her formidable gaze. All her life she had prepared for a position as concubine, which was the highest compliment and position a Manchu woman could achieve. This station she coveted more than the very breath she took. Of the girls present Ji-Kin Lau was considered the most beautiful, most cultured and learned of music and the fine arts.

There should be no reason not to be selected as one of two concubines to the Emperor. Once that occurred, and she obtained favored status with him, she would cautiously devise a way to usurp the Empress Dowager and rule China. Little did the Empress or Emperor fathom that she was also trained in military strategies and political fundamentals to command this country to greatness and power. That is where the current Empress Dowager failed, and China was slowly deteriorating before their very eyes.

Ji-Kin Lau covertly watched each girl as she was summoned before the Empress and Emperor to speak and be judged on intelligence, etiquette and refinement. Each girl shuffled forward swathed from their necks to below their feet in long, straight satin gowns. The bright and vivacious colors bespoke the unique flavor of each family house. The gowns were fastened across the chest from left to right shoulder with lavish embroidery on the sleeves, neckband, sideband and hem lending each girl their own personality. It was difficult to determine the thoughts and musings of the Empress who diligently asked questions, and listened to each response with avid interest. As the current girl was excused, Ji-Kin Lau was called to attend.

She approached the Empress, noticing the woman's assessing eyes narrow and her lips compress slightly even as the Emperor's eyes lit up with pleasure. He observed Ji-Kin Lau's flawless ivory complexion, her exquisite features hosting a tiny, rosebud mouth painted bright red, a small button nose and large angled eyes with indecently long lashes. While the Empress viewed her with envy the Emperor viewed her with favor.

"What would be your main focus as concubine to the Emperor?" Tzu Hsi's voice addressed the young girl.

"To serve his will, and to provide a future son and prince," Ji-Kin Lau answered. She conducted herself flawlessly, answered the questions pressed to her with deft aplomb and delicate animation, capturing the Emperor's constant attention, and even bringing a semblance of a smile from the Empress Dowager.

When her allotted time concluded she sagely bowed in reverence then returned to her position at the table. The evening wore on tediously with all the girl's expressing their nervousness and impatience, while Ji-Kin Lau remained composed. The fine delicacies lay out before them were tasteless as she went through the motions of pretending to eat. Her future would be fashioned today. A heady sense of anticipation filled her with excitement.

"Rise," the Empress Dowager finally commanded. Her voice of authority echoed in the immense chamber lined with eunuchs and Imperial guards. Each girl rose, their hands pressed together at their stomach as their heads and eyes remained lowered deferentially. This moment was all Ji-Kin Lau had cherished her every waking moment. Today she would be chosen future ruler of China!

"It is unfortunate that I may only choose two girls when each of you is more beautiful, poised and intelligent than the other," Tzi Hsu said as she lifted her right hand slightly. Long, talon like nails gleamed red, the length several inches long and bespeaking her wealthy position. There was a taut silence permeating the hall as she poignantly hesitated. "Yi-Shiang Chang and La-Mai Lee will remain."

Ji-Kin Lau felt the blood rush from her head. She sensed her ears burning as the shock of not being chosen struck her forcefully. Glancing up, inappropriate and brazen, she noticed the Empress's superior scrutiny directed solely at her. Tzi Hsu's small black eyes laughed at her, mocking her, as though she fully understood Ji-Kin Lau's ambitions. Peeking at the Emperor, she noticed a dark scowl covering his embittered countenance as he stared at her with obvious regret. A feral gleam entered Ji-Kin Lau's eyes as she bowed her head again in supplication. She silently followed the dismissed girls out of the Throne Hall.

Ji-Kin Lau strolled with regal dignity across the royal grounds, evaluating her present position in life and the decisions needed to change it. A shiver shook her as she felt an intent gaze focused on her. Glancing over her shoulder she recognized the Imperial Prince, Prince Tuan, with his red sash indicating his position within the government and the family lineage of the Empress. He was a cousin to the Empress and in a line with two others to potential reign should there be no male heir at any given point. Registering his keen scrutiny directed at her, Ji-Kin Lau blushed angrily and quickened her pace toward the carriage that would transport her from the Forbidden City.

"All I have strived for, diligently arranged, has been crushed at the decision of a woman once a mere concubine herself. This is my life and future she has destroyed! I know nothing except how to be ruler," she ground out bitterly between clenched teeth as tears threatened to drop from her tightly squeezed eyelids.

Quickly, she entered the carriage the Empress had provided while silently feeding her rage. Not falling victim to despair she suddenly filled her breast with sweet vengeance. There may not be a way to become Empress through this avenue, but there were other means of infiltrating and ruling the government. She was destined for greatness, which had been foretold by a mystic at her birth.

The carriages swept the despondent girls from the palace but it was the last carriage, Ji-Kin Lau's, which would raise mystified cries from her family by morning. Her family was no longer of any consequence. Not being accepted as concubine would mar any chance at having a wealthy, powerful life. In her family's eyes she would be a failure, and as such, would not be accorded even the smallest tolerance. Knowing her future would only be what she now made of it she took a deep fortifying breath.

"I will be Empress!" Flinging open the carriage door she threw herself from the slow traveling vehicle into the darkness of night.

Hunan Province, China
Two months later

"Her feet are not bound! She is not Chinese," a man growled loudly.

Ji-Kin Lau stood defiantly before the large group of Triad members, her dirty feet exposed but in normal condition. Anxiously waiting to be killed or accepted into their secret society she watched as the congregation grew. Attempting to enter the Triad was her only way to fulfill her mission in becoming Empress. Their renown for power throughout China was known, and they were growing. It was only a matter of time before they overthrew the current regime.

Very few Manchu joined the Triad. It was for Chinese ancestry preparing to overthrow the Manchu line, which was considered a virile race of hunters and warriors, rough and uncouth. They held the people of China under their dominion and had for many centuries. Traditionally, Chinese women bound the feet of their daughters at the age of seven, tightly winding strips of cotton around their toes and instep. The cloth would remain for years, causing acute pain and eventually the toes would atrophy. Finally, reaching adolescence, they possessed tiny 'lily-feet' admired by Chinese men. Manchu women never bound their feet.

"Enough!" Prince Tuan's beady eyes narrowed instantly at the disheveled, yet beautiful girl before him. He studied her intently for several moments before recognition surged through him. Rubbing his thumb and forefinger over his long, thin goatee, he thoughtfully considered the petite young woman before him. He remembered her. She was one of the girls not chosen as concubine to the physically deformed Emperor.

"Interesting," he mumbled to himself, then asked her, "How old are you, child?"

"Sixteen," she replied hesitantly. As his gaze traveled over her body lewdly, causing a shiver to race across her body. The coarseness of his gaze frightened her and excited her.

"That is a good age." His smile revealed yellowed teeth. "A very good age, indeed."

As a leader of the White Lotus Society, a branch of the five Triads, and a high council member to the Empress Dowager, Prince Tuan wielded great power. Not only was he privy to both the Manchu government and its political occurrences, but he was also the eyes and ears of the Boxer's. His Boxer's were Chinese villagers and Triad members who not only wanted the westerners out of their country but planned to overthrow the Manchu dynasty. He did not worry being Manchu, for they accepted him as one of their own due to his continual furnishing of information not accessible to outsiders. Once the Boxer's rose against the westerner's and drove them out of the country, the Boxer's would then turn on the Imperial guard and overthrow the Forbidden City where he would then rule as Emperor.

"There are many women with unbound feet," Prince Tuan stated in bored tones as his gaze lecherously slid over the petite form of the girl standing proudly before him. "Perhaps we should hear what she has to say?"

A chorus of voices echoed inside the elaborate chamber halls of the 'City of Willows'. The fortress bristled with armed guards surrounded by four gates, with four walls and a moat. Both beautiful and secure, a State within a State, it abided as a plebeian to a patrician city of the bureaucratic literati. Chinese from all stations of life filled the immense chamber. There was no distinguishing between them of wealth, status, or lineage. Their only concern: freedom from oppressive rule by the Empress Dowager and the westerners who had invaded their country.

"Let the girl speak," rang an irate voice from the crowd and the building became silent.

Ji-Kin Lau stared at Prince Tuan with both sudden recognition and clarity. She remembered the sensation of his gaze when she had left the Forbidden City several weeks ago. She now received the identical appraisal as excitement blossomed in her chest. He represented power. Seizing the opportunity she bowed humbly.

"I stand here as a loyal servant to this society. If you look beyond my ancestry you will discover I oppose the present sovereign. I desire only to witness the finale of western influence and Manchu oppression," she said clearly. "Though you view me as disparate, I too, have received personal retaliation and unreasonable subjection from the Empress Dowager recently. While she remains in power over this country we shall not reap the wealth or rewards she so greedily bestows upon herself. We shall not be liberated to live under our rule but to her proclamations!"

Silence saturated the vast group of people who nodded at her angry tirade before a hearty cheer was raised in agreement. Prince Tuan smiled magnanimously at the clever, aspiring beauty before him. He was reputed to have a propensity for low life, and justly so. For him there was nothing more exciting than objects considered taboo such as prostitution, drugs, robbery, murder and his personal favorite, rape.

Prince Tuan's licentious gaze traveled over the beautiful girl he identified with her thirst for status, affluence, and leadership. She would make an Emperor a majestic and ruthless Empress, exactly what he desired in a mate. He could almost taste her youth and virginity, though he preferred her younger. However, she would do nicely.

"I admire your eloquence and enthusiasm," Prince Tuan said as he smiled. His eyes flashed with lechery. "There is a place for you within this society. You will be initiated on the morrow."

A murmur of agreement filtered through the crowd as Ji-Kin Lau was led off the platform by two guards. They led her down a long corridor to a vast chamber with several adjacent rooms. Moments later, Prince Tuan entered.

"Leave us," he ordered his guards.

Ji-Kin Lau observed him as a nervous quiver danced along her belly. She realized they were alone in his private chambers and suspected what he wanted from her. The carnal flame of his stare allowed her to briefly bask in sudden feminine allure, although unsure of how to proceed with him. He was a dangerous man. It was evident in the darkness of his eyes, which revealed the treachery within his soul. She swallowed thickly as he removed his red sash and began unfastening his outer garments.

"We are alike, Ji-Kin Lau," he said smoothly. Prince Tuan's rich voice seduced her, calmed her, as he tread lightly toward her. His movements were fluid with his body barely restrained of its animal hunger as he slid off the remainder of his clothing. He stood before her totally naked. "You know what you must do if you wish to reign at my side."

With shaking fingers she released the holds to her tattered shift and shoved it over her small, still developing body. Staring at Prince Tuan's flagrant desire protruding from between his legs, Ji-Kin Lau bit her tongue to stifle the scream that threatened to rip from her throat. She had never seen a man naked before, knew nothing of the ways between a man and a woman. However, she would do anything he asked to rule China.

"Tell me your desire, future Emperor, and it shall be yours," she said obediently then cried out in fear as he grabbed her and threw her ruthlessly to the bed.

1897
Fukien Province, China

The market in the heart of the village lay near the coast hosting a myriad of shops, stalls and vendors who sold their wares. Many of them began closing as the end of another day fell. Outsiders from other countries seemed to be everywhere. Unwelcome were the foreigner's with their strange appearance, talk and aggressiveness among the quiet and timid Chinese people living there. It was odd seeing so many new westerners arriving in their province daily and frightening to think they were trying to take over China. Kai Chen Boussard did not want to believe these unusual men were here to rape her homeland of its natural resources and material wealth, but as the influx of newcomers increased dramatically and she witnessed many horrible actions by them against her people she knew it to be true.

Weaving through the crowd of people on the dirt road, Kai Chen spied her mother standing at a stall lined with large, silvery fish. Ying's petite frame was difficult to see with so many men loitering about the area, but her bright blue dress made it easy to spot her. Cautiously, so as not to attract attention, Kai Chen mingled with the crowd standing before the vendor.

"You should have waited for me," she said quietly in her mother's ear. The small woman's body tensed ever so slightly so that only Kai Chen could notice with her finely attuned senses. Ying turned slightly.

"I have told you, Kai Chen. It is better if you do not come to market. It is becoming too perilous for you," Ying coldly informed her, but the love shining from her small black eyes took the bite from her words.

"The danger waits for you also, mother," she returned knowingly and Ying's lips pressed together tightly as she recalled their last encounter here. Kai Chen watched her turn back to the vendor, silently accepting the statement as truth. Ying paid the vendor for her purchase then faced her.

"How is Ng-Kin this day?" Deftly, she placed the wrapped fish in her sturdy straw bag, stepping away from the stall with her noticeable limp. They proceeded south toward the coast where many enormous merchant ships lined the harbor, seeming huge and peculiar. A host of exotic smells greeted them as they passed a shop of spices. The heady sense of familiarity it lent surrounded Kai Chen like a comforting blanket.

"She is well, mother. I learned much from her with the teaching," she admitted. Kai Chen's face lit up beautifully as she spoke. "One day I hope to be as proficient as she with Wing Chun."

"You have far surpassed me with skill, child. Since the fall that broke my leg I have known that Ng-Kin would be your teacher. That is why she works with you now. She does not approve of pride in a person, yet I detect she feels it for you." The words were lightly spoken but they meant more to Kai than any material gift she could have been given. "Come. I would like to buy you fabric for a new dress."

"We cannot afford it, mother!" Kai Chen's worried expression belied her excitement. It had been several months since she had a new dress. Her body was developing quickly with her maturity and the clothes she wore were tight and worn.

"We can, and it shall be done." Ying waved Kai Chen's protests away with a slicing hand motion as they located the large shop filled with numerous bolts of fabrics. She noted her mother's odd expression of anxiety as she spoke. "An associate of your father's is arriving for dinner within the week and he has a son interested in meeting you."

Kai Chen's stomach clenched tightly upon hearing the words. She did not want to marry! There was so much in her life to accomplish and to experience. Marriage would forever hold her chained from her dreams. Inhaling deeply, she attempted to calm her frayed emotions.

"I do not desire marriage," she stated softly. She was content with her daily routine. There had never been a female friend, someone to share girlish dreams and secrets with, although she had longed for one. Her life as a half-breed and outcast had lent an inner fortitude for her to center on Chinese, English, and French languages. Besides, she was too old for such sentimental notions such as having a friend! Her life was now focused on more meaningful endeavors such as her martial art and her Buddhism. Her entire life she had never acquired friends because of her mixed lineage. That would not change now.

"Regardless, they are coming and you require a new dress," Ying chuckled at her daughter's barely controlled expression of placidity as they browsed for the perfect material.

For the next several minutes they bickered and debated in hushed whispers over the type of material and color they should purchase. Ying insisted on jade satin, which matched Kai Chen's eyes perfectly. Kai Chen insisted on a dull brown to remain inconspicuous.

"I am buying the green," the older woman stated firmly. They glared at each other intently, and then laughed at the other's stubbornness.

"As you wish, mother," Kai Chen relented. She did not welcome the appearance the dress would surely create, making her clearly noticeable. "I dare say you shall regret this decision."

Exiting the shop they turned north to head home. The dirt streets were less crowded as the sun set behind them in a bright orange glow, reflecting off the calm blue waters of the ocean. It was pleasantly warm with the slightest of breezes blowing inland from the sea. Many foreign men stared at Kai Chen and Ying, the difference in their appearance distinct. Kai Chen stood several inches taller than her tiny mother. Her features were unlike the oriental people as she looked completely American except for her large slightly angled green eyes and soft features holding a hint of classical, yet exotic beauty. Her deep auburn hair stood out against her clear, pale skin. It was common for people to ogle them. Kai Chen and Ying pointedly ignored the insult.

The sound of horses arriving within the market caught everyone's attention. People made way for the intimidating men by scurrying to the sides of the street. Kai Chen tiptoed to peer over a stack of baskets to see what caused the commotion and felt dismay.

Six Manchu soldiers arrived into the market area. They were dressed in military refinement that bespoke their position within the Imperial guard with red and gold accenting the uniforms. Scattering people out of their path as they brazenly rode into the village, they struck out at anyone not quick enough to avoid them. Arrogance held them erect on their mounts as they gazed carefully among the occupants lining the street. Kai Chen backed into the shadows and lowered her head, knowing better than to catch their attention. Ying attempted to pull her deeper into the shadows to keep her out of sight, but one rider stopped his horse directly in front of them.

"You. Woman. I order you to look at me." Kai Chen refused to raise her eyes. The soldier unsheathed his sword as he uttered a curse. Using the flat side of the blade he placed it under her chin and raised her face.

"Ah! Here is another half-breed," he declared, satisfied with his discovery. The other infantrymen stopped to pull their mounts toward the area that quickly cleared of villagers.

Vaden LeBlanc tarried in the market far longer than originally anticipated, but there were many goods he was interested in importing to America. Exiting the shop supplied with fine silks, satins and other priceless blends of cloth, he inhaled the fresh scent of the salty sea. This province was almost becoming a second home to him he was here so frequently. For the past ten years he had amassed a great fortune due to the wondrous exotic spices, fine materials, rare furniture and artifacts that only China could produce. However, the beauty of the land, the quiet people who toiled daily and their culture is what held him enthralled with the country.

"I could live here, you know," he admitted, causing his companion to visibly start at the proclamation.

"You must be insane," Sebastian Madden exclaimed. Glancing about the poorly constructed shops and stalls where people milled about, he snorted.

Vaden grinned at his best friend and slapped him on the back sharply. "You must open your eyes," he told him then chuckled. "Just look about, Sebastian! This is a world so rich with history, beauty and simplicity that you could never duplicate it."

"I would rather duplicate my wealth," the shorter man stated cynically. Impatiently, he ran his fingers through his short brown hair, which told Vaden the man's desire to head back to his ship.

"In time, my good man," he promised. He stepped aside to let two women exit the shop. Vaden's shrewd dark blue eyes immediately noted the difference in the women. The taller woman walked lightly next to the shorter one who had a pronounced limp. Listening to the tall woman's soft banter as they headed away from him made his loins tighten and reminded him it had been several months since he'd been bedded. Her delicate and musical voice sounded like a bird singing. As he observed their progress away from him the color of her hair caught his attention. Instead of the inky black color proclaiming oriental ancestry it was dark brown with red highlights and trailed past her buttocks enticingly in a long braid. The plain black dress she wore couldn't disguise the ripening curves of her body as she nimbly made her way through the market.

"What is wrong, Vaden?"

Sebastian's voice broke through his preoccupation as he stepped forward to follow her. He had never seen an oriental woman with her height and hair color. "I want to see something," he mumbled, pursuing her and the little woman she talked to with such animation.

"I will see you later. Do not forget to button your pants when you are done," Sebastian joked lewdly and headed toward the dock where his ship remained moored.

Vaden did not bother replying as he strolled casually behind the two women. It was easy to pursue them since he stood several inches taller than most men and supported a massive frame. Directly behind them now, Vaden listened to their conversation as they began to speak in English.

"I am still amazed at times that Wing Chun was named after Yim Wing Chun and not Ng Mui. Was it not Buddha who spoke to Ng Mui of the secrets? Should she not get the credit?"

The laughter of the tiny woman was lost among the many other sounds of the market and he could barely make out her response to this confusing and interesting topic. Vaden tried to stay close enough to hear, yet far enough away so they would not know they were being followed. It was a difficult task to blend in the crowd being a blonde American in China.

"Ng Mui was unassuming and a nun. As a humble servant to Buddha she would not wish to take credit. She was simply the teacher. The secrets needed a name and since Yim Wing Chun was the first in our line to keep the legacy it was named after her. It is as Buddha wills."

"Shi de," the tall woman agreed, "but I would have enjoyed seeing Ng Mui perform this martial art. She must have been amazing."

Vaden heard the two women giggle occasionally together as they continued to talk, reverting back to Chinese. As they neared the end of town where several roads led to various provinces away from the coast line, Vaden heard a commotion behind them. He spun around and his gaze immediately narrowed as he saw Manchu soldiers heading into the market. The determined pace of the horses entering the area gave him cause for mild concern. The soldiers were looking for someone. He could see their gazes hungrily search through the crowds of people as they separated.

Suddenly, the leader noticed the unusual woman he trailed. The tiny woman beside her tried pulling the taller woman back, but the man was already approaching them. Vaden frowned at the ruthless infantrymen. As was proper custom for the Chinese addressed by the Manchu he noticed the young woman kept her head lowered. The guard stopped his horse in front of her, his vicious comment about her being a half-breed fueling Vaden's anger instantly.

When the soldier pulled out his sword Vaden almost pulled out his gun. It would be prudent to discover their intent before taking action. It certainly would not do for him to get into an altercation while here on business, yet he refused to allow a group of soldiers to harass or hurt her or any woman.

As the tall, auburn haired woman lifted her head Vaden gained clear sight of her face and felt his heart almost leap from his chest. She was American! Her features held the delicate softness of an American woman with her heart shaped face and creamy complexion like fine satin. Her nose was straight and exquisitely dainty and her jaw finely sculptured. However, her eyes held his attention. The decidedly jade green color of them was so vivid they stood out as her most prominent feature. Dark, sinfully long lashes surrounded them enhancing their beauty. There was only a slight hint of angle to the shape of her eyes, the only real clue that she was partly Chinese.

She was utterly exotic and beautiful.

Observing the other soldiers join their comrade, Vaden frowned in concern. Had the young woman committed some crime that they were treating her with such disdain in front of the villagers? He knew some customs of these foreigners, but could not fathom why they were humiliating her like this unless she was some sort of criminal.

"The only thing a woman with mixed blood should be here for is prostitution. Why aren't you with the others?" The soldiers laughed at their leader who openly insulted the young woman in front of the dwindling crowds.

Vaden watched the tall young woman stand silently before them. Her expression remained composed as she let them badger her. The tiny older woman behind her held completely still with her head lowered. Fury rapidly built in Vaden at this disgraceful treatment of a woman. Were they only addressing her like vermin because she was of mixed heritage? It enraged him to witness such cruelty and reminded him of his own brutal youth. He knew exactly how it felt to be taunted and maligned because of station in life.

"Answer me, whore," the Imperial soldier bellowed when the young woman before him refused to speak. His face turned red with outrage as she stepped back from the blade still held under her chin. The tip sliced her skin as blood sprang forth on the porcelain surface to mar her exceptional beauty.

"I belong to no one or no place," she stated, her eyes never wavering as she surreptitiously handed her mother the bag she held.

"You dare talk to me like an empress? Did you hear her?" Turning to his men in astonishment the soldier then glared at the remaining villagers who viewed him with fear and dislike.

Vaden could see the disapproval in the eyes of the crowd, but also noticed that no man or woman stepped forward to aid this social outcast. It appalled him to think her own people would not protect her against such abuse, and it stoked his anger further. It was clear they were afraid of the Imperial soldiers and would do nothing to aid this woman.

"I think we must teach this young woman her place." The leader's left hand stroked the long, thin goatee and mustache on his face as his small black eyes roamed over her developing curves. He smiled evilly and his face became even more malevolent. "It will give me great pleasure to enlighten her in the ways of respect to the government."

As the soldiers slid off their horses the lingering villagers scurried frantically away until the market was seemingly empty, and yet, hushed whispers filled the shadows where they hid. Silence reigned in the once busy street as the young woman's mother turned and slowly walked away. Even British and German soldiers lingering in the marker refused to aid her.

Vaden's eyes widened in astonishment as the older woman headed north out of the market with unhurried broken steps as she carried her purchases. How could she just abandon her daughter knowing six men planned to rape her? Even in the worst society parents tried to protect their children!

The lead soldier sheathed his sword and approached the young woman. His grin revealed a cluster of rotten teeth. Using composed movements the woman wiped at the blood dripping down the front of her dark, worn dress. Not a flicker of emotion passed across her features as she bent over to set her remaining purchases on the ground. The soldier before her knocked them from her hands. The few items scattered across the ground causing the other soldiers to laugh with great zeal.

Unperturbed, the young woman stood before him again. Her demeanor surprised Vaden who watched in disbelief. Why wasn't she crying or cowering in fear? Why did she simply stand there with a calm assurance he certainly did not feel right now?

"You know where to take her," the lead soldier ordered his men as he seized her arm brutally.

"Forgive me." Her soft voice was heard clearly as she closed her eyes briefly in regret. Suddenly faster than a cobra's strike her palms struck the front of the soldier's chest. The impact resounded throughout the market as the man flew backward and landed on the ground with a decisive thump.

Vaden was unsure what she had done to the man who rolled on the ground, struggling to breathe. One second he had been grabbing her then he was hitting the earth with such force that it made Vaden flinch. Confused, he noticed the young woman slip quickly into the middle of the street as the other soldiers followed to attack her. Without delay he moved to help her as she waited without fear for their attack. He had only taken two steps when he saw the young woman adroitly stop and redirect each blow the men used on her. Three soldiers surrounded her and attacked at once, but with a mixture of kicks and punches she effectively stopped them as they fell to the ground and cried out in pain. Two more Imperial guards charged toward her with their swords raised.

Grabbing one soldier, Vaden spun him around. He slammed his fist into the smaller man's face and sent him to the ground, senseless. Reaching for the other soldier he noticed him already sprawled on the dirt road among his fallen comrades. His sword lay several feet away.

"You," the lead soldier shouted at Vaden. "You will leave now or die!"

Turning, he noticed the leader who had first been hit by the woman rising to his feet with his sword drawn. A menacing scowl was directed at the woman, leaving Vaden no doubt he was going to seriously hurt or kill her for defending herself. The gun in his jacket was suddenly in his hand and pointed at the soldier who gawked in astonishment.

"I believe it is you and your men who will leave," Vaden ordered, his eyes glaring intently at the soldier who now hesitated. He cocked the hammer back on his revolver and arched a thick blond brow, daring the other man to disobey then added, "Now."

The soldier glared at him for several seconds. Hatred blazed from his dark eyes as he ordered his soldiers to mount their horses. "You will suffer greatly for this, Foreigner," he spat as he joined his men who slowly rose to their feet holding arms and legs as they ineffectively attempted to mount their horses.

Vaden regarded the smaller man with contempt as he and his comrades finally mounted their horses. Hastily, they spurred their mounts' northbound away from the market. Relief at having aided this young woman surged through him. It was the morally correct action to choose. He would never allow a woman in distress to suffer at the hands of any man, let alone several. Placing his weapon back inside his jacket he watched the young woman demurely gather her fallen purchases.

"Are you all right?" What a ridiculous question, he admonished himself. Of course she was!

It amazed him that she had single-handedly beaten those men. He took great pride in being a former military man who had survived many battles. His athletic prowess was mightier than most in the art of fighting, but never had he witnessed a woman with such skill and composure defeat any man, let alone six. What kind of woman was she? And *who* was she?

Keeping her eyes lowered the young woman nodded once. She quickly turned from him to collect her belongings. Within moments she headed in the same direction her mother and the soldiers had taken. Fear for her quickened the pace of his heart. He would not rest easy until she arrived home safely. Trailing her he discovered how swiftly she moved. With difficulty he kept her in sight until they were a mile outside the market where she headed toward a small house located near a huge white church.

Stopping at the crossroads that branched before the chapel he watched with hungry eyes as a man and woman rushed from the quaint home to their daughter. The man dressed in black with the white collar bespoke his position as a missionary. His light brown hair was a banner proclaiming he was not Chinese. A cry of relief sprang from the tiny woman who held her daughter tightly in her arms as they stood outside their home. He felt his heart constrict at the loving sight of the young woman held by her parents. Once, he had possessed parents like hers but fate had ruthlessly snatched them from him while he was still a child.

The young woman glanced over her shoulder at him as her calm green eyes held his for several seconds. Those eyes, so uncommon and mesmerizing, would remain in his thoughts and remind him of Fukien province. Here he had witnessed a woman defend herself with an ability he had never seen before. His travels to China had never given him any idea such talent was possible, especially from a woman.

He noticed the missionary acknowledge him with a nod of his head. The Elderly man's gaze was penetrating as he recognized the familiar American attire Vaden wore. As the family turned to walk into their home the holy man raised his hand in a gesture of thanks, providing Vaden with a sense of wellbeing he had not experienced in quite a while.

☯

"Are you trying to destroy what little peace is left between our governments?" Sebastian's shout resounded in his large personal quarters of the ship where he and Vaden sat. Replete from a fine dinner of fish covered with delicate herbs and steamed vegetables, they now lounged comfortably in their chairs with fine brandy held in their snifters. "I assumed all you wanted was a piece of oriental flesh to fill a forbidden need."

"I resent that remark, Sebastian," Vaden growled as his fingers tightened on the stem of the crystal he held. Sebastian might be his best friend, but he certainly didn't know his desires. Sometimes he didn't believe Sebastian knew him at all.

"Duly noted," said Sebastian, his hairs rising in warning at his comrade's furious expression. It would not do to get on Vaden's list of enemies. Once considered an adversary they remained in that status for life. He was just as ruthless with them as he was with business transactions. Neither stood a chance.

Vaden closed his eyes as the fine liquor soothed his ire. It had been a long day and he needed rest, but it was difficult when the image of large, compelling green eyes surrounded by dark lashes haunted him. What would become of the beautiful young woman in this harsh culture that tolerated no deviation in heritage? Would his actions today lead to greater repercussions for her and her family by the Imperial guard or Chinese government? He sincerely prayed not, and yet, Sebastian had made a valid point. It wouldn't be wise to destroy what little tolerance existed between their governments and jeopardize his business in this nation. Presently, it was China who produced the goods that made him one of the wealthiest import merchants in the United States.

"What you need is a woman to bury your cock. When was the last time you took solace in the arms of a woman?" Sebastian paced the large room aboard his merchant ship that vied in size and speed to Vaden's.

Unfortunately, he didn't have the knack or flare for negotiating deals like his counterpart, leaving him to trail sluggishly behind with volume and money. However, when it came to women he was never without a cluster of willing, eager sexual partners.

"That is none of your business," Vaden said bitingly. His expression remained calm, but his eyes blazed with repressed fury. "I prefer to keep my personal life, personal."

"Oh, come now, Vaden! At each port I hail there are several women begging to know when you will next arrive. Your reputation as an exceptional lover is very much alive and well," the smaller man smirked.

Vaden refused to answer his friend's obvious attempts at fishing for information as he polished off his brandy with a single swallow. He refused to expound his sexual exploits for Sebastian's entertainment. Placing the delicate snifter on the table he rose and bowed his head. "Thank you, Sebastian, for the wonderful meal and delightful brandy. Good evening."

"All right, Vaden! Don't think I don't know you," his friend declared in a shrewd tone as he pursued him outside. "Come with me. There is a brothel along the docks with Chinese women who can perform the most incredible feats on a man, acts that can stir a man's lust never experienced before!"

With a strained smile Vaden walked down the temporary planks leading from Sebastian's ship to the wharfs. "Then I hope you enjoy yourself, Sebastian," he stated with boredom and turned toward his ship docked nearby.

"Fine!" Sebastian watched his friend saunter away with long strides. "Be that way! You don't know what you are missing."

"Oh, my friend," he mumbled deeply as he recalled witnessing the depravities of men at one such establishment, which in turn sickened him, "but I do."

☯

"You may never return to the market," Ying said to Kai Chen heatedly. Her harsh whisper seemed loud in the tiny kitchen. "The Imperial soldiers will be searching for you."

"I refuse to allow you to go to market alone! If I may not go then I implore you to let Ng-Kin accompany you," Kai begged. Her expression was one of rebellion and fear. The soldiers might be seeking her mother, too.

"Possibly," Ying smiled calmly as she held the green material purchased for Kai Chen's new dress. Deftly, she began spreading out the material.

"It will be so!" Kai Chen rose to her feet and planted herself before her mother who arched a delicate brow at her vehemence. Rarely did Kai Chen raise her voice, but it terrified her to think of her mother alone at market. Ying would now be subjected to the retaliation of the soldiers because of her actions. She would not permit it.

"We shall not speak of this again, Kai Chen." It was not a request.

Staring at her mother's stoic countenance Kai Chen clenched her teeth together angrily. It was disrespectful to argue with a parent and she had never done so in her life. However, she was very close to conducting herself in that very manner. Suddenly, a statement her grandmother made earlier while they trained that day came to mind.

You should not let your emotions drive your actions, child.

As though a cold bucket of water splashed over her, Kai Chen released a long sigh. "As you wish, mother," she said and turned to exit the room.

Ying smiled and said, "I love you, Kai Chen."

The whispered words were barely audible, but Kai Chen heard them as tears welled in her eyes. Darting back to her mother she enveloped her with a crushing embrace returned with equal fervor. "I love you, too, mother. If anything happened to you I would not survive."

"You would, daughter," Ying stated emphatically and pushed away to view Kai's tear stained face. "Never has there been a stronger person with greater character and fiercer tenacity. I have been blessed to have such a child."

"Yes, we are truly blessed," a familiar voice said from the kitchen doorway and both women started at his sudden appearance. They gazed at David Boussard with equal fever as he entered the small kitchen and embraced them warmly. Kai Chen and Ying smiled at one another, unspoken secrets passing between them. "It was the work of God sending that American to intervene with those hostile soldiers. Nevertheless, we are all going to be extremely tired come the morrow if we do not retire now."

Mother and daughter shared a secret look, knowing it had not totally been the American who had saved Kai Chen this day.

"Yes, father," Kai Chen said obediently and kissed her parents. Silently, she made her way through their home. The dining room was her least favorite room seeming cold and barren. She recalled many dignitaries and strange visitors joining them frequently for meals during the past several years. In the center of the room stood a heavy mahogany table surrounded by six chairs. Each was elaborately carved and polished to a fine shine with the seats stuffed with padding and covered with a light brocade fabric. A matching serving table adorned one wall where fine china, linens and silver were kept. Though her parents liked the dark, foreign items, she detested them.

Once through the living room furnished with ornate settees and tables, oriental rugs and dark, heavy draperies, she entered her bedroom. It was furnished with a large feather stuffed mattress and a bureau for clothing. A solitary cross was nailed above her door placed there by her father, but inside was a small alter containing ceremonial items for her dedication to Buddhism. Living in a dual world of religions she tactfully abided by her father's teachings, but embraced the Buddhism enlightenment and way. Dutifully she performed her evening prayer at the altar then removed her stained gown. Washing from a basin in a corner of her room she slipped on a sleeping gown then climbed into bed.

However, sleep did not come easy. Visions of the American stranger who had helped her today assailed her. Why would a foreigner assist her? Deemed a pariah by her own village she had never received any kindness. Didn't he fathom the reprisal that would occur toward her family *and* him for his involvement? He obviously didn't know better! Thumping her pillow soundly, she turned over and lay on her stomach.

"Foolish American," she said with derision, but her lips curved upward into a smile as she remembered his handsome face and piercing blue eyes. Those dark blue eyes reminded her of the sea on a stormy day, the passion of the winds promising death if challenged. His light brown hair with blond highlights gleamed orange with the setting sun reflecting off it. The thick waves reached his shoulders and were pulled back by a leather tie giving him a rakish appearance. He was incredibly good-looking compared to the dirty, unkempt foreigners filling their coastline, but even in a room of princes he would stand out. There was inherent strength in his face from his generous mouth and aquiline nose to the elegant ridge of his cheekbones and square jaw. This vitality transferred itself to his massive body, agile and muscular, a fact she had noticed but only fleetingly at the time of their brief encounter.

Kai Chen was stunned to think he had aided her although it had been unnecessary. By covertly handing her mother a bag it had been unspoken that she would handle the situation. Ying had walked home heartened by the knowledge of Kai Chen's expertise in defending herself. There was no reason the American should have helped her, but he had. The pleasure she had received had been alien. However, it had been equally surprising and gracious of him to ensure she returned home safely. Noticing him standing at the crossroads returning her gaze raptly lingered in her mind.

His aid was the first she had ever received in her life. Never, even as a small child, had one villager or outsider lifted a hand or voice in her defense. She was accustomed to and capable of protecting herself, primarily against the soldiers and foreigners. To have one extend their good will and compassion in a situation that boded ill for them both she considered honorable and unwise. The Imperial soldiers would devise a means to guarantee their vindication and to exhibit their ultimate authority against them all.

She knew how ruthless and barbaric the Manchu soldiers could be when dealing with the Chinese. Often she witnessed the unwarranted attacks on innocent kinsmen and felt a rush of apprehension for her parents. It would be merely a small time before they discovered where she resided and exacted punishment. Her mother knew this, but her father did not understand the finer elements of the Chinese uprising that was growing with enthusiasm, particularly that of the government. Now, she feared for the unidentified champion who had selflessly leaped to protect her.

Fighting memories and unwanted reflections that kept her from sleeping, Kai Chen closed her eyes and began to meditate. Clearing her mind she focused on her breathing and softly chanted her mantras. Within minutes she slept but her dreams refused to release the image of the good-looking American.

CHAPTER FOUR

All warfare is based on deception. Hence, when able to attack, we must seem unable; when using our forces, we must seem inactive; when we are near, we must make the enemy believe we are far away; when far away, we must make him believe we are near. Hold out baits to entice the enemy. Feign disorder, and crush him.
- Sun Tzu, *The Art of War*

"You are Imperial guards, trained for war against men, and yet, a small half-breed woman defeats you? To my utter disbelief you then speak to me of it?" Slamming his fist upon the ornate armrest of his chair, Prince Tuan then leapt to his feet and pointed to the man standing before him. "I should have you beheaded for such stupidity!"

The guard's body visibly shook with fear as Prince Tuan threw furious glances at the other men standing behind him.

"Your Highness, an American merchant aided her. Again, these foreigners are intervening with our work for you. They interfere with our country's laws and customs, our way of life. When will the Empress Dowager destroy this pestilence from afar? When shall China be free of the dogs that come to our country?"

Prince Tuan placed his hands on his hips as he glared at the man while considering his words. Suddenly, his expression changed and he raised one hand to casually begin to stroke his goatee as he started to pace the raised dais. There was much to consider here. Using the Imperial guards perhaps was not the avenue to correct this situation. His Triad members would easily take care of the woman. His guards would be better served with the foreigners. Calm settled over his once flushed countenance as he once again took to his chair.

"You say an American merchant aided her? Then let us welcome this merchant to our land and see that he does not wish to return. Find out what you can about this American in order for me to consider the choice of greeting we give him."

"Your Highness," the guard bowed in acceptance. "And the half-breed?"

"I shall see to her personally as soon as you obtain information on her. Be expedient with these tasks and do not tarry. I am a very busy Prince,"

Tuan sighed impatiently and waved them out of the room as though swatting at irritating flies. As the door shut behind the last soldier he turned to his cleric to confer. "What do you make of this…half-breed woman who fights as though a member of the Triad? I have never heard mention of her before, although there are more and more half-breeds among us daily."

"I have heard mention of a half-breed living in Fukien province, a young woman of great beauty. I do not know if she could be the same as the guard speaks of this day. Curious happenings, Excellency," the cleric advised sagely, waiting for Prince Tuan's reaction.

"Curious, yes," Tuan agreed as he stood again to resume pacing his chamber which was decorated brightly in red and gold as befitted his stature within the Imperial House. He was one of three familial princes in line to the Throne should the current Empress Dowager and Emperor find an untimely demise. The other two princes were of no consequence as their death sentence was a surety. All would happen in time, but for now he needed to focus on these current issues at hand.

"It will be simple enough to discover if the half-breed is the same who interacted with the Imperial soldiers," the cleric stated as he continued making notes to act upon for the Prince.

"I would like to know more of this beautiful half-breed you speak of," Tuan ordered, his interest piqued by the thought of raping a woman considered forbidden. He could not allow his insatiable lust to overrule his current state of leadership, but he certainly would not stop. Quickly, he returned to business. "Where is the Empress Dowager this day?"

"She is receiving guests. Many monks and nuns from different monasteries arrived to give blessings to the royal family."

"Indeed? They will need them," Prince Tuan purred knowingly. "You are dismissed."

"Yes, Excellency," the cleric smiled sanguinely and quit the chamber.

☯

Fukien Province, China
Three Days Later

"Kai Chen, you are so beautiful!" Ying's smile lit her entire face as she glowed with pride at her daughter.

"You are kind, mother," Kai Chen said as color blossomed in her cheeks from embarrassment. She smiled nervously, standing before her parents as they admired the fine needlework that had gone into making her new dress. The jade green color of the material matched her eye color. Black piping ran along the borders of the wrists, hem and neck. Her long hair hung in a thick braid over one shoulder. She looked like an exotic China doll come to life.

"Nonsense, you are my eyes now, Kai Chen. I can no longer see like before," her mother stated, a sadness creeping into her voice that could not be disguised. "Your stitches are fine and you have a gift for unique style. If only the Empress Dowager could see your splendid work she would have you as head seamstress."

Kai Chen's light, tinkling laughter brought wide smiles to her parent's faces. "You exaggerate, mother!"

Her father's expression suddenly grew solemn as he maintained eye contact with Kai Chen. "This evening," he began then faltered as he turned to Ying briefly for support. Seeing her single nod he continued, "…a prospective suitor is coming to dinner."

"I know, father," Kai Chen said softly, almost sadly. A tense hush filled the room as she kept her composure and lowered her eyes. Her face reddened as she contemplated what this meant as her heart sank in resignation. If her father's wish was for her to marry it was her place to agree with him. An obedient daughter did not to cry, lament, or object. She feared who he had chosen. There was no man in this country who would wed her knowing she was of mixed lineage. Her forced tranquility was physically draining. Her emotions warred within her, fear of changing the known aspects of her current life to something unknown and of meeting some unknown man who would most certainly gaze upon her with scorn and disfavor. The fear consuming her felt like talons of a mighty beast ripping her heart asunder. Why would they feel it necessary for her to marry someone soon, if ever? Her expressive green eyes spoke of her fears, even as a loud knock sounded from the front door of the house.

"I have not promised a betrothal, Kai Chen," her father chuckled, reading his daughter's expression. Hearing his words eased the strain she felt as her mother rose to answer the door. "It is your decision. We only want you to begin considering your future."

Kai Chen smiled tremulously as her father joined her mother at the front door to their home. With a slight whisper of satin, she glided into the shadows to see who her parents had believed suitable for her as husband. As the door opened she glimpsed a man whose age had to be older than her father's. Aghast that they would even consider a man his age asking for her made her stomach lurch and her breath catch in her throat.

Nervously, she wiped her palms against the sides of her slim hips to rid herself of the moisture. The strange American with graying hair, ruddy features and a bulging belly entered their home followed by a younger man.

Instant relief sprang within her and she sighed audibly at seeing the man who came after. He was nearer her age, although a good ten years older, and carried himself with great uncertainty. His agitated movements and flustered appearance caused her to smile sympathetically. Why, he appeared just as mortified of this situation. Immediately, her heart when out to him as she was perceptive to his position in this charade.

"Good evening, Colonel Baxter," David Boussard greeted his friend warmly as the two men shook hands. Turning to the younger man, he extended his hand, "And Mr. Baxter."

"Good evening to you, sir," came the tense reply as the young man took the chaplain's hand in a death grip.

Kai Chen muffled a giggle as she saw her father stifle a wince at the pressure of the younger man's handshake. Her father introduced both men to her mother then turned to locate her. Stepping out of the shadows, she kept her head and eyes lowered respectfully as her mother did.

"This is our daughter, Kai Chen Boussard," David Boussard announced proudly to the two men who stared openly in surprise at the tall young woman before them. "Daughter, you may extend American hospitality toward our guests this evening. They are from New York, America."

Kai Chen lifted her head, a warm smile lighting her face as she looked from father to son. "I am very pleased to meet you, Colonel Baxter, and Mr. Baxter," she said in her melodic voice as she extended her hand to each who grasped it lightly and placed a light kiss.

Covertly, she noted their double-breasted jackets and matching slacks with white spats worn over their shiny black shoes. Each held their short felt bowler hats with petersham hatbands and curled brims. Their clothing was similar to other extravagant foreigners entering their province.

"The honor is ours, Miss Boussard," the Colonel spoke in wonder as he continued to stare at her longer than was appropriate. Kai Chen knew that although she appeared American she dressed, spoke and conducted herself like a traditional Chinese woman. She watched as the Colonel shoved his elbow back into his son's ribs when he didn't respond promptly in kind. Biting her lip, Kai Chen observed the younger man's face flush with chagrin as he struggled to utter the appropriate response. Cringing inwardly at his obvious embarrassment she felt a sudden empathy for the man.

Ying dutifully took their guests hats, gloves, and walking canes then scurried from the room. Kai Chen's father was immediately dominated by the Colonel and talk of American trade, leaving her to gently place her hand on James Baxter's forearm and lead him into the interior of the living room. Sitting on one end of a flowered brocade settee Kai Chen observed the nervous man sit at the other end. She felt compelled to put the jittery man at ease.

"I was informed a week ago, Mr. Baxter, that I would be meeting you. I pray were you were not informed as your father knocked on the door," she whispered in a conspiratorial tone.

James Baxter lifted his gaze, caught her impish smile and visibly relaxed as his brown eyes brightened. There was a gentle quality to his eyes framed by spectacles, the glass thick which magnified them and giving him an owlish appearance. His wavy brown hair was parted to one side and combed straight back from his forehead. His sharp angled features spoke of his small body frame hidden by his suit. This was a man who did not work hard or toil. He was this, almost gangly in appearance. Most likely he had never raised his hand in anger once in his life.

"In fact, I was," he whispered uncomfortably. Kai Chen's impish grin caused him to relax. He shifted onto the seat closer to her so they could talk without being overheard.

"I am impressed at how well you are dealing with this considering the short notice," she offered sincerely. "What brings you to China, Mr. Baxter?"

Kai Chen felt his keen appraisal as he truly seemed to see her. The usual desire or condemnation was not reflected in his eyes. Instead he viewed her with calm tolerance and guileless interest.

"My father," he related dryly, throwing the man a frustrated glance. "He wants me to join the military, to follow his wake."

"You do not wish to do this," she confirmed with a soft knowing smile. His face flushed and his hands fidgeted with the buttons of this frock coat as he nodded and studied her intently.

"That's right."

"What would *you* like to do, Mr. Baxter?" The innocent and genuine question seemed to take him aback as she struggled for composure.

"I am an artist, Miss Boussard, and would like to pursue that as my life's work. A few of my paintings have been sold but I would truly like to see them in art galleries or museums." The declaration was not boastful; it was a clear yearning in his soul reflected by the rapt expression on his face.

"Then you must follow your heart, Mr. Baxter," she announced honestly. "If you do not, you will never find peace in your life."

James Baxter's mouth opened, yet no words came out. He stared at her as though she had just declared war upon America. Tilting her head to one side and throwing him an uncertain look she wondered if she had overstepped her boundaries in this conversation. A faint blush covered her cheeks and she lowered her gaze shamefully. Her parents would never forgive her for embarrassing their guests.

"You are absolutely correct, Miss Boussard!" His agreement was generated with such force and sudden determination it caused the others in the room to glance at them briefly with concern. "I will be eternally grateful to your realistic insight and exceptional wisdom for you are correct in that I will not be at peace if I do not follow my heart."

Kai Chen raised her gaze to see his beaming smile and nodded once in acceptance regarding his unworthy claims of her character. For years, Ng-Kin had spoken to her of suppressed yearnings of the heart and body. Although she knew of heart yearnings she had never felt a physical desire. It was curious how her grandmother knew the inner yearnings and contemplations of people. Her wisdom was truly transcendental. Perhaps she had passed on a few morsels of that wisdom to her?

"I apologize for speaking so brazenly."

"My dear, no apology is necessary," James implored. "It is refreshing to be truly heard for the first time in my life. I must admit that you are the only woman I have met engaging enough to hold conversation. Normally, it is either I or the other women who are dull and witless."

"Kai Chen, would you assist me with dinner?"

"Yes, mother," she said obediently and rose from her seated position with James standing next to her.

James and Kai Chen smiled as they held each other's gaze. Their friendship was solidified in those few precious moments. Neither felt romantic nor desirous of the other, but they were very much alike; alone in their self-made world and different from those around them. Fortunately, her parents loved her, and her grandmother understood and listened to her. Glancing at Colonel Baxter as she left to follow her mother, Kai Chen knew that James Baxter was not as fortunate. The rustle of green satin was the only sound heard as both women left to finish preparing dinner.

The remainder of the evening was spent listening to Colonel Baxter brag of current financial developments in America, as well as his military conquests and the decisions made for his son, James. Kai Chen then learned that her father had grown up and went to school with the Colonel, which is how they had been friends for so many years. Kai Chen remained polite and demure, never speaking unless directly spoken to and not issuing any comment toward any subject. Kai Chen found the Colonel difficult in listening to him plan James' future without any consideration toward what his son wanted, and amusing in understanding that life did not always turn out as one planned.

Sitting next to James again on the settee after dinner, neither spoke. Colonel Baxter continued to monopolize the conversation with derogatory remarks toward China's Empress Dowager and the Manchu government. He barked about the obstacles in dealing with the villagers in this province, and the incredible prices asked for rare commodities in this country. She surreptitiously glanced at James and saw he red hue of embarrassment on his face from his father's brazen and outlandish diatribe. It was evident the older man, his manner arrogant and careless from years of abused authority, refused to consider his inappropriateness toward his hosts while speaking. The steely glint in her mother's eyes made her bite her lower lip as she stifled a smile. China had its obstacles to overcome, but so did every country.

"Well," the Colonel boomed, patting his expanded stomach contentedly, "this has been quite an auspicious occasion. Madame Boussard, I thank you for the wonderful meal and delightful company. I hope to prevail upon you in the near future."

"Of course," Ying said pleasantly as she rose to retrieve their belongings. Seeing her mother's strained smile it was clear to Kai Chen that Ying would rather not accommodate him in her home again.

"Reverend Boussard, my friend, I will contact you regarding our little conversation," he began as he pointedly glanced from Kai Chen to his son, and then continued, "at your earliest convenience."

Kai Chen actually covered her mouth with a slender hand to hide her amusement as her father's brow dropped low and his lips pressed tightly, reflecting his disapproval of the Colonel's lack of tact. She was certain there would be no betrothal announcement forthcoming unless she pressed for it to happen.

"Please excuse my father's impertinence. He has commanded his entire life and understand nothing else," James stammered to Kai Chen in trying to cover his father's inappropriate statement. "It has been a pleasure meeting you, Miss Boussard. I would be honored for you to consider me a valued friend."

Kai Chen smiled brightly at him then bowed slightly as was Chinese tradition for respect. "I am the one honored."

"Good evening, Miss Boussard."

"Go in peace, Mr. Baxter."

"Hurry, your father will start shortly," Ying insisted, scurrying about the house as they prepared for their Sunday Lutheran religious service.

"I will wait outside, mother." Kai Chen giggled as she observed her mother scramble to find her best dress.

"Two minutes," the rushed woman promised and fled down the short hall to her bedroom.

Walking out the front door of their small home, Kai Chen inhaled deeply. It was a glorious Sunday morning with the sun shining brightly, the clouds white and fluffy, and the scent of lavender wafting with the soft breeze that came inland from the coast. Attending her father's Lutheran service was a duty and offer of respect, not a preference, but she would never consider insulting him with that knowledge. The Lutheran religion, although familiar, did not capture her heart as did Buddhism with its spiritual enlightenment and wisdom. She may look predominantly American but her heart, culture, and beliefs were traditional Chinese. She was definitely a child of two different worlds.

Kai Chen observed those villagers who adopted her father's western religion enter the white church located next to their home. Many parishioners were conventional Chinese families, but there were several new families consisting of American fathers and Chinese mothers, or Chinese mothers who had a mixed racial child out of wedlock. She knew she was the only mixed racial person in the area who appeared predominantly American, whereas the others had distinctive oriental features. Kai Chen prayed that all children of mixed lineage would be accepted within this strict oriental culture and received more tolerance than she had received.

"I am ready," Ying announced breathlessly as she exited the house to join Kai Chen. "Your father will be pleased to see you wearing the new dress."

Smiling in trepidation, Kai Chen walked along side her mother as they made their way to the church. She was not excited at all to be wearing the silken green creation, but her father had insisted. Her idea of wearing her sedate black and brown garments had been shoved aside as she obeyed her father. A sense of dread filled her, knowing the dress would attract everyone's attention and she would stand out. As if her face, height, and lighter hair was not enough!

"What a splendid morning," Ying proclaimed joyfully and turned to smile at Kai Chen. "What is wrong, daughter?"

Kai Chen's expression reflected her concern and alarm. "It is the Imperial Guard," she whispered in warning.

Her mother quickly turned to view several horses heading their way. A soldier held a bright red flag with a golden dragon emblazoned on it for all to notice. It announced a Prince of the Manchu government. The soldiers' formal black tunics and pants with ceremonial red and gold markings on their breast plates confirmed they were the Prince's entourage. Their large three pointed helmets exposed the front of their faces but were fashioned long in the back to protect them from being decapitated from behind while in battle. In all, they were authoritative, overbearing, and intimidating.

However, it was the Prince who rode with them that caught Kai Chen's immediate attention. His ceremonial dress consisted of red and yellow under robes covered by a deep yellow tunic and red sash. Atop his head was a small, raised circular cap with a long tassel dangling down the back. As they approached, she and her mother stopped walking and bowed respectfully. The entourage kept their brisk pace past them, although Kai Chen could feel their gazes upon her strikingly different appearance. She heard a sharp command given and all horses stopped instantly. Kai Chen seized her mother's elbow to propel them toward the church.

"Woman with the light hair, halt!"

Kai Chen paused in stride, urging her mother to continue with a gentle push of her hand. "I will be there shortly," she promised. "Do not worry."

Ying's faltering smile tore at her heart. "I do not fear for you, daughter. I fear for them and what the outcome may bring."

Watching her mother's limp increase as she trudged up the path to the church entrance, Kai Chen clenched her teeth painfully. Again, her American features drew unwanted attention. With her head still bowed, she patiently waited for his next command.

"Look at me, woman," Prince Tuan ordered in a deceptively pleasant voice, although a fine quality to the sound alerted her to use caution. She dare not refuse him.

Slowly, Kai Chen turned and lifted her head, meeting his intense gaze. Before her sat a man who radiated pure malevolence. His black eyes reflected a multitude of unspeakable sins and horrors in their inky depths, causing the fine hairs on her neck to rise in warning. Terror filled her for the first time in her life. As though in a trance, suddenly Kai Chen's senses dulled for only a few seconds as a vision came to her. This man was part of her fate. She perceived the link between them like a child connected to its mother by the umbilicus.

"What is your name?"

The sound of his deep voice slid over her soul like the promise of death as he urged his mount closer to her. He was so close he could reach out and touch her face as his expression changed to surprise as he noted her green eyes. Her throat convulsed as bile rose and she forced it back down, the thought of his touch in any manner making her ill. His obsidian black eyes raked over her slender body, visually raping her. Even though he had not touched her she felt violated. She knew he could see into her mind, heart, and soul. It was as if the gauntlet was thrown as he suddenly sat up straight on his mount. The expression on his face told her he gleaned her inner strength and that she would be a challenge to the death. Kai Chen felt the trance break as she put herself on guard. Although she appeared calm and humble, an inner cry to protect herself bellowed within her mind and heart.

"Kai Chen, great Sovereign," she answered softly, suddenly understanding that all of this was inevitable.

"Kai Chen," he purred as though tasting her name upon his serpent's tongue. His fingers stroked his long goatee as he licked his lips. Throwing her a smile that revealed his yellowed teeth he dug his heels into his mounts flanks as he spun around. Prince Tuan's macabre laughter echoed as he and his soldiers continued south to the cross roads before turning west toward Kingsi Province.

Hastily, she made her way toward the church as though the Prince were at her heels and chasing her. As she stepped inside she leaned against the vestibule wall, closing her eyes in momentary relief. Only momentary, for she had no doubt he would be back for her. This sacred haven would not save her when he returned. There would be nothing and no one to save her, except herself and her Wing Chun.

Kai Chen shivered as she remembered Prince Tuan's gaze roving over her body. His evil was no ordinary corruption. Within him stirred a sinister debasement toward all of humanity, a voracious hunger for ultimate authority and a penance for domination of anything considered a challenge. There was no doubt in her mind that he would annihilate anything that lay in his path toward those achievements

She was a challenge and would be one of his achievements. Buddha had given her a vision and had allowed her to see into his soul. But, Prince Tuan had also seen into hers. That invisible gauntlet now lay between them and his visual message had been clear.

He would return.

White Lotus Society
Fukien Province, China

"See to it the German shipment of goods is destroyed before it leaves our coast," Tuan ordered dryly to his cleric who diligently wrote down each order as he received it.

Casually, they strolled through the corridors of the City of Willows toward the training hall. Harsh grunts, sharp cries of pain and the pounding of feet and hands greeted him as he entered. Inside, several groups of Boxers practiced weaponry, fighting and assassination techniques. They mercilessly used each other for hand-to-hand combat practice with the loser obtaining serious injury. Wooden posts lined one wall where razor edged coins, knives and other instruments of death and destruction were thrown into them. Swords clashed together viciously as men and women carefully repeated motions to facilitate their perfection with the instrument. Long Bo's, or staffs, thrust forcefully into slower opponents who were then swept off their feet to land onto the hard floor with a mighty crash.

It was music to his ears.

"Where is Ji-Kin Lau?"

"She is training with the swords," responded the cleric who waited for his next order from Prince Tuan.

"So she is."

Tuan's eyes closed to mere slits as he watched the young woman shift her body easily across the floor, expertly blocking her opponent's strikes. While the other combatants used caution during practice Ji-Kin Lau was brutal and ruthless, as with everything she undertook. Excitement surged within him, filling his loins, as he watched her swing the pair of butterfly swords as though an extension of her body. Her motions were fluid, graceful and deadly, allowing no mercy toward her rival. In the past two years she had developed into the most deadly assassin within the White Lotus Society and five Triads.

Suddenly the image of a tall woman with dark brown hair and jade green eyes entered his mind. In Kai Chen's gaze he had beheld another warrior. He recognized a deadly calm adversary when he saw it. Though he knew nothing of her he had noticed brilliance in her eyes and soul. It was the expression he had seen in the nuns and monks at their temples. It was frightening as well as exciting; a minute form of enlightenment that very few individuals achieved.

Lust immediately overcame him as he imagined himself raping the foreign beauty. Kai Chen was obviously of mixed lineage and most likely virginal. An outcast, half-breed that no man would find worthy to marry. That she was not already a prostitute spoke of her parent's protection. A half-breed and a virgin. There was nothing that excited him more than an untouched maiden other than one considered forbidden, and she was unequivocally both.

"Send Ji-Kin Lau to my chambers at once," he demanded thickly, his passion rising as the notion of raping Kai Chen continued to blossom within him. Glancing down he saw the evidence of his desire rising and hastened from the hall. Flinging his garments from him he waited impatiently in his private rooms for Ji-Kin Lau to appear. When Ji-Kin Lau walked through the doors he grabbed her cruelly by the front of her tunic and flung her to the bed. Pouncing on her, living his current fantasy of Kai Chen through her, he violently shred her offending clothes away as she lay passively beneath him.

"Fight me," he gritted between clenched teeth, feeling his desire wane through her inaction. *You are Kai Chen*, he told himself repeatedly as he closed his eyes, envisioning large green eyes.

Ji-Kin Lau began to struggle aggressively and his passion flared anew as he imagined it to be Kai Chen. Flinging her onto her stomach he grabbed her hips and pulled her to him. Savagely, he thrust into her moist sheath as she joined him enthusiastically in their lustful frolic. Their shouts of release reverberated off the walls as they achieved their climax. Shoving away from her he frowned as he realized it was Ji-Kin Lau, not Kai Chen. The fantasy was over but he would have the reality. Of that there was no doubt.

"I am glad you are back, Tuan," Ji-Kin Lau purred, her lovely features roaming over him lewdly. It never ceased to amaze her how small his sex became after he was finished with her, belying the enormity of it during. "Much has happened while you were away."

"The cleric has informed me," he responded dully. His mind still lingered on arresting green eyes and a tight, virginal sheath. Although he had just climaxed and spilled his seed inside Ji-Kin Lau he was not sexually or mentally fulfilled. He lay in bed pondering his next move regarding Kai Chen, even while Ji-Kin Lau studied him intently.

She clenched her teeth together in anger. Prince Tuan was not attractive by any means with his harsh features, yellowed teeth, and beady eyes but he was hard, ruthless and arousing in bed, as well as in politics. Just the way she preferred it. Just the way she had been taught to relish it. However, there had been something particularly different having sex with him this time. It reminded her of when he had taken her virginity two years ago. At the time he had been a barbaric lover, causing her severe agony and savoring each moment. Since then he had remained rough but it had never been as angry and torrid as this. It was as though he wanted to take her virginity all over again.

Tuan was known to take young virgins frequently for pleasure and she didn't mind, but never had he fantasized of another while using her! It insulted her, degraded her position and threatened it. She would discover who this girl was he craved.

And kill her.

There would not be another who would usurp her position as future Empress of China or take her lover.

"Ah! Kai Chen it is good to see you," a nun greeted warmly as the tall girl entered the temple grounds.

Kai Chen bowed respectfully before the holy woman. "Sun Ma, it has been many weeks. You are well?"

"As well as this old body allows," the Elderly nun smiled toothlessly then cackled as she spryly headed toward the temple. Kai Chen followed, knowing her grandmother could be found within.

"Ng-Kin will be happy to see you. She speaks of you often."

"I am pleased to hear that she does, and how are your studies in the English language?" Kai Chen reverted to speaking English instead of Chinese and the nun cackled again with amusement.

"I could be doing worse," she replied easily in the foreign tongue.

"So I hear."

Ng-Kin exited the entrance to the worship temple as they approached.

"Granddaughter! What brings you to this temple today?"

"To see your welcoming smile," Kai Chen replied with an impish grin.

"That is a response I would expect from Sun Ma. You have been speaking with her too often," Ng-Kin declared with a chortle. The toothless Elderly nun laughed boisterously as she waved goodbye to Kai Chen before leaving them.

"I would speak with you concerning the Imperial Guard," Kai Chen whispered urgently and all traces of good-natured easiness disappeared between them.

"Come let us walk in the gardens."

Kai Chen walked beside her grandmother, their silent footsteps not leaving a trace in the dirt. "How are your parents?"

"They are well. Mother's eyes are no longer sharp for sewing and father's back bothers him at times."

"That is simply age. Agreed, they are well," the woman stated crisply and held her orange robes above her ankles as they walked across stones near a lily pond. Coming to a patch of grass, Ng-Kin sat and waited patiently for Kai Chen to do the same. Once settled, she asked, "What of the Guard?"

"I was stopped and questioned by Prince Tuan several days ago. He has yet to return but I saw it in his eyes. He will be back for me. I fear the altercation at the market with some of his soldiers and his arrival near father's church was not accidental. I am concerned for my parent's welfare."

Ng-Kin did not speak as she contemplated Kai Chen's concern. Her wrinkled skin was tanned from years of exposure to the elements. The inky blackness of Ng-Kin's slanted eyes deepened while she remained in thought. Her callused and worn hands lay loosely in her lap. A shroud of peace surrounded her, as always, leaving Kai Chen feeling comfortable and at ease. Although Ng-Kin had been at the temple as a nun for many years, she had once been married. After the death of her husband and Ying's marriage she had chosen to give up all earthly possessions and become a nun at the temple. For almost forty years she had resided at this temple.

"It is your welfare I fear for, Kai Chen. I ask you to remain out of view until I contact you. You understand," Ng-Kin ordered sternly.

"I will obey," Kai Chen promised. She would never disobey her parents, unless Ng-Kin advised to do so. Ng-Kin's word and honor she held above all others. Their relationship went beyond mere grandmother and granddaughter. They were best friends and understood each other's hearts. It was a kinship very few people in life shared.

"Go now and I will contact you soon," the Elderly woman said as she gave Kai Chen a serene smile.

With a nod Kai Chen quickly made her way from the secluded holy temple.

CHAPTER FIVE

Making no mistakes is what establishes the certainty of victory, for it means conquering an enemy that is already defeated.
- Sun Tzu, *The Art of War*

City of Willows
One month later

"I want the half breed Kai Chen from Fukien province taken to the Triad Temple in Hunan province. Her father is the Lutheran missionary of Fukien. It should not be difficult to find reason to arrest her," Tuan stated diabolically as he sat on the edge of his bed.

For weeks now Prince Tuan had been consumed with thoughts and fantasies of the half-breed woman with the green eyes. Not only did he wish to take her innocence, but he also wished to break the essence of something magical he sensed within her, her fighting spirit. He wanted to capture and destroy the warrior.

"Of course, Highness," the cleric said and bowed reverently.

"Instruct my members to use caution when apprehending her. I have word from a group of Imperial soldiers she is quite deadly and skilled in some form of martial art. It is understandable if she is injured slightly, but under no circumstances is she to be killed, permanently maimed, and most definitely not sexually assaulted in any manner. Is this perfectly clear?"

"Indubitably," the cleric bowed again.

"Good. I have plans for the exquisite Kai Chen that Ji-Kin Lau must not learn about. Is this clear as well?"

"I will sever the tongue of any member who speaks of this," the cleric informed his leader adamantly.

Prince Tuan chuckled. His amusement was clear as he leaned back on his elbows. "Speaking of tongues, you may use yours now." With relish, Tuan lay back completely on his bed as his male cleric kneeled between his spread legs and pushed his long robes up to expose his thickened manhood.

Ng-Kin, the Buddhist nun, remained hidden in Prince Tuan's room. She was disgusted by the vulgar act played before her between the two men. It was her duty to the Triad and her brothers and sisters of all temples to know everything Prince Tuan executed or planned. Observing his outlandish penchant for sexual deviance was one affront, but to discover he was scheming to use her granddaughter was the final one!

She would not permit him to touch Kai Chen in any fashion. Ng-Kin did not want to consider what Prince Tuan would do if he did capture her. Kai Chen was too valuable to her immediate clan of women with the legacy of their martial art, Wing Chun, and too spiritual and loving to be subjected to his licentious actions. Once captured, Ng-Kin knew Kai Chen would be physically restrained while he violated her mercilessly. No woman deserved the vileness of Prince Tuan and his sexual perversions. If he discovered Kai Chen's secret of Wing Chun she would be killed after great torture. He would want the secret for himself.

The ecstatic roar of Prince Tuan's sexual release resounded in the room. Ng-Kin saw a slight movement across the room and observed Ji-Kin Lau peer from behind a curtained wall. Ji-Kin Lau's eyes told of her hedonistic nature as she avidly scrutinized Prince Tuan in the forbidden act performed on him by his cleric.

"Very good," Tuan groaned with pleasure as the man before him rose to his feet, licking his lips as he bowed humbly. "You may go."

The cleric left the room quietly, wiping his mouth as Ji-Kin Lau slid from behind the curtain. Prince Tuan lay on the bed stroking his semi-flaccid manhood as he regained his strength. Ng-Kin frowned with repulsion as she witnessed Ji-Kin Lau silently shed her clothes and stand before him. Prince Tuan was unaware of Ji-Kin Lau's presence as he reveled in the aftermath of his sexual deviance. Ng-Kin's eyes narrowed as she considered Ji-Kin Lau thoughtfully.

Ji-Kin Lau had effectively slid into the room at some point and had not been heard nor observed by anyone, she reflected. Unease over this discovery filled her heart. Ng-Kin wondered how Ji-Kin Lau had mastered the art of stepping silently. Very few Elders knew the secret technique of complete silence. There was treachery among the temples anew, and it was clear by Ji-Kin Lau's uncanny ability.

Concern marred Ng-Kin's aging features as she glanced at the fresh wanton display before her. Prince Tuan had not known Ji-Kin Lau had witnessed the act with his cleric. Nor did he realize she watched him presently stroke himself. His excitement became evident in the swelling of his sex again. Prince Tuan now sported a full erection and Ji-Kin Lau was practically salivating in her desire as she nimbly straddled his waist and impaled herself upon him before he could react.

"What are you doing?" Tuan was outraged as he shoved at the woman on top of him.

"I witnessed your cleric, Tuan. It was exhilarating," Ji-Kin Lau announced breathlessly as she pumped her body up and down on him.

"How long have you been spying?" He spat the words at her. His fear that Ji-Kin Lau had overheard his plans for Kai Chen made him vicious as he bit down on one of her breasts painfully, drawing blood, even as his appetite for her grew.

"Only long enough to witness your sin," she lied and cried out in pain even as her eyes flashed brilliance in enjoyment. Ng-Kin knew Ji-Kin Lau had unearthed Kai Chen's identity.

"You enjoyed watching," he affirmed, seeing the libidinous glow to her dark eyes as she rode him. "Then you will love this."

Prince Tuan pulled her off him and rolled them over. Throwing her face down on the bed, he grabbed her hips and plunged his swollen member between her buttocks. Ji-Kin Lau's shriek of initial pain rang resonantly in the corridors of the City of Willows as he used her in a monstrous fashion that made Ng-Kin ill. Biting her lips to prevent herself from crying out at his heinous act, Ng-Kin quit the chamber and fled silently from the Triad temple to save her granddaughter, Kai Chen.

☯

"Quickly, my daughter, you must head for the Fukien temple before Prince Tuan's soldiers arrive," Ying cried out in fear.

"What?" Kai Chen stared at her mother in horror as the words settled in her mind like a black mantle.

"Ng-Kin overheard Prince Tuan order you be taken to Hunan province. She declares he will rape you and possibly kill you," she cried out, desperation evident in the way she clenched her hands into the material of Kai Chen's black dress.

"What shall I do at Fukien temple?" Confusion and distress tainted Kai Chen's exotic features as she digested the implications of what her mother meant.

"You are to become a nun. It has been your wish for many years, daughter. I have known this and so has your father," the small woman declared, her smile tremulous as she placed a dark cloak about Kai's body. "Go with our blessing, child, and know we love you most dearly."

Tears gathered and trickled down Kai Chen's face as her mother embraced her tightly. The fear in her heart of being captured by Prince Tuan and thought of leaving her parents overrode the joy of having her ecclesiastical desire granted. Once a nun at the temple, in hiding from the Manchu government, it would not be easy to see them again. She would remain primarily in seclusion in order to protect them all.

"You must run to the temple quickly, daughter," David Boussard urged, his features pinched as he attempted to control his fluctuating emotions. "I cannot protect you." The despair and shame of his admission was reflected in his voice.

Throwing her arms about him, Kai Chen held him tightly. "God shall protect me, father," she whispered softly in his ear. Though she did not believe in his God she did know how to appease his conscience. Stepping away from him she witnessed the bright shine of tears in his green eyes identical to hers. The dark ring surrounding the distinct green color only intensified its uniqueness and made her realize how different she was from others.

The sound of footsteps outside caused Ying to cry out in terror. Grasping her mother against her briefly in a quick embrace of reassurance, Kai Chen smiled.

"I will never be lonely for you will always be with me," she stated and placed a closed fist against her breast.

"My daughter," the woman cried in a subdued tone of loss as Kai Chen stepped away and headed for the kitchen door.

"I love you both."

With a final glance, she fled the small house like a spirit in the night. In the cover of darkness Kai Chen sped with sure feet across the familiar terrain of Fukien province toward her grandmother's Shaolin temple. The crickets continued their evening serenade without pause as she silently propelled through the forest like the wind. Even the ghosts of warriors past would not have distinguished her hushed progression as the warriors of the present invaded her parent's home.

A violent crash of the front door against a wall made Ying jump while being held in the circle of her husband's arms. Twelve figures clothed entirely in black surged into their home. Their faces were covered with black material, the only exposure their malevolent black eyes. They were not Imperial Guards, but Triad members.

"Where is Kai Chen?" The leader stood before them, legs spread wide and his arms crossed at his chest arrogantly. Other soldiers went into every room of the house to search for Kai Chen.

"She is not here," Ying declared, her anger building as they searched for her daughter. Objects were thrown against walls in outrage as they tried to locate the missing woman they were to kidnap.

"Where is she?" His vicious tone fueled her rage, but she held herself in check. She could not allow herself to openly fight these Triad members unless they threatened to physically harm them. However, if they did attack she would take great pleasure in killing all that her physical limitations would allow.

"Kai Chen was married two days ago and no longer lives here. She and her husband sailed to America," David Boussard lied. *God forgive me*, he prayed silently.

The Triad leader stared at the Lutheran minister standing before him. Skepticism was apparent in his narrowed black eyes as they raked over his tall, thin body. "If you are lying, death will certainly be yours."

"Death is all of ours at some point," the minister stated firmly.

"Get out of our home," Ying demanded fiercely, the verbal threat spurring her to defense. She would not tolerate these evil Triad members any longer.

Bowing in mock deference the leader spun around and left their house, his minions following. Ying slammed the door forcefully then threw herself into her husband's arms as tears coursed down her face.

"I pray to God they do not find our Kai Chen," she cried into his chest.

David Boussard held his wife closely within his arms, "As do I."

Shaolin Temple
Fukien Province

"Come, my child," Ng-Kin bade softly as they entered the temple where Kai Chen would remain for the rest of her life. "You must be prepared."

They entered the beautiful temple hidden in the deep recesses of the mountains. The elaborate structure took Kai Chen's breath away as she penetrated the sacred fortress. Golden Buddha's lined either side of the entrance inside, a heavenly scent of spice and lotus permeating her senses as they walked silently through the corridors. The temple was overwhelmingly spiritual, the sound of chanting mantras by monks and nuns almost musical in its creation. Candles and torches lit the antechamber as they passed through, providing a celestial ambience and inspiring devotion.

Ng-Kin wove her way through several passageways, delving deeper and deeper into the enormous temple. "This is where you shall shed all earthly possessions. Do not be afraid, Kai Chen. Though forfeiting your past life for this new one, I believe another awaits you beyond this sanctuary in time".

"I am happy to be here, grandmother," she smiled at her Wing Chun mentor and dearest friend.

"Then we shall proceed. You will begin as a laywoman Buddhist nun. If, in time, you find it Buddha's will then you may choose to become a full nun," the Elderly woman stated simply.

They entered a dimly lit chamber filled with candles. The scent was overwhelming and heady with the scent of lilacs. Two young nuns, Kai Chen's age, stepped from the shadows and bowed reverently to Ng-Kin who returned the gesture. Their heads were shaved almost bald and their orange robes glowed as though on fire as the flickering shadows from the candles shifted across the material.

"Sisters, this is Kai Chen. She is prepared to take her vows as a laywoman nun, and ready to relinquish all earthly possessions and transgressions," Ng-Kin announced. "When the preparations are complete show her to her sleeping quarters. Tomorrow, Kai Chen, you will be taken to the worship room for the ceremony."

"Yes, grandmother," she acquiesced and bowed deeply.

The older woman grasped Kai Chen's hands and squeezed them briefly. Kai Chen felt the callused palms and thick growths on Ng-Kin's knuckles from years of practicing Wing Chun. "From this day forth, you must call me Ng-Kin or sister. I am no longer grandmother."

"I will honor that, sister, but understand," Kai Chen said warmly as she kissed the woman's cheek, "you will always be my grandmother."

Tears sprang into the older woman's eyes as she nodded and released her granddaughter's hands. Quietly, Ng-Kin quit the chamber and Kai Chen knew a moment of fear. From this moment her life would change irrevocably. She would no longer be Kai Chen, daughter of Ying and David Boussard. She would be simply Kai Chen, Sister and Buddhist nun of the rebuilt Fukien Shaolin Temple.

Grasping her elbows, the young nuns escorted her into an adjacent chamber where a steaming bath awaited her. They spoke not a word as her clothing was taken from her and she stepped into the water. Each woman grabbed a sponge and scrubbed her body until it was red and clean then escorted her to a large table where they proceeded to massage scented oil into her porous skin. When finished they showed her how to fashion the orange robe about her body and completed the simple ritual with a meal of steamed rice and bland vegetables with her.

"You will share a room with us once the ceremony is over," one of the women stated as they strolled with her along the corridors. "My name is Lee."

"I am Sun," the other woman said and smiled shyly.

Kai Chen returned the smile. "I wondered if it was forbidden to speak."

"There is no speaking during the preparation. Instead, we pray to Buddha for your enlightenment," Lee stated simply. "Here is your room for the night. The ceremony will be long tomorrow. That is why we take such pains to give modest pleasure now."

"I appreciate your thoughtfulness," Kai Chen said earnestly and bowed to the two Sisters. When she raised her head they were gone.

It was difficult to sleep worrying about her parents and lying on the harsh pallet instead of her soft bed, but Kai Chen did not complain. This would be her life now. As a laywoman nun her existence would be decidedly more difficult in some areas, but the freedom to train in Wing Chun and devote herself to Buddhism would supersede it. She was spiritually content.

Morning came all too soon as Kai Chen was awakened by Ng-Kin. A white shawl was placed over her head and brief instructions given as they made their way to the worship room. Walking with her head bowed and her palms together, she knelt before the priest and Abbot of the temple. Each side of the temple was filled with monks and nuns on their knees bowed in devotion to the statue of Buddha on the altar before them.

"Brothers and sisters, today we eagerly embrace a new laywoman within our fold," the Abbot declared happily. Kai Chen's first name was chanted three times. "These items shall be your only worldly possessions."

At the Abbot's feet lay a wooden bowl, staff, and a scroll containing five vows. Kai Chen understood the vows she would embrace in this new life as Shaolin nun. Maintaining her position, Kai Chen listened as the Abbot prayed for several hours. Sitting with her legs folded under her, her buttocks resting on the heels of her feet, Kai Chen repeated her mantras to force herself into meditation.

A large gong sounded as the Abbot and monks finally moved and supplicated themselves before Buddha. After several moments they quit the prayer room. Kai Chen instinctively remained until the last monk and nun exited and rose to her numbed feet. Turning, she saw Ng-Kin waiting for her at the entrance. Since becoming a nun her grandmother rarely showed emotion, but now the older woman's eyes glowed with a semblance of pride and happiness. Kai Chen smiled. Gathering the meager items bestowed upon her, she followed her grandmother to her new room she would share with Lee and Sun.

"You did very well, sister. Now, I advise you to remember the five vows a laywoman takes. We will review these carefully and you must consider them wisely. The five vows given are vows that may never be broken and are easy to obey. If you become a full nun someday you may choose the other three hundred and sixty-five vows you wish to embrace in this life as a nun. If any of these vows are breached you will be banished from the temple," she warned in a firm and serious tone. "Remember the story I told you of Ng Mui?"

"Yes, Ng-Kin. I recall the monk Ma Fu-l broke a vow by having sexual relations with another monk's wife and his sister. He was banished from the temple in disgrace because Ng Mui divulged this personal knowledge to the Elders," Kai Chen recounted. "The story that is most important is the fall of the Five Elders in which Bak Mei killed Jee Sin."

"Ah! You have a good memory. It shall serve you well at this temple," Ng-Kin stated happily and grinned. "Come, child. Bring your new bowl. I am an old woman and in need of sustenance to keep this body functioning."

"I am hungry, too," she declared then whispered softly, "grandmother."

Triad Temple
Hunan Province

"What do you mean she got away?" Every member who stood before him in the training hall felt Prince Tuan's wrath.

"Her parents said she married two days ago and sailed to America, but one of my men thinks they saw her. He tried to follow her through the province but she managed to elude him. There is no way for us to know where she might be hiding now, Highness," the leader declared, his arrogance buffeted by the seething Prince before him.

"I want her found! Do not kill her parents just yet. She may very well return to visit them, and if not soon, we shall hold them as prisoners until she turns herself over to us," he mused deviously. "Off with you! Find her and do not rest until you do."

"Yes, Prince Tuan." The group of failed members bowed repeatedly as they backed away from the unpredictable leader before quitting the enormous hall.

Fury built in Tuan every second as his body screamed for sexual release. He had abstained from any carnal pleasures for weeks, savoring the moment when he would steal the fascinating woman's innocence. Now, she was missing and his sex weighed heavy with thwarted excitement.

Turning to his cleric, Tuan asked, "Where might a young woman go, a half-breed with no other family?"

Silence greeted him for several moments as the two men deliberated where Kai Chen Boussard would hide. Frustration filled him at his present loss, although admiration for the clever girl nipped at him. How could she have known there would be men coming for her? Who knew besides him and his cleric? Glancing at the small, thin man who had faithfully stood by him in every crisis, and before him on his knees in a most pleasing manner for the past twenty years, Prince Tuan knew he was not the traitor.

Suddenly, the memory of Ji-Kin Lau mounting him and her admission of seeing the cleric with him made Tuan wonder if she had not overheard his plans. She had never lied to him before, but as devious as Ji-Kin Lau was he would not be surprised if she had warned Kai Chen. But why would she? It thrilled Ji-Kin Lau to watch when he drained a virgin of her chastity. However, he had not planned on allowing her to watch him with Kai Chen. He had wanted that to be his singular entertainment. Besides, Ji-Kin Lau wished to rule by his side. She would do nothing to jeopardize her position as future Empress.

Sighing heavily, he studied his cleric and considered using him then frowned. No, he needed a chaste vessel to use, to get as close to having Kai Chen as possible. "Get me a virgin. I am in the mood. One of the girl's from a nearby village will suffice and make her young."

"Right away," the cleric said and shuffled off to please his master.

Ng-Kin stayed hidden in her secret spot she had used for years to spy on the Triad. She watched with some satisfaction in knowing she had thwarted his plans for the moment with Kai Chen, but with concern at what he would do to the girl brought to him by his cleric. Silently, Ng-Kin followed Tuan through the secret recesses of the Triad temple to his private quarters. Hiding behind a tall black screen covered with inlaid ivory dragons she waited patiently to discover his next move. It would be prudent to observe him as much as possible, although she must be careful. She placed herself in great danger by slipping into this Triad temple and possibly catching his or any other member's attention.

Almost an hour later a small Chinese girl was brought into Tuan's bedroom. Tears streamed down her pale face as she stared at the strange man who was rapidly removing his clothes. Her undeveloped body shook in fear as she wiped at her face. Her skinny arms and legs spoke of her malnourishment.

"How old are you, child?" Prince Tuan's voice was soothing as the girl struggled in the cleric's tight grip.

"Fifteen," she cried. "Please, do not hurt me!"

"Hush, child," he ordered harshly and fiercely gripped her arm. The cleric left quickly, shutting the door behind him with a soft click. "Do you not want to be consort to a Prince?"

"No!" The small girl fought to release his grip, her actions spurring his desire.

"Yes," he ground out between clenched teeth and ripped the clothes from her tiny body. "I will not hurt you if you pretend to be Kai Chen."

The screams from the girl incensed him as she fought mightily to escape. She stared at his sex straining toward her and cried out anew in horror. Hurling her naked body to the bed Prince Tuan threw her onto her stomach and impaled his thick desire through her maidenhead. Her screams of suffering only drove him to further cruelty as he grasped her black hair and sadistically yanked her head back toward him.

"I have you Kai Chen. Now I have you!" Over and over he violated her, yanking her head back as his ferocious shout of release camouflaged the sound of bones snapping in her neck.

Ng-Kin's eyes widened, horror reflected in them. She heard the sound of the girl's tiny bones breaking, of him killing her. Ng-Kin covered her mouth to mute her own cry of outrage. The sight of the young girl's virginal blood coated the sheets of the bed as Prince Tuan dropped her lifeless body as though discarding a dirty rag. He had brutally raped and killed that innocent girl! Squeezing her eyes shut to control herself of the atrocity she had just witnessed, Ng-Kin waited long suffering minutes to ensure her escape.

The cleric entered the room, expecting to help the girl from Tuan's quarters. Upon noticing the dead girl, his eyes widened with disbelief and he threw his master a terrified glance.

"Dispose of the body," Tuan said in bored tones as he sauntered across the room and began cleaning the blood covering his groin from a bowl of water. "Ah! I am temporarily rejuvenated."

Ng-Kin watched as the cleric nervously hoisted the inert body with no difficulty over his shoulder and made his way through the hidden recesses of the temple. Having witnessed this ultimate crime, Ng-Kin decided she would very carefully foist her knowledge of Prince Tuan's malfeasance to the clergy of the Forbidden City and the Empress, Tzu Hsi. Although corrupt, Tzu His would not stand for Prince Tuan's rape and killing of a child, especially if determined she was Chinese as he would have tainted the Manchu bloodline.

Kai Chen rose and bowed before the Abbess who smiled warmly at her. "Welcome, sister. I have heard many generous claims of you, given by Ng-Kin. We are honored to have a nun of your learning, skills and doctrine."

"I am honored." Smiling at the intimidating woman, Kai Chen felt the burden of her vows shroud her. As a laywoman nun of the Shaolin temple she could fight but never kill, she could love but never know the wonder of sexual contact. So be it. She was a half-breed; a social outcast who had never had a friend, let alone would ever know the love of a man. It was Buddha's will.

Ng-Kin met her in the corridor of the temple, a deep frown blemishing her lean features. Her pale face appeared drawn and exhaustion seemed to make her step less light. It was apparent a heavy burden filled her grandmother but she was a very mysterious nun who was not one to divulge information unless it was warranted.

"I must go to the Forbidden City. I will be gone for many weeks. Prince Tuan looks for you. He is a monster who must be stopped. The Empress will see to this once I pass on information to her clergy."

"Do you wish me to attend with you?" Kai Chen asked. Concern for her grandmother was foremost in her mind. Ng-Kin was now in her seventieth year. Although still incredibly deadly, she was not as agile, fast or powerful with her body. It was failing her as she began her trip to end this life.

The older woman stared at her granddaughter's stunning visage. Kai Chen's hair was braided and hung down her back. Her green eyes appeared enormous with her concern. The delicate curve of her face, flawless skin and infectious smile could capture the eye of every man, but would it ever steal one man's heart? It was a shame such beauty would not be appreciated, but she feared Kai Chen was correct in her thinking. Though accepted as a nun there may be no man who would accept her as a mate.

"No Kai Chen. This trip is mine alone. You will stay here and practice your Wing Chun. There is a storm coming and it will bring a change none of us may be prepared for, child. Honor your legacy and family. Honor Ng Mui and all she has given us by training as it may someday be your salvation," Ng-Kin stated solemnly. She turned away, moving with determination to prepare for her trip to Beijing and the Forbidden City.

☯

New York City

"Vaden, ole' chap!"

Sebastian Madden's friendly voice called out loudly amongst the host of people attending the fabulously expensive dinner party. Only the wealthy or prestigious had been invited, arriving in an elaborate horse drawn coach and some in the widely controversial automobile.

"Sebastian! Good to see you," Vaden declared as the two men shook hands vigorously. "It's been six months since I saw you last. I heard you were doing well with the new passenger liner in your fleet."

"Yes. I am pleased with the revenue. How is business in China?"

Vaden frowned pensively. "It may be faltering. I predict war soon. Not only are the people of China rebelling against the foreigners, they are uprising against their own government. The situation is grave."

"It is a heathen country, but it does have its pleasures," Sebastian stated with a wicked smile, and then chuckled briefly. "Your business is thriving, though difficulties are abundant in your most prosperous locale?"

"Yes. I have recently established trade in India and it is flourishing by leaps and bounds, exceeding China," he admitted and gratefully accepted the glass of champagne handed to him.

"You do have a penchant for prosperity, friend," Sebastian acknowledged as he raised his crystal flute in salute.

Vaden lifted his glass a notch and they swallowed the bubbly champagne as another was pressed into their hands by a passing waiter. Casually, he gazed about the elaborate ballroom for his new business contact. It would give him great satisfaction to add Germany to his list of countries of imported goods and would make him the wealthiest merchant in the country.

Searching for several moments for the tall man he had spoken with earlier in the week who assured him he would be at this event, Vaden finally gave up to regard several women. They were adorned with elegant ball gowns of silk in a myriad of colors and fashioned with daring necklines and flared skirts. Each tried to eclipse the others with flowers, ribbons, jewelry and furs. Men were decked in full evening dress, their tailcoats consisting of a continuous roll collar and their double-breasted waistcoats low cut. Pristine white stiff shirts complemented the stark black color of their suits. The only variance was the wearing of either a white or black silk bow tie.

"Sebastian! Sebastian Madden!"

A woman's high-pitched voice caught Vaden's attention as a lovely woman swept grandly toward them. Her honey blonde hair was styled in a sweeping bun with pale green flowers garnishing it, while curling tendrils framed her face. Coyly, she batted her long eyelashes at the two men to gain attention to her dark blue eyes.

"Why, Caroline Pennington! How decidedly stunning you are this evening," Sebastian asserted fervently as she pressed a lacy fan to her chest to bring attention to her heaving breasts.

Both men glanced down at her breasts which strained to burst free of the vivid green material of her dress. Vaden arched an eyebrow as he saw the rosy edge of one nipple peeping along the edge. Suddenly, the color of her dress caught his attention and he frowned. It reminded him of jade green eyes he had encountered in a China market.

"Thank you, sir, and who might your companion be?"

Bringing himself back to the present Vaden bowed slightly and took her proffered hand.

"Miss Caroline Pennington, I am pleased to introduce you to Mister Vaden LeBlanc, my best friend and foremost deadly business rival," Sebastian announced and chuckled at Vaden's pained expression.

"I daresay, Miss Pennington, he exaggerates my business achievements," he said in bored tones and kissed the back of her hand lightly.

"And I believe you are modest, Mister LeBlanc," she said breathlessly, obviously trying to impress him with a beatific smile.

"Please, call me Vaden, Miss Pennington. I abhor formalities," he offered politely, releasing her hand easily.

Leaning close to him as the room thickened with bodies, she whispered. "As do I, Vaden. Call me Caroline."

Her cool fingers slipped a small card inside his coat pocket before she was swept away by Sebastian for the first dance of the evening. Vaden arched a brow at her flagrantly flirtatious manner. Caroline Pennington appeared no different than many of the other money hungry vixens at this party. She simply wasted no time ensuring men knew she was on the selling block to the highest bidder. He was not interested. Not when a China doll with green eyes from Fukien province still haunted him on a daily basis.

"We shall talk business once I finish with this lovely morsel," Sebastian shouted to Vaden as they passed him while dancing.

Vaden lifted his glass and smiled but his eyes remained cold and his heart empty.

CHAPTER SIX

The victorious strategist only seeks battle after the victory has been won, whereas he who is destined to defeat first fights and afterwards looks for victory.
- Sun Tzu, *The Art of War*

Fukien Province

"I should change your name to Ng Mui," Ng-Kin declared breathlessly as she paused to regain her stamina. Her laughing eyes belied her weariness.

"None shall ever surpass the great Ng Mui, I fear," Kai Chen said seriously. With shrewd eyes she noted her grandmother was beginning to falter in her physical capabilities. No longer could the woman practice for several hours or strike with the speed of a snake or move with the lightness of a whisper. Since her return from Beijing a few months earlier the woman had been somewhat withdrawn and pensive. Although she had passed on the information to the clergy of the Imperial court regarding Prince Tuan, nothing had been done to stop him and his heinous actions. This spoke of inner treason within the Forbidden City in which the Imperial clergy planned to assist Prince Tuan with his plan to overthrow the Empress Tzu Hsi.

"It is time you train without me, sister. I am holding you back from further greatness. There is none alive who can defeat you. This, I know," the woman declared, pride and satisfaction evident in her pinched features. Pride was not an emotion allowed as a nun but if this was Ng-Kin's only transgression she felt Buddha would forgive her, for was He not the one to enlighten Ng Mui centuries ago with the very secret he had bestowed upon them all?

"How would you know, Ng-Kin?" Kai Chen scoffed with a chuckle. Throwing her grandmother a fierce scowl of disbelief at the woman's verbal approval, Kai Chen bounded across the sand with powerful legs. Propelling her body forward she hurled herself into the air, performing a series of flips and tumbles while using strikes and defensive motions with her feet and hands. Landing skillfully on the sand she spun around and repeated the motions exactly as she made her way back toward Ng-Kin.

"Wing Chun is an exemplary martial art. However, its full potential is different with each student or master. You possess an uncommon gift of physical prowess our lineage has never achieved before, but more importantly, you hold within your heart the elements of Sil Lum Tao, the way of the small idea, the core of the art's technique. You, my dear sister, are a great master," the Elderly woman proclaimed and bowed unpretentiously before her granddaughter.

Kai Chen stared at her grandmother with wide eyes, amazement reflected in the deep green depths. "I accept your most gracious compliments, sister, but they are taken lightly."

The old woman cackled with delight at Kai Chen's humility then brought up her hands and attacked. After years of training with Ng-Kin she was always on guard. Even while in the confines of the Shaolin temple the Elderly nun would attack Kai Chen when she least expected it. Lee and Sun thought it quite hilarious to be awakened in the middle of the night and enjoyed watching the sparring match between the two women in their small room. Upon occasion, even the Abbess was seen peering around a corner of the training hall to observe their unique relationship and talents with a grin spread across her usually severe face.

Their infectious laughter was whisked away by the breeze of the ocean as old teacher made way for new teacher. Although it was evident to both that Kai Chen's proficiency supplanted Ng-Kin's, the older woman was still as deadly as a poisoned dart.

"Enough," Ng-Kin confessed when Kai Chen cleverly removed the wooden blade from her gnarled grasp and held it to her throat. "This old body can no longer keep up with you."

"Can your body continue to secret away to the Triad temple to spy on Prince Tuan?" Kai Chen covertly studied her grandmother's expression as she sprung the question then released her. It was plain by the shocked appearance on the old woman's face that she did not know Kai Chen knew of her spying.

"You see too much, young sister," Ng-Kin stated sharply, her pleasant features suddenly drawn into a harsh mask.

"I see the grandmother I adore more than my life placing herself in grave danger. Who do you seek to protect? How are you able to invade their fortress unless you are a member?"

"You have followed me, sister." Disapproval was written in her rigid visage as she straightened her robe with shaking hands. Ng-Kin did not want Kai Chen to witness the horrors of the Triad temple. Although not an ignorant girl, Kai Chen was still very innocent in many ways of the world, especially between a man and a woman.

"Upon occasion I have followed you. I protect that which I hold dear to me; my religion, my family, and my Wing Chun," she whispered, grasping the old woman's hands in hers. "Tell me what needs to be done and I shall help you."

Ng-Kin sighed heavily and kneeled resignedly on the sand. Kai Chen sat next to her as they stared far out across the vast waters swelling, breaking then drifting inland to them. The tangy smell of the ocean and dried seaweed on the beach was familiar, promoting a reminiscence of the many times they had been here together. Ng-Kin appeared very old and fragile. Her fatigue of this life was clear.

"Prince Tuan is evil, Kai Chen. Even now, he has not forgotten you and seeks in every province to locate you. Through the years I have witnessed many abominations by him. Once, I tried relating to the Triad Elders of his demonic habits but they favored him greatly. I was forbid mentioning him in an opposing manner again. Afterward, the Abbess ordered me to infiltrate them for our temple's protection.

"Since that day I have strived to be particularly careful and ascertain every decision Prince Tuan makes and every action he takes. In his fanatical sickness he will not rest until he has defiled you and broken the ardent spirit he identifies within you, as he has done to countless others. I will not allow that," she pronounced vehemently.

"He will locate me eventually, grandmother," Kai Chen stated with certainty, remembering his invidious eyes the day he had approached her outside her father's church. "Your risk is no longer necessary."

The two nuns sat in silence and allowed the soft breeze to blow away the worries of the moment. Ng-Kin's heart was concerned. There was so much she wished she could share with her granddaughter, but Buddha had not spoken to Ng-Kin yet. When his spirit finally touched the older woman she prayed it was not too late.

"That is correct, young nun," Ji-Kin Lau whispered to herself as she watched the two nuns from her hidden position. A mercenary sheen lit her features as she observed the women gather their items and trudge along the coast toward the Fukien Shaolin temple. "Risk is no longer necessary as I have found you for Prince Tuan."

Imperial City
March 1900

"Send her to me," he ground out furiously between clenched teeth. Obediently, the cleric rushed from his master's private chambers within the Imperial City. Though none but the Empress Dowager, the Emperor, his concubines and their eunuchs lived within the Forbidden City, other officials and family members lived in the fortress surrounding their fortress.

Pursing his lips together while in thought, Prince Tuan wondered what would bring Ji-Kin Lau so far from the Triad temple in Fukien province. Never before had she dare enter the Imperial City after her failure to be concubine at the hands of the Empress Dowager. It must be of dire circumstance to bring her so far and to act so boldly. The footsteps of his cleric echoed down the hollow marble halls announcing his return, but he could not discern Ji-Kin Lau with him. Confusion marred Tuan's evil countenance as the cleric entered his chamber followed by the silent consort. He had never noticed before how quietly she moved, almost as though a spirit.

"Emperor," Ji Kin-Lu called out with relief and bowed before him. "I have tidings that shall lighten your mood and illuminate your life."

He stared at the beautiful woman before him who had come to him as a mere child and now was considered the most deadly society member within the Triad with her uncanny martial art ability. Not only did he desire her, he loved her; her unbridled spirit, brilliant mind and fantastic sexual deviance. He could never have chosen a better mate as future Empress. However, it did not quench the prurient need to ravish virtuous girls or be with men. There would always be a barbaric hunger within him for the killing of innocence and purity, and imbibing of the taboo, but he especially enjoyed destroying a strong spirit.

"Come to me, my love. I have missed you," he whispered softly as his desire for her flamed. "Cleric, you may stay."

Ji-Kin Lau lifted an eyebrow and threw a curious glance over her shoulder at the cleric who watched them avidly as their sexual tension mounted. A wicked smile curved her full lips as she slowly crawled toward her master on her hands and knees. Seeing the savage glow of Tuan's eyes at her submissive slithering made the ache between her thighs pulse.

"I have missed you also, Tuan," she responded in a husky voice as she spread his legs apart while he reclined on the huge bed. "Let me show you how much."

With the flick of her wrist a metal object appeared in one hand and in seconds she had sliced his clothes from his body. Deftly she snapped her wrist and the razor-edge coin sailed across the room sticking in the statue of a Buddha. Shoving his clothes aside she viewed his enlarged manhood and purred deep in her throat.

"Cleric, come and participate," Tuan demanded harshly, his desire raging as he yielded to his depraved fantasies.

The sound of the door locking brought a satisfied grin to Ji-Kin Lau's face as she stroked Tuan's desire with her hands and mouth then moaned with pleasure. She enjoyed her sexual power over Tuan, and yet, she refused to allow him fulfillment until she had imparted a taste of her information. Bending over him she allowed the cleric to remove her clothes, enjoying the feel of new, unfamiliar hands on her body.

"Do you not want to know what I have discovered, Tuan?" Her question lingered, almost unheard, as his groans of delight filled the room. Ji-Kin Lau's head was forced down roughly, her mouth and throat filled with his swollen member. The cleric's hands spread her legs as his tongue and mouth began to move over her wet entrance.

"What have you discovered?" Prince Tuan's voice was strained as he fought for control. His head rose to view his cleric and Ji-Kin Lau. His excitement grew as he watched the cleric grab her small, firm breasts while his mouth feasted between her thighs. Their taboo sexual tryst almost was his undoing as he felt his imminent release building to deposit in her mouth.

Lifting her head, Ji-Kin Lau purred proudly, "I know where Kai Chen Boussard is hiding."

Her hair was gripped viciously in Prince Tuan's fist as he stared at her with wonder.

"Where is she?"

Ji-Kin Lau saw the animal hunger in him, the drive to have this forbidden woman flaring in his eyes and felt insane jealousy surge within her breast. First she would have her desire quenched by him and the cleric then she would enlighten him with her find. However, the ultimate decision of what happened to Kai Chen Boussard would be hers.

"Let us finish this first," she groaned in sexual frustration and trailed her tongue along his turgid length. The grimace on his face as he fought for control made her smile smugly. Her own release was building as the cleric's tongue flicked over her wetness repeatedly.

"Yes," Prince Tuan hissed urgently as his ache for release grew. With eager hands he alternated licks and kisses with cruel bites and slaps on her body as his seed shot into her mouth and down her throat. He grunted with satisfaction as she rolled onto her back. Tuan watched as the cleric lifted her legs around his neck and entered her slick wetness. Soon Prince Tuan joined them again, and they were all crying out with release, appeased of their sexual escapade. Afterward, Ji-Kin Lau was revealing everything she knew of the Buddhist nun named Kai Chen.

Fukien Province
One week later

"Perfect, sister," Ng-Kin rejoiced as she watched the nun block, strike and shift her body with a magic seeming to emanate from her.

Kai Chen ignored her surroundings as she calmly focused on the Muk Yan Chong, or wooden trunk with three misplaced arms and one leg, as it spun on its base with each strike and block she inflicted. Using blinding speed, Kai Chen's hands and legs controlled the practice dummy as she let her mastery of her art flow. Perspiration lined the top of her dark top as she expelled a regulated breath. The black split skirt flowed easily around her legs, concealing the placement of her feet, which confused an opponent during combat.

The Dein within the temple grounds held various instruments of practice and destruction. One wall was lined with Pak Charn Dao or Twin Butterfly Knives, and Luk Dim Boun Kwan, eight foot long poles. Another wall consisted of sturdy round rattan shields used in conjunction with the broad swords, their edges honed. Shining fans hung on hooks, their deadly blades folded together. Although none of the weapons were used to kill by the disciples they understood the potential for death with each item.

"Kai Chen, we are finished," the Ng-Kin announced with satisfaction and finality.

Immediately, Kai Chen halted the rotating wooden dummy and glanced at her grandmother inquisitively. "Ng-Kin, I will never be finished. There is more to learn," she stated with a grin.

Shaking a crooked finger at Kai Chen the old woman cackled briefly and said, "You have achieved enlightenment from Buddha in many aspects, my child. I fear you did not listen to your heart when taking your vows, though."

Tilting her head to one side Kai studied to woman before her with a frown. "I do not understand."

"Kai Chen," Ng-Kin whispered softly and stood before her, "change is coming. Buddha has spoken to me. China will forever change soon."

"Tell me, sister," Kai Chen paused to listen carefully. Vivid green eyes searched Ng-Kin's expression for answers as she remained silent.

"There are several wars coming, child. Remember, Wing Chun is a salvation and a curse. It may save you, and perhaps those you love, but it is also a curse, a responsibility and legacy that you alone will carry. This burden, although a gift, must only be shared with a daughter selfless and pure of heart, even if not a daughter of your blood. Promise me and Buddha you will honor this legacy, the Wing Chun secret," Ng-Kin asked, suddenly aging greatly before Kai Chen's eyes.

It was as though they both knew Ng-Kin's end of this life was nearing. Tears threatened to fill Kai Chen's green eyes as she searched her grandmother's wise face for answers to the unknown. Kai Chen maintained her composure but her eyes shone with unshed tears.

"I promise to Buddha and to my sister, grandmother and friend, I will honor the legacy of Wing Chun and only choose a daughter worthy to pass the secrets, even if she is not a daughter of my blood," Kai Chen declared with dignity as an overwhelming sense of emotion tugged at her very soul. The honor of carrying such a legacy was so profound it felt all-consuming. Her heart swelled with love, joy, and a sense of fulfillment at being given such a gift and blessing.

Ng-Kin clasped Kai Chen's young hands within her own wrinkled ones. She bowed then said, "Daughter of my heart I leave with one last message. When the day arrives you find a man who looks upon you with favor, leave this temple, go to him and never return. You are the last of the Chens. You are the last of Wing Chun."

Silently, Ng-Kin leaned upon her staff as she walked across the dimly lit training hall where candles sputtered and died from hours of use. Kai Chen observed her grandmother leave the Dein then sighed in frustration and confusion. It was well past midnight and they should have been asleep hours ago instead of practicing, chatting, and bickering like two old peacocks, but Kai Chen was constantly restless. An agitation had centered in her breast months ago she could not ignore. It fuelled her with a sense of looming karma, shrouding the temple and focusing on her. An awareness of portent threatened her inner peace. Ng-Kin was right, change was coming. Soon.

Kneeling in the center of the stone floor of the Dein with her wooden staff beside her, Kai Chen allowed her hands to lie limply in her lap as she closed her eyes. Softly, she recited her mantras in her lilting voice. The constant sound of her voice and words lulled her into a trance as she became one with her surroundings, allowing the peace of the temple to pervade her focused mind. Bright light filled her inner being as her frustrations and concerns filtered away. The spiritual, mystical, and harmonious elements of her faith charged her with great joy, even as a dark shadow materialized near her. She remained one with the room, but allowed her focused awareness to alight upon the foreign entity that had invaded the Shaolin temple.

Change was here.

Immediately, her concentration was broken as a venomous force announced its presence in the enormous Dein. Not a sound was made by the evil but it saturated Kai's enlightenment as though black sticky tar had been poured over her soul. Maintaining her position she regulated her breathing as she continued her mantras and waited for the vicious attack she sensed approaching.

A whirring sound from behind her clarified the direction of the assailant. Kai Chen leaned to the left as she stood and aligned her staff upright beside her body. The razor-edged coins struck the wood as she spun around to confront her enemy. This was not a test by Ng-Kin or any other disciple of the temple. This was an open deadly assault by someone whose inner force radiated their hatred for her.

"Step forward, that I may know who violates this temple's harmony," she stated in a clear voice. To assault a monk or nun was considered punishable by death, but done inside a holy sanctuary was sacrilegious with the violator's death swift and just.

A small woman stepped from the shadows, her body encased in a black tunic and pants as she silently moved across the floor. The only part of her face exposed was her angled, beautiful dark eyes. Kai Chen could sense the malice radiating from the woman and wondered at its basis. She did not know this person, yet recognized in her heart the woman was here to exact a personal punishment.

"Kai Chen Boussard, come with me or die," the woman hissed. As she moved silently across the room, Kai Chen knew this woman to be deadly. Very few people had the ability to tread without sound or to move so effortlessly, each movement exact. This woman in all black was a tiny woman, perhaps five foot four, but something about her movements reminded her of herself, of Wing Chun.

"I have died many deaths in this life with hopes and dreams that will never come to fruition and you threaten to take yet another? How is it you know me and I have never seen you before?" Kai Chen's striking green eyes stayed in direct contact with the black eyes of her adversary several feet away. She noted the woman held several more coins grasped between the insides of her fingers.

"Do not trifle with parables, sister. Your death shall be final should you oppose my order, and it is of no consequence who I am," the small woman said between gritted teeth then demanded, "Choose."

"I will not leave my temple and do not wish you harm," Kai Chen said simply and clearly, arching an eyebrow as she witnessed her grandmother and the Abbess enter the temple with several other disciples. The disciples moved as silently as this stranger who had entered the training hall. Their skill was to be expected as all had been trained by Ng-Kin. They were here to observe this preeminent incident.

"So be it," the strange woman spat almost sweetly as both her hands lifted briskly. With a skillful twist of her wrists several razor-edged coins flew from between her fingers and sailed with incredible speed toward Kai Chen.

Agilely, Kai Chen gripped her staff and pushed away from it, somersaulting several feet from the spot where she had been standing. The coins sailed past and embedded into the Muk Yan Chong she had trained with earlier. Her staff echoed with a deep boom in the silent Dein as she struck the floor with the base of one end in warning as she landed easily.

"Do not further your folly. Return to the Triad and Prince Tuan unharmed," Kai Chen advised calmly, although she knew this encounter would end in tragedy. The day had finally come when Prince Tuan had located her. Oddly, he had not come himself or sent his soldiers. Kai Chen found this interesting and wondered at its significance.

"Foolish nun, I have witnessed your skill of a strange martial art, but you cannot conquer me." Employing remarkable litheness the woman vaulted toward her in a series of flips. A succession of pointed darts slipped from inside her sleeves and glided through the shadowy room toward Kai Chen.

Kai Chen snatched a round rattan shield from the wall beside her and caught the poisoned darts within the meshed defensive weapon then whirled it like a disk toward the woman, striking her mid-air. The black clad woman crashed to the floor with a ferocious cry as Ng-Kin and the Abbess nodded their approval from their protected positions. The woman agilely surged to her feet and immediately moved forward toward Kai Chen.

The first strike Ji-Kin Lau made to Kai Chen's face was easily blocked by the taller woman. Kai Chen bulleted the woman's face with a series of hand strikes before adeptly stepping aside to prepare for the next attack. She did not want to kill the woman, could not kill the woman as a laywoman nun.

No vows will be broken this day, Kai Chen told herself sternly.

An enraged scream emanated from the smaller woman. Kai Chen did admire the small woman's natural ability. She would have made a formidable opponent if she had been trained in Wing Chun. Unfortunately, her heart was evil and her knowledge of Wing Chun would have been used for mal intent which was not Buddha's will.

"I shall take majestic delight in assassinating you, Kai Chen," Ji-Kin Lau shrieked maliciously as she rebounded off the floor with incredible speed and ease. Though she promised Prince Tuan she would personally deliver Kai Chen to him she no longer wished to do so. Instead, all she craved was this woman's death. Kai Chen was nobody special with her unique looks and mysterious martial art. She was considered just another woman standing in Ji-Kin Lau's way toward inevitable greatness.

Staring at the composed holy woman before her, Ji-Kin Lau's eyes widened dramatically as she viewed her closely for the first time. Returning her regard was the greenest eyes she had ever seen, a dark ring surrounding the rare color and enhancing it. The nun's features were plainly not Chinese, but foreign in her exotic blend of races. She was arresting in her beauty, in her mien, and a wave of resentment saturated Ji-Kin Lau like never before.

"So, this is what Prince Tuan covets so greatly," she muttered between clenched white teeth. It was obvious to comprehend what he found so arousing. Not only was the sister lovely and chaste she was unparallel as competition for domination. And Prince Tuan craved the destruction of power and lived for the thrill of a challenge. But, within Kai Chen was also a passive strength even Ji-Kin Lau relished crushing and destroying. And she would destroy this nun. Even though consumed with jealousy she wanted to capture Kai Chen and witness the brutality Tuan planned, wanted to join him in his savagery toward her innocence and fortitude, and to physically maim and defile her uncanny beauty before killing her. But it would not happen this day. Kai Chen, although a worthy opponent, must be killed this day.

Leaping forward in calm resolve Ji-Kin Lau attacked with razors inserted under her talon-like nails. She sliced across the nun's raised arm. Blood spurted from the superficial wounds as the nun's injured arm delivered several numbing blows to Ji-Kin Lau's face in a matter of seconds. Stumbling back a few feet from the commanding impact, Ji-Kin Lau touched her swollen mouth inside the black head covering she wore and stared in astonishment at her fingers as she pulled them out. Her own blood trailed down the pads of her fingertips as she flicked her tongue out to capture the drops from the cut.

Narrowing her eyes on the nun's arm dripping blood down the front of her top, Ji-Kin Lau smiled ominously. A thrill raced through her and generated sexual excitement in her loins which lighted her exposed eyes. The nun was competent in her skill, but not the master of this confrontation. There was none she encountered who could defeat her. Her gaze moved and lit upon the weapons hanging about the training hall, causing her to almost laugh aloud. She was proficient with every weapon here. How did the nun presume she was better? Kai Chen had only resided within these sacred walls for little time and could never have attained the competence to defeat her. It had taken her a few years to become expert!

Snatching a pair of Butterfly knives Ji-Kin Lau whirled the blades effortlessly in expert fashion, her movements fluid and deadly as she sped toward the stationary nun. Employing a fierce cry she propelled within striking range of her victim. Fleetingly, Kai Chen's staff struck the front of

Ji-Kin Lau's shins forcefully then swept her feet out from beneath her. A flurry of skirts skimmed across her vision as Kai Chen leapt against the wall to secure an identical pair of Butterfly knives, before she landed soundlessly on the floor.

Springing to her feet like a flexible cat, Ji-Kin Lau confronted the nun who provided her with no outstanding presentation as to her talent with the weapons. The tall woman simply held them before her like a defensive shield as she awaited another onslaught. As Ji-Kin Lau stepped forward the sudden murmur of voices captured her attention and she turned her head. The training hall was lined with hundreds of monks and nuns who observed their intense battle with placid expressions.

Ji-Kin Lau's diabolic smirk and gaze suspended the disciple's discussion as she turned to admire her opponent. "I will not kill you if you surrender now," she promised, knowing it to be a lie.

"You will not kill me if I do not," Kai Chen responded calmly.

The blades in Ji-Kin Lau's hands shifted without hesitancy as her rage developed. How dare this half-breed be insolent and confident toward her? Voracious dark emotion amplified within her heart and heightened the thirst for more of Kai Chen's blood. Buddha would not save this disciple of his this day. Ji-Kin Lau moved forward and their blades clashed violently, swiftly.

The teeth gnashing sound of blades shearing across each other rang inside the training hall as the two women moved so swiftly they appeared a blur. Naively, Ji-Kin Lau let the red haze of fury sweep her into its vortex as she undulated her large knives against her prey. Kai Chen allowed the serene principles of almost fifteen years of habit, of Wing Chun, to guide the extensions in her hands. The flurry of blades was hypnotizing as over and over they clanked, pealed and rang in the training hall.

The monks and nuns watched in fascinated horror as their sister opposed the wicked black demon maneuvering with finesse and confidence. Their positions remained the same; the intruder the aggressor and the nun the defender, however, neither wavered in their expectation of being the victor. As the last few remaining candles along the walls of the hall began to sputter and die the silent disciples lit their candles, holding them aloft for the combatants.

Kai Chen continued her tranquil focus as she spryly avoided the smaller woman's rapid deployment of motions. This game was beginning to disturb her. She had taken the vow not to kill, but the woman was leaving her very little avenue for exception. Although she respected the noticeable talent of this stranger she did not wish to slay her or mar her in any manner. The decision was necessitated when the woman's blade slid along the front of her white banded top. Blood was not drawn, but the garment revealed a considerable portion of her stomach.

An audible gasp escaped from Ng-Kin and almost made Kai Chen falter as she glanced at her grandmother. The old woman's face was drawn and pale, her eyes bright with suppressed emotions as she clasped her knotted hands before her. There was dread in her dark eyes that related her fear of the outcome of this situation.

"I will not repress any longer," Kai Chen warned the woman in a firm tone then declared loudly for all her brothers and sisters to hear, "Forgive me!"

Revolving her blades with extraordinary speed and skill she disengaged her rival's blades easily. They spun haphazardly through the air and landed on the stone floor with a sharp clatter. Spinning her body around a second later, Kai Chen sent the fine edge of one blade downward in a slashing motion against the black cloth covering the woman's face. A scream of absolute agony plagued the customary serenity of the Shaolin temple as the woman fell to her knees, holding her ravaged face as blood spurted through her fingers.

"I - shall -," Ji-Kin Lau croaked, but never finished as she collapsed to the stone floor.

Kai gazed down at this anonymous woman and remorse for causing her grievous injury centered in her breast. With a heavy heart she bent down and removed the black covering on the woman's face, noting the once exceptional loveliness of her oriental features, which were now hideously defiled. An open gash tracked from her left temple, across and down her nose, cheekbone and lips to the right side of her chin. With immediate attention she would survive, but remain permanently scarred.

"See to it the stranger receives treatment and is returned to her Triad temple," the Abbess stated in a flat tone but her eyes blazed with emotion. "She should be put to death but I believe her punishment has been meted out appropriately and to the satisfaction of Sister Kai Chen and this temple."

The heads of the monks and nuns within the temple nodded in agreement of the Abbess' words as they began to depart. Kai Chen's face reflected her sorrow.

"I do not find satisfaction in the injury I have caused, but I realize the necessity. Many thanks are given I did not kill her," Kai Chen mumbled quietly as several nuns lifted the woman's body and carried her from the desecrated training hall.

"We vow not to kill because we value life. There may come a time soon when all of us may break this vow," the Abbess murmured and touched Kai Chen's shaking hand. "Trouble is rising in this land, sister, reminding me of the fall of the Shaolin temple of Ng Mui many years ago."

"When word and sight of this reaches the Triad temple there will be grave repercussions," Ng-Kin whispered to them.

"I agree, but we shall continue peacefully until that day arises," the Abbess declared.

"I have chosen the wrong path this day," Kai Chen doubted her actions, her stricken expression piercing the heart of the Abbess as the woman embraced her with affection

"You had no choice this day, child," the Abbess maintained. "The decision was made for us when that evil woman entered our peaceful temple. Does your arm need tending, sister?"

Ripping a piece of her already rent top, Kai Chen wrapped it around her bleeding arm and knotted it. "I will be fine, Abbess."

Ng-Kin nodded once in agreement and the three of them wearily began cleaning the Dein of the befouled blood staining the once virgin floor. Kai Chen knew of personal choices and their consequences. Unfortunately, once made they could rarely be recanted.

☯

City of Willows
Two days later

Prince Tuan's enraged shouts echoed throughout the temple as members frantically sped to prepare themselves for their uprising. Weapons were honed and counted, groups were formed and specific missions given in preparation for the eradication of all foreigners in China and the supplanting of the Empress Dowager. However, his main focus would be to destroy Kai Chen and everything she held close to her heart.

"I want the very finest assassins from the five Triads to assemble here. Their mission will be to destroy every monk and nun within Fukien Shaolin temple. Specifically, I want the severed head of Kai Chen Boussard, the half-breed nun with green eyes," he ground out bitterly between yellow clenched teeth as spittle flew from between his lips.

The cleric wrote down each order as it was spouted off, his hand quivering in fear. It was the wildness of Tuan's eyes that frightened everyone within the temple as they had never seen such uncontrolled rage from the Prince. All within the temple knew he was on the edge of insanity due to Ji-Kin Lau's current condition.

Tuan glanced at Ji-Kin Lau who lay sleeping in his bed with her face bandaged. He had seen her disfigurement when the physician had checked the wound. Her injury was hideous to gaze upon with the oozing red gash puckered and swollen while still fresh. The nuns had neatly stitched her face, but the scar would be prominent and permanent. Never would Ji-Kin Lau be beautiful again.

His fantasy for Kai Chen was changed. No longer did he lust for her innocence, her inner strength and control. No longer did he relish her virgin's blood on his groin. He wanted it on his hands as he gripped her cleaved head instead. Kai Chen had taken from him something more desirous than a fantasy. She had taken his future Empress. With Ji-Kin Lau's face butchered she could no longer serve by his side. There was no place for her on the throne for she could never be looked upon with favor or acceptance by him or the people they would rule. It was a traumatic disappointment for him.

"Cleric, I want the members gathered quickly," he ordered, spittle flying from his lips. The wildness in his red rimmed eyes increased as he stormed out of his private chambers. Wrath towards the heavens filled his chest at the warped turn of events unfolding. Where would he ever find another to supplant Ji-Kin Lau? As future Emperor he would have many concubines, but he needed one extraordinary woman to rule by his side. None could replace Ji-Kin Lau.

His voracity for any sensual encounter had been squelched by the sight of Ji-Kin Lau's face. It would take many days, even weeks, to grieve over his current loss of her position. New plans were necessary and they would require time to consider carefully. With a frustrated sigh he wondered where he could find another innocent like Ji-Kin Lau who was as intelligent, mercenary and virginal as when she had first come to him. It was highly doubtful there was another like her.

CHAPTER SEVEN

The art of war teaches us to rely not on the likelihood of the enemy's not coming, but on our own readiness to receive him; not on the chance of his not attacking, but rather on the fact that we have made our position unassailable.
- Sun Tzu, *The Art of War*

June 1900
Fukien Province

"Vaden! We must leave the coast immediately. There are reports war has broken out north of us in Chekiang province. The Imperial City is being taken over and the Boxer's are traveling south toward this coastline," the captain yelled harshly. Just as quickly he delegated other tasks to his crew to prepare to leave China.

"This is a passenger-cargo merchant liner. I refuse to leave until the last of the goods I purchased have been loaded and my paying passengers are aboard. See to it both is accomplished and then we may leave," Vaden stated bluntly and spun on his heel. He quit the tastefully decorated dining room of his ship.

Word had been brought to him for two days now of uprisings exploding throughout China. Massacres done by the Chinese were embellished by his overwrought crew members who cried out stories of beheadings and savage tortures prior to death. However, truth be told by his informants, the Chinese and Manchu Imperial guard were both heavily outnumbered by numerous foreign countries prepared for battle. Though the skirmish was heading his direction Vaden refused to leave without the shipment he had purchased or his passengers. Only half of his shipment was in the cargo hold with the remainder to be completed by the end of the week. Obviously, this situation pressed for expedition.

There was only one hundred passengers on his liner this trip, but the cargo he obtained would make up for the lack of income from them. Normally he held over one thousand passengers, but news of the disruption in this country had frightened many from their normal excursions. At the moment he considered it a blessing. It would be tragic were any of his countrymen aboard his liner killed in this foreign land by the upheaval occurring. It would be even more disastrous if forced to leave without them aboard.

Suddenly, the image of brilliant green eyes, porcelain skin and dark hair with a hint of red flame came to him as he entered the private rooms of his ship. He was curious what had become of the unusual woman he had witnessed repel six men. After that incident he had questioned several people before finally discovering her name was Kai Chen Boussard, her father a Lutheran minister from America, her mother Chinese and her grandmother a Shaolin Buddhist nun. Though he had been in Fukien province several times since their initial encounter, he had not spied her in over two years. From time to time the memory of her flawless beauty and initial shyness would catch him off guard before the remembrance of her incredible physical skill shattered it.

"Most likely she is married with a babe suckling at her breast," he said aloud then moaned at the vision his words invoked. It was easy to imagine her, her hair lying thickly over one shoulder as a beautiful blond babe with green eyes hungrily grasped one of her distended nipples between its lips for nourishment. Mentally berating himself for thinking such intimate and asinine thoughts he quit his rooms and headed outside. It would be advisable to check on the girl and her family. Perhaps they wanted to leave this country with its current revolts but did not have an outlet to escape? Even though the girl and her mother would be considered illegal aliens in the United States due to the Chinese Exclusion Act signed in 1882, it should not be difficult to obtain citizenship through the minister. He was American.

Convinced it would be the gentlemanly and politically correct thing to do, and that it had nothing to do with his curiosity toward the green eyed young woman or his repressed desire for her, he surrendered to his brazen impulse and left the ship.

Several Days Later
Shaolin Temple
Fukien Province

"The temple shall be guarded by our brothers and sisters," Ng-Kin stated to Kai Chen as they swiftly made their way across the harsh terrain. "We must assure your parents safety."

"My burden of guilt is great, grandmother. If I had simply conformed to Prince Tuan's wishes and left with the masked woman this predicament of the temple would not be happening." The pain reflected in her face was insignificant to the misery of her heart. Kai Chen had thought to avert any further disaster in being a half-breed nun cloistered in a temple, away from Prince Tuan and the community. No. She had been discovered and the culminating events had provoked an even more disastrous chain of events.

"It is Buddha's will, child. Prince Tuan has planned this uprising for several years. Your action toward his assassin did not initiate this war," her grandmother said before laughing bitterly. "It thwarted one of his many plans, nevertheless."

"Which plan?" Kai Chen glanced at her grandmother with interest as they raced silently on bare feet through the forest along the road leading to her family. She would have preferred to travel more rapidly, but Ng-Kin was no longer agile or capable of extended endurance.

"The woman you disfigured would be the next Empress, child. She is as desirous as Prince Tuan of ruling China. However, she is ultimately more dangerous than he as she has been trained well in martial arts by an Elder of the Triad and knows many clever secrets. Beware of her, Kai Chen, for she shall never pause in her revenge for the grave and permanent injury you caused. Now she is disfigured she shall never rule as Empress and her torment is extreme in this realization."

Kai Chen threw Ng-Kin an appalled expression at this information. "Why would a future Empress want to deliver me to Prince Tuan rather than send her minions?"

"Ji-Kin Lau is the most deadly Triad member ever trained since the demise of the Five Elders and death of the great Abbess Ng Mui. She witnessed your skill with Wing Chun and took it upon herself to win ultimate favor with him by capturing you herself. However, in her great arrogance she did not fathom your mastery, nor did she perceive you toying with her in the training hall," she asserted. "She was so full of her own essence she could not detect yours, which shined bright and constant."

"It is sad such talent she possesses is used for evil," Kai responded dejectedly as they moved silently through the forest. "Imagine her greatness were she to channel her energy toward enlightenment."

"It was not meant to be. Again, it is all about choice and Buddha's will," Ng-Kin disclosed, her wisdom invariably making perfect sense. "This is why the secrets of Wing Chun must go to someone pure of heart and worthy."

Nearing the clearing of trees leading to the cross roads by her parents house, they paused for a moment for Ng-Kin to catch her breath. The sound of fierce battle was nearby. Men cried out in death and roared with anger as the echo of swords rang in the early morning. The sounds of shots from guns and cannons being fired resounded throughout the area as the battle loomed closer to David and Ying Boussard's house. Kai Chen and Ng-Kin could smell the acrid burning of smoke nearby.

"I pray we are in time," Kai Chen whispered desperately as they crept forward to observe the spectacle.

Two dozen Imperial soldiers savagely beheaded numerous foreigners who lined the roads as they fought for command of the territory. A canon exploded sending several Manchu infantryman and their horses to their deaths. The cries of the foreigners were eerily similar to the battered Chinese, showing how similar all people are no matter the country. A deep sadness filled Kai Chen's breast as she observed the degradation of humanity, of how cruel humans could be to one another. As the progression of warriors wandered south toward the village, Kai Chen and Ng-Kin dashed from the wooded concealment onto the dirt road leading to David and Ying Boussard's home. Keeping her pace in check as they ran, Kai Chen attempted to supervise her emotions which threatened to overrule her wisdom.

Rounding the bend to the cross roads Ng-Kin cried out in alarm. Kai Chen glanced toward the direction of her parent's home and observed dark smoke billowing from it. Flames licked up the side of the white church, practically engulfed by the fire. As she stared in dread her grandmother's soft cry of warning greeted her again.

"David! No!"

Kai Chen frantically searched for her parents and noticed her father in front of their house. He stood proudly before Prince Tuan who wielded a deadly broadsword in one arm and a rattan shield in another, while astride a powerful horse. In her father's hands was a gun. Staring in amazement at the peaceful man who loathed violence, Kai Chen witnessed him lift the weapon and shoot two Imperial soldiers charging toward her mother, Ying.

Ng-Kin immediately gripped Kai Chen's arm to hold her in place as they both watched Prince Tuan raise his sword and sweep it through the air. Initially, it seemed as though Tuan had caused no injury to the minister but a bright red ring of blood around his neck appeared just before his head toppled off his body.

"No!"

Kai Chen's intense wail was broken by a hand placed over her mouth as she observed her father's body fall limply to the ground. Her heart beat savagely in her breast, her eyes widened in horror, and her stomach lurched as the realization her father was dead buffeted her mind. Anguish filled her and threatened to consume her, as Ng-Kin's soft words whispered in her ear.

"Do *not* let your emotions drive your actions, child. Focus. We are Wing Chun," the old woman chanted mystically as she released the pressure that held Kai Chen from battle. "You have taken the oath not to kill, Kai Chen. All vows will be broken this day."

"Shi de," Kai Chen affirmed in a soft voice, her tear filled eyes fixed on Prince Tuan's gloating countenance. "Vows will be broken this day."

Vows she had taken with pure heart and steely intent were now meaningless. Her father was dead by the hands of Prince Tuan. Never had she felt such blinding rage or such intense grief. Her heart was nearly pounding out of her chest as her mind raced for control over her emotions. A steely focus flowed through Kai Chen as her gaze narrowed on his face. The first vow she would break would be not to kill.

"Come. We must help Ying," Ng-Kin whispered in her ear, the first hum of true desperation she had ever heard from her mellow grandmother in all the years she had known her.

"Yes, we must hurry to mother," Kai Chen repeated, her gaze finally breaking away from the man she would destroy. "This day all disciples will break vows."

Vaden LeBlanc couldn't believe his eyes!

Staring with dread at the scene before him, he knew his offer came too late. The minister lay decapitated in the exact spot he had seen him stand with his wife and daughter over two years ago. The green eyed enchantress was nowhere to be seen. Her mother stood just behind the spot where her husband had been killed. Frowning as he scanned the area, Vaden noted two bright orange robed figures steal toward the small house on fire. They dressed like the monks and nuns he had occasionally seen wandering through this province carrying staffs in their hands. He had noted that some shaved their heads while others kept a full head of hair. As he continued to watch he noted their movements were sure, soundless and swift as they bolted around the house.

"Are they crazy? They'll be killed," he muttered to himself as he checked his revolver. He had six shots and extra bullets in his pocket for reloading. He would have to make do with what little he possessed.

Carefully, he moved through thick foliage toward the scene before him. When trudging through the village to extend his offer to this family he had been shocked to discover the battle was already raging toward the coast. He had not been prepared to be involved in a larger form of skirmish. Once he offered assistance to this family they could return to the safety of his ship and get under way to America.

Glancing up as he prepared to move forward again he stared in confusion at the drama before him. Two women fought violently in front of the house where the minister lay dead. One looked young with long black hair trailing down her back, dressed in all black, but something about her face seem distorted, almost disfigured. It was difficult to discern from his hidden position within the cluster of trees off the road. The other woman appeared older, familiar, and he suddenly gasped as he realized it was the wife of the minister who resisted the savage attacks of the other woman.

"Cease your amusement Ji-Kin Lau and simply kill her!"

The command came from the man on the horse as he observed the two combatants with impatience. Vaden leaned forward to gape as the older woman's hands and arms rapidly issued a series of blows, sending the younger woman spinning to the ground. Immediately, the tiny woman bounced to her feet and with a shriek of fury conducted a succession of kicks and punches. The wife of the minister was deadly with her fighting skills but her crippled leg limited her ability, which the younger evil woman in black took advantage of. Swiftly, the woman in black struck at the knee of the crippled leg, breaking it, before striking her in the face and chest multiple times. The strikes rendered the older woman almost incoherent as she dropped next to her dead husband.

"Your daughter did this to me," the tiny woman screamed at Ying and drew her hair aside to expose the grotesque scar running diagonally across the length of her face. Reaching down, the disfigured woman grasped the prone woman's hair and thrust her face toward the body of her husband. "And I shall do this to her!"

"You will never defeat Kai Chen for poor imitations never endure," declared the woman stoically, blood trickling from her lips. She refused to cry out as a foot slammed into her chest. Bones snapped loudly and pierced her internal organs as her slender hand reached out for her dead husband's lifeless hand. Blood now pumped from her mouth as death hovered near.

Vaden felt bile rise in his throat at the barbaric display unfolding before him. It was terrible to witness the atrocities of men, but for a woman to be so physically ruthless was anomalous. He had been raised in a world of violence where men were the domineering faction and women were soft, meek, and respectably defenseless. This country had never shown its true virulent secrets before, but he had just witnessed one of them. The women of China were as lethal as men.

"Ji-Kin Lau!"

The authoritative voice grabbed Vaden's attention as a new scene in the tragedy unfolded. He changed his position as he tried to see the two monks, or were they nuns? For the life of him he could swear they looked like women. Certainly, the one who had just spoken sounded like an old woman!

"Ah! It is Ng-Kin, the Triad traitor. Oh, and the lovely Kai Chen Boussard of Shaolin temple. How fortuitous you have arrived in this moment of triumph," Prince Tuan trumpeted loudly.

Both nuns gazed down at Ying who held the hand of her dead husband and stared at them with a bright sheen to her eyes. Her soft gaze spoke of her delight in seeing them, of her physical suffering she adamantly refused to give voice to, and her fear for them. As Kai Chen stepped forward to lend her mother a comforting touch before her death, Ji-Kin Lau slammed the heel of her foot down. The grisly sound of Ying's skull being crushed sent waves of nausea through Vaden as he watched Kai Chen stumble before she stopped.

"You are next," spat the tiny woman who faced Ng-Kin then she turned to Kai Chen. The disfigurement of her face was appalling, but the absolute loathing in her eyes was far worse. "Kai Chen, you are a foolish nun! You should have killed me when you had the chance. Now I will destroy all you treasure before destroying you."

"Prepare to die, Kai Chen Boussard," Prince Tuan shouted as he spurred his horse forward.

Vaden could not budge. He tried to move, he wanted to move, but he was held transfixed as he stared at the orange robed woman who was the same beautiful young girl he had seen two years ago. Only now she was a nun wearing an orange robe with her long hair plaited and hanging down her back. Her face was as striking as he remembered with a more mature visage, even more entrancing than he remembered. Shaking his head in disbelief he observed her bare feet carrying her swiftly across the ground. She was charging toward the horse with her staff as the rider of the animal flashed his broadsword.

"She will be killed, just like her parents," he whispered in horror. Shock rendered him motionless. As the events played out before him all he could do was stare. Never in his life had he witnessed such destruction and treachery. The people of China were merciless in their campaign for domination. How did all western countries presume they could vanquish them? It would take years!

Suddenly, the penetrating shriek of a woman caused his hair to rise on the back of his neck. It was like the Gaelic folklore banshee, a high screeching wail warning a family that one of them will soon die. Shuddering where he stood Vaden stared at the harrowing performance several yards away. Although he was not in the immediate fray his body, mind and spirit felt as though it were part of their battle. His emotions screamed for action but his body refused to initiate it as he watched in dread. The tiny woman with the butchered face was attacking the older nun brutally as her scream vibrated shrilly.

Vaden's gaze was torn between two simultaneous horrors. One scene was of the young nun, Kai Chen, who had somehow managed to avoid the Prince's broadsword and was flying through the air with her leg extended out, before twisting her body several times in an amazing, almost inhuman move. The kick struck the man powerfully from behind, flipping him off the front of his horse to the ground with a violent thud. The other scene was between the Elder nun who used her hands faster than any professional boxer he had ever seen, and the young woman whose sadistic will generated an inconceivable range of strikes and blocks. Youth and pure evil intent was effectively overwhelming her older and obviously tired opponent. He had never seen anything comparable to this in his entire life!

"Join your parents in death, half-breed," Prince Tuan roared angrily.

"We shall always be together, whether in this life or another," Kai Chen asserted, whirling her staff so rapidly it was only a blur before her antagonist's heated gaze. In the blink of an eye the wooden pole struck both his wrists and splintered the bones. The man's bellow of pain announced his injury as he dropped to his knees, both hands dangling at awkward angles. Without pause, penitence or pardon she thrust one end of the staff into his open mouth then nodded with satisfaction as it exited the back of his head. Hurling the staff from her hands as though blemished she watched his body topple to the side with the staff still protruding from the front and back of his head. Kai Chen then pivoted around to see Ji-Kin Lau standing over her inert grandmother.

"Tuan!"

"Ng-Kin!"

Both women cried out in misery as their loved one lay on the blood soaked ground, dead. Whirling to face each other, annihilation the only intelligible consideration between them, they unexpectedly heard the larger battle returning to their location. Triad members headed their way, ready to assist Ji-Kin Lau. Both women gave pause for a fraction of a second but their intent was clear as they circled each other.

"Surely, you will die this day!"

Vaden heard Ji-Kin Lau rave hysterically as her Triad members made their way toward them. Americans propelled forward with their modern weapons of destruction. Vaden watched the tiny oriental woman with the deformed face. Her outrage was palpable as the American's slaughtered her Triad members and her certain means of killing Kai Chen.

"You have violated my temple, my family and my honor, Ji-Kin Lau. Because of you, I have broken vows," Kai Chen declared calmly, even as anguish rooted in her breast. Vaden watched, choked with emotion, as she glanced at her dead grandmother whose broken body lay a few feet away.

Everyone who mattered in her life was gone. She was now completely alone.

"I have broken vows, so anything I do now does not matter," Kai Chen stated, a steely edge to her firm voice.

You carry the Wing Chun legacy. It matters. It is everything, an inner voice reminded her.

"This is not over. I will never stop, never rest, until you are dead," the small woman hissed evilly with promise, and then sprinted away from the foreigners who were charging toward Kai Chen with their guns raised to shoot.

Vaden observed Kai Chen face the strangers who were intent on killing her as Ji-Kin Lau fled into the interior of the forest. Kai Chen turned her gaze upon her grandmother whose face reflected peace in her death. Kneeling beside her grandmother she gently closed her dark eyes which no longer carried the inner gleam of life. Vaden noticed the defeat etched on the young nun's face as she cradled her grandmother's head in her lap. Tears rained down her cheeks as she tenderly stroked the old woman's hands and pressed their foreheads together. Dashing from his place of concealment as though finally released from some intrinsic barrier holding him back, he surged forward to stop the multitude of British soldiers from killing her.

"She is American! Stop!"

Several soldiers paused to glance at the man who bolted past them with fantastic speed, his words penetrating their crazed minds. The soldiers paused in their charge and stared at the nun whose intense green eyes shifted to them. Realizing she looked American they redirected their rage and pivoted away to resume their bloodshed elsewhere.

Vaden's dark blue eyes locked with hers as recognition flared between them.

"I remember you," the woman's charming voice said in English.

"I remember you, as well," he stated. Curiously his gaze traveled over face noting her profound beauty. The past two years had brought a maturity to her appearance that was bewitching. Her beautiful long hair fell over one shoulder as she used strips of cloth from her orange robe to wrap around her grandmother's body, binding the legs and arms against her body so they would not move. "My name is Vaden LeBlanc."

"What is it you search for, Vaden LeBlanc?"

Her question produced a frown as he pondered an answer. What *was* he searching for? Why was he here instead of safely on his ship headed back to America? When had he lost his sanity and believed he could play champion to this family? As their gazes met Vaden lost all reflection as a numbing awareness enfolded him. He was drowning in her intense scrutiny. She somehow saw into his mind and his heart. Kai Chen imprisoned him by simply delving into his soul with the talons of her question and mesmerizing green eyes.

"I came to help your family," he responded then relaxed as her gaze swept from him to the woman she held so tenderly in her arms. "Why did you become a nun?"

"As you can see I no longer have any family. We all have different quests in life. It was my calling to define myself as a nun but that is changed now," she murmured sadly and gently place her grandmother's head on the ground. "There will be very little splendor left in China after this war. Return to your country while you can."

Bending down, the tall nun grunted faintly as she hefted the limp body of her tiny fallen grandmother in her arms then hoisted her over her shoulder. Kai Chen's face reflected the pain in her heart as she glanced at her parents and chanted a simple Lutheran prayer over them. Dispassionately, she then walked over to the man she had killed. Placing her bare foot against his skull she jerked the staff out of Prince Tuan's mouth. Without another word she proceeded away from the house and church now totally engulfed in flames.

"Wait! Where are you going?" He was confused. How could she walk away and not bury her parents? Where did she plan to take her grandmother? She would not get very far carrying the heavy weight of the dead woman.

Kai Chen saw no purpose in answering the American and continued to lumber along the dirt road, leaning on her staff gripped lightly in one hand to balance the weight of her grandmother on her other shoulder. Persistently she trudged with her burden, never wavering as the miles passed and the terrain grew rougher. Her lumbering steps swept her into the high mountains. She would return to bury her parents once she had deposited her grandmother within the temple where she belonged.

Vaden followed her more out of curiosity than desire. How long did she think to travel with her load before she collapsed? The mountains were dangerous and steep, rocky and unforgiving, as they climbed deeper into the dark forests. Though Kai Chen toted the woman on her shoulder her pace remained brisk and unrelenting. He was stunned at her physical endurance and emotional strength, her ability to bear her personal mourning so peacefully. She had just lost her entire family, killed a Prince of the Manchu dynasty, and yet, remained as composed as still water.

"Still water runs deep," he reminded himself then grimaced at his musing as he scrambled to keep up with the determined nun with the haunting eyes. What variety of skills did this unconventional woman possess? How long, and what sort of training had she acquired to fight so masterfully? Who was this unorthodox paradox, this odd mixture of

American and Chinese heritage? Vaden was determined to discover the depths of Kai Chen Boussard, if she would allow him.

"You persist in being a foolish American," she suddenly snapped at him. Pausing in her lengthy stride she turned to view him with stormy green eyes as she caught her breath. "Two years ago you acted unwisely and jeopardized yourself and my family in your chivalrousness. Why do you follow me now?"

"I am defining myself in a new quest," he said glibly. Noting her scowl at his poor sense of humor he grinned cheekily and blushed for the first time in his life. How did this quiet, modest woman compel him to feel ashamed? He felt guilty for making fun of her faith and philosophy of life.

"Then you shall search far and in many lifetimes for you shall never find what you seek by following me," she stated emphatically, shifted the weight of her grandmother on her shoulder slightly, and then began to climb the rough region anew.

Several minutes later they broke free of the dense wooded area into what was once a beautiful temple surrounded by gardens, now destroyed and littered with the dead bodies of monks and nuns. The accepting expression on the Kai Chen's face caused Vaden to falter. He watched her impassive features take in the destruction of her home, of her adopted family. It was ironic he should witness the complete loss of every person and thing she considered precious in her life. The experience was comparable to his as a child and it evoked painful memories he shoved aside.

He sat quietly upon the ground for hours and observed her collect the bodies of her fallen brothers and sisters, her energy never lagging, her face displaying no emotion as she carried severed limbs and heads inside the ravaged temple. She had spurned his offer to help with the bodies, demanding he leave. Impulsively he tarried outside, afraid to violate the sanctity of her home or to offer his assistance again. Somehow, he should have known she would not want or allow his help.

The creeping blackness of night swathed the area as he paced the grounds. Walking to the door he peered into the interior of the temple. The sight of broken golden Buddha's toppled across each other lined the entrance. A few candles burned, reflecting eerily inside the silent tomb the woman had disappeared. What was she doing? The question burned more brightly than the waning candles that began to sputter, then extinguish, like the lives of those entombed within.

"I have much to do, stranger. Why do you remain here? What do you seek?"

Vaden almost leaped out of his skin at her totally silent approach. "How did you do that? I was standing right here and you didn't make a sound!"

The woman stared at him with a flat expression as she waited for her answers. What did he seek? He felt his throat constrict as he allowed the truth to surface. There was about her an essence of harmony and fortitude that called to him. Her inner peace and beauty drew him to her like a moth to a flame.

What did he seek?

He sought her.

As the realization struck him like a thunderbolt, he flinched. There had been many women in his life but none had ever captured a part of him until now. Two years ago he had first beheld her and accepted he was physically attracted to her, but having learned so much more about her he admitted he was entranced with her spirit and some undefined element within her. Kai Chen Boussard was the most unique, fascinating, beautiful woman he had ever come across in his life.

"I took many vows when I became a nun, stranger. The vow not to kill was one, which I broke this day. Also, I pledged celibacy among others," she stated pointedly as her intuition honed his intent. "I shall not break another."

When the day arrives you find a man who looks upon you with favor, leave this temple, go to him and never return.

The memorable words raced through Kai Chen's mind as she gazed upon the tall, broad man standing before her. In his eyes was something she had never seen before. She had seen the love of her parents, her grandmother, and her brothers and sisters of this temple in their gaze. She had seen lust in the eyes of men, envy in the eyes of some women and disdain in the eyes of most, but never had she seen the expression shining in the scrutiny of this foreigner.

Could it be - ?

"That is changed now," he reminded her swiftly of her own words.

Kai Chen blushed profusely and pressed her lips together tightly. So, she had said that! However, that did not give this American the right to play verbal games with her. She did not have leisure or the desire to flirt with this man.

"Go from here and leave me in peace," she exclaimed loudly as alien emotions battered her. Before her stood the handsome man who had come to her rescue two years ago, the man she had once secretly dreamed of upon occasion. Excitement, a small sliver of fear, and a suppressed desire threatened her inner serenity and drove her actions. Just as her grandmother had warned her to beware all her life!

Vaden stared in astonishment at the woman who had not raised her voice the entire day and now yelled at him. If he did not know better he would swear she was afraid of him or the possibility of what might be between them. The thought gave him great satisfaction as the edges of his lips curled into a smile. His gaze took in her flushed cheeks and bright eyes, the only other indications she was emotionally unsettled.

"You are not safe in this country any longer and you have nobody here to care for you. Come with me to America where I will protect you," he offered sincerely. He hated to think of her killed by the Manchu government when they discovered she had killed Prince Tuan.

"There is none who can protect me, save Buddha," she proclaimed. With tears in her eyes returned inside the dark temple leaving Vaden to find his own way not only to his ship, but in life.

Fukien Province
One Day Later

"I have now broken a second and third vow," she moaned with regret then sighed heavily as she remembered her oath not to steal and not to lie. By declaring to the American, Vaden LeBlanc, she would not break another vow she inadvertently had for now she had stolen onto his merchant ship bound for America like a thief in the night. Only hours ago she had silently passed several crew members who stood guard outside to protect the large vessel from attack by Boxer's, Imperial soldiers, and vagabonds. Cautiously, Kai Chen made her way deep into the belly of the ship to hide. Now she sat huddled in a vacant storage room, waiting to discover what fate had in store for her.

The past twenty-four hours had been filled with grieving, fleeing the Triad members sent to assassinate her by Ji-Kin Lau, and simply surviving. After torching the Shaolin temple, its recesses lined with her grandmother, brothers and sisters, she had ceremoniously thrown her orange robe and meager belongings into the inferno. Dressed in a simple black gown with a black cloth wrapped around her head to hide her dark auburn hair she had turned her back on the life she had loved so briefly. Though she was formally no longer a nun, having broken vows, her heart would remain loyal to her Buddhist religion.

She had barely made it from the Shaolin temple when several Triad members had attacked her. Feeling displaced without the staff she had kept devoutly by her side for two years, she focused on the other aspects of Wing Chun training she had spent her entire life perfecting. This demanded she let her attackers get within arm's reach of her to use economy of motion and straight forward attacks, instead of the elaborate

Wu Shu, or Kung Fu, techniques the majority of Chinese employed. Her martial art was unpretentious by using upper body strength with multiple hand attacks and defense by controlling, or "trapping" one or more of her opponent's limbs. Whereas, the Wu Shu was ostentatious with its sweeping arm and leg motions that were easily manipulated. Once she easily disposed of them she returned to her parents' house.

After burying her parents and being hunted by more Triad members and Imperial soldiers, Kai Chen realized she could not remain in China and endure. The Wing Chun legacy must continue, as promised. She could not continue running for the rest of her life like a criminal. Her only chance of surviving was to find a merchant ship sailing to America. On feet fleet as a deer she had sped to the coastline to discern if any ships still remained then had easily boarded one. She could easily have supplanted herself in front of the handsome American and asked for his help, but she knew he would want or even expect more from her. She refused to be in that position. Prince Tuan had wanted to control and break her. She would not allow any person that strength over her life.

The sudden sound of feet now running past her, the steam engines of the ship coming to life, frightened her. It terrified her to leave the only life, culture, and country she had ever known, but it was more horrifying to think of the life she would lead were she to stay in China. How she would survive in a foreign land without getting caught, she did not know, but she had to attempt it. Certain death awaited her here.

"Is the last of the shipment on board?" The familiar voice of Vaden LeBlanc with his wavy blonde hair and dark blue eyes was audible over the loud sounds of the engines.

"Aye, Vaden. 'Tis all there," another man said nervously. "I don't think we can hold off the heathens much longer, sir. I'll be glad to leave this godforsaken place."

The sound of their voices drifted off and Kai Chen released the breath she had been holding. If she closed her eyes she could recall the handsome stranger who looked upon her with kindness. He had offered to protect her, to take her with him but she had been so surprised by the suggestion and so consumed with personal grief she had shoved it aside. Now she was no more than a common thief by creeping onto his ship, instead of going to him directly and accepting his gracious proposition.

"What am I becoming in this life?" The question brought tears to her eyes as she closed them, crying softly until sleep took her for the first time in days.

Meanwhile, Vaden stood next to the captain as his ship sailed quickly away from Fukien province. This would be his last voyage to this country until the Boxer Rebellion was finished. From what he had encountered it could be years, but that did not disturb him. Kai Chen Boussard did. He felt guilty, inadequate, and angry that he had not done more to help save her family, to aid her and guarantee her safety.

"I am not her keeper," he reminded himself bitterly. "She had a choice and made it."

Still, the image of her retreating inside her temple alone haunted him. How would she survive? Who would she have to help her? Who would be there to appreciate the value of her? She was exceptional in beauty, skill, intelligence, and insight. He valued those attributes and understood her misfortune. Vaden could not define it exactly but there was an invisible link to Kai Chen Boussard that he could not deny.

"We will be home in a few months, sir. We are now on our way to your new port of income. Bombay, India!"

"Very good," Vaden replied without enthusiasm.

Leaving the captain to his duties he strolled casually throughout his ship. This newest passenger-cargo merchant ship pleased him greatly. It was comfortable with amenities his full cargo ships could not utilize; game rooms, huge elaborate dining hall, public rooms, smoking rooms, an infirmary and separate accommodation for his seamen. Though not as luxurious as Sebastian's fast ocean passenger liner strictly for passengers and no cargo, his was affluent and he charged lesser fares.

A woman in a satin green dress greeted him cordially and he returned the gesture automatically, but his thoughts immediately went to the woman he had left in China. He had thought of Kai Chen Boussard frequently the past day since leaving her at the temple. Although she was mysterious and alluring, she was also charming and wise. No woman had ever captured his attention like Kai Chen Boussard. Even her name was fascinating with the mix of Chinese and French.

"Let her go," he advised himself sternly, but some things were easier said than done.

CHAPTER EIGHT

If you are far from the enemy, make him believe you are near.
-Sun Tzu, *The Art of War*

Bombay, India
Three weeks later

"What have we here?"

Kai Chen froze at the man's unfriendly voice. Holding a plate of food in her hands she turned to view the old cook who glared at her. His small eyes darted from the stolen assortment of delicacies on the plate she held to her large green eyes staring at him in fear. They traveled down the length of her shabby, torn gown to her bare feet.

"Stowaways! Bah! Your face is too different to be from this heathen country. Where are you from?" he demanded as he placed his hands on his wide hips and leaned forward to better look at her, blocking the only exit with his massive frame.

"China," she said directly, her compelling gaze holding his suspicious one.

"You don't look like any Chinese I ever saw," he huffed with a gruff voice and quirked a heavy brow at her head. "Why are you wearing that cloth?"

"I am hiding my hair," she answered simply.

"Why are you hiding your hair?" His face contorted with uncertainty as he felt himself fall under her musical voice and peaceful aura.

"Some nuns shave their heads and some do not. I was a nun and did not, but I am no longer a nun. It is an unusual color and is quite noticeable." Tilting her head to one side slightly she gazed at him thoughtfully. "Are you the one who makes this wonderful food?"

Holding the plate before him for his view she saw his body draw up with self-importance at her compliment. She was sincere with her praise. Never had she tasted such varied and splendid fare nor viewed such complex designs in some of the foodstuffs. It was a marvel.

"I am head chef on this ship," he asserted proudly then grinned. "My assistants help but I create it all."

"I do not know what items I have eaten these last few weeks, but they are fit for the Empress Dowager," she stated ingenuously.

The man bowed at her high tribute then frowned. "You are a clever tongued woman for a stowaway and a pilferer. A nun, huh?"

Skeptically he stared at her then gaped as she removed the dark cloth on her head to reveal her long dark auburn colored hair which tumbled to her waist. His eyes widened further in surprise as he observed her balance the plate of food on one raised knee as she replaced the wrap on her head again. Humbly, she handed the plate toward him.

"I understand I have committed serious offenses and am prepared to pay atonement," she offered in her sing song voice.

The heavy chef studied her pensively for several seconds then his eyes opened wide in astonishment again. "I just noticed! You speak English!"

"Of course, my father was American. I also speak Chinese and French," she told him as she placed the plate on the metal counter beside her. She laid her hands down on the wooden chopping block and closed her eyes.

"What are you doing?"

Kai Chen turned her innocent green gaze to his astonished countenance before replying, "I am waiting for you to exact your punishment for my crime."

"What punishment?" His confusion was genuine as his brows lowered in a grimace.

"The severing of my hands for stealing," she told him.

"What?" His shout of revulsion was earnest as he shuddered visibly. "I would never do that to anyone simply because they were hungry."

"You are a very generous man. Very few would be so honorable. What shall my punishment be then?"

For several seconds the man was speechless. He exhaled audibly as his lips quirked with the semblance of a smile. "What is your name, dear?"

"Kai Chen Boussard." There was no sense lying and compounding her other offenses.

"Sit with me while we talk, Kai Chen Boussard," he bid her and swept his arm toward a table with several chairs. "And bring the food."

She smiled shyly at him and bowed as she picked up the plate with only a few meager items, and then joined him at the table. For the next hour Kai Chen and the Elderly man chatted as a deep respect and admiration grew between them. When her plate was empty the man shuffled across the room and brought back a veritable feast for them to dine on. Back and forth they related personal triumphs and tragedies as their friendship flourished.

"You know, Kai Chen," he began as he licked the chocolate mousse from his fingers, "you are the most fascinating woman I have ever known."

"Then you must not know many women, Chef Smithers" she stated guilelessly then frowned as he burst out laughing. "I do not understand your humor."

"That's the beauty of it," he declared as he wiped tears from his eyes. Her innocence was unpretentious and beguiling. "You are serious."

Kai Chen tilted her head and pondered their conversation before grinning. "I understand now."

They both laughed and polished off the remainder of the delicious chocolate mousse from a huge bowl with their fingers. Never had she eaten something so sweet and wickedly delightful. It seemed almost sinful to enjoy something so palatable.

"I haven't eaten with my fingers since I was a babe," the chef proclaimed in a conspiring tone. "That'll be our secret."

"Your secret will remain safe with me," she told him solemnly and he guffawed anew. Smiling at him she tried to adjust to his unusual sense of humor. "I am ready for my punishment now and respect your decision."

"Now wait a minute here, little lady," he warned as the amusement disappeared from his face. "I'll have none of that! You are a woman of the cloth, a fine lady, and I happen to have a soft heart for stowaways. There'll be no punishment."

Kai Chen pressed her hands together and bowed as she sat in her seat. "Venerable sir, I am in your debt."

"Ah! Go on with you." He collected the assortment of empty dishes and trudged over to the large basin. "The only thing I ask is that you not come into my kitchen again. I'll be pleased to see you are served meals. Where are you hiding?"

"In one of the cargo holds," she said and noticed the man flinch. "It is quite comfortable and dry."

"Pishaw! I'll not have you living in a hole like some guttersnipe. Come dear, I'll make sure you are adequately provided for," he offered and held out a beefy arm.

Rising to her feet she slipped her arm through his as they left the immense kitchen. Cautiously they made their way to the second deck, just above the cargo hold she had been hiding. With a circumspect knock at one of the doors, he waited for an answer. When one was not forthcoming he tried the knob and it opened.

"Here are your quarters, demoiselle," he trumpeted with flourish and swept his arm aside for her to proceed inside. The room was small but cozy with a narrow berth, desk and chair and private lavatory with shower. Pale pink wallpaper with minute white flowers covered the walls and soft mauve carpeting on the floor.

"It is elegant, fit for the Empress Dowager," she said in awed tones as she slowly touched the cherry oak desk with her hand. "I do not deserve such lodging."

"This is far from elegant," he grumbled then chuckled at the perplexed look she threw him. "You should see Vaden's private quarters. Now *that* is elegant."

At the mention of Vaden's name Kai Chen blushed then paled. This was his ship. Should he discover her on board she wondered what type of retaliation he might demand. Though he had offered her refuge a few weeks ago she had spurned it. Somehow, she did not presume his reception would be a happy one now.

"You are very compassionate given the circumstances," she credited him and saw his face turn red with embarrassment.

"Nonsense, we'll be anchored off the coast of India for a few weeks. Now, you stay here and don't get caught wandering the decks," he cautioned and headed for the door. Turning, he added in a gruff tone softened by his twinkling eyes, "And stay out of my kitchen!"

Kai Chen pressed her palms together and bowed as the man closed the door with a soft click.

The warm air caressed Kai Chen's skin as she cautiously made her way through the dark of night. Although Chef Smithers had told her not to venture from her room she could not be without the fresh sea air. It was invigorating, refreshing. She needed to move her restless body and keep in shape and stay flexible. Though no longer in China she was still responsible for her legacy of Wing Chun. She had failed as a nun and she would not fail with this. So, in the dark of night she would sneak outside to practice her martial arts and discover the confines of Vaden's ship. Her favorite pastime was watching people dance within the grand ballroom.

The sound of music greeted her as she silently walked the huge ship. The tinkling of a piano lured her toward the area where bright light filtered out from a large entrance. Prudently she made her way to the door and peered inside to gasp in wonder. The beauty of the room struck her each time she saw the huge crystal chandeliers hanging from the tall ceiling of the grand ballroom, twinkling gaily as though in accordance with the lively atmosphere. A group of musicians were at the far end of the room, their elegant attire matching the fine decor. White linen tablecloths with sparkling glasses and fine dish wear covered the tables arrayed strategically for movement of the patrons. Although there were at least one hundred people in the ballroom there were countless empty tables. The dance floor had several couples on it as the music continued.

Kai Chen stared in awe at the beautiful gowns the women wore with their fine jewelry glittering majestically, proclaiming their wealth. The delicious smell of various culinary works of art made her stomach grumble in protest which she easily ignored. Smiling at the men and women who glided across the dance floor Kai Chen carefully noted their movements. As she saw them whirl and coast easily in various patterns a familiar face caught her attention. Vaden LeBlanc was sitting at a table alone. He lounged comfortably in his chair observing the couples on the floor also. On his face was a blank expression as if he were not really seeing them but thinking of something else. A glass of wine was held up before him as though he would drink from it, but he didn't move.

She examined his face closely for the first time. He was a striking man with sharp, chiseled features. His tanned complexion from years of being in the sun accentuated his mane of gold blonde hair, but his dark blue eyes drew her to him. They were so compelling and expressive. She could read his thoughts and heart in them, and they told her he was a good man. He was an honest man.

He suddenly turned to look in her direction as though sensing her scrutiny. Kai Chen jumped back instantly before he could see her. Hearing the sound of approaching people she slid into a dark corner, waiting silently as they moved past her and into the elaborate dining area. The image of Vaden LeBlanc's handsome face, of his huge body relaxed in the formal attire he wore, stayed with her as she quietly slipped from her concealed position to make her way to another part of the ship where she could enjoy the memory of him.

☯

September 1900
New York Harbor

"We must move quickly," Chef Smithers whispered as he observed her carefully wrap her hair in a new piece of black cloth he had given her.

"You have been so very kind to me, like a father," she told him kindly with tears in her eyes. "When I was hungry you fed me. When alone, you gave me companionship. Now you give me clothing fit for royalty."

"Nonsense!" The man blushed profusely as he considered for the thousandth time how very humble and appreciative she was of the basics in life. Being with her had caused him to reevaluate certain aspects of himself and the things he took for granted. Her subtle influence would forever change the ways he viewed himself, others, politics, and religion.

Brushing her hands down the black tunic with narrow white piping on the wrists, hem and short upright collar, Kai Chen smiled beautifully. It was a striking outfit with matching black billowy pants that gathered at her slim ankles. Sturdy black slippers covered her feet, the feel of them peculiar having went barefoot most of her life. A dark satchel slung over her shoulder held two other outfits he had acquired for her.

"How will I repay you?"

"Go on with you! I don't want repayment," he blustered and handed her a slip of paper. "I spoke to a friend of mine knows a man named Fong-La, who owns a laundry shop in Chinatown. It is hard work but you should make some money. I only wish I could do more to help you. Are you sure I can't take you to the woman's address I got for you?"

"Your generosity knows no bounds," she told him earnestly then smiled almost sadly. "No, the woman does not know me."

Observing the confused expression on Chef Smithers face, Kai Chen sighed heavily. In her own time and way she would somehow approach her only remaining relative, her father's sister, but now was not the time. This new world she found herself in would take some time to become accustomed. Perhaps she might stand a chance to start anew in America? The odds were certainly against her in China.

"It's dark enough outside. Let's go while the getting is good. Fortunately, as primarily a cargo ship we can avoid Ellis Island where all new immigrants must register," he declared then chuckled as a thought struck him. "To think I'm smuggling an illegal alien into the country! Makes me feel like one of those Tong members I've heard about, slinking around in the dead of night."

"Tong?" Kai Chen frowned as she threw him an inquisitive look. The sound of Chef Smithers shoes squeaking as he valiantly tried to remain silent made her grin. Given time she could have taught him the art of walking silently.

"They are the Chinese mafia, a secret society," the man whispered as he peered around a corner to ensure their safety. "Assassins and drug lords."

"Very much like the Triad in China," she deliberated and assumed they were somehow connected. If they existed in Chinatown she would have to tread very carefully to remain as cloistered as possible. Were they to discover her and her illustrious past connected to Prince Tuan and Ji-Kin Lau, her persecution would commence again in this new land.

"From what you have disclosed to me of the Triad, yes, the Tong and Triad are very much alike," he admitted as they prowled down the gangway to land. As their feet touched soil he heard her breathe a sigh of relief. Grasping her hand he squeezed it gently in reassurance. "Come this way, Kai Chen."

She did not bother to glance about the area with too much curiosity. There would be plenty of time later to discover this new world to which she now belonged. It was important she obtain lodging and a job to survive in this foreign country. Kai Chen wondered how well she would be received by this laundryman when he discovered she was a half-breed.

"It being late summer the laundry will be a hellish place to work. The heat is already unbearable, and it is twice as hot inside the shop. I hate this for you," the man grumbled unhappily.

"Do not worry. I am accustomed to extreme temperatures," she advised him. Kai Chen considered him so very kind to care for her. Her musings shifted however as they entered the first of several novel villages. The numerous exotic neighborhoods they traveled through astounded her; Germans, Russians, Jews, Swedes, Italians, Polish, French, Welsh and Blacks. Their mode of housing, clothing, foods, economics, and language varied as they traveled through each one to reach Chinatown. It was dark, mysterious and frightening, with dim lights reflecting eerie shadows along the cobblestone streets. Unfamiliar noises sent Kai's heart racing in her breast as she gazed at sudden movements and loud screams or crashes with wide eyes. Dark figures lurked at every corner, their deep sinister calls in various languages adding to the enigma of this bizarre environment she found herself in. She prayed the light of day would diminish the evil she sensed skulking in the souls of some of these foreign immigrants, and hoped this new life she strived to attain would not be her death warrant.

"I fear to go further, dear lady," her companion and aide admitted shamefully. "I frequent these communities but dare not enter Chinatown at night."

"The Tong is your fear?" Kai Chen glanced at his dark scowl and wondered if her Chinatown was infinitely more dangerous than those villages they had just passed through. The idea did nothing to assuage her qualms.

"There is more in Chinatown to fear than the Tong," he confessed and threw her a concerned glance. "I only bring you here because you are accustomed with the culture. If I was certain you would be safe elsewhere I would take you there without hesitation."

"This will do," she said in a low tone, hearing the familiar strands of lilting music and the sing song voices of China stemming from the businesses and homes before her. "I thank you for the benevolence you have shown me, honorable friend."

"I thank you for enlightening my life," he stated gruffly. Pressing his palms together he bowed and heard her tinkle of laughter.

"It was not I who did the enlightening," she said mysteriously and returned the bow before disappearing silently into the shadows of the night.

The soft voice of a woman singing brought a wistful smile to Kai Chen's otherwise stern expression. She did not like hiding in a darkened alley until the sun could rise and light her way to the laundry shop she needed to find, but she had no other choice. An astute sense of danger and self preservation kept her from approaching those men skulking about in the deep of night to ask for directions. She could not afford to take chances in this new country, in this new life she was creating for herself. It would be to her benefit to remain as unobtrusive as possible.

Finding an abandoned spot she crossed her legs in a lotus position as she sat in a black shadowed corner to the entrance of a closed doorway. Kai Chen allowed herself to close her eyes. She would not sleep for her senses would be alert to even the slightest of sounds, but the peace and calm her meditation brought would suffice. Besides, she didn't need much sleep when there was so much in life yet to accomplish. Sighing softly, she let the familiar melody of the song the woman sang lull her into a light slumber.

Only a few hours had passed when the crunching sound of pebbles brought her instantly awake. Opening her eyes, and instantly wide awake, Kai Chen inhaled deeply through her nose and listened to the approaching steps of someone making their way stealthily toward her. From the cautious movements they made she was certain they were attempting to sneak for an attack. She frowned as an unfamiliar fear rose within her breast. She did not like being alone in this new world but she was realistic and knew there was no other alternative for her. This was only the beginning of many new experiences she was likely to encounter. There was no doubt this America was going to be completely different from her homeland, China.

"Sh-h-h! There she is. I told you she was around here," a man's voice hissed softly to his partner.

Kai Chen's frown deepened as she recognized her native Chinese dialect. Her own kinsmen were once again going to assault her. Would she never be free of the trials of being not only an outcast, but a woman? Would men continually seek to punish her or use her for her difference in appearance? Would she never have a simple life? She doubted it all greatly.

"They are looking for more girls down by the docks," another man replied. "This should be simple enough. She is alone. We won't know how much we will get for her until we get a good look at her, but it should fill our bellies for a week or more."

"Yes," the first man murmured quietly as he moved toward the shadows where Kai Chen hid.

Sagely she waited and watched as they advanced. Within seconds they were standing before her and reaching for her in the darkness. She remained seated as she leaned forward and struck out with both hands. The sound of bones snapped as her palms struck one knee of each man. She felt the shift of their bones snapping as they broke. The sound echoed in the quiet alley. Their cries of agony suddenly filled the night as they fell to the road, each clutching a dislocated kneecap.

"Forgive me," she whispered sadly as she clutched her cloth bag and slipped into the alley, away from the disquieting wails of the men who meant her harm for their own benefit.

Striding briskly from the alley she made her way to the center of Chinatown. Her heart was racing frantically as she recalled the feel of bone breaking under her hands, and it was heavy with the burden of causing another injury. It seemed all too clear now the burden and blessing of Wing Chun. The knowledge could save her life, but what of her heart and conscious at hurting others so grievously?

Looking over her shoulder she could see a pinkish cast to the east as the sun began its ascent. Soon morning would arrive and she could make her way more comfortably to the laundry shop of Fong-La. She had not questioned Chef Smithers how he was able to make this arrangement for her and she was curious as to the reception she would receive, but so long as she had a place to stay, an occasional meal, and was not discovered she did not mind.

Wandering the streets which were rapidly beginning to come alive with activity as the sun rose higher in the sky, a hint of a smile touched her lips. There was so much of China here in this small community. The bright colors of red, purple and gold decorated many shops. Various dragons decorated the windows, doors and signs of restaurants and other businesses. The heady smells of pungent ginger and garlic filtered past her as she stopped in a shadowed doorway of a Lutheran Chinese church. Seeing her kinsmen exit their homes and shops she felt her eyes fill with tears.

The sight of their pale skin, their straight inky black hair and sloped dark eyes reminded her of her lost homeland, of her mother and grandmother she would never see again. Though the sight of these strangers brought an odd sense of relief to her she was anguished at the memory of all that was unsalvageable in her life--the deaths of so many, the loss of her position within the temple, but mostly, the odd sense of having lost a part of herself. She knew with each choice a person made a path was chosen. Her belief was strong in that she had chosen wisely in many instances and unwisely in others. However, she could not go back to choose differently as lamenting over what could not be was unhealthy and illogical. This was her life now and she must make the best of it.

A soft click behind her announced a door opening. Stepping forward she made to leave the small alcove that hid her but a strong hand on her shoulder detained her.

"How are you today, child?"

Turning to face the pleasant voice of the man who lightly restricted her escape, Kai Chen bowed humbly. Never would she think of disrespecting a man or woman of any religion as to walk away without acknowledging them would be a very high insult, indeed. Instinctively she wanted to defend herself at the touch of another person's hand on her body.

"I am well. Many thanks for your concern. I pray all is well with you," she responded with an easy smile. As she straightened she noted the startled expression flicker across the minister's face as he saw her American features. Rapidly, his glance slid over her outfit which was standard within the American Chinatown community and his brows rose even higher.

"All is well, child. I have not seen you here before."

Kai Chen hesitated in response. There was such open concern and kindness in the missionary's light brown eyes she felt compelled to be honest. She instantly thought of her father as she noted the man's light hair and fine features. There was tenderness about him reminding her of her father.

"I look for a laundry shop owned by Fong-La. Where might I locate it?"

The tall man's countenance changed from concern to consternation as he said, "If you are looking for work you should not go there. He will work you hard and pay little."

"Your concern lightens my heart but I am obligated," she advised him in her singsong voice.

He paused for several seconds as though wanting to say more before sighing heavily. He noted her stoic expression and knew that being an illegal immigrant and half-breed she would take whatever form of servitude she could obtain. "Should you need my assistance you are free to come here any time, child."

"Many thanks," she smiled warmly and bowed again as he gave her directions to Fong-La's laundry shop. She sped away without saying more. Making her way northwest toward Fong-La's she set a swift pace before the sun rose completely to announce to all of Chinatown she was there and not truly one of them. For several blocks she darted along the street and finally came to Fong-La's shop. It was not large and appeared very plain from the outside. Peering down the side alley she saw a side door open with steam rolling out and walked toward it. As she stepped inside a blast of damp heat struck her face and made her catch her breath.

"Who are you?"

Kai Chen glanced at the black woman who confronted her with an obvious glare of dislike on her face. Another black woman stood beside her, scrubbing a white shirt against a board as she threw an inquisitive look at her. Two Chinamen watched her enter the back of the shop, their frowns displaying their disapproval of her as they ironed shirts and pants rapidly. Another Chinaman held a thick wooden paddle in his hands and stirred a mass of shirts in a massive metal tub boiling with water and soap. He did not bother to look at her as he continued stirring the steaming mass.

"I am looking for Fong-La," she stated and gazed about the tiny area. The small workroom was cramped with equipment and it was sweltering hot. Sweat was already saturating her clothes and plastering loose wisps of hair against her neck and face.

"I am Fong-La," announced a man who came out of a room to her right. "You are Kai Chen?"

"I am," she said and bowed. As she straightened she noted the men and women in the room had stopped working. The stunned and wary expressions on their faces spoke their disbelief that she was part Chinese. She looked American except for the very slight angle of her eyes.

"You are half-breed," Fong-La declared, surprised at the discovery then nodded thoughtfully as he approached her. Slowly he walked around her, gauging her physical strength by her uncommon height. As he stood before her he grasped her hands and examined them. For a moment he seemed pleased to note the roughness of her skin and calluses on her palms, but as he leaned closer to inspect them a sharp gasp escaped from his parted lips. "It cannot be!"

Kai Chen watched as his small, dark eyes darted up to meet hers. It was obvious the fear and respect on his face as he stepped away from her and bowed humbly. "Many moons have passed, Fong-La. I no longer serve the temple," she whispered. The man raised his upper body to gaze at her anew.

"Many things about you were not disclosed to me. This is a most curious situation, one I must reflect upon," Fong-La insisted and turned to his other workers. "Back to work! I do not pay you to gawk!"

Immediately the men and women resumed their tasks, throwing Kai Chen glances which spoke of their mistrust toward her. Kai Chen was treated differently from the others working for Fong-La. Initially, it caused a deep malcontent between her and the others working there. They felt she was taking away from money they could potentially make. However, soon it was obvious she was capable of handling the business much better than Fong-La. She was frugal with expenses and kept his accounting books meticulous and somehow managed to pay her coworkers a little extra. This endeared her to them more than anything else she could have done.

Her acceptance by them was much easier than by the customers entering the laundry shop or by the inhabitants of Chinatown. The customers were taken aback at seeing an American looking woman working for Fong-La, but gossip quickly spread by unknown persons of her mixed heritage. In time they grew accustomed to her and relaxed enough to speak about more than their laundry specifications.

The inhabitants of Chinatown treated her as was customary. At first they continuously threw her wary glances or spat out profanities but never were so bold as to confront her physically. With her usual calmness she let the vocal assaults slide off her back and ignored them. Over time she was accepted or ignored by the local Chinese people. However, the other cultures that entered Chinatown were not as forgiving. The youth gangs of Italian, Irish, and Blacks continually looked for her, or someone, to assault. Anyone was a target from the brutal attacks by the young men, but they had a particular penchant for Kai Chen who easily eluded them with her fleetness of foot and quick wit. For them it was a challenge as to who would capture and hurt her first. For Kai Chen it was just another nuisance in this new world she found herself.

She hoped in time that she would be able to blend in with the people and culture of Chinatown without causing upheaval but she instinctively knew it was a simple dream that would never come to fruition. No matter the place or time she was forever outcast. She was a half-breed that would never truly be accepted by any culture or any person.

December 1900

"The half-breed does not say much," Li-Chin said as he shoveled more rice into his mouth with the thin chopsticks, staring at her warily.

"Kai Chen only speaks when there is something worthy to say. She is a hard worker and very smart. Already, she has made my profits rise by doing my bookkeeping," Fong-La declared triumphantly, knowing his friend would be jealous at his sudden monetary gain.

"You cannot trust a half-breed," Li-Chin spat, throwing a distrustful glare at Kai Chen. It was clear he was aghast at Fong-La's apparent naivety in allowing anyone other than their own kind to handle his business, especially his money.

"Hah!" The small laundry man shouted a laugh, scooping up a large portion of stir-fried meat with vegetables and savory sauce. He ate it with enthusiasm before saying, "You know nothing! Look at her hands. Tell me what you see."

The restaurant owner, Li-Chin, Fong-La's dearest friend, leaned over the table and stared at Kai Chen's hands as she silently ate the delicious meal before her. For the past hour she had sat silently with the two men as they talked business in the empty diner. Fong-La was good to her, better than Chef Smithers or the Lutheran minister had predicted. Once he discovered she had a knack for making him more money, Kai Chen had become invaluable to him and he treated her kindly. Though the work was tedious and hard at times when she worked with the other staff, she was already accumulating a sizeable amount of money that she had stashed safely away.

"I see nothing but a woman's worn laundry hands," the man scowled in disgust and resumed eating his meal.

"Kai Chen, extend your hands to Li-Chin," Fong-La requested kindly.

Kai Chen threw him an exasperated look before dropping her chopsticks and placing her hands flat on the wooden table. Once again the man leaned close to her hands and studied them. Suddenly, he fell back into his seat with a shocked expression on his face.

"She cannot be!" His dinner was forgotten as he lifted his gaze from her hands to her face. There was pure astonishment and disbelief written in his countenance as the truth about her became quite obvious to him.

Fong-La leaned over to his friend and whispered quietly in his ear. "You are the only one who knows, Li-Chin. Do not start rumors that will hurt her. Befriend her and she will protect you."

The squat little man's head bobbed up and down furiously as he continued to watch Kai Chen as she resumed eating, her head lowered and her eyes downcast. He was amazed. Never had he seen a half-breed Buddhist nun nor heard of one who had left her temple and continued to live outside it. It was truly astonishing.

"I will remember," Li-Chin proclaimed and they returned to their meal, but his curious glance returned to her several times. For the next hour the two men talked and drank tea as Kai Chen patiently waited for Fong-La. It did not bother her to tarry. There was nowhere she had to be. It was Sunday, a day of rest. It was her only day without work.

Abruptly, the men stopped talking as the door to the restaurant opened and four huge men entered. They were dressed in baggy pants and dirty shirts, their caps askew on their heads. They towered over Fong-La and Li-Chin by several inches with the size of their brawn and muscle intimidating. In their hands they carried baseball bats and their expressions carried the look of smug expectation.

"Well, what've we here? Two Johnny's and their Chinkie woman," the apparent leader of the pack announced. He was by far the largest in size with a pock-marked face and rotten teeth. His heavily muscled body was daunting as he easily tossed a chair aside in a threatening manner.

"What do you want?" Li-Chin's face was pale, his throat working convulsively as he cowered away from the frightening men. Fong La was just as pale as he threw Kai Chen a pleading, almost desperate look.

"We want all your money," the red headed leader demanded arrogantly. "Now!"

"You hoodlums get out of here before we call the leatherheads," Fong-La warned but his voice quivered with fear.

Kai Chen's hands unfolded from beneath the table as she sized each man up immediately. She noted the other men were large in size also, but did not speak. They let their leader do all the talking as they waited for him to give the order to act. The small band of men reminded Kai Chen of the Imperial soldiers or Triad members in China. There was always one leader who did all the talking and the others simply waited for their cue to act out against everyone.

"Boys that sounded like a threat to me. P'haps a coupla broken bones'll set 'em straight," the redheaded man declared, causing the others in his gang to laugh. Their faces were bright with anticipation as they stepped forward. They tapped their baseball bats against the palms of their hands as preparation and mock warning as to what was coming next.

Kai Chen stood. "Violence will only beget violence. Do not choose this path."

"Sit down, Chinkie woman. We have som'em special planned for you after we finish with them."

The redheaded man's mean brown eyes met Kai Chen's vivid green, calm gaze. He blinked stupidly for several seconds, trying to comprehend what an American woman would be doing here dressed and acting like a Chinese woman.

"Ya' heard da man. Sit down, woman," another man bellowed impatiently and came from behind Fong-La toward her.

Kai Chen waited until the man grabbed her shoulder before acting. Swiftly, she captured his arm with one hand, and with several blows to his mid-section and face with her free hand she then spun him forcefully to the ground. His bat shot across the room like a cannon ball as he moaned in pain on the floor, barely conscious.

"You will leave now," she announced firmly as every man in the room stared at her with a mixture of incredulity and anger.

"You'll pay for that, bitch," one of the other men yelled as he ran around the table toward her with the bat pulled back and ready to swing. As he neared her he swung the bat forward to connect with her head.

Fong-La and Li-Chin cringed as they watched in fascinated horror. She stepped boldly into the strike, rather than away. For a brief moment they expected to see blood explode around them as the bat hit her. There was no way to possibly stop the force of that swing or avoid it. But as the man's arms extended, Kai Chen shoved her body against his and captured his beefy forearms under her armpit. Her free hand shoved against one of his elbows causing its dislocation. His wrists struck her back sending the bat sailing toward the watching men without it striking her. The men fell back with a cry of surprise to avoid the projectile heading their way as she allowed the man before her to fall to the ground with screams of anguish. Refocusing on the phenomenon happening before them, they saw the second man lying on the ground beside the first. Fong-La and Li-Chin sat next to each other, their smiles beginning to widen on their faces as the leader and his last man both propelled forward to attack her.

"I told you," Fong-La said to his friend as he nodded toward Kai Chen.

Astounded at Kai Chen's extraordinary ability they watched as she skillfully felled the other two men. All men lay on the floor, crying out in obvious pain from their injuries as she calmly returned to her chair where she tucked her legs beneath her, bowed her head and whispered, "Forgive me."

The door to the restaurant flung open as two policemen walked in with their clubs raised, the obvious Irish descent announced as one of them spoke. "What's da ruckus? We were told by some people outside dere was a -," he stopped as he saw the four men lying on the floor. "Landsakes!"

"These four men tried to rob Li-Chin. You can see their weapons. Fong-La and Li-Chin were only protecting their business and defending themselves, benevolent officer," Kai Chen spoke with her head still bowed.

"Seems as though we've finally caught up with da Delaney brothers. Dirty hoodlums," the other officer said as he and his partner each hauled the men to their feet. Throwing them up against the wall they began to pat them down and check their pockets.

"Aw! You don't need to overhaul us, copper. It was the woman, she did this to us," the leader complained, but groaned loudly as the officer rammed his billy club into the man's back.

"Shut up, ya filthy moll buzzer. We know ya been pickpocketing women off the streets, ya rounder," the older police officer gritted between his clenched teeth. "Ya never know when ta quit, do ya boys?"

"Da cooler will do ya fine, until ya get sent to da calaboose," the other officer informed them, and then added with a threat, "We still might put ya in da sweatbox."

The four robbers blanched. There was nothing worse than the sweatbox where the police forced confessions from criminals through the third degree of questioning. It terrified even the most hardened of criminals. They had seen men crippled afterwards from the type of solicited admissions the leatherheads coerced from them.

"And ya say 'twas the woman who did this to da lot of ya?" The other officer crowed with laughter, causing his partner to laugh in unison. "Now Oi've heard it'all!"

"All right, boys. Let's go. And no funny stuff or I'll brain ya!" The older officer turned and looked at Kai Chen who had raised her head. His eyes widened at the sight of her green eyes and obvious American features. Opening his mouth to speak, he suddenly snapped it shut and ushered the young men out the door.

"I thank you most profoundly, Kai Chen. I am forever indebted," Li-Chin promised and bowed humbly before her. Were he to tell his other friends what had occurred here tonight they would laugh at him as if he were high on opium. How Fong-La had happened upon this wondrous woman did not matter.

What mattered was that the Tong would be interested in knowing about her and might pay him most handsomely.

CHAPTER NINE

He who knows when he can fight and when he cannot, will be victorious.
-Sun Tzu, *The Art of War*

January 1901
Chinatown

Kai Chen entered the laundry shop through the side alley door with her arms carrying supplies and groceries to last the work crew for one week. It was her duty and Saturday ritual to acquire the items necessary for the upcoming business week in Fong-La's shop. However, she was becoming concerned. Fong-La was disappearing more and more during the week, leaving her in charge. She was uncomfortable dealing with the customers and more used to toiling in the back with her friends. Her worst fear, she dreaded the day the Tong arrived and she need deal with them. Each week they arrived to blackmail and extort money from Fong-La, leaving him with little money to pay his workers upon occasion.

Setting the bags on the floor Kai Chen paused as she heard a woman laughing. Arching her brow she twisted her lips sourly as she contemplated Fong-La's present partner. It would be the prostitute, Chun. She came every Saturday evening to provide Fong-La with his sexual diversion and enjoyment. Normally, she did not arrive until Kai Chen was already asleep. She was early tonight. Very early.

"You are so big, Fong-La. However will you fit inside me?"

Kai Chen frowned as she heard the woman's insincere raillery. Chun's sarcasm was evident though Fong-La thought her genuine. Kai Chen cringed as she quickly began to put the items away so she could retire to her chambers, away from the woman's lewdness and Fong-La's moans and grunts. She did not know the first thing of what a man did to a woman other than the terrible memory of seeing a girl raped once. She had only been about six years old herself and although she did not see exactly what the man did to the women, it had frightened her.

"Take me in your mouth," Fong-La insisted as his voice rose in excitement.

"I do not do that normally. You know that. It will cost you extra," the woman demanded harshly.

"Fine. Just do it," he ordered urgently. Within seconds the sounds of his hedonistic groans and her lips smacking were heard from behind the closed door.

Turning to flee from the embarrassing scene Kai Chen heard Fong-La's shout of sexual release, spurring her to her room upstairs in haste. Heat suffused her cheeks as she sat on her hard pallet and shoved aside the memory of what she had just heard. What happened between a man and woman was private and she was sure she never wanted to discover it for herself.

February 1901
Chinatown

Kai Chen wiped the perspiration from her brow as she folded another shirt perfectly and centered a paper band about it. She was thankful for the sweltering heat of the laundry shop as freezing winds blew inside with the customers. It was a bitterly cold winter with snow almost to her knees, making her yearn for her climate in China. Stacking a band of shirts together she diligently began folding another set.

The front door blew open with a fierce gust of wind, causing her to wince as the frigid air swept about her. A small tinkling bell chimed long after the door closed again. Glancing up she noticed four men in black coats and hats. Their oriental features and menacing scowls immediately alerted her to their origin. She had seen them numerous times before but had never dealt with them. Fong-La always dealt with the Chinese mafia, or Tong, in his own manner. The Tong was known to be ruthless and was never disobeyed.

"May I help you?"

Fear threatened to grip her but she pushed it down. It was not that she was afraid of them, she was afraid she would have to kill them and then be on the run again.

"We are looking for Fong-La," one of the men declared sharply, his eyes narrowing on her face. Gazing into her unique large green eyes he spat on the floor. His disrespect for her could not be more evident.

"I will find him," she offered in their Chinese dialect and calmly left the front counter of the shop to find her employer. A knot filled her throat as worried thoughts consumed her. Fong-La was in no condition to see anyone. As a matter of fact he was in no condition for anything.

Scurrying to the rear of the business where his small room was, Kai Chen knocked on the door. The sound of Fong-La vomiting into a basin made her grimace as she imagined the horrible poison being expelled from his ravaged body. He had been using opium delivered by Chun, the prostitute, for a couple of months now since his business profits had raised. His addiction was taking its toll on his body and business.

"The Tong," Kai Chen whispered through his door and heard the man moan in misery.

"You handle it, Kai Chen. I cannot," he groaned deeply before his body tried to purge the illicit opium again through more vomiting.

"I will try," she stated and turned from the dying man's room. The workers in the rear of the shop stared at her in concern. They were aware of Fong-La's condition and were waiting to be told they were no longer employed. It was all their greatest fear but they foresaw the inevitable.

Returning to the front of the store, Kai Chen said firmly, "I fear Fong-La is grievously ill and is unable to speak with you. He has requested I help you."

"You?" one of the men barked angrily and they all laughed at her. "We do not deal with half-breed vermin. We will speak with another who works here."

"You will speak with me or no one," she told him calmly.

An irate silence greeted her as one of the men stepped forward and leaned over the counter into her face.

"I will first cut out your insolent tongue before gouging out your blasphemous green eyes if you do not respect my order," he hissed between rotten teeth as he slipped a wicked-looking blade out from the sleeve of his coat.

Their eyes locked, his in rage, hers in refusal. Adamantly she stood before him as he spun from her with a savage yell. The knife he held whirled from his hand as she easily leaned to the side and avoided it. As the blade embedded itself into the wooden wall behind her the man's eyes widened a fraction. Refusing to bow in deference she waited patiently for his next words or actions.

"What may I help you with?"

For several moments the men only gaped at her as they reconsidered their mission. Nobody evaded an attack initiated by the Tong. Uncertainty was etched in their visage as they wondered who this unusual outcast was. They need discover as much about her as possible, as soon as this confrontation was finalized.

"We are here for payment," the man who threw the blade demanded insolently.

"Payment for what?" Kai Chen knew but she wanted to see exactly how much of Fong-La's money was disappearing to them.

"For his opium habit, for the prostitute we furnish him with every Saturday night, and for allowing him to continue his paltry establishment here in Chinatown," he snapped irately and held out his hand. "That will be one hundred dollars for this week."

Kai Chen pressed her lips together to maintain her composure. One hundred dollars! That barely covered the operating expenses of his business. The bad weather had cut his revenue in half. If she gave them the money they demanded there would be nothing left.

"I will give you thirty dollars and no more. If you wish to continue blackmailing Fong-La, it would behoove you to take it and be thankful you may do so another day. Take it all and he will be out of business and you will get nothing in future," she told him firmly.

The shocked expression on the Tong leader's face reflected the same of his companions. Never had anyone from any establishment dare speak to them as she did so now. The Tong would ensure Fong-La, this woman, and his business would not last long. They would be reporting this back to their leader, Mock Duck, immediately.

"Give me the money," he agreed. His face was flushed red from his fury but what she said made irrefutable sense.

Kai Chen used the only key around her neck to open the moneybox. Counting out the bills she thrust them toward the evil man who snatched them from her. Deftly he grasped her extended hand and scrutinized it carefully before dropping it from him as though burned.

"Nun," he whispered in stunned bewilderment. His eyes stared into hers again. "I have only seen marks like these on the monks and nuns in China."

"You know nothing," she whispered to him and easily slipped her calloused hand from his. She hid her hands within the folds of her loose black top. Continuing to hold his gaze she waited as another man leaped forward to shake the dazed man who held the money in a trembling hand.

"What is wrong with you?" the man hissed at his evil Tong brother who could only stare at Kai Chen's large green eyes. "Let's go!"

The men hustled their muddled Tong member out of the shop even as their furtive glances returned to her, unsure and hateful. Kai Chen turned to pick up another stack of shirts and noticed her co-workers peering around the doorway to the entrance of the shop where she stood. They stared at Kai Chen with their faces beaming fear, respect and gratitude.

"Thank you, Kai Chen," one man said generously. "I would not be able to feed my family if I did not get paid."

"Nor would I," a black woman proclaimed with tears in her eyes. "You are so brave to confront them."

"I am more foolish than brave," she replied with certainty as she waved them back to work. "They will be back and when they do I fear our days will be numbered."

With a heavy heart and weary sigh she folded the stiff shirts lying on the counter before her automatically. Melancholy filled her breast and she allowed it to stay briefly. Softly humming a sad tune, she recalled hearing the words as a child. It was a haunting song where the sun set one evening, never to rise again.

Downtown New York City
The next day

Kai Chen peeked from behind a large oak tree, one of many lining the bricked street in the exclusive and fashionable neighborhood. Staring at the immense home before her, she sighed. It was a beautiful house painted soft yellow with the intricate and detailed trim painted white with splotches of green accent here and there within it. A solid white picket fence surrounded the immaculate lawn and bare rose bushes placed strategically for effect. She was sure the Empress Dowager would be envious of such a magnificent home.

Like clockwork the stained glass front door opened and a small, slender woman emerged with an extremely tall man. Her fur lined wool coat covered her as if a bear were swallowing her whole as she attempted to ward off the bitter cold. Sturdy shoes adorned her feet as she cautiously stepped down the several cleared steps leading away from her home. A pert little hat with an array of flowers was perched atop her graying hair. It was an impractical adornment against the fierce winds that could sweep her off her feet, let alone sweep the ridiculous item off her head, but she looked simply adorable with it.

"Now, don't worry about me, Manfred. I shall be back shortly," the small woman informed her assistant gently in her melodious French.

"Let me call a carriage for you, Mistress Minot," the man beseeched in concern. Kai Chen smiled at the situation. She had memorized this scene between them after seeing it for the last couple of months.

"Non! I need the fresh air and exercise," Kai Chen replied rapidly in French then listened.

"Non! I need the fresh air and exercise," said the woman as she took infinitesimal steps along the cleared walkway leading toward the sidewalk.

Giggling behind her hand Kai Chen mentally responded with their rehearsed lines and within seconds the man and woman duplicated them exactly. They were a funny little couple she had decided, and was particularly taken with the humor and sweetness of the woman. Having followed her aunt for the past several months, Kai Chen had vigilantly used her free time from the laundry shop to protect the dear woman from harm as she unwittingly traipsed throughout New York City. It was clear the woman had no sense of self-preservation by going alone.

Observing the woman stroll briskly along the cleared sidewalk she was reminded sharply of her father. Although the woman was slightly older than her brother their features were similar. She had fading light hair and those hereditary large green eyes that were a Boussard trait. Her sharp features were softened by the twinkling of happiness in her eyes and the continuous smile on her painted rosy lips. Seeing her brought a rush of emotion to the surface as she remembered her father's welcome smile given freely to everyone and his expressive eyes that reflected his peace and love toward humanity.

The urge to walk up to the woman, to introduce herself was so poignant and fierce Kai Chen actually took a step forward then halted. How could she meet her father's sister appearing as she did? The woman had been informed of Kai Chen's existence when she was born but it was clear from her parent's conversation she did not know Kai Chen was half Chinese, or that David Boussard had married a Chinese woman. It was never revealed to her why they had not told the woman the truth but Kai Chen had never felt it her place to question her parents.

"How I wish I could look American, act American, and be American so I could meet you and you would not feel ashamed," Kai Chen whispered to herself sadly as she stealthily pursued her aunt before reprimanding herself. "Wishing is not the Buddhist way, Kai Chen. You are acting and sounding like the foolish American!"

Thinking of Vaden LeBlanc gave her warm thrill that raced through her. His image was permanently transfixed in her memory; his dark blue eyes, warm and sincere, which spoke of his inherent kindness. The difference in his thick, wavy blond hair that gleamed like the sun itself when light struck it compared to her darker thick straight tresses. His angular, attractive features made her heart flutter like the wings of a butterfly. However, there was something more about Vaden LeBlanc, something different about him she considered even more seductive. Inside him was radiance cloaked by dark pain that spoke to her spirit. She felt it when they first met. She noticed the brilliance glittering in his penetrating gaze. Although she had not seen him since that evening on his ship as he held the glass of wine she did think of him nightly as she lay on her hard pallet within the laundry shop.

She believed their lives had been predetermined by kismet, long before they had entered this world, but only Buddha knew for sure.

☯

Chinatown
Two days later

Vaden's breath turned into a white mist in front of his face as he and Sebastian crossed the slush filled street to avoid carts burdened with fresh produce from the docks. The exotic smells of spices lingered in the air about the tiny Chinese restaurants he enjoyed frequenting. It reminded him of Kai Chen Boussard and her world. A world now changed forever by the Boxer Rebellion. An international force of troops, approximately twenty thousand soldiers from the countries of Austria-Hungary, France, Germany, Italy, Japan, Russia, the United Kingdom and the Unites States had arrived in China to overtake Beijing and rescue all foreigners and Chinese Christians.

The Dowager Empress, Tzu Hsi, had fled the Forbidden City disguised as a peasant woman, taking her incompetently suppressed son with her. China accepted their loss during the Boxer Rebellion, relieved to be free of the hands of a cruel and manipulative Manchu female leader for now. They rejoiced in the new peace terms, but knew until Tzu Hsi's death that she would attempt to re-establish her regime. Although the Empress was well hidden they began to create new boundaries for peace within China.

Gusts of wind buffeted Vaden while he and Sebastian discussed these vast global changes occurring in the world. To avoid being battered any further by winter's bitter bite, he and Sebastian quickly entered one of the better dining establishments in Chinatown. Sitting at a large table they were immediately greeted by the proprietor who suggested the special of the day. Ordering one for each of them Vaden shook his head sadly as he placed the linen napkin in his lap.

"We have lost contact with each other, Sebastian. For almost a year now we have been so wrapped up in our business transactions we have not made the time for simple pleasures," Vaden noted frankly and looked at his best friend.

Sebastian had aged dramatically in the past few months. Fine lines were etched around his eyes and creased his face. He had lost weight and his skin had a slight pallor to it. If Vaden didn't know better he would swear his friend was lost to the opium so widely used by the wealthy. But, he did know better! Sebastian might entertain himself having wild orgies with women and gamble occasionally, but he did not smoke opium.

"Yes, life has been too demanding for us Vaden, old chap," the dark haired man declared and sighed dramatically. "I, for one, have decided to delegate more responsibility to my employees and relax. You should consider doing the same."

"I just might do that," Vaden admitted seriously, and then chuckled at Sebastian's wiggling eyebrows. "However, I won't join you in your trysts with women."

"Your lunch," announced the owner, who placed two large delicious looking platters of food before them with a flourish. Chicken with vegetables and a savory sauce covered a huge mound of steamed rice and several little side items. "Enjoy."

"Thank you," both men replied and dug into the food with zeal, momentarily forgetting about small talk.

"I must admit," Sebastian said several minutes later as they continued the appetizing meal, "Chinatown incorporates a flair that no other village possesses. However, the Italian's produce this heavenly veal dish that cannot be mimicked. Have you been to Alfredo's yet?"

"I don't get out as often as I would like," Vaden admitted as they finished their meal. He threw several bills on the table as they put on their coats, gloves, scarves and hats to once again battle the raging winter outside. "Thank you for joining me, Sebastian. We need to get together more often."

"Definitely, old friend," the shorter man acknowledged and slapped Vaden on the back with mock force. "Nothing should come between two friends who have been through hell together most of their lives."

"I will second that motion," Vaden responded adamantly. Pulling his coat about him to help ward off the bite of the gusting winds, Vaden walked outside followed by Sebastian. A fierce gust of wind seemed to rip through his clothes and settle into his bones.

"Damn cold winter this year," Sebastian said between clenched teeth as he pulled his coat closer about him, too.

The sound of yelling boys caught their attention and they both leaned forward to peer at the small group running toward them. As they drew near, Vaden stared at a figure running in front of them through the wet street. Dark brown hair with red highlights was drawn back in a neat, long braid. Her clothing was dark and worn but it was her tall body that struck him as familiar. A fleeting impression of Kai Chen Boussard filtered through his mind but he shoved it aside. He must have a mental malady. She would not, could not, be in America or New York! What was wrong with him?

But as the figure loomed closer and the sight of haunting green eyes flashed briefly at him he felt his heart almost rip from his chest. It was Kai Chen Boussard! She was sprinting at an uncanny speed from a group of older teens who were jeering her and swinging large clubs.

"Chinkie, Chinkie, half-breed,
Sitting on the fence;
Trying to make a dollar
Out of fifteen cents.
Chink, Chink, foreigner
Eats dead rats;
Eats them up
Like gingersnaps."

Vaden was livid at the ridicule they heckled her with. No human should be treated like that, especially a woman! His fists clenched as physical violence toward the street urchins threatened to engulf his better sense. It was a shock and pleasure to see Kai Chen, and he noticed Sebastian followed her lithe figure also. Sebastian's face wore the expression of a man totally confused in seeing Kai Chen's American face, but wearing clothing distinctly proclaiming her Chinese.

Vaden glanced at her again. Kai Chen's gaze met and locked with his for a brief second. Recognition flared in her beautiful large eyes as she swiftly leaped over a huge puddle filled with ice, water, and slush. Lithely she landed on the other side without slipping or touching the frigid mess as the boys behind her attempted to do the same. As the first two jumped they fell short of the other side by a good two feet, slid and fell back in the center of the water at least a foot deep. The others followed suit until they all lay floundering and screaming in the icy mess.

Sebastian burst out laughing at the sight of them trying to get up but continually knocking each other down. Immediately, Vaden darted after the woman who had haunted him for the past several months. He would not lose her! How she had managed to get to America or why she was here did not matter. What mattered was finding her, making sure she was taken care of by him, and getting to know her better. His soul would not rest otherwise.

"Kai Chen! Wait," he yelled loudly as he pursued her on the icy sidewalks in his slick black dress shoes. Sprinting after her was dangerous for him in his current business attire, but he would gladly swim through a river of piranha naked if it would get him to her.

Her hesitant glance over her shoulder advised him Kai Chen knew he was pursuing her, and she did not want him to catch her. Like a doe being hunted, she darted sprightly through alleys and over garbage littering the alleyways as Vaden stalked her as though his life depended on it. And in some infinitesimal way it did. There was a bond between them, a cognizance of each other's inner self, drawing and binding them together.

"Damn it, Kai Chen, wait!"

His shout reverberated off the bricks of the buildings as he chased her relentlessly through Chinatown's almost deserted alleys and back streets. Turning a corner he skidded on the slick soles of his shoes and slammed into a wall with his shoulder. With a loud grunt he lunged forward after her again. As long as he kept her in sight he would catch her. Forging ahead like a man possessed he saw her dash inside an open side door to a business. He had her now! Catching his breath, which came and went in deep gasps from his effort in keeping up with her in the harsh cold weather, he entered the noisy laundry shop. Inside three oriental men and two black women slaved over steaming ironing boards and boiling washtubs. Their surprised expressions at seeing him almost made him smile. Obviously customers came in another door. However, he was not a customer.

"Where is she?"

Immediately, the three oriental men started shouting at him in their foreign dialect with their hand gestures threatening as they walked toward him. The two black women went back to their work as though nothing of import was happening. It was clear they were protecting Kai Chen and refused to help him.

"I only want to talk to her. She is my friend," he said in clipped tones laced with anger as their threats became clear. If he did not leave they were threatening to make chop suey out of him.

"Honey, if she is your friend then why is she runnin' from you?"

Vaden glanced at the black woman who chuckled at her own witticism as the other woman joined her in the good laugh.

"I ain't never seen Kai Chen with any friends. We're her only friends and family."

Frustrated, he stormed, "Kai Chen Boussard! Get out here before your friends get hurt."

Sagely Vaden sidestepped one of the men who stalked him menacingly. The little China man continued to berate Vaden in his unique dialect. Kai Chen's voice from the rear of the laundry shop halted the men who continued to openly yell at him. They returned to their duties but watched him with vigilant dark eyes.

"Foolish American," she called with her musical voice. "Come."

Vaden held back a smile as he recalled her calling him a 'foolish American' last they met. Treading quietly to the rear of the shop he frowned as the pungent smell of death overwhelmed him. It was easy to identify the source as he glanced into the room where Kai Chen sat next to a man. His body was shriveled, only skin and bones, the muscles long since atrophied. Jaundiced eyes stared at the ceiling blankly and a ghastly green liquid flowed out the side of his gaping mouth.

"Dear God," he groaned at the hideous sight of the dead man. Unfortunately, he had seen the exact scene in opium dens as he had tried to save members of his crew from the same fate.

"Your god, nor any other, will save him now," she stated quietly and placed a sheet over Fong-La's body. They both looked at the opium in her hands she had struggled to purchase to keep Fong alive just a bit longer. Standing, she faced Vaden squarely and tilted her head to one side as she studied him.

"You cut your hair."

Vaden smiled at her sudden turn of conversation. He was not surprised to see how calmly she acted even though her employer was dead. He had seen her in worse conditions and knew of her inner strength. What bothered him was that death seemed to follow in her wake.

"I would have shaved it, but there are few Shaolin temples here in America," he jested and actually saw her smile. He held his breath as he absorbed her radiance. She was absolutely stunning with her large green eyes and her pretty white teeth. Glancing back to the dead man he asked, "Who is that?"

Kai Chen gazed at her employer before sighing heavily.

"Fong-La, the owner of this laundry shop. I will have to inform the authorities."

The work stopped in the room as the employees heard her announcement and realized they were out of a job. Throwing the opium in a nearby garbage can she moved out into the workroom to talk to her friends.

"No, missy! You ain't gonna do that. Why, they'll ship you right back to China," one of the black women cried in outrage. She had heard their brief conversation and rushed over to embrace Kai Chen warmly. "We'll find us another sweat shop, honey. Don't you worry none."

"Kai Chen, are you an illegal immigrant in this country?" Vaden stared at her in astonishment before bursting out laughing at the dark humor of it. The image of a former nun resorting to stealing into another country struck him as oddly funny. The five workers glared at him menacingly as he continued to chuckle.

"I am," she admitted honestly as her face reddened in shame.

"Why didn't you let me help you earlier?" With a frustrated sigh he shook his head. "All right, I will take care of Fong-La with the authorities then you and I are going to have a long chat."

"I must help my friends obtain work or their families will suffer," she objected as the concern on their faces touched her tender heart.

Vaden glanced at the extremely thin men and women. All of them looked malnourished, unhealthy and exhausted. It was not difficult to imagine the type of lives they led. He had lived it once. They obviously had cared for each other in this hellish place and respected Kai Chen greatly. Clearly, Kai Chen appeared more concerned for her friends and co-workers than she was for herself. Her selflessness struck him forcefully and gave him one more reason to care for and respect her.

"They will be taken care of, Kai Chen. I will see to it they secure a better job with a decent salary," he offered kindly. The obvious surprise, relief and thanks on their faces touched him deeply. There were so many people in the world suffering. He did not have any idea what type of position these people were qualified for, but he would find something suitable and less arduous.

"We are but strangers to you. Why would you help us?"

"You and I are not strangers," he said with tacit meaning to Kai Chen as her blush deepened at his words. "If they are your friends then they are mine, also."

"We accept your generous offer." Promptly Kai Chen pressed her palms together and bowed. The others followed suit with beaming grins.

"How long will it take you to finish the current orders," he asked, inspecting the cramped and horrid conditions of the small workroom. How they managed to survive during the summer he could not begin to envision.

"A couple of days," she replied and saw the vigorous nods of her five friends.

"Fine. Place a note on the door stating this establishment is closing and will no longer accept laundry. All items presently ordered must be picked up by the end of next week. I will handle the rest," he said, his business acumen taking control as he considered what needed to be done to conclude these affairs. "Did Fong-La leave a will?"

"A will?" Kai Chen tilted her head and considered the word. "I do not understand."

"A piece of paper leaving instructions by a person in case they die," he informed her. Her blank mien answered his question. "Never mind."

Walking toward the door to leave, Vaden suddenly turned and glared pointedly at Kai Chen. "Don't you dare consider eluding me because I will hunt and find you, China doll."

A deeper blush filled Kai Chen's face as the black women chortled out loud with laughter. She nodded with acceptance and threw a caustic scowl at her two friends who chuckled even harder. Buddha's will intervened, placing the foolish American in her path again.

"Kismet," she clarified softly to herself.

Watching with fearful eyes and a hopeful heart as his broad shoulders squeezed out the doorway Kai Chen knew her life was once again changing in another unexpected direction. Waving to the two men in the laundry to follow her she directed them to Fong-La's room where they would prepare his body in death.

Tong Headquarters
Chinatown

"What is it you wish from us, Li-Chin?" Mock Duck was the brutal leader of New York's Tong. He wore a chain mail shirt over his chest, carried two guns, and a small hatchet up his sleeve at all times. His angelic face was deceptive, as was his seemingly kind disposition which led his prey into a false sense of relaxation. This strategy worked in his favor in all of his illicit dealings.

The small framed restaurant owner quivered with nervousness. The Tong's reputation for mercilessness with everyone was known. They were powerful and not to be trifled with in any fashion. Located on the corner of Pell and Doyers streets, known as ground zero or 'Bloody Angle' due to the numerous slayings there, the Tong's rival wars were renown across America. They integrated racketeering, gambling, drug trade, and prostitution, among other monetary deeds such as assassinations and bribery.

"I have information regarding a half-breed woman working for Fong-La," he offered nervously, holding his hat in his hands. His fingers fidgeted with the rim of the hat as he shuffled from foot to foot.

"Shi de, we are aware of her. You offer us nothing new," Mock Duck smiled but his eyes were cold and empty.

"She is illegal from China, a Buddhist nun," Li-Chin began to stutter as Mock Duck leaned back in his chair as though bored. "She has a martial art ability I have never seen before."

Suddenly, the gang leader leaned forward and pursed his fingertips together. He had heard from a few of his men of this woman in a laundry shop but had scoffed at them. A Buddhist nun in New York's Chinatown? His gaze never wavered from Li-Chin whose body was shaking fiercely. Mock Duck remained silent as he waited for more information. Soon Li-Chin retold the story that occurred in his restaurant and where Kai Chen could be found.

"Reward Li-Chin once this story has been confirmed," Mock Duck stated, the smile on his innocent looking face never reaching his eyes that were empty of any emotion at the moment.

Li-Chin bowed several times as he backed toward the door, afraid that if he turned his back it would find the sharp edge of a knife.

CHAPTER TEN

"When the enemy is relaxed, make them toil. When full, starve them. When settled, make them move."
— Sun Tzu, *The Art of War*

LeBlanc Estate
One week later

"I am very uncomfortable," Kai Chen murmured. Her head lowered as she entered Vaden LeBlanc's home. The massive white structure was larger than the Shaolin temple ground where she had lived. It made her envision the Imperial City with its grandeur. She did not belong here. She would never fit in!

"You will adjust," Vaden asserted confidently and placed a strong, tapered finger under her chin. Lifting her face he saw the uncertainty and concern. "Kai Chen no longer exists. You are Kay Boussard."

"Kai Chen will always remain," she told him sternly and placed a fist against her breast in defiance. Though her name was legally changed, and she was no longer an illegal immigrant thanks to Vaden, her spirit was not changed.

Vaden grinned and nodded in acknowledgment. "That is true and Kai Chen is also who I first met a few years ago. I have never forgotten her."

"You do not know me," she countered pointedly, unsure how to handle this intense and powerful man.

"But I do," he said with a chuckle and placed his fist over his breast.

Her tremulous smile brought lightness to his heart. Kai Chen knew the language they spoke. They were alike in so many meaningful ways they had yet to discover. She relished discovering more about him and his life.

"Foolish American! You should not say such things." Embarrassed, Kai Chen turned her face from him to hide the smile she could not contain or the excited glow of her expressive green eyes.

"That is true. No words are necessary when you already know how I feel," he retorted quietly.

Kai Chen felt her heart soar as his words settled within her heart. What he said was true and she perceived it with all her senses, which were heightened around him. Warmth surged through her as his hand caressed the side of her face lightly, forcing her to look at him.

"Your vows belong to the past. You are no longer a nun. Begin considering your future as an American, Kay Boussard. Being a legal United States citizen you are a free woman to do as you please. China no longer owns you," he murmured as he closed the distance between them. Grasping her hands within his, he offered sincerely, "Give me a chance."

When the day arrives you find a man who looks upon you with favor, leave this temple, go to him, and never return.

Her grandmother's words danced around in her mind as Vaden leaned forward and pressed his lips lightly against hers. The intimate nearness made her heart mount with wonder as desire flooded her. His spicy scent, persuasive touch and earthy maleness were like an aphrodisiac to Kai Chen as she opened her mouth to receive his contact. Never did she envision a man gazing at her with adoration as he did now. It scared and thrilled her as his tender hands held her face and his mouth moved possessively over hers. Her heart raced as his tongue faintly touched hers. His fresh breath mingled with hers as a throaty moan escaped him.

"This is only the beginning," he breathed against her lips as he stepped away from her. "Come. I'll show you to your room."

Kai Chen trailed beside him, confusion and wonder from his kiss befuddling her mind. They swept up the grand marble staircase as she noted a magnificent crystal chandelier centered in the enormous foyer. The prisms reflected light beautifully as she gazed about his mansion in wonder. She knew Vaden LeBlanc was an extremely wealthy man and wondered how she would fit into his world. There was so much to learn and she was unsure not only of herself, but this arrangement.

"We will be busy this week. I have a fashion consultant arriving tomorrow to assemble you a trousseau," he advised her. "Your English is superb, but I would like to downplay your foreign enunciation, so there will be an instructor to assist you. Do you speak any other languages?"

"French," she answered automatically, her mind whirling at all the preparations he had planned simply for her. She felt like a queen, a very undeserving queen in a strange world. Her life had not equipped her to mingle with the aristocracy. Kai Chen was a simple farm girl and nun. More importantly, she was a woman with the Wing Chun legacy to maintain.

"Very good," he stated with enthusiasm as he regarded the rare scowl on her face. "What is wrong?"

"I am afraid," she said candidly as tears welled in her expressive eyes, "and overwhelmed."

Vaden stopped at the landing and wrapped his powerful arms around her in a protective embrace. His lips lightly brushed across her forehead as he pressed her against him. Kai Chen stiffened at the curious feel of his body flush against hers. The emotions he evoked were potent and erotic, unfamiliar and new, saturating her with the remarkable awareness of being cherished and secure. These feelings jeopardized her sense of control.

"There is nothing to be afraid of. I will not allow anything or anyone to harm you."

Tears slipped down her cheeks as she gave way to emotions she had suppressed and controlled for so many years. Her expressive release was intense as she suddenly cried for the loss of her parents and grandmother, for the loss of her brothers, sisters, and life at the temple she had treasured, and for the loss of life she had taken so mercilessly during the Boxer Rebellion. Allowing herself to open up this chamber of sentiment was like releasing a massive dam as she vented against Vaden's shirt.

Tenderly he stroked her back with his hand as he held her against him protectively. He murmured nonsensical things into her hair as she grieved for her loss of integrity of the vows she had taken, as she allowed self-pity to engulf her for the first time in her life, and as she simply let another person into her heart. It took her many moments to compose herself from the floodgates of emotion that had been opened.

"Kay Boussard," he whispered against her cheek and she lifted her tear stained face. "I am relieved to see you are human, after all. For many years I wondered if you were simply a spirit haunting me."

She giggled with a soft hiccup and pressed her face against his smudged shirt. "What is it about you that causes me to reveal myself? With you I am a different Kai Chen," she admitted grudgingly, almost angrily.

"No, not different, simply exposed and human, a woman," he distinguished and felt her soft nod against his chest.

Pressing a handkerchief into her fists he patiently waited for her to compose herself before continuing down the hall. They stopped in front of a set of double doors and he grinned boyishly.

"This is my room if you ever need me."

A dark red flush blemished her pale skin as she shielded her uncertainty. Turning across the hall he opened another set of double doors wide to the vast room. Kai Chen tentatively entered and then gasped at the beauty of the room. It was almost virginal in its appearance as though never used before.

"It's exquisite," she exclaimed and stared at the dark blue carpeting, curtains and bed coverings in awe. They were the exact color of his eyes. The white furniture and matching chairs before the white marble fireplace made the room feminine and fit for a princess.

"I had it redecorated for you," he stated simply.

"You should not be so foolish," she informed him, then turned and threw him a mischievous grin, "American."

"Ah! I see you are learning impertinence quickly. Who has been teaching my China doll bad habits?" His teasing almost made her laugh.

"What is a China doll?" Tilting her head to one side her hair swept over one shoulder as she examined his face seriously. "I do not look Chinese, nor am I a doll."

Vaden's rich laughter rang loudly throughout the room and echoed down the hall, making his staff raise eyebrows in surprise at the rare sound.

"You do not realize it yet, Kai Chen, but you are going to be a hit with the upper class with your innocent earnestness. They will consider it classic dry humor. They like nothing better than sharp wit."

"I do not think I will meet these nobility," she announced and placed her worn black satchel on the floor. "I do not think I will adjust to this life at all."

"Nonsense. As clever and resourceful as you are, you will be untroubled by all of this quickly. I understand you are not accustomed to this lifestyle but you were meant to be happy. I want to offer you that opportunity," he stated solemnly.

She faced him and saw the flames of sincerity and passion in his eyes. Before her stood a man who was willing to give her a new life of wealth, happiness and protection, as well as love if she would permit him. Was it not what her mother had found in her father, what her grandmother had been trying to teach her?

"I will speak frankly," she began and took a deep breath to calm herself, "I want to understand your intention toward me."

"My intentions right now are to help you and get to know you, nothing more," he said honestly and turned to leave the room. "Over time we will talk of other intentions."

"Why help me? I am a virtual stranger." Though they had a unique affinity toward each other, she wanted to distinguish whether he recognized the element she had discovered when first seeing him over three years ago. Would he understand the tie between them, the connection that had sent her running to her grandmother for advice?

"You are no stranger," he stated firmly as his gaze locked with hers, "you are the other half of my soul."

LeBlanc Estate
That evening

Kai Chen's expression was one akin to horror as she stared at the elaborate table extended before her in the dining room. Although accustomed to the western practice of sitting at a high table with chairs rather than the traditional Chinese foot high table and cushions on the floor to eat, she had never dined in a setting with such opulence. There were three forks, three spoons, three knives and three different glasses at each place setting. She was unfamiliar with the finesse of elegant dining and dreaded the notion of making a mistake in front of Vaden, and of embarrassing herself and him.

Glancing down at her worn black tunic and pants she felt her cheeks warm. A sense of unworthiness engulfed her and her conscience urged her to flee. Yet, knowing what awaited her in China kept her rooted to the floor. Better to suffer small indignities of ignorance than to suffer physical torture before death. Deftly she picked up a silver spoon and studied the flawless engravings before replacing it. Leaning forward, she scrutinized the delicate crystal glasses, fragile china, and unblemished linen tablecloth. The items were priceless and beautiful, almost too precious in appearance to touch. It astounded her to consider how great Vaden's wealth must be. She surmised he must live as grandly as the Empress Dowager and wield as majestic a power to have acquired such a lifestyle.

"I see you found your way." Vaden's familiar voice sounded in the room and she felt her heart speed up with excitement.

Standing tall again, Kai Chen turned to find him entering the dining room dressed casually in a pair of sharply creased black trousers and a dark maroon smoking jacket with thick rolled collar and cuffs, his stark white shirt and black tie exposed by the V formed where the jacket was closed by the black sash at his waist. He appeared relaxed, yet she could sense his control as he approached her. Vaden's fixed gaze stroked her face like a velvet caress and she shivered noticeably.

"I allow my instinct to guide me," she confessed softly and lowered her pale gaze to her rough, calloused hands from years of hard labor and training in Wing Chun. Though she did not have the delicate hands of a cared for woman, hers were slender and strong. Light scars crossed the tops of her hands and a few of her knuckles were slightly swollen from years of punching and breakage, but they were still feminine.

"Interesting," he murmured as he stood before her and placed his hand under her chin. Raising her face their eyes met. "Do you always follow your instincts?"

"No. I also follow logic and my heart," she whispered as his magnetism and physical proximity bemused her senses.

It was a heady feeling, the emotions he wrung from her without effort, and she felt her body sway toward him of its own volition. Catching herself before she actually touched him she placed her hand on the back of a chair to steady herself. Vaden's secret smile brought a blush to her creamy skin and his soft, husky laughter deepened it.

"Kay Boussard, are you telling me you are a romantic?"

"You may construe it as you wish, American," she told him as her embarrassment continued. His laughter and the exquisite sensation of his hand sliding across her jaw made her heart lurch and desire fill her belly. A thrill of excitement heated her body as he guided her to a chair. Vaden seated her then sat at the head of the table beside her. Immediately, a servant entered with a cart holding a tureen of soup which he quickly set about serving first her then Vaden. He disappeared just as promptly.

Kai Chen stared down at the steaming soup and inhaled. It smelled wonderful, and appeared colorful and odd.

"What is this?"

"It is a thick, hearty soup I enjoyed once while in Louisiana. It is extremely spicy and flavorful, like many Cajun dishes. Try it," he advised her as they placed their linen napkins in their laps. He picked up the rounded spoon next to his right hand.

Kai Chen watched every move he made and followed suit exactly, memorizing each detail. This art of fine dining would be a new experience that must be perfected if she were to be seen in public or amongst his important friends and business associates. Her father had taught her basic American manners and customs but this elaborate formality would be quite different. Picking up her soup spoon she dipped it into the bowl full of vegetables and fine slivers of meat. Cautiously, she placed the spoon against her mouth and let the contents slide inside. The incredibly spicy concoction made her mouth feel as though it was on fire, though the flavor was delightful. After two more mouthfuls her body felt over heated and a fine sheen of perspiration was noticeable on her face.

"It is delicious but perhaps too spicy for me. I am used to bland meals," she confessed as she polished off the glass of water before her.

"Of course, I sometimes forget you have lived a very simple life but I want to awaken you to so many new experiences," he enthused as he watched her expression carefully.

The servant returned and removed their dishes, replacing the soup with two plates filled with seasoned chicken, red beans and rice, and a savory vegetable medley.

"You will enjoy this more."

Kai Chen carefully chose the correct fork and knife to cut the meat. It was a delectable meal with the items not near as piquant as the soup had been. The chicken covered with a slightly zesty cream sauce practically melted in her mouth and the vegetables were crisp and flavorful. Clearing her plate she sighed softly with contentment and noticed Vaden's broad grin.

"That was the most incredible meal, although, Chef Smither's is by far a better cook," she told him then became silent as she realized her confession.

"You were on my ship?"

Turning to stare at Vaden with wide, frightened eyes, Kai Chen knew she must tell the truth.

"I smuggled aboard your ship before you left China."

Vaden's laughter rang throughout the room as a curious servant and cook peered around a door to stare at him before quietly retreating with smiles on their faces. For the second time in one day his mirth had astonished his staff.

"It's simply incredible! You were on my ship for months and I did not even know it. How is it you are able to simply vanish and appear like a ghost?"

Kai Chen bowed her head in shame during her confession but at the sound of his laughter stared at him again. His obvious humor of the situation had surpassed his ire and he was now joking about it. She was confused, but pleased, that he was not angry with her.

"I was discovered by your chef in his kitchen. He was very generous to me. Do not punish him for his secrecy."

"Obviously he was generous as he did not say a word to me," Vaden chuckled as he grasped her hand and squeezed it. "Although I feel piqued you did not allow me to help you when I offered I am glad you are here now. That is all that matters."

Her blush deepened as his thumb brushed across the top of her hand intimately, causing her heart to pound. She had no experience with men, knew nothing of the wiles of women and their fine arts of seduction. However, Kai Chen did understand the lust of men. She had seen it in their eyes and heard their filthy words. With Vaden, though, she sensed desire and something more. It was the tenderness shining in them that informed her he wanted more of her than simply her body.

"You are very gracious," she murmured softly as he helped her from her chair.

"I can be selfish. Do not think otherwise," he advised her dryly as they headed toward the sitting room. "You deserve fine gowns and jewels, to be cared for and loved like any other woman. We both deserve happiness, Kai Chen."

"Everyone deserves to be happy, but each person must look within themselves to find that happiness. Other people nor material items cannot supplant what must already be there. They can only enhance it. Have you never noticed that what you consider the poorest man, can still walk about with a smile and offer a kind word, or that some of the wealthiest people ride about in their carriages with a petulant frown and deep scorn etched across their faces although they appear to have great material wealth? Each of us has an individual responsibility to discover within ourselves what it is about life that will make us happy. If we rely on others or material goods we shall forever seek the truth and never find it," she reflected perceptively. Observing his thoughtful countenance she grinned ingenuously.

"Your philosophies astound me, Kai Chen. When I behold you I see a lovely young woman but when you speak you sound like a wise old prophet. At times, I admit, I am quite speechless," he chuckled as they entered the warm sitting room housing a cheery fire.

"I shall accept that compliment," she acknowledged and bowed slightly.

Vaden's rich laughter caressed her like a warm hand stroking her body. Delicious shivers raced down her spine as he escorted her to the settee placed before the fireplace. His nearness bemused her already heightened senses and made her pulse race as though she were trekking the mountains of Fukien Province.

"I am glad I have enhanced your happiness," he grinned.

Kai Chen's tinkling laughter filled the room. She gazed about the comfortable sitting room and decided she liked this room in his vast house the best. The rich colors of brown, burgundy and cream were warm and cozy, allowing her to feel comfortable for the first time since stepping through the entrance to his home earlier that day. The walls were lined with numerous books and curious artifacts were strategically placed around the room, lending a decidedly masculine atmosphere.

"This is a wonderful room," she suddenly announced as she turned to Vaden.

"I agree," he said, pouring a brandy. "Would you care for a drink?"

Kai Chen arched a delicate eyebrow as her lips pressed together firmly.

"I do not drink alcohol," she reminded him stoically. Her back was stiff and her hands were clasped tightly in her lap as she sat on the edge of the settee.

"Ah, yes! One of the many vows you pledged," he responded as his gaze slid over her as easily as mercury rolling across a tabletop. "You are no longer a nun."

"That may be so, but I retain my own personal principles. I have broken some vows and may break others, but I shall not break this one."

"Well said," he grinned and raised his snifter of brandy in salute as he strolled casually toward her like a predatory lion preparing to strike. "I admire your fortitude, spirit, and integrity. You would not be the woman I care for should you lose those attributes."

Kai Chen stared into the leaping flames of the fireplace as she nodded her head once in silent acceptance of his carefully thought out concession. Memories of her Shaolin temple in Fukien Province with its constant fire burning in a deep well centered in the shrine filled her mind. Images played themselves out as she recalled her last days in China.

Meanwhile, Vaden sat next to her remembering his own personal hell.

☯

December 1865
White Plains, New York

"Sleep in heavenly peace."

The last strains of the soft music from downstairs died away, as did the angelic voice of his mother who hovered over him like the Christmas angel he had seen atop their tree. Although the angel on their tree flew high above his head where he could not reach, this angel was close enough that he could smell her sweet perfume and feel the warmth of her kiss on his cheek as his lids closed and sleep swept him away to that magical resting place he traveled to each night. He dreamed the peaceful nonsensical dreams of a protected, loved, and innocent child. The visions were elusive, yet comforting, and a slight smile curved his small mouth upward. In this safe place he could soar like a bird, run faster than a deer or jump higher than a kangaroo. Never did horrible events or images confront him or threaten his tranquil slumber.

Until he heard his mother scream.

At first his dream changed. In it he could hear his mother's voice singing 'Silent Night' to him, but then it mutated into shrill screams he had never heard before. The shrieks from her were alien sounds that frightened him. Fighting against this terrible nightmare he somehow awoke and sat up in his bed. Squinting and rubbing his eyes to view the familiarity of his room he heard the awful screams continue. Though they were like the screams he had heard in his nightmare they were now amplified and real.

"Vaden! Oh, my God! My son!"

The screeching sounds from his mother blared like some wild animal in pain. The frightening screams did not even sound like the softly spoken woman he had known his short ten years of life. However, the desperation in her voice told him that something dreadful was happening and her words expressed her concern and terror for him.

"Mama? Mama!"

His little boy's voice called for her with uncertainty, but as her screams became increasingly sharper and piercing his panic grew until he was screaming for her in return. Throwing back the thick, warm blankets that kept him warm from winters' cold talons he jumped out of bed and ran to the door. Grasping the handle he flung it open, only to see an eerie glow in the hallway.

"Vaden! Jump out the window! Jump! Don't come into the hallway!"

Hearing his father's deep command, and a slow agonizing groan from his mother, Vaden stepped back into his room and slammed the door closed. The muffled screams of his father continued to urge him toward the window of his bedroom, even as he realized his mother no longer called for him. Grabbing the edge of the window he shoved until it slid upward. A frigid blast of winter air and snow blew into his face and chest, causing him to gasp for breath. Looking back at his bedroom door he saw smoke beginning to roll under the slim seam at the bottom from the hallway.

Fire.

Turning back to the window he leaned over the edge and saw the long drop. He was a least fifteen feet from the ground. If he jumped he would break a leg or even his neck. Staring down at the snow covered earth Vaden saw the bushes lining the side of the stately wooden home and decided to try to land in them. Maybe they would break his fall and his injuries would be less.

But what of Mama and Papa? Why weren't they yelling for him anymore? Why weren't they outside waiting to catch him? Where were they? Vaden glanced over his shoulder again and coughed as thick smoke continually poured into the room. The door was now beginning to glow from the heat of the blaze on the other side, lending a false sense of warmth to the room exposed to the icy winter that blew through the open window. As he brought his leg up to climb onto the ledge he spotted his boots and coat by his rocking chair. Running across the small room he slid his bare feet into the ankle high boots and shoved his shaking arms into the warm coat. With quivering legs he ran back to the window and hoisted himself onto the ledge.

"Papa? Mama? Where are you?"

He called over and over for them to come outside to catch him, but they didn't come and they didn't answer. Tears rolled down his face as fear began to rip his confidence in his parents asunder. They loved him! There had to be a reason they were not here for him, but what could it be?

A fit of coughing seized him as smoke entirely filled his bedroom and began to pour out the open window. Flames lit the dark room as the contents became greedily consumed by the fire.

Jump, Vaden! Jump!

The voice of his father seemed to echo in his head as he peered down at the snowy bushes that seemed so far away. He was afraid to jump, but was also afraid to wait any longer. Already he could feel the heat of the flames nearing him. He could feel the intense heat on his cold cheeks as he searched for the courage to leap into the unknown below.

"Mama! Papa!"

He called one last time, praying they would be there for him as they had been his whole life. But they didn't come and they didn't answer. With a final look into his room, which was now an inferno, he simply let himself slide over the edge. He did not want to see himself falling or the ground flying up to greet him. Squeezing his eyes shut tight he felt the weightlessness of falling. For a few brief seconds he flew into the wind imagining it must be the same for birds, before he the impact of crashing into the bushes below turned his world entirely black.

"Vaden? Are you ill?"

Reality came crashing down upon him as the memory of his very first nightmare ended. Opening his eyes, Vaden saw the fire before him burning low and quickly dying before he turned to view Kai Chen. Her gaze was filled with concern as she leaned toward him as her slender cool hands touched his brow.

Was he ill? Not exactly, but he had been afflicted in some intangible way for the past twenty years. Maybe the nightmares would finally end with her. Maybe he would be able to experience mellow, safe dreams again and someday deliver the same for his own son through the comforting presence of the woman who had entranced him. Although he would never again hold dear the innocence of his own youth he could hope that for his own children.

"I'm fine, simply tired," he replied gruffly and then sighed heavily. He did not allow himself to ponder on his expanding feelings for Kai Chen. She was not prepared for the possibilities blossoming between them just yet. Vaden knew he must tread carefully with this unusual woman who had taken over his thoughts.

"I am concerned. Most people claiming they are fine do not break a glass in their hand," Kai Chen informed him softly and looked pointedly at his hand.

Vaden frowned as he looked down at his right hand holding the brandy snifter. He had been clasping the short stem between his long, strong fingers and had snapped it without apparent effort while he had been remembering. His gaze slowly drifted up to hers where they locked. Time seemed to stand still as her probing green eyes seemed to delve into his soul, exposing his lost inner child he kept protected from any further harm.

"I understand your pain," she said to him and then astonished him further by scooting back on the settee and crossing her legs underneath her. Taking the broken glass from him she placed it on the table next to her and simply held his hand between hers. The gesture was of simple kindness and friendship, a camaraderie he had never experienced with any person before.

For hours they sat on the small sofa, no words spoken or needed as they healed one another with their silent communication. Kai Chen was more than astute; it was as though she could see into his very mind, heart, and soul. Somehow they understood each other's thoughts and emotions without a word said between them. Never before had he felt so attune to another human being's needs, fears, and desires. Never had any person read him as openly as Kai Chen did, without really even knowing him. With her he experienced the beginnings of an elusive wholeness he had been searching for since his parent's death.

The fire before them had died long ago, but neither moved. It was as though they needed to heal some small part of each other before letting go for a while. He could not imagine sharing a relationship like this with anyone else. The thought of Caroline Pennington sitting beside him, comforting him with a simple touch and complete silence, was incomprehensible. There was no other woman unique enough to understand him like Kai Chen, nor was there any man who could appreciate her value as he could.

"It is time," she finally whispered and gave his hand a soft squeeze. The slight pressure was as intimate as a kiss.

"That it is," he agreed as he stood to bank the fire.

Never had he spent a more peaceful, relaxing or healing evening. Vaden knew she had mended a small part of him that had been lost for many years. Turning to thank her he noticed he stood in the room alone with the broken glass on the table gone.

CHAPTER ELEVEN

"Engage people with what they expect; it is what they are able to discern and confirms their projections. It settles them into predictable patterns of response, occupying their minds while you wait for the extraordinary moment — that which they cannot anticipate."
— Sun Tzu, *The Art of War*

March 1901
LeBlanc Estate

Vaden observed the interaction between Kai Chen and the couturier the next afternoon with fascination. Both were bent over a series of drawings depicting daywear, couture wear, eveningwear, underwear, leisurewear and accessories, though she adamantly refused to look at bridal attire. He suppressed his mirth at her calm demeanor as the man insisted she view the selection of bridal gowns. With each refusal the man became more flustered.

"Shall we compromise, sir? If you leave the designs with me I will view them when I have time," she offered with a bewitching smile.

The man sighed with obvious relief as he wiped at his brow with a white kerchief. Vaden snorted with a chuckle, knowing Kai Chen was not ready to look at bridal designs, if ever. For several minutes she and the couturier worked together to select several tasteful items, which pleased the couturier immensely. That was, until she began asking him to make subtle changes to his individual designs. His affront was evident in his flushed face and compressed lips until he saw the attractive changes she was suggesting, creating an entirely new appearance to the beautiful gowns.

"You have a fantastic eye for detail, mademoiselle. Would you consider allowing me to re-create these changes for a new line of women's wear?"

The calculating look on his face did not go unnoticed by Vaden who stepped forward from his area of concealment.

"I am sure Miss Boussard would allow you to do so, given a grace period in which she may have singular possession of such designs," Vaden demanded subtly.

The man practically leapt out of his skin at sound of Vaden's voice and the excited flush of his face turned to an ashen pallor.

"Good day, Mister LeBlanc," the man hastily greeted. "Certainly the lady shall be the sole possessor of these grand gowns to display in public for all to admire. What time frame would you consider equitable?"

"Three months from the date of delivery," Vaden said firmly, noting the greedy gleam in the small man's eyes. Glancing down at the pictures he saw the exotic flare she had suggested, noting the distinguished and attractive changes. She did have a talent for fashion and the rapacious couturier wanted to reap great rewards from it.

"That is extremely equitable," the man declared, knowing he would be sitting on pins and needles to bring out a new line of fashion that would take New York, maybe even Milan and Paris, by storm. However, he knew better than to double cross Vaden LeBlanc. Anyone who knew Vaden knew better than to tread with such folly.

"I will await your written contract adhering to our verbal agreement," Vaden agreed amicably and saw the man pale further. "Kay, dear, are you ready for lunch?"

"Actually, I am hungry," she admitted as she curiously listened to the verbal exchange between the men.

"Shall we?"

Vaden held his arm aloft for her. The small, thin man lurched to his feet as Kai Chen rose gracefully from her chair and accepted Vaden's extended elbow.

"When should we expect the delivery of her chosen garments?"

"Within the month, most assuredly, sir. In the meantime I have had her fitted with some excellent selections in stock. Those shall be ready within days and delivered posthaste," the man professed adamantly and bowed sharply as Vaden gave a satisfied nod. Quickly, Vaden escorted Kay from the spacious drawing room.

"I would ask how your morning has been, but from what I witnessed moments ago it appears to have been entertaining," Vaden stated then chuckled at her amused expression.

"It was enjoyable. Living in Chinatown I saw ladies parading their finery, but I never imagined I would wear it someday," she professed as she walked beside him.

"You will turn New York on its ear when you do," boasted Vaden proudly, seeing her cheeks turn a delightful pink at his words.

They savored a wonderful lunch of crisp salad with herb dressing, baked salmon and sweet stewed tomatoes. The conversation was light and congenial between them as he worked to bring Kai Chen out of the reserved shell she had encased herself in all her life. This precious time they spent together was a learning experience for both of them. For the next two weeks Kai Chen spent her mornings being measured and questioned by the couturier and his assistants regarding her clothing, spent leisurely lunches with Vaden, and spent her afternoons with several tutors who worked with her diction, formal deportment, and the basics in fine arts and music. She was a willing and resourceful student who endeared herself to everyone, making very few requests and only one demand. However, each evening Kai Chen would disappear on his grounds for hours at a time before dinner, returning disheveled but with a glow of satisfaction that made him intensely curious.

"I must continue my training," she informed Vaden one afternoon as they dined.

"Training?" His perplexed look made Kai Chen inwardly wince.

"My martial art is Wing Chun. I cannot forsake it. It is my heritage and my obligation to maintain it. It is a family legacy." She explained as she waited nervously for his response. He seemed to consider her words carefully before speaking.

"There are several questions I have concerning this Wing Chun, and the people and culture of China," he declared.

Vaden recalled the extraordinary feats he had seen her perform, in addition to the destruction of her family by the disfigured woman. Still, he did not want to hurt her by bringing up a painful subject. He knew how difficult it was to talk about such tragedy. He had never spoken of his parent's death since it had happened twenty years ago. Vaden watched Kai Chen close her eyes briefly before nodding in acceptance. He realized this would be hard for her in remembering certain events, but he needed answers to some of the incredible things he had witnessed.

"Tell me of your martial art first," he asked with honest interest as their empty plates were removed. Sweetened hot tea was placed before them.

"It is an art that has been perfected by the women in my family for over three hundred years, a legacy passed from mother to daughter since the initial fall of the Shaolin temple of the Buddhist nun, Ng Mui. She was the Mother of my art. Her only student of the complete art was the founding Mother of my family generations ago, Yim Wing-Chun.

"None, but the women of our house know the entire secrets of Wing Chun. Even my father did not know the women of our family practiced it. Many know Wing Chun as just a simple martial art, but it is more than that. You are the first outsider, the only man, to know this much," she advised him, her words impacting the seriousness of what she revealed.

"The basics of my art are known by the Triad Elders in China, but I am the only one holding the true full secrets of it. As you have witnessed they are deadly methods that cannot be placed in the wrong hands of evil minds. I, too, must one day bequeath this knowledge to my own daughter or granddaughter. Should I never have a child, I must wisely choose a worthy female student."

Vaden stared at her, dazed at her revelation. Never would he have imagined the burden of such a mission placed upon her or the women of her family. He was fuelled with surprise to consider the length of time it had been a tradition, or more like a curse. Angry at what he did not fully understand, he wondered why the men in the family had not been given this physical and arduous task of maintaining such a lethal martial art. Instead, their women had shouldered and suffered the brutality that would inevitably accompany it. He was also filled with admiration and respect for the commitment and excellence Kai Chen and the women of her family had achieved in this extraneous responsibility.

"You will have many beautiful daughters one day, Kai Chen, and also handsome sons," he said with implicit meaning and observed her face flame. "Will you pass this to your sons, too?"

"The custom of only passing it to a worthy daughter is one that will eventually be broken in time. I shall only teach those who are worthy. Even the most wonderful of children are incapable of fulfilling such a serious obligation at times. There are special means, tests if you will, that determine the spirit, mind, and aptitude of a potential pupil. It is a most grave responsibility for both teacher and student." Kai Chen appeared reflective as she spoke.

Vaden sipped at his hot tea as he studied the tall, athletic woman sitting next to him. She was the most complex person he had ever encountered. Though exceedingly feminine in appearance and demeanor she had the physical skill to annihilate several men within a matter of seconds. With a sense of caution toward her feelings he continued asking questions.

"Who was the woman with the disfigured face?"

Kai Chen's expression immediately changed from calm serenity to controlled fury as her eyes met his in an intense stare. He detected the barely restrained urge to flee, but she gripped the steaming cup of tea with strong fingers instead. Vaden knew speaking of this part of her life was difficult.

"Ji-Kin Lau, former future Empress of China," she said in clipped tones, her gaze now fixed upon the tendrils of steam rising from the delicate cup.

"I don't understand," Vaden stated in confusion, a frown marring his features as he leaned forward with interest. "What would a former future Empress be doing in the middle of a battle, and with your family?"

Quietly, Kai Chen explained the entire set of circumstances leading up to the moment when her family was killed, the part her grandmother played within the Triad and the information she had secretly obtained. She then told him of the battle with Ji-Kin Lau and the disfigurement of the lovely woman who might one day rule China. Completing the incredible tale of political intrigue and deviant yearnings, Vaden sat back and absorbed the amazing story. The lives of these foreigners were inconceivable, and yet, he knew power, politics and domination in world affairs by those who coveted such positions was a worldwide trait amongst many.

"Is there a chance they know you are in America? Would they come to find you?"

"Yes, they will come for me if they discover I am here," she told him with confidence and threw him an understanding smile. "If you wish me to leave, knowing I might place you in danger, I will understand."

Vaden's troubled expression changed to fierce determination as he shoved away from the table to stand beside her. "You are going nowhere, madam! This is your home and we shall never speak of you leaving again."

Bowing her head at his outburst, Kai Chen suddenly felt his hands on her shoulders. The warmth from him radiated throughout her body as her heart leaped in joy. Home. He had told her this was her home, here, with him. Her heart knew it to be so. Her destiny lay with this man who gazed at her with such devotion and tenderness. Great gladness filled her breast as the image it conjured played in her mind.

"As you wish," she softly spoke as his hands slid down the sides of her arms in a loving caress.

"Knowing why you need to preserve your art and the threat of retaliation against you, I am more than willing to supply you with the time and instruments you need to fulfill your legacy, Kai Chen," he whispered against her ear. Then his lips fleetingly brushed against her neck before he stepped back.

Delicious, erotic shivers coursed through her body at the intimate touch of his warm lips on her cool skin. His spicy scent lingered around her even as she heard him walking away from her. The comforting proximity of his body was gone but it seemed to hover about her like an endearing cloak. Vaden LeBlanc's respect was felt within the core of her soul, leaving her winded and dizzy. Never before had she experienced the emotional love of a man other than from her father. This felt different, more intense and stirring. Kai Chen realized she had much to ponder concerning Vaden LeBlanc and her new future.

LeBlanc Estate
Two weeks later

"Your diction is practically flawless. Actually, your voice is enchanting with its musical tone and should entrance every man you meet, and it will be the envy of each woman," Vaden acknowledged over dinner as they polished off the last of the chocolate mousse.

"I am conscious of each word before I speak and I have been practicing. However, your flattery is quite outrageous," she reprimanded with a smile that belied her harsh tone.

Kai Chen sighed with repletion as she placed the dessert spoon beside the dish. Quickly, the delicate china and crystal was whisked away by servants as Vaden rose to escort her to the sitting room as was their nightly routine.

"My flattery is not outrageous and I will thank you to accept it graciously," he demanded with a devilish twinkle in his eyes.

Kai Chen nodded once in acceptance before she turned her face away so he could not see her blush. It made her decidedly uncomfortable to receive so many compliments throughout the day. She did not think she would ever adjust to his flattery.

"The dress you are wearing is quite fetching and the style truly becoming. You shall be a great success amongst the women of the upper circle who consider themselves fashion queens," he mused thoughtfully as he studied the cream silk and satin crepe evening dress. The low V-shaped neckline in front and back exposed Kai's porcelain skin. The edges were decorated with gold and green beaded and sequined flower motifs matching the looped-up back train, short cap sleeves cut in one with the high-waisted bodice, wide belt under the bust and draped ankle-length skirt wraps over the back. It was somewhat oriental in appearance and absolutely unique.

"My mother was a fine seamstress and I enjoy sewing too, though I have not done much sewing the past couple of years, except at Fong-la's laundry. These gowns are so cumbersome and I refuse to wear a corset," she admitted frankly with a shy smile. Kai Chen allowed Vaden to escort her to the lovely flowered settee. It was their favorite spot in the room where they would sit before the fire and either speak of insignificant happenings, or simply enjoy a companionable silence.

"The reaction you will receive tomorrow night wearing one of the lovely creations will be quite interesting." His glance slid to the enticing cleavage of her ivory breasts and she felt as though he actually touched her. A delicious shiver raced through her body. Then his words registered in her mind.

"Tomorrow night?" Her brows furrowed as she scrutinized him.

"Yes. There is a function we are attending tomorrow night," he said as he poured himself a brandy. "Care for one?"

"I took the troth not to drink alcohol. You know that," she reminded him in exasperation and then bit her tongue. It was unlike her to unveil her emotions, but he had shocked her with his announcement of her attending a public function so soon.

"You are no longer a nun," he flung at her smoothly as he replaced the decanter. "You may have one drink."

"I will honor my vows unless I am given no choice," she informed him decisively again, sitting with her back stiff and her hands folded primly in her lap. The long white gloves encased her arms past her elbow and kept her warm as a sudden chill raced over her.

"Including the vow of celibacy," he asked nonchalantly as he gazed intently into her wide emerald eyes. His gaze held hers over the rim of the glass as he took a drink of the amber liquid.

Kai Chen stared at him as though physically struck as the color fled her cheeks. For the past several weeks she had been considering that very vow and her loyalty to it. Although she was no longer a nun she was still very devout in her belief and faith in Buddhism, as well as her pledges made to Buddha at the temple. Granted, she had broken three of them already but was that an excuse to break them all? However, to have a commitment with this man or a future, would she not have to break the vow of celibacy to be married? The arguments went round and round in her head and her heart, every day and every night, as she pondered what to do.

"Unless I am given no choice," she repeated on a choked cry as her emotions escalated. How could this man bare her inner conflicts like raw nerves? The controlled martial artist and nun she knew herself to be were somewhere. Or were they forever lost to her like her homeland, China? Standing up she threw him a scalded look, which she actually felt toward herself.

"Thank you for a wonderful evening. Good night," she replied with a calmness she did not feel. She turned to leave the room, but Vaden clutched her arm and pulled her against him. Their bodies touched suggestively and she felt his hard arousal press into her lower stomach.

"You have no choice," Vaden informed her decisively with a deep groan. Hungrily, his lips claimed hers as his hands held her to him. She could not resist his magnetism as her traitorous body melded against his and she returned his kiss with equal fervor. His tongue slid against hers, dancing with its new partner as she whimpered her pleasure. The taste of the brandy he had imbibed was upon her lips as her desire for him escalated. Her arms twined about his neck. Kai Chen did not know the sensation of being drunk, but she imagined the impact of her present feelings might be comparable. Her head was spinning, her body felt heavy and languid, her control over coherent thought and physical restraint was lost.

Sensing the lost of command of her passions turned her moans of pleasure into small cries of fear as she suddenly fought for release from his charismatic lure. Her body yearned for more of his touch, more of his magic, but her mind was fighting against him more fiercely than any battle she had waged in China. For her this struggle was one she knew she would never win.

"Don't pull away, Kai Chen," he murmured against her lips. She was almost seduced by the deep huskiness of his voice, but her apprehension at the force of her emotions toward him surfacing made her vie for her freedom.

"Do not make me hurt you," she insisted as tears gathered in her eyes.

He stepped back from her with a jagged sigh and raked his fingers through his short blond waves. The sexual tension still connected them as though a fine silken strand of a spider's web was linked to their hearts. Both were breathing heavy as they fought to break the spell, the intrinsic tie.

"I apologize for my insistent actions. Tomorrow we are to attend a museum exhibition of a newer artist. Dinner is to immediately follow. Be prepared to leave by six tomorrow evening," he informed her abruptly before stating pointedly, "Good night."

Having been dismissed so suddenly by him, Kai Chen's eyes widened in astonishment. Vaden had never spoken to her using this clipped tone before and it distressed her. Where was the man who had smiled at her, lavished compliments, and treated her like a priceless gem? Who was this angry, cold man who stood before her now, dismissing her like a servant who had displeased him?

"Good evening, sir," she replied with a shaky voice as tears threatened to fill her eyes. Throwing him a confused and hurt glance she slipped away soundlessly and sped to her room. She understood the sexual frustration he was experiencing, but refused to yield to it. More than her vow her personal honor held her back. Was not marriage the time for surrendering her chastity? Did it mean so little to these Americans they would appease immediate desires without commitment or betrothal?

"We are but humans, all given needs," she tried to remind herself.

Carefully, she unhooked the back of her dress and slid the gorgeous creation down over her slim hips. Walking over to the immense closet hosting numerous gowns, shoes, hats, gloves, coats and accessories, Kai Chen hung the dress. The fantastic array of items seemed alien to her. She was not accustomed to possessing so many material items, or such expensive ones. Viewing the assortment of gorgeous gowns she promptly turned off the light and closed the door to block the sight.

Completely naked she sat before the blazing fire in her room with crossed legs and her wrists lightly resting on her knees. With thumbs and center fingers touching she gazed into the leaping flames. Meditation would allow her to reason judiciously, would fortify and remind her of who she was and who she would remain. This, she did nightly to keep in touch with inner peace, but somehow she knew there would be none for her this time.

"Although I have resisted much in this short life I understand this is one fate I shall never overcome," she admitted, then sighed. Her desire for Vaden was just as keen as his for her. "It is only a matter of time."

The passions Vaden had awakened in her were ones that could never be doused by logic or vows.

Vaden paced in his bedroom like a caged animal, waiting for deliverance from the sexual confinement that held him. Although he knew Kai Chen would surrender to their mutual desire in time his current tormented need for her would not be appeased. Most men he knew would simply run to any willing woman for release of the sexual frustration devouring them, but none but Kai Chen would ever pacify the ache in his heart or his body. Unless he could have her he wanted no other.

Tugging at the cravat at his neck he tossed it onto a nearby chair impatiently. Vaden reminded himself they needed time to adjust to one another before he asked for her hand in marriage, let alone force his sexual advances upon her. It worried him that there was no female chaperon in his home to qualm any vicious gossip concerning his intent toward her. He considered it prudent to check into acquiring one for her before it was discovered she resided here. Having another woman between them in the house would make it safer for Kai Chen from his honorable, although lustful, intentions.

Satisfied with his current plan Vaden began divesting himself of his clothing. Completely naked he slumped onto a chair and fought with his raging desire that burned more fiercely than the fire before him. The noticeable thickness rising between his thighs pleased and angered him. It had been so very long since he had been with, or even desired, a woman. Since meeting Kai Chen in Chinatown it was as though he had awakened from a dormant sleep to discover he had needs, wants, and desires. She made him feel like a man who had suddenly come alive.

Ignoring the flagrant throbbing of his manhood he concentrated on tomorrow night's outing. For Kai Chen it would be her debut into a new world of excitement, glamour, and wealth. Unfortunately, it would also expose her to the vicious, debasing tongues of those envious of her distinct beauty, grace, and charm. A part of him wanted to spare her this experience into his world. He would much rather keep her sheltered away from greedy eyes and wagging tongues, but it was impossible with the life he led. Once his wife, she would be expected to be by his side.

And he wanted her as his wife.

There was no other woman he had ever considered sharing his life with, having children with or giving his heart to hold. She was the missing link to his soul and could never be replaced by a facsimile. It was Kai Chen, Kay Boussard, for him, or no one.

As his musings inevitably returned to the woman he was falling in love with so desperately, his desire sprang anew and the deep pounding in his sex gripped him hard for immediate release. Allowing his thoughts to wander to sensual couplings with his China doll, his hand obeyed the screaming in his loins and brought about a temporary release he had been craving for so very long.

Manhattan Museum
The next evening

"I do not like this, foolish American," Kai Chen told Vaden sharply, a dangerous warning in her musical voice.

"You will do fine," he told her, then added flippantly, "If you can defeat six men at once, kill a Prince, and carry your grandmother for several miles to a temple in the mountains, you can do anything!"

Kai Chen's shocked countenance made him inwardly flinch but he refused to allow her to succumb to her fears. She was a legal citizen now, an American. To gaze upon her unique and beautiful face none could tell she was half Chinese. She spoke more eloquently than a polished politician and carried herself with the grace of a queen. Kay Boussard was going to throw New York into wondrous turmoil.

"That was uncalled for," she imparted abruptly.

Her voice sounded tight, reflecting the strain of maintaining her emotions. The door to their carriage was opened and Vaden stepped out onto the cleared pavement.

"So it was," he apologized sincerely and offered his hand to assist her from the vehicle.

"Your viper's tongue will cost you one day, sir," she wisely noted and heard his deep laughter echo in the night. "Those who use words to hurt receive it tenfold."

"Then I am certainly in trouble," he agreed, his humor restored as he stared at her uncommon beauty. "Kay, you truly are so very lovely."

"You play a dangerous game, American," she cautioned, but a smile lit her features as they walked up the numerous steps to the huge museum before them. "One minute you are insulting, then next extolling. Men like that are not to be taken seriously."

"You play a dangerous game too, Kay Boussard," he whispered seductively in her ear as hordes of people joined them on the steps to enter the congested building.

"I play no games. Even as a child I played very few of them," she stated proudly and felt her heart leap at the sound of his genuine laughter.

Several people turned to gaze at them, their sly expressions revealing they considered Kai Chen and Vaden a newlywed couple enjoying an intimate flirtation.

"What amusement is it you presume I trifle with?"

"The game is one you shall never win. It is the game of desire," he said huskily in her ear.

A shudder raced down her spine at his declaration and she pulled the stark white fur closer about her. The thick, heavy mink swept around her ankles and collared her throat, leaving her warm and protected from the night's winter chill. Vaden's soft chuckle only compounded the effect of his words.

"Now you claim to be a prophet? Such blasphemy," she declared lightly then smiled as his laughter deepened.

As they waited in the growing crowd gathering before the doors to the brightly lit interior of the museum, Vaden was hailed numerous times. He returned the greeting with a short wave as the slow moving crowd suddenly surged forward to present their private invitation to the museum proprietor.

"It seems you know everyone attending," Kai Chen observed with one arched brow raised. Her heart raced with excitement and uncertainty as she took in the bright lights, large mass of strangers and unique surroundings. This new world made her head feel like it was spinning as she tried to take in all the incredible sights and to digest all of the amazing experiences.

"I would not profess to know everyone, but running in the same financial and social circles leads to meeting the same people frequently," he admitted unpretentiously. "We are all patrons to the arts, partly out of vanity and self-indulgence, and partly genuine interest. From what I understand about this artist tonight, it is mainly for interest. He is highly praised."

"I do not know much of art. Hopefully, I will not embarrass you," Kai Chen informed him in a serious tone.

"Nonsense! Half the people here know less than you," he told her seriously as he handed his invitation to one of the director's

"Good evening, Mister LeBlanc. It is a pleasure to see you again," the Elderly man expounded enthusiastically, then nodded and smiled to Kai Chen. "Good evening, Miss."

"It is good to see you also, Mister Jenkins. Another successful investment it would seem," he responded as he nodded toward the filled building.

"Yes, indeed. Enjoy yourselves."

Vaden issued the man a warm smile as they entered. Merging into the crowd effortlessly he directed them across the foyer where several employees were taking coats and hats. With practiced ease he slipped the spotless white fur off Kai Chen's shoulders. His eyes lit with appreciation at the dazzling dress she wore, both daring and novel in design.

The pink silk-satin evening gown had a high-waist, emphasized by a cream silk cummerbund and rosette with long end ribbons carrying a matching embroidered and beaded floating front panel. The bodice was ruched across her breasts with embroidered cap sleeves sporting short handkerchief points and the skirt was gathered at each side of the front panel to form low panniers and a long train. Long white kid gloves encased her toned arms. On her head was a small tiara set with minute gemstones, giving her the appearance of royalty. A three stranded diamond necklace, diamond drop earrings Vaden had purchased specifically for Kai Chen completed the glamorous ensemble. Not only was the style decidedly oriental, the soft colors enhanced the richness of her thick hair swept upon her head in a loose bun with tendrils framing her ivory complexion. Her green eyes never seemed more outstanding.

She truly was a China doll come to life. *My China doll*, Vaden possessively contemplated.

"I have never seen a more beautiful woman," Vaden said to Kai Chen with a hushed whisper, bringing a rosy glow to her cheeks. He observed her demurely look down. Following her gaze to her clenched hands, Vaden felt his heart soar. Kai Chen, Kay Boussard, was his. This was the woman he had been waiting his entire life to make his wife. Very soon, he would.

"Thank you," she murmured faintly, her cheeks soft pink from his compliment.

"Shall we?"

Extending his arm, he waited for her to accept it as they made their way into the swarm of aristocrats who had come to see what their money had been spent on this venture. For several minutes they strolled casually among the bodies of guests who milled in groups to greet each other and catch up on the latest social gossip.

"Vaden LeBlanc! I do declare, darling, where have you been?"

The woman's high-pitched voice caused him to cringe inwardly as he recognized it. Caroline Pennington. He had strategically avoided her for months, but this evening he would have to pay his dues. Though she was an attractive woman he found her frivolous, spoiled and brazen, in addition to doing nothing for his libido. He could not imagine being cursed by fate in having her for a wife.

Turning to face the calling voice, Vaden observed her manufacture her way toward him. As usual her breasts were virtually oozing out of the bodice of her tight gown, the color an audacious red. Miniature live red roses were placed around her head like a coronet with crimson ribbons dangling down the back. The first thing he thought of when he saw her was the red-light district in Europe, which housed hundreds of prostitutes for a man's every pleasure no matter how perverse.

"Vaden, my darling man, it's been too long," she cooed as though broken hearted. Reaching him she launched herself into his arms. Pressing her vividly painted lips against his she then stepped away and viewed him with a distinctly predatory look. Nonchalantly, Vaden slipped a white handkerchief from inside his evening coat and wiped the scarlet color from his mouth.

"It is always a delight to behold you," he embellished greatly as he replaced the folded white linen inside his coat. He observed her eyes narrow on Kai Chen in calculated competition. In them he could discern curiosity, suspicion, rivalry, and fear.

"Who is your companion?"

Vaden's smile turned genuine as he glanced at Kai Chen's serene face. He would rather conceal her than subject her to Caroline, but instead he became the gracious gentleman as courtesy dictated.

"Miss Caroline Pennington, I would like you to meet Miss Kay Boussard."

Caroline nodded once toward Kai Chen as she smiled cheerfully, but her expression of pleasure was clearly forced. She was none too thrilled to see Vaden with another woman and her cold eyes conveyed it clearly.

"A pleasure," she replied cordially as her glance raked over Kai Chen assiduously. The dark scrutiny did not go unnoticed by any of them.

"Likewise, Miss Pennington," Kai Chen expressed in her musical voice, her eyes not missing the venom now pouring from Caroline Pennington. The undercurrent of hostility from the other woman was like a banner being waved. Vaden wondered if Kai Chen thought Caroline one of his former mistresses. By all appearances Caroline acted it.

"That is a decidedly original gown you are wearing, Miss Boussard. Where did you buy it?"

The verbal insult was not understood by Kai Chen but was by Vaden as his eyes gleamed dangerously at the blond vixen standing before them. Caroline knew well the dress was not manufactured in a factory or shop, but specifically made by one of the top couture's in New York.

"I did not buy it, Miss Pennington. It was made by the couturier Vaden hired," Kai Chen told the woman innocently.

"Is that so?" A feral iridescence lit Caroline's dark blue eyes as she threw him a cunning examination. "I didn't realize you were so personal with Miss Boussard, darling. So, this is where you have been hiding yourself. No wonder I can't seem to keep up with you," she said bitingly and then smiled sweetly.

"Business keeps me engaged," he retorted coldly.

Obviously Caroline had been hunting him like a dog on a fox hunt. He could see this encounter escalating in a negative fashion and began to spy about the crowds of people to find someone to help entertain Caroline. It was clear she was going to insinuate herself by his side for the remainder of the evening if she could manage.

"Oh, posh! You haven't returned any of my messages, darling. I am under the impression you are avoiding me," she stated guilelessly, but her lips were pressed tightly together and her cheeks were flushed in anger.

"Nonsense, Caroline. Tell me, have you seen Sebastian yet?" It was a tedious chore trying to keep personal conversation from passing her lips.

"Yes, he is across the room speaking with Colonel Baxter. Shall we join them?"

Kai Chen's eyebrows furrowed as she tried to recall the familiar name. Memories assailed her and the sudden image of a short, squat man with a loud voice and pompous attitude made her visibly wince. Then she remembered his son, James Baxter.

I would be honored for you to consider me a valued friend.

Throwing an anxious glance at Vaden, Kai Chen noticed he seemed none too pleased at the mention of the Colonel's name. He glanced at her and the panic in her expressive eyes must have sent him a silent warning, because he suddenly extended his arm.

"Caroline, pardon us if we proceed to the exhibition. I am quite anxious to see his son's astounding work," he stated with enthusiasm and bowed to the affronted woman whose countenance revealed her displeasure at being cast aside.

"Of course, my dear, as I am sure we shall run into each other throughout the evening," Caroline said with false sweetness as she smiled with effort before sailing away from them.

Kai Chen tilted her head to one side thoughtfully as she studied the outraged flurry of Caroline's skirts as she traversed the vast room.

"She is jealous and she is not very good at guarding her emotions."

Vaden took a step forward to usher Kai Chen toward the exhibition, but faltered at her simple statement. Caroline jealous? Glimpsing over his shoulder he followed Kai Chen's observant gaze where Caroline stood next to Sebastian Madden and Colonel Baxter. However, her attention was not on the men she stood with. Caroline's furious fixed gaze was on Vaden before it darted to Kai Chen malevolently.

"Possibly, but I have never given her reason. We are nothing more than acquaintances," he advised her as they strolled easily through the throngs of people. The sincerity of his tone rang of the truth he spoke.

Heads turned, glances slid over Kai Chen by men and women as they absorbed her unusual beauty and extraordinary dress.

"You and I are more than simply friends."

"You have something else planned instead of friendship," Kai Chen imparted knowingly as a pretty blush lit her cheeks.

Leaning close to her ear, he whispered, "I do."

Her embarrassment deepened as he chuckled at her timidity. The next hour passed swiftly as they stopped at each painting to view the artistry of James Baxter. Kai Chen was impressed with his talent, for not only did he capture a scene vividly the colors were ideal for each setting. Turning toward Vaden to ask him a question she observed Caroline Pennington making her way through the congregation with her gaze locked on them. Trailing right behind her was a dark haired man who she suspected was Sebastian Madden, and following him was the ostentatious Colonel Baxter.

"Vaden, I need to locate the ladies' room," she said as calmly as possible.

If Colonel Baxter recognized her, and she was certain he would, her new identity would not be worth the piece of paper it was written on.

"Of course, right this way," Vaden told her and made to escort her there.

"It would be better if you simply direct me," she insisted. The confused expression on his face changed to annoyance as he heard Caroline call his name.

"Go down this corridor and to your left. I will wait for you here," he advised her and pointed to a narrow hallway not far from them.

Kai Chen nodded and nimbly manipulated her way through the assembly just as Colonel Baxter's booming voice welcomed Vaden to his son's exhibition. Breathing a temporary sigh of relief, Kai Chen located the ladies' room and entered. To calm herself she sat on the edge of a mauve brocade settee in the outer lounge with her palms pressed together and her head bowed slightly. Closing her eyes she meditated and within minutes the shaking of her hands, body, and heart quieted.

Worried thoughts persisted as she heard several women walk past her. Would she forever run from people she knew from her other life? Was this new pretentious existence she led simply another veil to hide behind before fate exposed her? She was tiring of running, of lying, of living a lie, but she did not want to be sent back to China and into the hands of the Triad, Manchu government, and certain death.

"Pardon me. Are you all right, my dear?"

The sound of an Elderly woman's voice speaking to her was familiar.

"I am fine. Thank you for your concern," Kai Chen replied and lifted her gaze to the anxious woman standing before her. Large green eyes identical to hers widened a fraction before the older woman collected herself. It was obvious the older woman recognized the similarity in their eyes.

"Certainly," the older woman murmured in a shaken voice and paused as though she wanted to say more. She smiled and quit the lounge.

Kai Chen was unnerved by the encounter. She had actually spoken to her aunt! What a prophetic evening this was turning out to be. First, she discovers Colonel Baxter in the museum, and then learns James is the artist whose exhibition is being shown, and now she meets her only living relative. It was all very peculiar, but life seemed to be odd at times and she was accepting of that.

CHAPTER TWELVE

"Even the finest sword plunged into salt water will eventually rust."
— Sun Tzu, *The Art of War*

Standing, Kai Chen straightened her gown and prepared to leave the ladies' room. She only prayed Colonel Baxter was no longer with Vaden. As she peered around a corner she noticed James Baxter striding toward her. Before she could step back into the ladies' lounge he spied her. His eyes widened dramatically and his mouth fell open, even as his thick glasses slid down his sloping nose.

"Kai Chen?" His hushed whisper caused her to blush as he neared her. "Is it really you?"

"My name is Kay Boussard," she informed him in a conspiratorial whisper. "I pray you will not speak of my other life in China."

Several men and women walked around them before James finally pulled her aside to a dark corner where they could speak privately.

"What are you doing here?"

"It is a long and difficult account."

"I imagine it is at that," he said with a smile then shook his head in disbelief. A lopsided smile returned him to the dear man she had met a few years ago. He had a glow of happiness about him that had been absent then.

"You have done well." Her meaning was obvious and he blushed humbly at her praise.

"It was you who lead me on the correct path. For that I owe you," he admitted earnestly. "Who are you here with tonight?"

"Vaden LeBlanc," she told him and saw his shy smile widen. "He has helped me become American. That is why I changed my name."

"He is a good man, Kay Boussard. How did you come to meet him?"

"It is a long and difficult account," she repeated and he laughed outright. "I fear your father will recognize me and this would cause much misfortune for me."

"Do not fear, Kay Boussard. I will keep my father busy for the remainder of the evening," he promised and clasped her hands tightly for a moment. "It is so good to know you are well and as beautiful as ever. I heard of the terrible destruction of the Boxer Rebellion and worried for you. Where are your parents?"

"They died during the outbreak," she informed him, not wishing to speak of their true demise at this time.

"I'm so very sorry to hear it. They were wonderful people," he stated sincerely. His soft eyes and warm smile lightened her momentary grief. "I would like to see you again so we may talk longer."

"I would like that very much. You may find me at the LeBlanc Estate."

"Ah, I will make sure to find time to visit you soon. Take care until then, my dear." Squeezing her hands one last time he walked out of the shadowed corner.

Kai Chen followed him then stopped short as she saw Vaden several feet away, leaning against a wall with an expression making her heart leap in her chest. Suspicion was evident from his compressed lips and narrowed, blazing eyes to his arms folded across his chest and one leg crossed casually over another. There was nothing blasé about the aura of irritation emanating from him, however.

"I was wondering what could be taking so long," he stated tersely as his gaze followed James Baxter as he walked into the men's lounge. "It seems you have made a conquest."

"Nonsense, James is a very dear friend."

"James? You are on a first name basis with him?"

Vaden's simmering rage and jealousy was suddenly apparent.

"I have known him a while," she divulged and saw his eyes widen in surprise. "He and his father were in China a few years ago. They had dinner with my family."

Sudden clarity of her eagerness to leave for the ladies' room made him smile. He felt like a fool for his mistrust. She had been avoiding Colonel Baxter and had unwittingly run into James. The fear of being identified as Kai Chen must have been terrifying for her and here he was acting every kind of jealous dolt, compounding her fear.

"Your secret is safe with them?"

"Only with James. His father was quite angry when my father refused to a betrothal with his son," she told him. "I fear his retaliation at the slight I am certain he feels was issued by my family."

"Then by all means we shall call it an evening and go to dinner," Vaden offered, apparently relieved to discontinue the exhibition.

"That sounds lovely," Kai Chen agreed and boldly placed her gloved hand on the lapel of his black formal coat. "I do not like crowds."

A fierce, possessive gleam entered Vaden's smoky blue eyes as he clasped her hand within one of his large ones. Carefully he propelled them through the crowds of people, retrieved their coats, and soon they were outside in the frigid air awaiting their carriage.

Kai Chen's alleviation at being away from Colonel Baxter and potential disaster was obvious as she sighed heavily. Vaden apparently sensed it too, as his arm crept about her and pulled her close against him in a gesture of comfort. The warmth of his body kept the bite of winter from holding her in its ferocious clutches as she snuggled against him and prayed it would always be this way between them.

Triad Temple
Fukien Province

"Where is she?"

The thunderous shout echoed throughout the empty training hall of the City of Willows. Ji-Kin Lau paced the worn floors like a crazed demon as the trembling cleric attempted to pass to her his newfound information concerning the disappearance of the Buddhist nun, Kai Chen. Though Prince Tuan had been diabolic and perverted in his mechanizations, Ji–Kin Lau was fanatical and horrifying in her thirst for revenge and bloodshed. The cleric feared her more than he had ever feared Prince Tuan.

"It was said she left on a ship headed for America. I contacted the Tong and received a response confirming this," the small, thin man said rapidly to hopefully dissipate her insatiable rage. "She has been seen in Chinatown in a laundry by a few of their members. They explicitly remembered her green eyes, but the shop has closed and she has disappeared."

"I shall not wait one more day," Ji-Kin Lau screamed at him maniacally and turned on him with a feral gleam to her black, cold eyes. "We will leave on the morrow for America and locate her ourselves. With her eyes she will not go hidden for long."

"Yes, Ji-Kin Lau," the cleric immediately responded. Bowing reverently before her, he suddenly felt a sharp pain as she grasped his single long braid.

"I have finished mourning for Prince Tuan and require your services." Her meaning was unquestionable as she pulled his body against hers roughly and rubbed her pelvis against his. "You know what I like."

Uncertainty was written on his face as he nodded in acquiescence of her demand. Silently he followed her to Tuan's chambers, which she had taken over since his death and prayed he did not fail her debauched desire; else his head would be rolling.

Manhattan Museum
New York

"I did not meet her. Where is she?"

"They have left for the evening," Caroline hissed angrily, her flushed face broadcasting her fury. "She is a pretty, but there is something very mysterious about her. I have never seen her in our social circle before nor have I heard her name. We should find out who she is before our plans are ruined!"

The thoughtful mien of the man standing before her brought a beatific smile to her pouty red lips. How she adored this man! For years their love had been growing but until he achieved financial success of epic proportions her father would not allow her to marry him. It was strictly forbidden for her to wed unless her potential husband's fortune was as great as her fathers. Then he would be assured of her monetary security in life.

"That should be simple enough, but if what you say is true and Vaden is enamored of this woman then we must go a step further. I will take care of the problem, my pet. Do not worry so," he consoled her and reached out surreptitiously to tweak one of her pert nipples between his fingers.

Caroline's excited gasp and gleaming eyes instantly filled his loins with lust as he hastily glanced about for a private place they might share a quick erotic rendezvous. Seeing a door leading to the lower level of the museum he grasped her hand and they covertly made their way downstairs. Exhilaration at their current search for an illicit, public bout of lovemaking filled them as they found an unlocked door and entered a room snowed under with historic artifacts.

Preserving the darkness, they savagely kissed each other. His hands swiftly stripped her of the scarlet dress, exposing her nude body underneath. She hadn't bothered wearing underclothes, which excited him even further as his aching member strained to break free of his constrictive trousers.

"I want you, darling," she hissed in his ear. "I want you rough, hard. Hurt me, give me pleasure and pain."

"Anything," he mumbled as his hands feverishly worked at pulling down his pants. His swollen length finally exposed, he lifted her up and sat her on a nearby table. She spread her legs wide, displaying herself for his anticipated touch.

With harsh, eager hands he grasped her breasts. Moaning, he leaned down to lick then bite at her enlarged nipples. Her moan of pleasure urged him on as he felt her cool hands grip his distended length and stroke him to mindless sexual arousal. He could feel the quickness of his release coming and pulled away from her. Kneeling down before her he buried his face between her legs and groaned with sweet torment as her muskiness invaded his senses.

Hearing her sharp intake of breath and groans of delight was music to his ears as he lapped at the entrance he would soon thrust himself into. As the sound of her enthusiasm quickened and she neared her peak, he quickly stood, grasped her hips and impaled himself into her. Their satisfaction of finally being coupled was violent as he ruthlessly plunged into her repeatedly, deeply, until they were both panting from exertion and impending deliverance.

"That's it," she cried against his mouth seconds before her sharp cry rent the air and her feminine muscles clenched around him, bringing his own voracious orgasm. For several seconds after he continued to ram into her as he let his body drain itself of his seed.

"You are going to kill me one day doing this," he teased breathlessly. Her lips trailed across his softly before she shoved him away with impatient hands.

"That is highly doubtful. You are a degenerate," she informed him seriously as she slid off the table and bent over to retrieve her gown. The feel of his hand delving between her thighs again brought a smile to her lips.

"With you in this position, it makes me want more."

"If you are man enough for seconds, help yourself," she offered lightly, doubting his ability.

"Then I shall," he said as his hands moved her back to the table and bent her over it. Within seconds he was propelling into her again as though it was their very first time, bringing forth from her a shriek of contentment.

Tong Headquarters
Chinatown, New York
One week later

"There will be a delivery coming from China the end of this month," he assured Mock Duck who sat across from him with a displeased expression on his face. "The Boxer Rebellion has made it terribly difficult to obtain opium and I no longer deal in importing. My ships are strictly passenger liners now, making it exceedingly arduous for me to dock along the coast. Rest assured you will have your product soon."

"You have always been prompt. We shall excuse this one misfortune in timing," a different Elderly man decreed as the council remained silent while he spoke. "There was another issue you wished to speak of?"

"Yes. I need a spy."

"You need a spy? Pray tell," Mock Duck demanded, his expression revealing amusement at the request.

"Vaden LeBlanc has met a woman who is distinctly novel. She has materialized from nowhere and is not known by anyone within our social circles. I require an informant to discover as much about her as possible, for fear she may threaten our designs to acquire his holdings," he cautioned.

The council members spoke to each other in their native tongue over this new event, their furious banter quickly coming to a halt as Mock Duck spoke again.

"So be it. Jun-Ma Lee shall work with you. It will be your responsibility to see he is planted in LeBlanc's house."

"Your assistance in this is appreciated."

Nodding once in assent, Mock Duck and the Tong council members rose to withdraw from the large room. With a pleased smile on his face, Sebastian Madden pivoted on his heel to expeditiously inform Caroline of his good news.

April 1901
New York

"May I help you?"

The Elderly butler, Manfred, smiled generously at Kai Chen as she stood at the entrance to Suzette Boussard-Minot's stately home. His grey eyes were kind but his sudden frown tainted the peace reflected in them.

He was staring at her green eyes surrounded by an almost black ring identical to that of his employer. Confusion, concern, and propriety battled for placement as he held open the door for her to enter.

"I would like to speak with Suzette Boussard-Minot," she informed him softly as her gaze took in the warmth and taste of the finely decorated home.

For a moment the man hesitated. His expression betrayed his thoughts. He recognized the similarities in their features; the unique eyes, the finely arched eyebrows and high cheekbones. She looked very much like a younger, taller, more exotic version of the woman she asked for.

"Certainly," the man bowed and helped her remove her knee-length red fox fur coat.

His quick glance approved of her splendid pink linen tailored suit with long fitted jacket. The vented sides were trimmed with silk braiding and the buttons covered to match the detail on the slim fitted sleeves, bodice, mock waistcoat, side panels and hem of the flared skirt. The fine cream silk blouse sported a high stand collar and waterfall jabot. A cream straw hat with brim turned up at front and back, and trimmed with stiffened pink silk ribbons and a silk posy complimented the ensemble. Her white kid gloves covered the scars on her hands and kept her warm. She was the epitome of elegance and wealth.

He escorted her to a cozy sitting room where a fire blazed a warm welcome.

"Miss, if you will wait here for a moment?"

"Thank you, sir."

Kai Chen glanced about with a shy smile. The comfortable room decorated with feminine touches lent a grace and style that was distinct. Photos lined the mantle of the fireplace, drawing her to it. There she saw her father as a boy, standing next to his older sister with his arm placed about her affectionately. The next one was of them as adults, her father wearing black pants and the long black matching coat that flapped about his ankles when he walked, adorned with a single white stiff collar. Suzette was beautiful with her light hair, pretty smile, and beautiful gown. Kai Chen recognized herself in the woman's features, more than her own mother.

Emotions of love and loss for her parents swelled in her breath as she remembered their caring guidance and kind words. They had loved her unconditionally, had never spoken to her harshly or in anger, nor had ever raised their hands to her in punishment. How she missed them! Oh, but to feel their embrace again. Sighing heavily, she let the memories return to their resting place.

Suddenly she sensed a presence behind her. Turning, she saw her aunt. Suzette Boussard-Minot's face expressed surprise as she recollected their meeting at the museum. As their eyes locked Kai Chen smiled and knew the woman recognized who she was in her heart, even if her mind had not done so yet. Crossing the room, Kai Chen held out her hand.

This was the moment she had been waiting for so long. Finally she would meet her aunt, her last living relative. She felt fear race through her, wondering if this woman would accept her. Though Vaden had given her every possible advantage in this new world with clothing and classes Kai Chen still felt different, outcast. However, she refused to think of this woman denying her the Boussard heritage.

"My name is Kay Boussard. My father was David, your brother," she said quickly, as though afraid she would not have the nerve if she wavered longer. In time she would tell this woman the truth of her heritage, but not now.

Several seconds passed as the small woman scanned Kai Chen's face earnestly.

"I should have known," the woman said as her tears threatened to spill. "You have the eyes."

Kai Chen smiled as the woman embraced her in greeting. There was nurturing love in the tiny woman's clasp reminding her of her grandmother. Breaking apart, they moved to sit upon the settee near the fire as the butler discreetly shut the doors as he left.

"You must have much to tell. I am eager to hear how you found me and how your parents are," Suzette enthused as she retained Kai Chen's hand in hers. "For so very long I wanted to meet you and your mother, to see David again."

The pained expressed in the older woman's face spoke of her loss, of the hurt she was trying to keep secreted within her breast. Kai Chen knew of this pain and prayed she could lessen the woman's grief.

"I obtained your address from father long ago, but I regret to inform you that both he and mother are dead. They were killed during the uprising in China," she whispered and squeezed the woman's hands as her mourning became obvious.

Slipping a lacy handkerchief from her pocket, Kai Chen gently pressed it into her aunt's hands as the woman wept for her lost brother and unknown sister-in-law. Manfred returned carrying a tray, which he placed before them on the small serving table. Kai Chen automatically reached out to serve them as her aunt collected herself.

"No cream, dear, just sugar," the woman sniffed daintily before wiping at her eyes again. "Oh, dear, to experience such tragedy and happiness all in one moment is overwhelming. Here I sit with my niece of whom I've thought of so often, only to discover my beloved brother is gone. Still, I must not grieve overly much. He was a man who placed his life in God's hands and chose the path to share that with others. I am sure he is at peace."

"He is," Kai Chen concurred as she carefully handed the woman a delicate cup and saucer. "I was fortunate to be saved by a very generous man who brought me to America. It has taken me some time to adjust to the cultural differences of this country, and to find you."

"Last week at the museum," the woman began and took a graceful sip from her cup. "When you looked at me I saw my image as a young woman, and saw my brother in your eyes. I wanted to say something to you then but did not want to seem imprudent or mad."

"I was startled as well and sensed your hesitation."

Kai Chen refused to admit she had known all along whom Suzette was. It would only lead to more questions. Questions she was unprepared and unwilling to answer.

Smiling, the small woman placed her cup and saucer on the tray and turned to Kai Chen. "Would it be inconvenient for you to spend the remainder of the day with me? I would like to simply talk."

"There is nothing more I would rather do," Kai Chen said with tears in her eyes as her heart inflated with joy. Everything in her life was perfect right now.

☯

LeBlanc Estate
That evening

"Vaden LeBlanc! I do declare," Caroline Pennington preened loudly as she pressed her uplifted bosom against his chest blatantly. "I thought you had forgotten all about me!"

"Who could forget a woman as lovely as you," he replied dryly.

Placing a discreet kiss on her cheek he grasped her arm stroking down his coat toward the front of his pants brazenly. Slipping the wandering hand into the crook of his elbow, he escorted her into the elegant dining room.

"You make me forget myself, sir," Caroline purred seductively in his ear as she pulled him down for the intimate proclamation.

"Caroline, we have been over this before," he said impatiently and stopped before a chair. Pulling it out, he waited for her to be seated then assumed his place next to her at the head of the table. "I refuse to become intimately involved with you. I am committed to another."

"I understand," she said in clipped tones, her eyes hard as diamonds as she glanced at his fair hair and handsome features. "I knew one day some woman would break that icy reserve you encase yourself in. Would it be Kay Boussard, perchance?"

Vaden only raised an eyebrow at her and refused to reply as dinner was served. It was impeccable timing on Caroline's part that she arrived just as he was preparing for dinner. Kai Chen had sent a message that she would be dining with her newfound aunt before returning home. Caroline basically invited herself to dinner. She now sat beside him to dine on luscious prime rib with flavorful au jus, piping hot seasoned vegetables, and fresh sliced bread was piled on their plates. A dark burgundy wine filled the etched crystal flutes resting on the virgin white linen tablecloth as soft music filtered into the room.

"You certainly dine as though expecting company," she stated innocently and observed his nonchalant shrug.

"I enjoy the finer things in life, whether or not I entertain," he told her as he sliced into the medium rare meat.

Of course, he had expected Kai Chen to return by now but she had not. Vaden wanted to claim her for himself and never share her with anyone but he knew the importance of her meeting her only living relative. It would be the same if he was in her place.

Caroline smiled sweetly at his statement as she cut a dainty piece of the beef. For months now she had unsuccessfully tried to manipulate herself into Vaden's personal life. She knew he was a man of suppressed desires, saw the flame of eroticism in those dark blue eyes of his, but he never allowed any woman near. It was as though he had taken a vow of celibacy and was determined to follow it to the end. However, that would simply not do. She was resolute in being his wife. No amount of fortitude on his part, or the promise to any other woman, was going to thwart her intention.

Caroline talked amicably during dinner, their wine glasses repeatedly filled until another bottle of the expensive wine was opened. Dessert, a tart lemon meringue pie, was served with coffee as the table was cleared.

"That was a splendid meal, Vaden. Thank you for asking me to join you," she said softly, her eyes narrowing as he pushed back from the table.

"It is my pleasure," he stated politely, but the sincerity did not quite reach his expression or tone of his voice. Caroline had invited herself. He would have preferred her to leave at once but would not be so rude as to force her to leave.

"Won't you have liquor with me?"

"Yes, we shall have liquor before you leave," Vaden announced, his irritation almost evident as he escorted her from the lavish dining room to his study.

Caroline smiled with calculated purpose. *Who said I was leaving?*

"I was just mentioning to Sebastian today that I was thinking of ordering several cases of the Beaujolais wine we enjoyed so much at his last affair," Vaden admitted, keeping the conversation away from personal issues, which was a difficult task around the flirtatious and aggressive Caroline Pennington.

"Wasn't it simply delectable? Father and I spent days in Paris deciding over which wine to bring home until we discovered it. I'll have it at my wedding reception when I marry," she said guilelessly as she watched him cross the room, admiring his height and breathe of shoulder. "Someday..."

"I look forward to being at the event," he announced gallantly as he collected two large brandy snifters and filled them slightly with the amber liquor.

"As do I," she purred in response and let her eyes roam over the opulence of the sitting room filled with priceless antiques, divine artwork, and tasteful furnishings. One day soon this would be hers.

Accepting the snifter from him she smiled and batted her eyelashes as she reclined on the settee languidly. Adept with her cunning she tipped the glass slightly as she raised it to her lips. The strong liquor splayed across the front of her pale pink gown as she cried out with mock shock.

"Oh, dear, it's ruined," she wailed, observing the spot widen as the material soaked up the liquid.

"Nonsense, I will have it taken care of," Vaden offered instantly. Setting his glass next to hers on the table by the sofa, he quit the room.

Caroline giggled with excitement as she withdrew a small piece of paper. Unfolding it carefully, she poured the white powdered contents into his glass and swirled it around with her finger until it dissolved. Reaching inside the front of her tight bodice she pushed up her heavy breasts, the nipple of each barely showing. Hearing his footsteps she crushed the tiny paper in her hands and stuffed it behind her in the cushion of the settee as he entered the room.

"Here we are." He held a small bowl of water and a cloth. "Simply dab it on the stain and it should suffice until you have it cleaned properly."

"Thank you, dear Vaden. What would I do without you?"

Blotting the fabric at her chest with the cloth she watched his eyes linger on the exposed skin of her breasts, then narrow as they caught sight of her barely revealed nipples. For several seconds they lingered on the spot then he turned away to free his hands of the bowl and cloth.

"You would survive, my dear," he stated wryly and picked up his drink.

"But not nearly as happily."

Lifting her glass again, Caroline watched with slyness as he polished off his drink quickly and returned to the decanter filled with brandy. Daintily she sipped at hers and waited. The effects of the powder should take affect soon, very soon.

Vaden refilled his snifter and blinked several times as the glass wavered before his eyes. Replacing the decanter with a loud thump, he shook his head and grasped the edge of the table. What was wrong with him? He had only drunk a few glasses of wine and one brandy. That was nothing compared to his usual allotment.

"I believe I'm turning into a pantywaist," he scoffed aloud harshly as he shook his head again. A strange fuzziness invaded his senses. Turning toward Caroline he saw her reclining on the ornate sofa but there seemed to be three of her. No, four!

"Why, Vaden, whatever is wrong, dear? You don't appear well," she said, her voice sounding oddly distorted and deep.

As though in slow motion she rose from the sofa and walked toward him, her eyes gleaming with satisfaction.

"I don't quite know," he muttered thickly, placing a hand to his spinning head.

"Everything will be just fine," she cooed as she positioned her arms around his waist to help him. "I'll take care of you."

"Don't - know - whas -," he said, but suddenly stopped.

He was cognizant, but unfocused. The wide steps leading upstairs waved before his eyes as he stumbled up them. It seemed to take forever for him to reach the top.

"Which way to your room, my love," Caroline asked in concern as she watched one of his hands rise slightly and point.

Anxiously, she led him to his grand chamber with muted brown and gold colors. Heavy draperies kept the room dark as a cheerful fire blazed in the fireplace across the room. Elegant Italian provincial furniture was displayed in the room as her gaze alighted upon the massive four poster bed. Helping him to it, she watched as he fell back sluggishly against the soft mattress.

With a suppressed squeal of excitement she saw his eyes close. Quickly she began to undress him. Her eyes noted his muscular body, trim and fit from years of physical labor. In a matter of minutes Vaden was totally naked. She removed her dress with impatient hands. Staring at his flaccid manhood laying between his thighs, she licked her lips with surprise.

"Well, if he isn't hung like a horse," she quipped then tossed the rest of her undergarments across the room. Sliding her body over his and straddling his pelvis, she felt the wetness of desire pulsing between her thighs.

"Too bad the potion renders you impotent, big boy, but then again, you'll never know that. Will you?"

The lids of his eyes lifted slightly as she rocked her body against his and placed his hands on her full breasts. His brow furrowed in distress as she undulated above him, then cried out in mock ecstasy and fell against his chest as though replete from his lovemaking. For several seconds she lingered there then peeked at his face. Vaden's eyes were open and he was vaguely aware of what was happening, but he had no physical control. Her plan was working beautifully.

"You are mine," she whispered softly along his jaw as she let her lips trail over his and then slid her body beside him. Her body screamed for fulfillment as the excitement of her plan made her lust soar. Knowing she would be replete come the morrow she slid into a peaceful slumber.

Throughout the night Vaden slept and would then awaken as though some nightmare had occurred that he couldn't recall. At one point he thought he heard the door to Kai Chen's bedroom close. By morning, as the effects of the potent drug wore off, Vaden knew his nightmare was reality. Beside him lay Caroline, naked with one leg thrown over his groin as if it were a common happening between them.

Lunging out of bed as the realization of what this situation signified, Vaden felt his heart plummet. The details of what had transpired with Caroline were sketchy, but he vividly recalled her riding him in passion as she cried out with release. Bile filled his gullet as he stared at her in horror. Had he drank more than usual? Never had he been so sot with drink he couldn't distinctly remember details. How could he have let down his restraint with this woman? He had never desired her, had went out of his way to be pleasant to her, but evasive. What madness had overcome him last night?

Furious at this culmination of events he glanced about the room and noted their strewn clothes. It appeared as though they were impatient lovers in a sordid tryst. Nothing could be farther from the truth and it made him ill. There was only one woman who had been in his thoughts for the past several months and she had green eyes the color of the grass on a summer day.

"Hello, my darling."

The sound of Caroline's voice made him flinch. Vaden turned to see her seductive smile as she boldly let her gaze rake over his body. He stared at her, seeing her slender legs, tiny waist and heavy breasts with taut nipples, and felt absolutely no desire for her. Though she was beautiful and most probably would have stirred his lust several years ago, only one woman had the capability to do that now. And because of this predicament Kai Chen could possibly be forever lost to him.

"Caroline, I -," he stammered, unsure what to say or do. Obviously, he had bedded her in a drunken stupor and would now be liable for the consequences.

"Oh, Vaden," she said with a sigh, "last night you were wonderful. I never knew you felt this way toward me."

"I didn't know it myself," he mumbled angrily under his breath as he strode across the room and slid into his dress slacks.

Caroline watched his powerful body as he thrust his mighty legs into the pants. She could see he was troubled by this circumstance and smiled contentedly. His guilt would rend the appropriate action from him. There was no doubt.

CHAPTER THIRTEEN

"One may know how to conquer without being able to do it."
— Sun Tzu, *The Art of War*

Niagra Falls
The next day

"I tell you Sebastian," Vaden stated harshly as they strolled along the snow covered street, "I do not know what came over me. It was as though I had been drugged!"

"Drugged?" The color in his friend's face paled at the implication. "Are you suggesting Caroline Pennington drugged you and took advantage of you? Do you understand how ridiculous and coarse that sounds?"

"I know," Vaden said wearily then sighed as he removed his black hat and ran his long fingers through is wavy hair. "My behavior was outlandish and I am searching for excuses, I guess. But damn, I'm not even attracted to the woman!"

"Well, you were once," his friend jested callously and flinched at the outraged glare Vaden cast him.

"Your humor is greatly lacking," Vaden ground out between clenched teeth. "As a matter of fact, it is totally tasteless."

"Sorry, old chap. That was uncalled for," the smaller man apologized, but secretly chuckled at his verbal thrust.

"I have been avoiding her since it happened yesterday," Vaden admitted, his face revealing his displeasure. "It sickens me to think I basically fucked her and don't remember it."

"That is a pity. Caroline is quite the beauty. That's one body a man would find hard to forget."

With a smirk, Sebastian gazed at the huge rush of water from Niagra Falls streaming downward into a misty haze. The terrible cold and snow of the last several weeks had finally let up and it was actually comfortable outside. The sun was shining and the temperature had risen. Indeed, it was almost as though it was a sign of good fortune.

"I wish I could forget the whole nightmare," Vaden growled angrily, frustration filling his entire being.

Unfortunately, it would never happen. It was an incident that would haunt Vaden's every waking moment in thought, and every nightmare as he dreamed. Since it had occurred he had avoided Kai Chen, had basically avoided everything, even work, as he mulled and tormented himself over what had transpired and what he would do. Vaden had implied he would ask Kai Chen to marry him and then he had taken Caroline to bed. Was he depraved from years of abstinence? Or was he simply that lacking in morals, though he consciously tried to behave differently?

"Well, I definitely suggest you at least offer her marriage. Heaven forbid she and her wealthy daddy start a scandal," came the warning Vaden had been telling himself for two hours. "And I would not put it off much longer. Heaven forbid there is already a babe in her belly!"

That night Vaden locked himself into his bedroom, disgusted with himself and not certain what to do. Never had he felt more sickened with his actions than he was at this moment. How could he feel the beginning of love for Kai Chen and bed another woman so callously? This action was totally out of character for him. Regardless of what Sebastian claimed there was not a woman at every port pining for him. He considered himself a man with standards, morals, ethics, and they did not include randomly bedding women or using them for his sexual entertainment.

Flinging himself upon his huge bed Vaden glanced at the clock and groaned. Four in the morning. He was physically and emotionally exhausted but his mind was racing frantically. For the second time in his life he felt tears on his cheeks. His spirit was consumed by Kai Chen Boussard, a woman of unparallel beauty whose essence had captured him as no other woman could or ever would again. Although a part of him screamed inwardly that this could not be happening, his mind hazily recalled the events with Caroline Pennington. His heart was breaking at these bizarre turn of events. Vaden allowed his emotions to consume him as he realized he had most likely lost his China doll, his Kai Chen, because of this situation.

Finally, Vaden fell into an uncomfortable and restless sleep as he dreamed…and remembered.

"This is Mr. Garwood. He is the headmaster of this orphanage and you will obey him completely or suffer the consequences. Is that understood?"

The Elderly man sitting at his desk glanced up at him. His cold eyes held malevolence in them that rendered Vaden speechless. He experienced another new fear since his parent's death. Their funeral had only been two days ago. Two days of wondering why they had been taken from him, where he would go and who would love him. Now he knew some answers. There would be nobody to love him and this was his new home. Correction, this was his new hell. The other hell was in knowing his parents would never come back. They were forever lost to him.

He nodded quickly, afraid to speak.

His chin quivered as he fought back the tears, the hurt, and the fear. Staring at the mean looking man before him, his hair only fine gray wisps, his beady eyes narrowed and hating, and his hawkish nose protruding from his face with thin lips compressed tightly, Vaden knew he had stepped from one nightmare into another.

Would these nightmares never end? He didn't like them! He wanted his mother and his father and the safety and security and love he had experienced for ten years.

"What? We have another heathen brat to feed? Agh! What pathetic story trails this child?" The mean looking older man spat out as his gaze roamed over Vaden with considerable interest.

"His parents were killed in a fire. He has no other relatives. The estate is comfortable and the solicitor was more than happy to give us a generous donation for taking him," the woman's nasal reply seemed almost comical if it were not for the horrific circumstances.

"Isn't that unfortunate," said the man sarcastically as he stood. Walking around his desk he towered over Vaden with clenched fists. "You will learn the rules and follow them exactly. Any deviation, however slight, shall not be tolerated. It gives me great satisfaction to mete punishment to those fail."

"Yes, sir," Vaden replied then reeled backward in pain as the man's hand struck his face brutally.

"One of the rules is never to speak unless asked a question. Is that clear?"

Two new emotions surged within Vaden's breast. The first was one that would carry him for years to come, one that would strengthen his fortitude and spirit. It started as a tiny flicker, then flamed brightly as the man before him casually wiped the blood from Vaden's mouth from his hand with a stark white handkerchief.

It was anger.

The second was one that would forge his future, would give him ideas, dreams and stamina. It was one that would come to fruition in a manner that would have repercussions long before he would ever leave this orphanage.

It was revenge.

Vaden awakened immediately.

Though he had worn rags, had been treated and fed worse than the dogs roaming back alleys in the heart of the city, had not received the best of education, and had been ruthlessly beaten by the headmaster of the orphanage, he had never once despaired. His reflections moved forward to his days as a Navy sailor. Even when he had been in ferocious battles at sea and wondered if all was lost, he had never despaired. Or when his first merchant ship was attacked and the goods were stolen from a foreign pirate ship, he had not despaired. As a child losing his parents he had not despaired, although he had grieved. He had been too innocent to understand despair.

Despair was a new emotion for him.

However, that was changed now. The resignation toward his current plight with Kai Chen consumed him like the plague. Death was preferable right now, but then his hope for a life with Kai Chen would surface. Why he held a small candle of hope for her, for them, he didn't know, but it was inside him burning strong and constant. Her incredible image flashed before his closed eyes and instant desire surfaced in his loins. Moaning, Vaden rolled over on his stomach and pressed his face into the soft pillow cushioning his head. Yes, he had bedded several women in the past with whom he had considered a relationship, but he had never felt the consumption of need that sprang in him as he did when he thought of Kai Chen. She was like a breath of fresh air in his stagnant life or like a cool breeze across his burning skin. Her beauty was unsurpassed, her calm serenity a balm to his soul. The passion he felt for her knew no bounds.

Her innocence and her purity had been saved for him; he believed they were meant for each other. But now he may no longer possess Kai Chen due to his recent actions. Instead, he was now possessed. He was possessed by a horror that was far greater than any he had ever known. Caroline could be pregnant with his child from their brief coupling. Until he knew for certain, the next month would be spent speculating about it and it aggrieved him, but what he considered far worse was facing Kai Chen with the truth of what he had done.

Kai Chen's movements were so rapid that Vaden could not keep up with each one as he watched in bewilderment. Her wrists, elbows, arms, shoulders, hips, legs, knees and feet moved like a whirlwind, dizzying with speed and accuracy. The Muk Yan Chong, with its extended arms and leg, spun back and forth as she practiced trapping the limbs of her imaginary opponent. It strengthened her upper body with resistance training called *Chi Sao*, or sticking hands, she had told him when the wooden dummy had initially arrived. Although he now spied from a hidden portion of the room he somehow knew she sensed his presence.

"You may join me, foolish American," she grunted between strikes then stepped away from the new item. It did not have the character, the hours of blood, sweat, and tears of many monks and nuns that the Muk Yan Chong in her temple had. Many lifetimes need pass before this one had the marks and worn wood to tell any story.

Vaden entered the room in his house turned into a training hall especially for her. His intention was to merely observe her positive inner strength, her outward beauty and her remarkable skill, but as he neared her his intent changed. He wanted to taste her lips, feel her tongue mate with his as their blood rushed in heated desire together. He needed to feel the imprint of her toned and satiny skin against his as they melded into one another. He yearned to bury himself in her sweet innocence and make her his for the very first time, every time.

"Teach me," he appealed to her suddenly, throwing caution to the wind and ignoring the sharp warning that cried for him to run, to leave before he committed another grave sin. Instead, he stood directly in front of her and let her green eyes shine with trust.

"You must be of pure mind, body and spirit. Do you have these qualities?"

Her light bantering brought a grin to his face as she danced away from him faster than the wind. Spinning around to find her, he saw her slide behind him as their game of hide and seek ensued. For a full minute he spun around crazily, trying to keep up with her twirling movements until he realized she was no longer near him. She was across the room with a cheeky smile on her face.

"No. There is nothing pure about me, except what I feel for you," he said deeply as his eyes locked with hers. Like a lion stalking its prey he moved toward her. Almost within reaching distance she suddenly darted to the side as their cat and mouse game continued.

"Then I cannot divulge my secrets," she declared and giggled as he chased her across the shiny wooden floor.

"I don't want your secrets, only you," he growled as he caught the edge of her black tunic and pulled her to him. Their bodies met, hers malleable and submissive, his hard and demanding.

"Then I am yours," she whispered just before his lips claimed hers.

Her words struck a chord within him, igniting the savagery of his pent up frustrations and desires. This was the woman he should be marrying, having children with and spending the rest of his life loving. She was the woman who set his passions aflame and was the only one who could douse them. He wanted no other.

Permitting his primitive emotions to surface his kiss took, demanded, and branded her as his. Their lips met, tongues gently touching before they eagerly slid against each other. His hands slid beneath the black top she wore, lightly touching her creamy breasts and the puckered nipples that seemed to reach out for his touch. Continuing the onslaught of his kiss he lowered her to the floor. Opening her slender thighs, his body slid against hers as his hands stroked her heated flesh, fingers tugging at her straining nipples as he buried his face between her breasts.

How he wanted her!

The pulsating desire of his sex was unstoppable as were his actions. He was consumed by lust as her hands slid under his shirt and stroked his back. Her light touch issued a fierce groan from deep in his throat as he lay between her spread legs. He shifted his pelvis against her, grinding his thick manhood in imitation of the act he knew would be heaven between them. As he switched his weight he found her hands unexpectedly unfastening his pants. His thoughts and emotions whirled as he realized he was committing an atrocious sin by allowing this, but her slender fingers tentatively fondled his manhood, driving him beyond sanity. Reason, morals, and repercussions faded against the glorious feel of her fingers gripping him.

Hovering over her, his pants around his hips, Vaden watched in fascination as Kai Chen instinctively began to stroke him with her hands as she lay on her back. With a low moan of pleasure he closed his eyes and yielded to her guileless touch. Heaven and hell were clashing here on earth as he tried to fight against the raging tide holding him, but he could not win. Her naive hands were taking him, driving him to the edge of completion.

"Kai Chen!"

One of his mighty hands clutched hers fiercely and quickened her movements as his body trembled with release. As his shout of fulfillment echoed in the empty room and his seed spilled, his mind reeled at the extraordinary fervor she had brought forth from him.

"Vaden?"

The sound of her lilting, questioning voice cleared his muddled senses as he comprehended the enormity of what had just occurred. Peering down into her face, her cheeks red and her hand still clutching his slowly waning manhood, Vaden almost shouted in victory. He had bedded many women in the past, but never had he experienced such complete and utter joy and satisfaction without actually bedding her. And he had never felt so soiled by the knowledge that he had betrayed her with Caroline.

Her eyes were bright with desire, anticipation, and curiosity at what had transpired between them. Her lips quivered slightly as her gaze moved down. Following the movement of her eyes, he saw the evidence of his physical release on the flat plane of her stomach that had been exposed. Freeing her hand against his now flaccid organ, he shrugged out of his shirt without hesitation. With infinite care he wiped his seed from her taut stomach and pulled together the ravages of her tunic.

"I am sorry, Kai Chen. I did not mean -," Vaden broke off as anger toward himself, toward his weakness of flesh, and toward life, devoured him.

It must be true! These actions proved how vile he had become. Kai Chen deserved better; a man who would treat her with the respect she deserved, whose physical desires would not lead him to bed other women. He considered himself despicable.

"Please," she said, beseeching him with her expressive eyes, "do not be sorry. I have never experienced anything so profoundly beautiful."

Her words were like music to a deaf man, but it was too late.

Lincoln Center
Two days later

Countless men and women stared at Kai Chen as she glided beside Vaden, the whispered excited and approving comments made of the gown she wore. She focused on the man beside her in order to keep from stumbling at their keen scrutiny. Vaden returned her gaze, adoration evident as they climbed the wide staircase that led to the second floor.

"It seems your gown is causing quite a stir among the nobility. You are stunning," he murmured softly in her ear.

Kai Chen blushed prettily as he accepted two glasses of champagne from a passing waiter. He pressed one into her gloved hand while clasping the other tightly within the crook of his elbow.

"Foolish American, you know I do not drink alcohol," she told him, changing the subject of her appearance.

But as she turned she caught her reflection in a full-length mirror. She barely recognized herself in the gold colored silk-satin dress that shimmered as though alive. The under bodice gathered onto a silk-chiffon yoke with short inset sleeves decorated with ropes of glass beads and an asymmetric beaded and fringed chiffon shawl worn over one shoulder. The narrow skirt with long train lent a distinctive oriental look, one of royalty. Her hair was pulled back severely in a chignon with bird of paradise plumes attached from behind. Amber drop earrings and a matching necklace completed the glittering ensemble that was the envy of every woman in the theater.

Vaden leaned toward her intimately and murmured, "You don't have to drink it, Kai Chen, just smile and pretend you are enjoying yourself."

Her blush deepened as she turned to him and replied, "There is no need for pretense. I am savoring each moment. Never have I seen dancers like these ballets."

"Ballerinas," he corrected.

Smiling at her mistake she let his blue eyes captivate her, transport her back to the training room where she had witnessed a man's pleasure and release for the first time. His gaze flashed hotly and she knew that he too, thought of that erotic moment. Tearing her gaze away from his she concentrated on the bubbles lifting upward in the fluted glass she held. Kai Chen compared her life to this strange drink. When would her bubble of happiness pop? When would she find herself running again? When would her fairy tale life with Vaden suddenly turn?

A series of bells announced the second half of the performance. Vaden escorted her to their balcony seats above, yet so very near, the stage. Carefully, she placed the glass she held on the table to the rear of their cushioned seats and eagerly awaited the continuation of the beautiful female swans, sweeping her heart away with their magical dancing.

As the presentation began anew, picking up the scene where it had been interrupted, Kai Chen contemplated all of the enchanted places and things she had never known possible. Her life, her tiny world in China, had never given her any inkling to the wondrous events or achievements taking place around her. The sedate dances of her people seemed timid compared to the sanguine athletics of these women and men who leaped, twirled and stole her breath. She absolutely loved the ballet.

Vaden noticed her entranced expression as she shrewdly observed and attempted to memorize each move the dancers made. Her intensity was that of a fellow artist, whose physical capabilities would or could match theirs was she to know their secrets. It was that probing gaze that carefully separated each move, each subtle nuance and filed it away in her sharp memory. A smile curved his lips as he imagined her pirouetting across the training hall at his estate until she was as perfect as those she admired.

For the remainder of the evening he did not notice the performance on stage, but instead, watched Kai Chen as her fingers and eyes danced. As the last note was struck and the curtain fell, her sigh of complete and utter pleasure sent a thrill through him. Deafening applause seemed to shake the building as the audience showed their approval of the exquisite performance. It dawned on him that for the first time in seven years he had missed Swan Lake.

"Oh, Vaden! Never have I had such a thrilling experience," she blazoned enthusiastically and gripped his right hand between her gloved ones.

"Never?" The question was a subtle purr from Vaden, a seductive question that made her face turn crimson as he leaned toward her.

"Shame on you, Vaden, seducing this poor woman in front of hundreds of envious women," a man's laughing voice declared and they broke away as if caught stealing the champagne glasses they had been given earlier.

"Sebastian Madden. Your timing leaves much to be desired, as do your insinuating words and viperous tongue," Vaden said lightly as he stood to shake his friend's hand. He appeared cordial, but Kai Chen sensed Vaden's anger he held in check at Sebastian's tart words.

"Touché," the shorter man conceded and turned his curious gaze to Kai Chen. "My, my, what beauty we have here this evening!"

Vaden reintroduced them to each other, his baritone voice clipped and aloof. The theater was emptying rapidly as patrons left for private parties they had been invited to. He noted their inquisitive stares as they strained their necks looking upward to see them. He and Kai had been invited to numerous gatherings, mainly because word of her mystery, beauty, and voguish apparel. They were dying to know who the obscure debutante was and her relationship to Vaden LeBlanc.

Returning his attention back to Sebastian who was fawning over Kai Chen like a bee over a flower, Vaden frowned. Resentment of his friend's apparent profound interest in her made his hackles rise. It should not bother him the way Sebastian's words dripped honey or the way his eyes visually caressed her flawless skin or the way his voice dipped and rose seductively as he tried to attract her with his worldly charms. That was Sebastian. He had always been that way with women, from those who were decidedly obese or homely to those who were voluptuous or glamorous. Every woman was a conquest to him.

However, it rankled that he would execute his charms on *his* woman. Anger suffused his being as he gritted his back teeth together for control. His hands itched to reach out and break Sebastian's fingers, which stroked Kai Chen's gloved wrist so methodically. His fists clenched and unclenched as he fought not to pound them into his friend's jaw as he flirted outrageously with her. Never had he felt such uncontrollable insanity, jealousy, grip him.

"Have you seen Caroline yet? She was here with her father earlier," Sebastian informed Vaden with calculated finesse.

"I have not seen them this evening," he stated indifferently.

Turning to Kai Chen, Vaden smiled warmly and extended his arm. She took it with an expression of gratitude at having Sebastian's fawning put to an end.

"Please excuse our abruptness, but we are expected elsewhere. Do contact me one day next week."

Vaden's words were laced heavily with meaning, not lost on Sebastian who bowed stiffly and stood aside to let them pass. As they made their way out of the expansive and ornate building to the waiting carriage, he noticed Sebastian walking quickly toward Caroline. She stood next to her father with a group of patrons, her gaze coldly following him as Sebastian approached her. Fury practically oozed from her as her icy blue eyes alighted on Kai Chen. Vaden knew if he did not do something about this appalling situation that was building, his troubles were going to compound.

Escorting Kai Chen out into the cold evening, Vaden decided it would be better to remain out of Caroline's way. Until he knew if she was pregnant or not, Vaden would simply avoid Caroline. It would not do to have Kai Chen's reputation tarnished by a scandal due to the woman's viperous tongue. With that decision made, he informed the driver to head straight home instead of the party they had planned on attending.

"Vaden?"

Kai Chen's worried voice broke him from his musings and he opened his eyes.

"I have a fierce headache. You are not disappointed at missing the party, are you?"

"Of course not! I am actually relieved. It was a very trying evening for me with everyone staring," Kai Chen confessed with a hesitant smile, which alleviated his woes. "I have an herbal remedy that would help your pain, but we would need sail to China for the herbs."

Her light banter made him chuckle as he listened to her sweet voice. Kai Chen was actually joking with him! His worries of Caroline disappeared under the lightness she enveloped him with. Her words were more medicinal than any herb, her touch more gratifying than any aphrodisiac as she moved to sit beside him. The remainder of the ride was spent with the two of them lightly jesting back and forth, their soft laughter easing away the dark clouds that seemed to hover about them. Although they were able to push the clouds aside momentarily, they remained constantly lingering nearby.

"That's it, deeper," she urged, reveling in the feel of his hardness as he shoved into her forcefully. Straddling his waist as the carriage bumped along, assisting his powerful thrusts with each jolt, she pretended he was Vaden. She imagined seeing him nude, his large member rising against his thigh. She was sure he was magnificent in size, and a sensual lover. It was he she now envisioned ramming into her, his harsh groans spurring her on toward release.

"Oh, yes. You are so wet," Sebastian murmured, suckling her heavy breasts as her snug muscles clenched about him. "So tight."

The fantasy of Kay Boussard riding him, sucking his seed from him with her narrow sheath, drove him as his hips bucked wildly. She was so exotic looking, so meek and demure, so boldly innocent. He could imagine her lily white breasts with rosy tips straining toward him, her nest of dark curls separating as he forced himself past her snug entrance. There was nothing as exciting as the tightness of a woman's sex, except a woman's mouth.

As his fantasy changed he neared his peak. He imagined he could feel Kay Boussard's moist lips stroking the tip of him, her teeth grazing along the length of him as she took him deep into her throat. Over and over, deeper and deeper, she would take him until he exploded. And she would greedily swallow his essence until he was drained and satiated. The image was too much. With a fierce groan his seed shot into Caroline who rode him and grunted with her own satisfaction. Though he would never marry anyone other than Caroline, he would never remain faithful. Nor would she. They were both immoral when it came to sex, but they appreciated each other for it. It kept the excitement and spice in their relationship. They were made for each other.

"Goodness! That was exhilarating," Caroline purred contentedly as she took his tongue into her mouth and sucked on it suggestively. Both were panting heavily from their exuberant escapade.

"It always feels like the first time with you," Sebastian asserted as she finally slid off of him and readjusted her skirts and the bodice to her dress. Tucking himself back into his slacks and correcting his messed attire, he glanced at Caroline's face. He knew she had been thinking of someone else while he used her body as he had done.

"It does, doesn't it? Tell me," she began and looked at him ingenuously, "what did you think of Kay Boussard?"

"She is attractive, but I prefer a certain blond," he said breathlessly and leaned over to place a brief kiss on her lips.

"You may prefer me, but you lust for her. Just as I do Vaden," she informed him smugly and saw his face flush. "Don't deny it was her you were just fucking."

"You are so crude at times, Caroline. Shall we discuss something more refined? I think it time you began pressing Vaden into marriage. He is quite enamored of Miss Boussard and it could cause a serious problem if we do not nip it in the bud, so to say."

"We have to wait. I am still trying to locate a doctor to help us. Besides, I need at least two more weeks before I can pull off this charade," she snapped at him, angry at his verbal slap to her vulgarity.

"Fine, but no more than two weeks. In the mean time, I will check with Lee and see if he has unearthed any information concerning this puzzling woman who has suddenly entered Vaden's life. For our sake, I pray she is of no consequence to anyone."

"Why?" Caroline's sudden interest brought her closer to him as she snuggled for warmth from the slight draft entering the carriage.

Impatiently he barked, "Because I would hate to think of the sensation it would cause when she is found raped and killed."

☯

LeBlanc Estate
The next morning

Kai Chen enjoyed the feel of Vaden's warm body. Opening her eyes, she viewed him sitting beside her. An enormous tray was across his lap littered with the delicious aroma of breakfast. In his hands was the morning paper, which he scanned thoughtfully as he waited for her. He was wearing only a maroon robe, his bare legs exposed beneath the edge as he leaned against the padded headboard of the bed. She had heard him enter her room and had sensed his presence, but had not dared move until now.

"What are you doing in my room?"

"Well, I wanted you for breakfast but the cook would not allow it, so I brought this instead," he quipped with a mischievous grin as he leaned over to place a lingering kiss on her parted lips. "Sit up so we can eat before it gets cold."

"This is totally inappropriate, Vaden! What if a servant walks in?"

"They would not dare," he declared knowingly, remembering the verbal holocaust he had initiated years ago after a new servant's impromptu entrance into his study. "Besides, there is nothing inappropriate about eating in bed."

"But I am undressed," she whispered, her face pink with embarrassment as she realized her admittance.

"Even better," he growled deeply and let his lips trail down her neck to the blanket tucked securely under her arms across her breasts. Forcing himself away from her he placed the tray between them on the massive bed and served her.

"There is enough food here to feed four people," she cried out in astonishment then giggled as he heaped large amounts of seasoned scrambled eggs, thick slices of ham and browned toast on a plate and handed it to her. "I'll never eat all this."

"You had better try. You will need your strength today," he promised, but refused to say more as he prepared a plate for himself and dug into the food with enthusiasm.

"Why?" Kai Chen asked between mouthfuls of food, enjoying the comfort of having him beside her, even if the situation was highly improper.

"You will see," he teased, and then added, "and dress warmly."

"All right," she acquiesced, polishing off the scrumptious meal. Sighing contentedly, she glanced at Vaden who was filling his plate again. She had never noticed how much he ate before. He was a big man who obviously required a great amount of sustenance to get through the day.

"What are you staring at? Didn't your mother tell you it is impolite to stare at someone while they are gorging?" His lopsided smile and playful bantering had her laughter filling the room.

"Actually, it is occasional custom for the wife in China to observe her husband and sons eat before she or her daughters do so," she informed him with a grin as he cleaned his plate before placing it on the loaded tray.

"Sounds primitive to me. I want my wife beside me in everything I do." His eyes flashed provocatively as he picked up the tray and placed it on the floor beside the bed. Sliding closer to her, he saw her eyes widen in apprehension. "I will not bite. I just want a little nibble."

"Vaden," she warned, "I do not think -"

Her words were stopped by the forceful plundering of his mouth as his arms pulled her to him. His arousal had been hard and demanding since he had awakened this morning, but now it was throbbing, hard as granite, as he thrust his hips evocatively against hers. Kai Chen's moan of need, the feel of her satiny flesh in his hands drove him further. Shoving the blankets aside he lifted his mouth from hers to view her naked body.

"Just a nibble," he promised as his lips left a searing trail down her neck to her aching breasts. Her sharp cry of pleasure as he lightly tugged at each nipple sent his blood boiling. Vaden knew he needed to stop now before he couldn't, but her soft whimpers of delight goaded him onward. It was already too late. She was the most beautiful woman he had never seen, smelled, touch, or tasted. His hand slid to her hip as his mouth trailed to her stomach. Then he was leaning back, spreading her lean thighs and drowning in the sight of her feminine folds barely hidden by her dark curls. Eagerly he delved between her legs, stroking her nub with his thumb as he slid a long finger inside her.

"Oh, you are tight and wet," he growled with desire, savoring the feel of her silken muscles clenching about him. Withdrawing the solitary digit, he inserted two, deeply, and felt the barrier that he would someday break. A shudder raced through him as his desire escalated. He wanted her now. He could not wait any longer.

"Vaden, something is happening," Kai Chen whispered in wonder as he removed his hand and replaced it with his mouth. Within seconds she was crying out her release, bringing him to the brink of his own release as he felt her body tense and shudder. Her sweet, soft cries of fulfillment as he continually ravished her musky entrance with his lips, tongue and teeth drove him wild as he glanced up to see the ecstasy reflected on her face. Finally, she lay still as he leisurely continued to caress her intimately.

"Vaden?" Her soft voice was questioning and held a note of wonder. Her slender, strong hands touched his head. He moved from between her legs as she sat up. "Teach me. I want to please you in the same way."

Her words evoked erotic images in his mind.

"Are you sure?"

Her smile and bright eyes spoke of her love, of her desire to satisfy him, and he removed his robe. Lying on his back he wondered how he could go through with this. He knew that he would take her virginity if he allowed this to continue, but his body screamed for her, for only the gratification she could bring.

Tentatively she kneeled before him, her nude body perfect, flawless, lean, and toned. Her breasts were high and full, her waist tiny and her hips narrow, tapering down to long, firm legs. The alabaster color of her skin was creamy and pure against the dark mahogany of her hair. Then, as her hands surrounded his rigid maleness and she bent over him, he felt his sane world disintegrate. Her lips barely caressed the tip of him, causing his hips to rise off the bed as he groaned.

"That's good. Use your lips as you open your mouth," he directed her. He guided her as she attained a rhythm that set his heart pounding savagely as her hand stroked the base of him and her mouth worked magic on the length of him. He had already been excited beyond reason and now was reaching his apex. He had to stop her before-

"Kai, I can't stop-," his hoarse cry was muffled by the hammering in his head, the rush in his loins, as she continued to take him in her mouth until he was exploding over and over, until finally satiated. Slowly he drifted back to reality as he felt her lips slide off of him. Opening his eyes, he beheld her bemused expression.

"Kai Chen?"

"I am ready," she told him earnestly, her eyes alive and bright as she crawled across his body. The feel of her body against his was more incredible than he had ever dreamed. He was in heaven right now.

"Ready?"

"I am ready for you to be inside me," she told him sincerely as she wrapped her arms about his neck. "Though we have not been legally joined by marriage, I am ready."

"Unfortunately, it will be a while before I am ready," he stated wryly, trying to clear his head and recapture his coherent thoughts.

"I do not understand," she said, looking at him in confusion.

"Sometimes, once a man -," he began to tell her then stopped and laughed heartily at her serious frown. "I am sorely tempted to do as you ask, but there is a problem I have to take care of first."

"What is the problem?"

"Nothing I cannot handle."

With a light slap to her bottom he pulled the blanket over them and held her against him. He loved the feel of their bodies together, their hearts racing as one. He was compounding his quandary with Kai Chen by having sexual encounters with her that would eventually lead to her innocence being stripped. It was only a matter of time, but he wanted it to be right. He wanted her as his wife.

But that could not happen until he resolved the dilemma with Caroline.

CHAPTER FOURTEEN

"Can you imagine what I would do if I could do all I can?"
— Sun Tzu, *The Art of War*

"I recall seeing this when I first arrived to America on your ship," Kai Chen announced with zeal as they approached the base of the Statue of Liberty. "She is most impressive and beautiful with a very earnest expression."

"So she is. I never paid much attention to her facial expression before," Vaden exclaimed in surprise. Turning to Kai Chen he leaned close to whisper in her ear, "I have always wondered what she wore under the dress."

Kai Chen's shocked gasp and pink cheeks made him bark aloud with laughter. People nearby turned and smiled at the handsome couple she and Vaden made; one so tall, fair and masculine, the other exotic, delicate, and lovely. As Kai Chen saw Vaden's brilliant smile and conspiratorial wink, she suddenly remembered her first lesson in Wing Chun, taught by her grandmother.

The breeze blew off the sea, lending a slight relief to the hot summer day. A day when she had just turned five and her grandmother was explaining their family responsibility.

"Wing Chun is in your blood, child, as it has been for generations. Though each has attained perfection in many levels, the basics, the secrets, have never deviated. Nor shall they with you," Ng-Kin said, her small black eyes seeming to bore into hers.

"I do not want to do this," Kai Chen declared mutinously, her arms crossed and her bottom lip protruding in a fierce pout.

"First, let me tell you a story. Then you may decide," said the orange robed nun, her grandmother, who moved with such fluid and grace, with so light a step there was no trace of her footprints in the sand. Grabbing a thin stick nearby Ng-Kin drew a symbol into the sand then stood back for Kai Chen to see.

"What is that?" Even as a child she felt the familiarity of it, the pull of the symbol as her grandmother explained.

"This is the Tao of Wing Chun Do symbol. In the center are white and black symbols, each chasing the others tail in a never ending circle, distinguishing their individuality; but both encompassing the other in harmony and endless continuity. Within each half curved circle is an eye, white in black and black in white, signifying that no matter how strong something is there should be some gentleness within; no matter how gentle something is there should be strength.

"Surrounding the relentless circle are three solid lines on the top. They signify Yang, black, male; extreme hardness, strength, firmness and dominance. The three broken lines on the bottom signify Yin, white, female; extreme softness, yielding and subtleness. To the right are three lines; one solid in the center and two broken outside signifying Older Sister, soft and yielding on the outside but with an inner firmness and strength. To the left are three lines, one broken inside and two solid outside signifying Older Brother, firm and strong outside, yet springy and flexible inside. Together, Older Sister and Older Brother represent the non-traditional or changing way of life. They are not restricted to tradition and form, but seek to expand for total personal growth. The spaces between each trigram show each is an individual; the circular pattern shows each individual belongs to the same family."

Kai Chen stared as though mesmerized at the picture in the sand. Though she was uncertain of all Ng-Kin had said, the words had lulled her into acceptance. In that moment, she accepted her obligation, the will of Buddha.

"It is your destiny, child," the nun said with a tolerant smile, "it is one you shall embrace with your very being some day. You, Kai Chen, will be Older Sister."

"You will be Older Sister."

And Vaden was Older Brother. Together they formed the complete circle, the heart of the Wing Chun Do symbol.

"Are you ill, Kai Chen?"

Vaden's anxious voice broke her from her reverie as she stared into his concerned blue eyes. Throwing her arms around his neck, oblivious to the stares and murmurs of people nearby, she cried softly, "I have never been better."

LeBlanc Estate
The next afternoon

"Foolish American," Kai Chen said with a sigh of frustration and turned to see Vaden standing in the doorway to the training hall. He had broken her concentration for the first time in ten years, simply with his presence.

"How do you do that?" he asked in confusion and sincerity.

"Do what?"

"Know when someone is near," he clarified and entered the darkened room, shutting the door behind him. There was a single white candle burning two feet in front of her.

"Through meditation comes heightened awareness. Would you care to learn?"

"I would be honored if you would teach me," he admitted, surprised at her offer.

"Come sit beside me." She patted the polished wooden floor once with a slender, slightly scarred hand and returned to her pose. "Choose a sitting position that is comfortable for you. It is not necessary to sit lotus as I do."

Vaden looked at her crossed feet tucked under her, then mimicked her. She nodded once in acceptance then grasped his wrists and placed one on each knee. Though her touch was gentle there was strength about it.

"Relax your body and concentrate solely on your breathing. This is most important. Take a deep cleansing breath and release. Now, breathe in your mouth and out your nose slowly," she directed, showing him the proper technique to use.

"Good. Now, clear your mind of all thoughts and distractions and focus solely on the flame of the candle. Channel all energy toward it, see the flame flicker and dance about."

Kai Chen watched as Vaden was calmed by her soothing voice as he performed exactly as she directed. Smiling with satisfaction as his eyes began to take on a glazed appearance she repositioned herself and followed him to a place of perfect peace.

Vaden was never more aware of Kai Chen, could hear her faint breathing even as he began to slip away from reality from her hypnotic, musical voice. The flame frolicked before him, coaxing him, guiding him, reminding him . . .

"I see you have broken the rules, yet again, Vaden LeBlanc," Mr. Garwood said with a fanatical gleam to his evil eyes. "Isn't that a shame? After six years you would think you would know better than to be awake this time of night."

The evil headmaster of the orphanage stood stiffly before Vaden, their eyes now level. Vaden was older now. He and the headmaster were comparable in size now that Vaden was sixteen. Vaden's blue eyes flashed defiance and open hostility at the man who had concocted another excuse to abuse him, who did it frequently to all the boys. However, Vaden was one of the lucky ones. He had not been sexually molested by him. Yet. Mr. Garwood liked to wait until the boys were seventeen and ready to leave his tender, loving care.

"I have not," Vaden declared angrily, his fists clenching as adrenaline surged through his hormone riddled body which was rapidly developing into manhood.

"Are you also calling me a liar?"

A hush fell over the large room where fifty boys stared in muted horror from their beds, their ages ranging from three years to seventeen years. All had been abused repeatedly by the brutal headmaster; all physically, all emotionally, some sexually. Every boy there was terrified of defying him, of speaking to him, of simply living anymore, but they did not have the heart to kill themselves or each other to end their utter misery.

All except Vaden. Vaden constantly defied the headmaster, and was constantly punished severely for his rebelliousness. Every day that passed an uncontrollable rage grew in his breast for the man who treated them worse than prisoners or dogs on the street.

Vaden had had enough and now wore his boldness and anger like a protective cloak as he attempted to shield his brothers from any further verbal or physical mistreatment from the sinister man. Since he had turned fourteen he had begun to rise up against Mr. Garwood, and the man took great satisfaction in hurting him the most. Vaden was now the older man's size with youth, boundless energy, and wrath on his side.

"Yes, I am," Vaden said between gritted teeth, waiting for the man to lash out with a brutal fist. A collective gasp sounded from his friends as the older man drew back his fist.

But Vaden took the advantage. Lunging, he threw his youthful body filled with fury and pubescent testosterone at the hateful man. A hearty cheer rang throughout the room from the boys who witnessed the fight as they both fell to the hard floor with a mighty crash. Vaden landed on top of him as a bony fist shot up and connected with his jaw. Spinning to the side, he was suddenly pinned on the floor as the headmaster straddled him and proceeded to strike him repeatedly about the head and body with vicious fists. Blood poured from Vaden's nose and mouth, and he could swear he heard the sound of a bone breaking.

Pain shot through his body, but he refused to give up. With a mighty growl Vaden grabbed the older man's arms and lunged off the floor as they began to roll. The sounds of his brothers urging him on lent him the physical might and spirit to pin the hated man to the floor. Over and over, harder and harder, he planted his fists into the man's face and body. Relentlessly, he returned to the man the pain of years of abuse until four of his older brothers caught his weary arms and pulled him off.

"You bastard! If you ever lay another hand on any of us again, I'll kill you," Vaden spat, blood flying from his mouth as he glared at the beaten man on the floor. The pounding of footsteps heading their way alerted the group that other adults were coming.

"This isn't over," the headmaster groaned, his eyes promising death to the bleeding young man.

"Yes, it is," Vaden promised and kicked the headmaster forcefully in the ribs with his booted foot. The sound of bones splintering and breaking could be heard and almost made Vaden vomit onto the floor. He watched the older man's eyes widen with shock. No sound came from the headmaster's open mouth as blood pumped from it and he lay quietly on the hard floor.

"You killed him, Vaden," one of the boys whispered in a mixture of reverence and horror.

"God, forgive me," he croaked as his world spun crazily about him and blackness gave him temporary comfort.

Come back to me, Vaden, the seductive voice demanded.

Kai Chen.

He could hear her voice, but could not see her. Blinking once, Vaden saw the flame of a candle in front of him as his recollection faded. Then he turned and saw her pale face. Tears were slipping down her cheeks as she pulled him to her in a powerful embrace.

"I thought you lost," she sobbed into his neck as he placed his arms about her. "What happened?"

"I remembered," he revealed harshly as he held her tightly. "I merely remembered."

☯

Brooklyn Bridge
Two days later

"Isn't this lovely? Rarely do I take a ride across this bridge. It brings back such bittersweet memories of my Jean-Paul," Suzette said with a sigh, paused reflectively then continued. "We used to do this every Saturday afternoon, and then have a scrumptious luncheon at some romantic restaurant.. Jean-Paul was so terribly romantic."

"You miss him very much, but you have been blessed to be so loved," Kai Chen commented and watched as the elderly woman threw her a poignant look.

"I am twelve years older than your father, almost sixty-five years old, and I question how a young woman can seem so perspicacious."

The twinkling in her aunt Suzette's eyes told Kai Chen she was lightly jesting, yet complimenting her. However, Kai Chen had no idea what 'perspicacious' was. There were so many American words and phrases she did not understand just yet. She would ask Vaden what it meant tonight when she saw him at dinner. In the meantime, she would merely pretend to understand.

After viewing the Brooklyn Bridge, Suzette insisted on having lunch at one of Brooklyn's finer restaurants. They were directed to the center of the room by the maître d, all eyes on Kai Chen as they studied her unusual beauty, grace and distinct outfit. Their interest doubled when they recognized her aunt who was the most generous patrons to the arts in New York.

"My, but aren't you incredibly lovely in that suit." Suzette exclaimed delightedly as her gaze traveled over the brownish-pink tailored wool-serge suit. The jacket consisted of a high waistband, wide revers, narrow velvet collar, inset sleeves decorated at the wrists with three pearl buttons and vertical pockets on the natural waist position. The matching narrow skirt came to just below her ankles with the cream silk blouse flattering her slender figure with a high round neckline. A gold and amber brooch adorned her throat. Her straw hat with wide upturned brim and large crown was draped with brown silk to match the outsize bow trimming. "I do believe I have never seen anything quite like it."

"You are very gracious," Kai Chen said with a smile as they were seated. "Tell me of my father. What was he like growing up?"

For the next two hours they dined on succulent beef smothered in a rich, creamed sauce, steamed asparagus and creamy, whipped potatoes, followed by cherry tarts covered with a light sweet glaze. Suzette spoke of her late Jean-Paul and their wonderful marriage that had unfortunately, never engendered any children, and of David Boussard. Kai Chen told her of his life in China, of his unwavering faith in his religion and his devotion to it.

"What was your mother like? How did David meet her? She must have been very brave to travel from America to wed him then live in a strange country."

Kai Chen tried to maintain her composure as she carefully placed her folded napkin on the linen tablecloth. *How to answer without deception*, she asked herself as she struggled to maintain her integrity.

"Mother was a kind, loving woman with black hair and dark eyes. I do not know the complete story of their courtship but he met her in China. And yes, she was a very brave woman," Kai Chen hedged, trying to answer honestly, yet knowing she lied. She lied by omission. Though no longer pledged to her vows it pained her still to lie to this sweet woman.

"I am sure she was a delightful woman, a good mother and wife," Suzette expounded with a tremulous smile. "I would have liked to have known her."

Raising her hand slightly, a waiter immediately arrived and Suzette insisted on paying the luncheon bill. Soon they were draped in their thick furs and inside a carriage returning them to Suzette's home. They alighted from the coach greeted by the beginning of rain. Dashing inside the stately home they shook off their furs and giggled as they tried to fix their askew hats.

"I do not believe I have moved that quickly in years," the older woman stated breathlessly as they moved to her sitting room. "We should have been prepared. Parasols are always proper regardless the weather."

"We are hardy. I do not suspect a little rain will hurt us," Kai Chen claimed with a grin as they settled themselves comfortably on a settee. Within minutes the butler was entering with a tray of tea.

"Oh! This is lovely. There is nothing better than hot tea on a rainy day."

"Especially with a friend," Kai Chen declared with a smile, bringing tears to Suzette's eyes.

LeBlanc Estate
That evening

"Kay, this is Lee. He will be our permanent secondary butler," Vaden announced as though it was an everyday occurrence. "Sebastian asked me to employ Lee as a favor."

Kai Chen nodded once toward the thin oriental man and caught herself as she prepared to bow. His upper body bent forward in respect as their eyes met. Immediately, she sensed something odd about him but was not sure what bothered her. Her time around Vaden was changing her. Her ability to intuitively assess people seemed to be faltering.

"He speaks very little English. Since you are proficient in Chinese I thought you could teach him."

"I would be honored, Vaden," she said, but felt her skin crawl at the way Lee's eyes roved over her meticulously, as though memorizing every detail about her. It would be wise to remain very circumspect around this man.

"Many thanks, gracious lady," Lee said in Chinese and Kai Chen inwardly cringed. Servants gossiped and this one would be no different. Vaden announcing she spoke Chinese would be talked of amongst the staff, which would then filter out to others. She only prayed it did not come back to haunt her by people asking questions of how she learned to speak the language. She watched Lee follow Vaden to his new quarters where the other servants were located.

For the next week Kai Chen took an hour each day and worked with Lee and his English, but she did not enjoy it. There was a sneaking quality to him she did not trust and made a mental note to herself to follow him one day. She was interested to know why he disappeared for a few hours each day and what he was doing. It also bothered her how he seemed to lurk about every corner and moved as silently as Ji-Kin Lau. Was she discovered then? Would the Triad arrive here to capture and kill her at Vaden's home? She would not doubt it could happen.

"You are still as lovely as ever," James proclaimed as he rushed forward to greet Kai Chen.

"You are too kind," she replied with a smile as he grasped her hands within his.

Vaden observed them as he poured himself a whiskey. He had spent a lonely, miserable day without Kai Chen as she visited her aunt. Now he would share her with the prolific artist, James Baxter. He grimaced as he realized he selfishly wanted her for himself. Alone. Just the two of them sharing dinner, conversing, quietly sitting before the fire as they usually did.

"Vaden, I profusely thank you for rescuing my friend," the thin man stated frankly as he accepted a whiskey from him.

"The circumstances were certainly unique. Wouldn't you agree, Kay?"

Kai Chen's eyes danced mischievously as she broke away from James and tucked her arms into Vaden's. She could see the fire burning in his gaze whenever another man was near her. He was jealous, a feeling she was discovering herself at the thought of him around Caroline Pennington.

"Definitely," she agreed.

"Dinner," came the announcement from the open doorway of the sitting room.

Kai Chen looked at the new servant, Lee. His dark eyes peered intently at her before looking humbly downward. There was something suspicious and not right about the servant that she could not shake, yet he had done nothing circumspect. When he was around she found her defenses rising and yet, was not sure of the cause. Maybe because he was Chinese it reminded her of her lost homeland and the reason why she had fled.

"Very well. Shall we?"

Vaden escorted Kai Chen with James walking on her other side.

The evening sped by as they enjoyed the delicious meal. By the time dessert arrived Vaden was comfortable with James and was mentally kicking himself for being so insecure with his feelings. Never had Kai Chen done or said anything inappropriate, unless it was with him. A slow smile curved his lips but it quickly vanished as James brought up Caroline Pennington's name.

"She has been asking around for you, Vaden," the man informed him innocuously.

"I am a very busy man, but knowing Caroline she will catch up to me eventually," he asserted dryly, causing James to chuckle.

"Well, knowing Caroline as *I* do, it would behoove you to remain very busy."

Vaden's laughter eased the discomforting seriousness of the conversation as he enjoyed this light joking. James threw him a pointed glance that told him she was nothing but trouble. Nodding once, Vaden silently agreed and they rapidly changed the subject.

"Shall we adjourn to the sitting room for after dinner drinks?"

"That sounds delightful," James concurred.

Vaden assisted Kai Chen from her seat as the three of them walked arm in arm down the long hallway. Kai Chen was centered between the two men, her arms captured lightly by each as they amicably chatted, stopping occasionally so James could view a painting. Eventually they made it to the sitting room where a merry blaze in the fireplace lent warmth to the room.

"Brandy?"

"Fine," James said and accepted the snifter.

"Your tea, Miss Boussard," announced Lee as he entered the room with a large serving tray.

"Thank you, Lee."

The man left the room soundlessly and she made a mental note to observe him more carefully. His silent walk was more than mere coincidence. As she spent more time observing the servant she realized his placement at their home was more than sheer coincidence. He was most likely a spy, but for whom?

"Vaden, I would like to extend my gratitude for you having me this evening. I know I arrived without invitation, but my schedule is such that plans change without notice."

"It was a pleasure having you here, James. You are welcome any time," Vaden offered, and knew he meant it. James was a pleasant man and certainly no threat. He was just a devoted friend to Kai Chen, the woman who had changed his life so drastically one evening several years ago.

"Well, I really should be heading home. However, I have a request of you, *Kay*," James said pointedly with a twinkle in his eyes.

"Of course," she accepted as he played along with the charade she was committed to.

"I would like your permission to paint a portrait of you."

"I -," she began, but halted. She was not sure how to respond. She was flattered and surprised. Kai Chen's gaze met Vaden's, her uncertainty reflected in emerald depths.

"Think on it. I do not need your answer this evening. Here is my card. Let me know," James stated and handed her the small white card. Leaning down, he kissed her cheek briefly. Turning to Vaden, he shook his hand. "I will have another exhibition shortly. However, this will be a private auction. I hope you will attend."

"Most certainly we shall attend. I am always looking for new artwork," Vaden assured him as they walked into the foyer. Lee assisted James with his coat and hat. "I hope to see you soon."

"As do I. And personally, I would stay clear of Caroline were I you. It is purported she is generous with her favors."

Vaden stared at James as he tugged on his dark gloves. There was only one thing he could mean!

"Would you please define that last statement?"

James took a step back, afraid he had spoken out of line, but saw the concern and suspicion in Vaden's face.

"There are words to the effect she is bedded already," he whispered in an attempt to be discreet, then added, "and not by one man. There have been many."

Tong Headquarters
One week later

"It is advantageous that the shipment has arrived," said Mock Duck, leader of the Tong council. His eyes raked over the dark haired American slowly. "Who is this woman, Ji-Kin Lau, you speak of?"

"I do not know her. All I have gleaned is that she arrived from China on my ship, demanding to know where to locate the Tong from one of my men. Shortly afterward she disappeared on the docks and they have not seen her since," Sebastian Madden told him.

"Curious," Mock Duck hissed before reverting to his native language as he and his council deliberated over a course of action to take.

"If it helps, my men said there was something very bizarre about her. Her face was totally covered by a scarf, except her eyes, and she was never seen during the light of day, only at night," Sebastian interrupted. Immediately the men stopped talking and scowled at him.

"Helps? I cannot see how that insignificant information helps," the leader spat. "Do not speak again."

Sebastian bit his tongue. He wanted nothing more than to bash the insolent Chinaman's teeth in, but these men were ruthless and did not play games. He had witnessed how sly and unemotional they were in dealing with their prey or their business transactions. It would not do to displease them, but he had pride, too. Unfortunately he would have to suck up his pride at the moment. He was in dire financial trouble.

The Boxer Rebellion had stripped him of his importing business and he had lost several of his ships. Now his passenger liners were threatened by political wars breaking out in Germany, France, and South America. He was so far in debt right now that unless Caroline married Vaden quickly, acquired his fortune then disposed of him, Sebastian knew he was going to lose it all and end up in prison.

"When will your next shipment of opium arrive? The demand is far greater than the supply you have been issuing," Mock Duck asked him sharply and Sebastian visibly flinched.

"It is no longer financially viable for me to secure opium. I will have to find another location to procure it or find another drug," Sebastian divulged, hoping this Chinese mafia would not behead him where he stood for making this decision without their input.

A hush fell about the room as the Tong leader rose and walked toward him. There was a smile on his angelic face as he halted in front of Sebastian, although his eyes remained lifeless, cold.

"I understand, Mister Madden," the oriental man said and extended his hand.

Sebastian sighed with relief as he took the gesture of friendship and bonding. It was all right. They were going to work with him. All of his worry had been for naught. Relieved he had been wrong as to their reaction to his declaration he grinned and gripped the man's hand.

Suddenly, his arm was being jerked forcefully behind him, the tendons in his shoulder ripping and the bone snapping. Screaming in agony he was shoved to the floor face first. Blood spurted from his nose and mouth as he hit the wood, pain blinding him from every inch of his body. A foot slammed between his legs and into his crotch as the very breath was knocked from him.

Gasping for breath, bile rose in his throat at the savage agony shooting from his prized manhood. Vomit pumped from his mouth as he used his free hand to clutch his crushed groin, the other arm lying at an awkward angle behind him.

"You should not have made that decision alone, Mister Madden," the man said with a beatific smile as he squatted before him. "Perhaps this will remind you, should you think to do so again."

A fist slammed into Sebastian's face as a creeping numbness took him to a place of relief from the horrific agony inflicted upon him.

☯

Chinatown
That evening

"You will locate the leader of the Tong and express my desire to become one with them. Explain we are from the Triad, their homeland, and of what our mission is here. They will consent to my admission. If not, I shall become their new leader," Ji-Kin Lau said glibly to the cleric who lay beside her.

"Yes, Ji-Kin Lau."

"What is wrong with you?" Grasping his flaccid member she yanked him to her, enjoying his yelp of pain. "For weeks now you have been unable to service me!"

"I do not know," he winced as she raked her nails across his spongy flesh that refused to harden. "I will try harder."

"Bah!" Shoving him away from her, she stood and glared down at him evilly. "You are not a man! Leave my sight and do not return until you have news from the Tong."

"Yes, Ji-Kin Lau." Scrambling rapidly, the cleric dressed as he stumbled across the room. His body trembled with fear as he threw nervous glances over his shoulder as he neared the door.

Ji-Kin Lau smirked as she strolled casually toward him, her naked body glorious to behold, her face a nightmare come to life with its disfigurement. Sliding her hands over his shoulders she then clasped his throat and squeezed ever so slightly. Her talon nails broke the skin as she purred softly into his ear, "Do not try to disappear in America, cleric. Make me hunt for you and you will suffer beyond comprehension."

"Never, Ji-Kin Lau! I will return quickly," he promised, sliding his feet into his soft black slippers.

"I will expect this to be operational, as well," she commanded and gripped his wilting member savagely. His cry of pain was music to her ears. "Very good. Be gone."

Ji-Kin Lau watched as he scurried from the room, bent over in pain from her vicious grasp she had eventually released. She needed a man. A real man! It had been almost a month since the cleric had been able to perform. Strutting across the room, Ji-Kin Lau donned her clothing and wrapped a dark scarf about her face. Within minutes she was slipping through a back door to one of the many brothels littered among the back alleys of Chinatown.

Smiling cattily, she peered into each room as she passed looking for just the right one. A real man, better yet, men.

"We have been waiting for over an hour for her! Where is she?" demanded one of four huge American men who stood towering over a small man.

"I swear she will be here soon. It is difficult to find a woman able to handle such men as you," the Chinese man replied quickly, soothing their ego and pride as he backed warily out of the room. "I will be back with her momentarily."

"Here I am," Ji-Kin Lau said throatily as she sashayed into the small room past the eager group of men. The proprietor stared at her, not recognizing her and at the moment not caring. If she wanted to service these four men at once, why would he object? He had already taken their money.

There was only a large four poster bed in the room with black leather straps attached to each post. Ji-Kin Lau liked the looks of it immensely. Observing the four large men she stared at their swollen, throbbing members already swelling in their pants and literally salivated. Finally!

"You may do whatever you wish with me, but I ask you not to remove my scarf covering my face. It will lend an air of mystery," she purred to them as she began to remove her clothes.

"Sure," the men chorused as the proprietor closed the door behind him with a sigh of relief. Quickly they shed their clothes, vying for position around the makeshift bed. Within minutes Ji-Kin Lau's arms and legs were tied to each post and she was shrieking wildly in horrendous pain and glorious ecstasy as they took turns using her in every conceivable manner.

Not long after, they began again.

Pennington Manor
That evening

"Bring him upstairs, quickly," Caroline hissed quietly. Her voice was urgent as the servants carefully lifted Sebastian's battered and bleeding body off the marble floor to her father's house.

"Clean the blood off the floor and bring medical supplies. Then send for a doctor."

She stared intently at each servant. "Keep word of this. I will have your job and your head should you awaken my father or speak of this to anyone."

The fear in their eyes was answer enough as they took the injured man upstairs and placed him in a spare bedroom in the east wing. She and her father used the west wing of the house. He would never know Sebastian was here.

Caroline looked at her love's swollen and pummeled face, which was distorted from the beating it had taken Sebastian did not even look like the man she had known for so long. What had happened to him? Who could have done this, and why? Shoving her deliberations aside she prayed he would survive. With his injuries he appeared as though dead already.

"Carefully now, place him on the bed," she directed. "Remove his clothing so we can see his wounds. I daresay some are internal by the look of him."

The two men quickly and conscientiously removed Sebastian's clothes. As they removed his pants, they both gasped and turned a sickly green color.

"Dear Lord!"

"Oh, my God!"

Both men's cry of astonishment and revulsion brought Caroline to the bed to see what abhorrence they were staring at. As she reached the side of the bed she felt bile rise in her throat and quickly turned away. Blood covered Sebastian's groin where he had been severely and permanently damaged. Never had she seen a more gruesome and hideous sight with his testicles smashed beyond repair.

Turning back she noticed his legs were not injured, although his sides, chest and back were covered with bruises and swelling. There was no doubt several of his ribs were broken. A doctor would have to determine whether he had internal harm. One shoulder was distorted at an odd angle, horribly swollen and almost black. His face! If it were not for his familiar thatch of dark hair, she would never have known it was Sebastian.

"I have never seen anything so terrible," one of the servants whispered as he carefully placed a clean sheet over the unconscious man. "It would be a blessing were he to die."

Caroline felt outrage sweep through her at the comment, but as she looked down where blood seeped into the sheet covering his groin, she suddenly felt herself crumble. She had to agree. Sebastian's manhood was destroyed. If his injuries did not kill him, the knowledge that he would never sexually perform as a man again would.

CHAPTER FIFTEEN

"Strategy without tactics is the slowest route to victory. Tactics without strategy is the noise before defeat."
— Sun Tzu, *The Art of War*

Sitting back against the leather cushioned seat of the carriage, Vaden closed his eyes and tried to vanquish the offensive remembrance of Caroline's breasts swaying before his face as she rode him to fulfillment over a month ago. That night was still a blur to him. Vaden knew he had to have been duped. He had not been drunk that evening of Caroline's visit. How would he get himself out of the fix he was in? How could he dismiss Caroline and what he had done to her as if she were nothing but a common trollop? Yet, how could he marry her and remove Kai Chen from his life? She was the other half that made him whole.

Vaden lamented his current predicament with Caroline. It was one he did not desire, but the point was moot. He was in it and there was no getting out. The only decent course was to marry Caroline and be subjected to a life of misery. Forever he would lose his China doll.

"Why? Why?"

His verbal rage was muffled within the carriage as he slammed his fist against the frame of the vehicle. He had asked himself that question many times. Why had this happened to him again? Why was it Caroline, instead of Kai Chen?

"It is simple, you lecherous bastard. You were drunk, lusting for Kai Chen and took another to replace her a month ago," he answered himself. "It still does not explain that night and his unusual behavior, or his inability to remember what happened."

Arriving home, he surged out of the carriage and stormed inside. He entered his library and paced the room like a caged tiger as he tried to consider another course of action other than marriage to Caroline. He could not think of any course of action that she or her father would willingly accept if she was pregnant.

Standing before a tall window, Vaden stared outside at the billowy white snow covering the expanse of land that belonged to him. Soon, it might be Caroline Pennington's, also. The idea made him shudder. In her own way Caroline was a beautiful and vivacious creature, but he could see into the depth of her soul, her cold and calculating eyes, and discerned she was frivolous, narcissistic, and manipulative. He understood her desire to be with him. It was not solely for him, it was for his wealth. Combined with her father's riches she would inherit one day it would make her one of the most affluent women in America.

Caroline had flirted outrageously with him but he had never been tempted to bed her. However, in one night of stupidity he had apparently used her like some cheap prostitute. Now it was time for him to make retribution as a responsible man and a gentleman, if she was pregnant. It did not soothe the ache in his soul, nor quench the hope in his heart that somehow, someday, Kai Chen Boussard would be the wife he had always longed for.

☯

Three weeks later

Idly, Kai Chen loitered about the foyer of the LeBlanc Estate then went to the sitting room. The memory of Vaden's mouth on her femininity could not be forgotten. Never would she have thought she could behave so brazenly or find his intimate touch so exciting. Vaden's gratification moments later, and knowing she was the cause of it, had made her feel wanton, powerful and erotic. It was highly stimulating knowing they could bring each other to climax so easily without fully consummating their physical union. She had never considered herself a sexual person, had taken the vow of celibacy to avoid such thoughts and desires, and had kept busy her entire life to keep her pure views.

Until now.

Now, Kai Chen wondered where this newfound intimate discovery would lead her with Vaden. Certainly to his bed. It was inevitable. The image of his manhood in her hands, large and swollen with desire, lingered in her mind. It had been the first time she had ever seen a man nude. She had not seen him in the training room, even after he had spilled his seed on her body. And Vaden's body was beautiful. He was hard and muscular, especially his chest and stomach, but it was the unusual body part of his that she found so curious. She had discovered when he was aroused the organ inflated and throbbed demandingly in her hand. Once spent, it became somewhat smaller and soft, the event truly fascinating. Even more curious was the fluid that came from his body, which she knew could impregnate her.

An inner voice within her cried out in anger because nobody had ever talked with her about the differences between men and women. Not even her mother or grandmother. As a child she had once hid in a grove of trees and watched as a foreigner raped a Chinese woman. Though she had not seen what he violated the woman with, Kai Chen had known instinctively it came from his pants. The man had rutted and propelled his body against the screaming woman until Kai Chen had run away, fearing he would do the same to her if she was discovered.

Although she recalled this incident, Vaden's amorous pursuit of her had never frightened her. The intimate actions they had performed on each other had aroused her to a state she knew no other man could. Her heart raced just thinking of touching him again, of him touching her. This new awakening of her body yearned for more, more of his expert loving, more than they had done thus far. She wanted him inside her.

As though reading her thoughts the sound of a door opening announced Vaden's presence. Then his hands encircled her waist and drew her inside the room. The door closed quickly behind them. The familiar scent and touch of Vaden was like an aphrodisiac as she let herself relax against him. She felt the warmth of his body against hers, his stiff arousal pressing between her buttocks. It brought forth a sound from her, a mixture of surprise, desire, and satisfaction. His answering groan as he nuzzled the side of her neck sent shivers down her body where they landed at the pulsing between her thighs.

"You are presumptuous, Foolish American," she sighed seductively, her hum of excitement in her voice urging him to further action.

"You are driving me wild, Kai Chen. Let me taste your sweetness again," he growled in her ear, his implied promise of fulfillment in the tempting words.

The image of him between her thighs, drinking her essence, sent a bolt of passion through her that she could not contain. Her body shivered as her breath was released in a long sigh. Immediately, his hands slid upward and clasped her breasts, his fingers flicking the hard pebbles through her dress.

"I have thought of nothing but you for days. I must have you," he murmured as his teeth nipped at the tender flesh of her neck. "Do not deny me."

"I will never deny you," she replied as her emotions overrode her better sense, and his. Denial was futile.

A discreet cough engendered the wedge needed to detach them from their emotions and each other. Guiltily, Kai Chen stepped away from him and kept her face averted to hide her humiliation at having been caught in such a torrid embrace. Vaden spun around as if slapped violently to glare at the uninvited intruder. It was the new servant, Lee. His head was lowered and his black eyes downcast so they could not see his satisfied mien. Vaden moved his body to protect Kai Chen behind him.

"Sorry to disturb. Knock, no answer. Madden, sir," the man said in stilted English.

Vaden's fury was evident as he viewed the man who remained humbly bent before him. He had not heard a knock at the closed doors to this room. He had not heard the man open a door and enter. He would have to speak with his staff to correct the man's faulty habits. His privacy would not be violated by anyone! And what the devil was Sebastian Madden doing here? The man was in terrible condition.

"Send him in," Vaden ground out angrily as he worked to control his tangled emotions. His body still screamed for release within Kai Chen's virginal folds as his outrage at having been caught in an illicit position with her scorched him. Extending a hand to the woman he loved, he caressed her cheek softly before placing distance between them. Suppressing his physical desire he poured himself a drink and gulped it like a man who had been without water for a week and had just found a well. He glanced at Sebastian as the man limped into the room, his arm still in a sling.

"Ah! There you are! I have had a time trying to track you down. Never thought I would find you home in the middle of the day," Sebastian said in a gravelly voice as he entered the room with a distinct limp as he walked. Vaden noted the bruising to his face had virtually healed.

Vaden greeted him with a twisted smile and held up his snifter. "Like one?"

"It is too early in the day for my tastes. Well, who have we here?" The shorter man's interested gaze alighted on Kai Chen who stood near the settee demurely. "My, it is the lovely Kay Boussard."

With a slight nod she asked with her musical voice, "How are you, Mister Madden?"

"I am alive," he said cryptically as he captured her hand. Turning her slender hand over he pressed his lips to her wrist then backed away at her disapproving frown.

"If you will excuse me, gentlemen," Kai Chen blushed as she exited the room in a flurry of skirts.

"Your little hummingbird is a shy creature."

Vaden glowered at Sebastian and slammed his glass on a varnished table nearby. Sebastian rarely paid social calls to anyone anymore since his disfigurement. He wondered at the occasion.

"Yes, she is. What is it that brings you here, Sebastian?"

"Is she living here?" Sebastian's eyes gleamed with curiosity as he noted Vaden's expression darken at the personal question. "Surely you know your dalliance with her need end quickly before you marry Caroline. If you must have her, put her up as mistress in town."

Vaden's control nearly snapped as he grabbed Sebastian by the coat lapels and scowled at him. Frosty daggers seemed to emanate from his eyes as he leaned into his friend's face. There was no doubt as to the fury exploding inside of Vaden at this insult made against Kai Chen.

"Never, *ever*, speak of Kay like that again," he threatened menacingly. Thrusting the startled man from him, Vaden stood before Sebastian with spread legs with his hands on trim hips. He was enraged! How dare Sebastian talk about Kai Chen as if she were nothing more than a common whore? How dare he insult him with the suggestion of keeping her as his mistress?

How dare you continue the seduction of Kai Chen, his inner conscience retaliated.

Instantly his fury abated as he recognized some truth to Sebastian's words. For some time now he had avoided telling Kai Chen the reality of their situation. He kept hoping some miracle would occur, that Caroline would declare her love for another man, inform him she was not pregnant or he would simply die in his sleep. But, none seemed to happen and he had to face Kai Chen eventually with his damnable news. By continually putting it off and lecherously seducing her he was only worsening matters.

"I think you need help, Vaden. This is getting out of hand. Correct?"

Rubbing a calloused hand over his face, he stared at Sebastian with utter misery.

"I am in love with Kay, but may have to marry Caroline if she is pregnant. I have been waiting for her to show up on my doorstep any day to make the announcement. There is nothing worse than being torn between passion and honor."

"You truly are in a fix, old man."

Wearily Vaden turned and strode over to a fine winged chair and collapsed in it.

"I know."

Later Evening
LeBlanc Estate

The sudden slam of a door brought reality crashing back to Vaden as he sighed with vexation. A woman's high-pitched voice caught his attention as his eyes narrowed dangerously.

Caroline Pennington.

Anger surged through him anew at the desolate unfairness of it all. For years he had done nothing but dream of green eyes and gorgeous auburn hair against ivory skin. Then, in one night of barely remembered insanity he had ruined any chance of ever having Kai Chen.

Foolish American. The phrase echoed in his head as her musical voice repeated it over and over.

"Oh, Vaden! Darling! Where are you?"

Groaning, he stalked across the room and poured himself a tall whiskey. He dreaded the confrontation about to occur, but what in hell had he expected? If he was not going to the dragon then he should have known she would come to him! Downing the drink in one gulp he slammed the glass down on the polished wood of the table.

The doors surged open to the sitting room as he turned dejectedly to greet her. Caroline dashed in, dainty, blond and dressed in a deep green velvet gown with her breasts practically heaving over the bust line. The sight of her skin made his flesh crawl as the memory of her large, swaying breasts sagging before his mouth during their illicit evening came to him. Her fair hair was swept up loosely into a fashionable bun with ribbons woven around it, but the color seemed brassy and harsh compared to Kai Chen's thick tresses that gleamed like fine mahogany.

"Why, here you are! Vaden, darling," Caroline purred as she pressed her chest against his seductively, "we must speak in private. I have news to convey."

"We are alone, so privacy is assured. What is it now?"

Disengaging her arms from around his neck easily, Vaden escorted her to the settee where she pulled him down beside her. He felt as though a noose was closing tightly around his neck as she practically devoured him with her insidious gaze. Although he comprehended the import behind her visit, he prayed it would not be so.

"Why it is simply the most unexpected news," she declared and paused for affect, then continued, "I am pregnant!"

LeBlanc Estate
The Next Afternoon

The sound of a carriage outside snapped Kai Chen out of the preoccupation consuming her. Looking out a window she saw Caroline Pennington emerging from the elaborate coach. Her black hat, gloves and shoes were the only things showing, other than the gorgeous, thick black fur swirling around her ankles. With her blond hair and flushed complexion she looked every bit the grand lady.

A persistent foreboding troubled Kai Chen as she heard the doorbell ring. Within moments, the sound of Caroline's high-pitched voice was ringing loudly, falsely. It was not difficult to grasp the woman was artificial with her congenial words and generous deeds. It was also apparent from their previous encounters that Caroline did not like her one bit.

Kai Chen was worried about Vaden. She had not seen him since Lee had interrupted them in the sitting room the previous day. He had not been at dinner or at breakfast this morning. Clearly, something was wrong as he had disappeared without a word.

Kai Chen turned in the foyer to greet Caroline as she entered with an ostentation that brooked on vulgarity. She acted as though she was queen of this house and would do as she pleased. Caroline's sharp, assessing eyes immediately focused on her in surprise then contempt and satisfaction.

"Well, if it is not Kay Boussard! What a coincidence meeting you here," the blond declared sincerely.

"Good day, Miss Pennington. It is no coincidence. I live here."

As though the wind had been knocked from her sails, Caroline's mouth fell open. Quickly, she composed herself and strolled casually across the room. With a slightly shaking hand she gazed at herself in a large mirror. Satisfied with her own beauty Caroline's gaze lifted to meet Kai Chen's emerald green stare.

"How long have you lived here, Miss Boussard?" There was an underlying current of hostility and smugness to her words.

"That is none of your concern, Caroline," Vaden advised her coldly as he stepped into the foyer from the sitting room and shut the tall doors behind him with a soft click. Both women glanced at him with different expressions on their faces. Kai Chen's held confusion and wariness, Caroline's spite and triumph.

"Oh, but I think it is my concern since I am marrying you, Vaden," she said with dramatic flair as she turned her twinkling blue eyes toward her adversary.

Kai Chen's face turned a ghostly gray as her eyes widened and her throat worked convulsively. It could not be true! Vaden had implied they were to marry. They had loved each other's bodies intimately and had rejoiced in it although they had not fully consummated their union. She had even designed a wedding gown for herself and given the instructions to the couturier. Kai Chen had simply been waiting for Vaden's official proposal of marriage.

Now, searching Vaden's face for denial to Caroline's claim, Kai Chen saw his crestfallen features instead. His guilt, shame, and sorrow reflected from his dark, stormy blue eyes. A sharp pain, deep inside her heart, soon radiated throughout her body as the knowledge that he had used her and lied to her filtered through her mind.

Caroline noticed the unspoken interplay between them and seized the moment with both hands viciously. "Vaden! Why, you haven't even told her I am carrying your child?"

Kai Chen felt the world crumbling beneath her feet as she kept her stoic gaze fixed on Vaden, willing him to deny Caroline's allegations, willing him to assert his love for her, willing him to claim all was a lie. But instead he stalked across the room angrily and liberally filled a snifter with brandy.

"Vaden?"

Kai Chen's delicate voice sounded weak and pathetic as she waited to hear him speak. By the pained expression on his face and Caroline's self-satisfied air, she knew it to be true. He was marrying another woman who he had made love to and who was carrying his unborn child.

Pride, a trait not considered acceptable in her religion, was the only thing keeping Kai Chen standing on her feet as the blood drained from her head, leaving her cold and numb. She had never permitted herself to undergo the rueful sentiment of pride until now. Now, it was the only detail sustaining her in this, her most recent nightmare.

All of her life she had pushed aside the belief she would ever find the love of a man, had known she would never marry or have children because of her lineage. Then Vaden had come along and opened her mind and heart to a new world, full of virgin notions and unrealistic dreams. She had let herself be lured into trusting him and her secret wishes. It was a painful learning experience, one she would never forget, aside many others.

"Is this true, Vaden?"

"I was recently informed of her condition," he admitted as he gulped the fiery liquid until it was completely gone then poured himself another.

"Recently? I told you yesterday," Caroline interjected heatedly.

Vaden's face flushed bright red. Whether it was from shame or anger Kai Chen did not know or care. He had not told her. He had not respected her enough to admit to his betrayal. This hurt her worse than any physical assault she had ever received. Her heart felt as though it was splintering into several large fragments with agonizing slowness.

It was breaking.

"If you will excuse me," Kai Chen said with as much calm dignity as she could muster and smoothly walked to the doors.

"Kay, wait!" The desperation in Vaden's voice almost stopped her. Almost.

"Vaden! I warn you, I shall not suffer this arrangement. You cannot think to marry me and keep her as mistress," Caroline snapped and actually blanched as he loomed over her.

He was enraged, ready to kill by the wild expression on his face. They heard the doors close quietly upstairs. Kay Boussard was leaving. Good! Lifting her gaze to meet his Caroline gulped visibly, but stood her ground. She had to play her part fully or possibly lose all she and Sebastian had carefully worked for.

"Let me clarify things for you Caroline. I do not love you. I have never loved you. Nor will I. *Ever.* We will be wed out of circumstance. Do not expect me to ever beget you with child again. Enjoy your life here for it shall be a lonely one," he said coldly and finality.

"You love her, don't you? You actually love that little nobody! Why would you want her tall, shapeless body when you could have mine?" she demanded from him as she ripped open the bodice of her gold gown, exposing her heavy breasts indecently.

Vaden's disgusted look actually made her flinch as he stalked away from her, bounding up the large staircase. Caroline felt total humiliation at his snub and was incensed that he preferred Kay Boussard. Every man she had ever known had told her she was the most beautiful woman, the best lover they had ever known.

Every man except Vaden. He had never disguised his indifference toward her. His current contempt toward her only added fuel to her spiteful fire. So, Vaden though himself in love with Kay Boussard. Well, when she got done with the enigmatic woman no man would want her. With a satisfied smile Caroline pulled the bodice of her gown together and proceeded upstairs to show Kai Chen what Vaden's lust for her had just accomplished with her torn bodice, albeit the story a little lie.

"You will leave my room now or I will be forced to harm you."

The softly spoken words were loud enough for Caroline to hear as she hid in the shadows of the hallway. Harm him? How did Kay Boussard think she could hurt Vaden? The idea was preposterous! Covering her mouth with her hand to quell a giggle, she listened as she tiptoed quietly toward Kay's bedroom door.

"Kai Chen, listen to me. I can explain," Vaden growled savagely. The despair in his voice made Caroline almost sick with revulsion. She had never heard Vaden beg a woman for anything and it was truly unmanly, a side of him she had never known existed.

"Caroline has explained sufficiently. I will not ask you to leave me in peace again," she warned as her voice hardened. "Allow me to depart with dignity, Vaden."

"I will not lose you, Kai Chen! I love you!"

Caroline's eyes expanded as she heard the familiar name. Sebastian had said the Tong was looking for a woman named Kai Chen. It couldn't be! A feeling of great elation enveloped her as she fought to contain her excitement. So, Kay Boussard was not who she claimed to be. It explained much about her; her exotic looks, her unusual voice and panache, her air of mystery.

"You lost me the night you impregnated Caroline," came the clipped rejoinder from Kay Boussard. "Please leave my sight. I do not wish to gaze upon you ever again."

"I refuse to-," Vaden began heatedly.

Caroline strained to hear what was happening. Material ripped. The sudden sound of Kay Boussard's soft grunt and Vaden's fierce yell of obvious pain echoed in the hallway before the sound of a loud crash emanated from the room, and then complete silence. Had Vaden just killed her? Shock at the sudden turn of events brought Caroline out of the shadows to discover what had happened. Creeping to the opened bedroom door she peeked in and saw Vaden lying on the floor. He was unconscious, or dead. Kay Boussard, or Kai Chen, was standing beside him bearing an expression of anguish on her pretty features. Tears streaked her pretty face as her fingers lingered on Vaden's neck.

"What have you done?" Caroline whispered in horror, capturing Kai Chen's attention.

"He is not harmed and will come around shortly. It will give me time to leave," she stated with a broken voice as she continued to pack her meager belongings.

Caroline stared at the huge man. How had she done it? There was no blood, no broken vase or weapon anywhere to be seen. How could she have felled a giant like Vaden without using something? Suspicion and fear lanced her breast as she saw Kai Chen pointedly glance at her exposed breasts. Clutching the remnants of her bodice together Caroline actually blushed. Though she did not mind a man staring at her magnificent endowments, she certainly did not want this woman!

"Vaden is a lustful man, as you can see," Caroline told her smugly as she pulled her bodice together. She gloated as she noticed her verbal dart hit home as Kai Chen flinched. "There is no one woman who can satisfy him. Did he claim he loves you? You are not the first he has claimed to love and will you be the last. Our marriage has been arranged for years.

Our families have always planned to join, to build one great financial empire."

Kai Chen said nothing as she completed her packing with shaking hands. Her silence angered Caroline, but it did not matter. Within minutes her competition would be gone and Caroline would assert herself as mistress of this estate, and of Vaden. With her newfound information on Kay Boussard, of who she truly was, her position in this challenging game was finally secure.

☯

May 1901
Home of Suzette Boussard-Minot

"My dear Kay, I am so dreadfully sorry. Of course, you are welcome here. I am thrilled you chose to come to me," the small woman cooed affectionately as she pulled Kai Chen into her arms for a healing hug. "I just cannot believe that man would do such a thing! He seemed to adore you."

"Shi de. People can be great deceivers," Kai Chen sighed, her eyes red rimmed and swollen from crying.

"Shi de? I do not understand," Suzette declared in confusion as a look of dismay crossed Kai Chen's face.

"I am sorry. I reverted to Chinese," she stated quickly. "I am weary and my homeland language takes over. Forgive me."

Suzette's eyes danced merrily as she escorted her niece into the sitting room where Manfred arrived with a tray of tea and sweet biscuits. Waving him off with a conspiratorial glance, the elderly woman doted over the distressed Kai Chen by preparing her tea and patting her hands. Feeling the slight swelling of the young woman's knuckles, she inspected the rough skin and gasped.

"My dear, whatever have you done to your hands?"

Kai Chen's expression continued to reflect distress as she tried to pull her ungloved hand from the older woman's grasp. Her head was spinning and her thoughts crumbling as she felt the daunting oppression of keeping secrets weighing upon her already feeble emotional state.

I am tired of the secrets and lies. I can no longer continue this charade. I must be honest with this woman and face the outcome, Kai Chen told herself solemnly as a heavy sigh escaped her parted lips.

"There is much to tell you," Kai Chen said then proceeded to explain to her aunt about her parents, her mother being Chinese, the story of her escape from China to sitting beside Suzette now. She did not mention the Wing Chun or its legacy as it would most certainly overwhelm the woman. "I never meant to deceive you or hurt you. I simply wanted-," Kai Chen attempted to clarify but Suzette held up a hand with a kind smile to interrupt.

"Kay, thank you for sharing so much of the past with me. I do not care that David married a Chinese woman. You are still my only family. I have come to know you and to care for you deeply," the woman exclaimed as tears threatened to spill from her eyes. "You have been through so much. I am just sorry you did not come to me when you first arrived here. But I do understand your fear of rejection."

Kay embraced the woman as they both wept for so many things, but also for relief and acceptance of having each other. For a few hours they continued to chat while composing themselves. Manfred arrived to announce dinner, breaking up their reminiscing of their different pasts. And for the next few days they began a wonderful discovery of New York, each other and their deepening relationship as family and dear friends.

Tong Headquarters
Chinatown

"I have news of the nun, Kai Chen," the informant, Lee, eagerly report to Mock Duck. "She was residing at Vaden LeBlanc's estate but has since moved out to live with her aunt across town. I have seen her performing her martial art. She is a force to be reckoned with, but not impossible to defeat."

Mock Duck listened with fascination as he pressed his fingertips together forming a steeple shape, which he rested his chin upon lightly. Lee continued to update all information obtained on the mysterious nun and happenings at the LeBlanc Estate. As he finished, a commotion outside caused everyone in the large room to become silent. Suddenly, the door burst open with the wood splintering in pieces. The shattered pieces flew across the room in all directions. A huge piece shot through the back of Lee's neck and out the front of his throat as he slid quickly to the floor in death.

The guards who had raised their weapons to shoot at what they perceived to be the police or rival gang members, cried out in surprise and anguish. Mock Duck watched in amazement as a single blade imbedded itself into each guard's left eye. As they dropped their weapons and fell to the ground, leaving him without his usual band of members for protection, Mock Duck watched as a masked feminine form proceeded into the room.

"Are you the Tong leader who killed my cleric?" Ji-Kin Lau asked in a deceptively mild tone.

Mock Duck noted the numerous razor-edged coins she held between her fingers and knew he dare not move. If this one woman had successfully thrown six blades into the eyes of his six guards then he would have to tread carefully to plan his attack to kill her. As if reading his thoughts, Ji-Kin Lau offered him a distorted smile. The only thing he could see of her face was her eyes and lips. One eyelid had a scar, as did one side of her mouth. Her movements were pure silk as she walked silently, seductively, smoothly across the wooden floor toward him. There was a powerful quality to her that spoke of her deadly ability. He suddenly knew he was in trouble.

"I did not kill your cleric," Mock Duck said in a smooth tone of innocence. "I do not know your cleric."

"Ah, do not lie to me Mock Duck. I am from the Triad in China. I know all about your Tong operation here, and I know all about *you.*"

The woman's voice held the boldness of truth, her manner spoke of complete confidence with her martial arts skill, and her actions told of her domination in all things she wanted. And she wanted his position within the Tong. As he shifted to raise his arms and fling his axe hidden within the sleeve of his coat, several of her coins sliced into his arms. Blinding pain ripped through him as the razor-edged coins rendered his arms useless as they severed muscles, ligaments and tendons.

"Tsk, tsk, Mock Duck. First you lie and then you attempt to assault a Triad member?" Ji-Kin Lau whispered as she walked around the table to stand beside him. Bending down to gaze into his widening eyes she asked him, "Do you know what happens to someone who does those things?"

Before he could answer, Ji-Kin Lau gripped his head and with a quick, vicious snap, broke his neck, flinging his body backward. He slid across the floor, even as Ji-Kin Lau grabbed the falling chair, swung the back around to face the broken door and straddled it. Several Tong members who were just entering the room stared at the massacre before them, their faces registering alarm and incredulity. Dropping their weapons immediately, they faced the woman who sat behind the table watching them with a completely bored and relaxed expression.

"If you wish to own this American country with me, stay. If you plan to obey me without question, stay. If you have reservations, questions, or plan to thwart me in any manner, regardless of how slight, run for your life now for it will be your last opportunity," Ji-Kin Lau stated as she held out a finely manicured hand to glance at her sharp nails.

The members immediately dropped to prostrate themselves upon the wooden floor before her. Ji-Kin Lau smiled, her lips twisting grotesquely as she glanced down in front of the table where the informant, Lee, had divulged all he knew about Kai Chen Boussard. It had been opportunistic timing on her part in overhearing all of this prior to taking over the Tong here in Chinatown. Surely, this was Buddha's will in ending Kai Chen's life, and her fate to rule a country. Even if it was not China.

CHAPTER SIXTEEN

"Move swift as the Wind and closely-formed as the Wood. Attack like the Fire and be still as the Mountain."
— Sun Tzu, *The Art of War*

LeBlanc Estate
Two Weeks Later

Vaden threw himself upon the settee where he had spent so many memorable evenings with Kai Chen, only now to wallow in his misery alone. For the past two weeks he had not been to work, had not socialized, had not accepted visitors, had not eaten or bathed. A scruffy beard was already forming on his face, dark circles under his red eyes reflected his lack of sleep, and he knew he looked like a guttersnipe. He freely admitted he had not done a damned thing, except drink himself into oblivion. Presently, he held a bottle of expensive brandy in one hand and a beautiful crystal brandy snifter in the other hand. Letting out a loud string of curses he slammed the glass into the fireplace.

"Who needs a glass?" Vaden's roar of rage filled the sitting room. He understood his house staff was distressed at the change in him since the situation with Caroline Pennington had been announced, and with Kai Chen leaving. He did not particularly care what anyone thought of him right now. Even the announcement of the new servant, Lee, suddenly disappearing did not matter to him. All Vaden knew was that his life was completely ruined. He had lost an angel and acquired a bitch.

"Nobody to blame but me," he growled in disgust.

Taking a large drink from the bottle of brandy he repositioned himself on the settee, his fingers digging into the seams of the cushion. A piece of paper scratched along his nails and he rose up on one elbow to grab it. Pulling the white paper from the back cushion he opened it up to read. A white powder filtered from the paper onto the dirty shirt he had worn for three days.

"What the-?" Vaden said in confusion as he saw no writing on the small piece of paper. Bringing the paper to his nose he inhaled and instantly recognized the sweet, cloying scent of opium. There was also another distinct smell, something familiar. As he sat upright, suddenly alert with the brandy bottle forgotten, Vaden closed his eyes and smelled the outside of the paper not tainted by the opium. Perfume.

Caroline Pennington.

Suddenly, he leapt to his feet and paced the room, trying desperately to recall the night she had interrupted his dinner. Placing the brandy bottle on the table his mind began to recall everything that led up to when he had basically passed out. He and Caroline had dined then came to this room for an after dinner drink. She had spilled liquor on her dress and he had left the room to get her items to clean her dress. *He had left the room!*

Vaden slammed his fist onto a nearby table as the realization that Caroline Pennington had drugged him finally hit him with the force of a tsunami. A feral wrath consumed him as he stuffed the paper into his pants pocket and strode from the room. If it was the last thing he did, he would discover the truth from Caroline himself and then throw her to the societal wolves who would greedily consume her and then outcast her. Heaven forbid he discover anyone else in on this ruse to keep him from Kai Chen Boussard.

Not bothering to bathe or change clothes, Vaden shouted for a servant to saddle his fastest horse, and then with deadly purpose headed straight for Caroline Pennington's family manor. Her father wielded much political and financial power in New York and was well respected, but once he got wind of his daughters manipulations Vaden was certain the woman would be in dire straight with her daddy. She had gone too far with this farce! Even as rage filled his breast a sense of joy began to fill him.

I will marry Kai Chen right away if it is the last thing I ever do, he promised himself as he kicked the horse into a mad dash across town, passing carriages and even motorists in their newfangled automobiles. His lathered horse arrived at the Pennington Manor at breakneck speed. Reigning in the heaving beast, he handed the care of the animal over to the servant who met him at the front of the house. Vaden barged into the beautifully kept home without announcement.

Hearing Caroline's muffled whimpers to his right, Vaden purposefully strode toward the library and flung open the doors. A high pitched scream rent the air as Caroline pulled her legs together and dropped her dress to cover herself. Sebastian Madden jumped back from between her legs, wiping his mouth as he stared in surprise at Vaden's entrance. The blood drained from both of their faces as they realized not only were they caught in a compromising position, but Vaden was now fully aware he had been duped by both of them.

Plucking the paper from his pocket, Vaden sauntered over to Caroline and flung it at her. He noted the blood drain from her face as she recognized the item used to drug him. Sebastian had the moxy to summon up the courage to appear outraged, but cowered in fear as Vaden sneered at his once best friend with disgust.

"Of all people, after all we have been through together," Vaden pointedly bellowed at Sebastian. His perusal moved to Caroline and narrowed menacingly. His eyes were brilliant with his vehemence, causing the blonde to squirm uncomfortably. "I will ask you one time, and you had better tell me the truth. Are you pregnant with my child?"

Caroline's expression turned calculating for a mere second before she cried out in absolute terror at the wild ferocity of his crazed gaze as Vaden painfully gripped her upper arm.

"The truth!" His ferocious demand loudly echoed throughout the house as servants ran into the room to see the commotion.

"No, I am not pregnant with your child. It is Sebastian's!"

The room was utterly silent as Vaden felt his heart soar with relief, even while he watched Sebastian sink backward onto the floor dumbfounded.

"You are really pregnant?" Sebastian's question had Caroline flashing angry blue eyes at him.

"Yes! I am ruined. Good luck dealing with my father when he finds out that not only have you defiled me with child, but that you are financially ruined," she screamed harshly. Her face twisted in a nasty scowl as her eyes raked over Sebastian in loathing.

Vaden watched Sebastian's skin become a ghoulish gray pallor at her words. For a moment he almost wanted to laugh at the turn of events. He had not realized Sebastian was in financial trouble, but completely ruined? And Caroline truly was pregnant by Sebastian? The irony was almost too much for him to digest.

"You both deserve each other and all the misery you will undoubtedly produce together. Never come near me or Kay Boussard again if you value your life and everything you hold dear. Cross me again and I will ensure you have nothing left to live for," Vaden said through gritted teeth before turning on his heel and storming out of the house.

"One down, one to go," he avowed with determination and satisfaction. He would make himself presentable and pull himself emotionally together before speaking to Kai Chen. He had much to do before he confronted her with everything, and he wanted it to be perfect. There was no way he would ever lose his China doll again.

Kai Chen woke with a start.

Change is coming, her grandmother's whisper seemed to echo in her mind as she darted from the soft, downy bed. Donning the black outfit Chef Smither's had given her that first day she had stepped onto American soil, Kai Chen prepared herself. Wrapping her thick, long auburn tresses in the black scarf and tucking it tightly around her head, she sensed an impending destiny that had come full circle.

"Ji-Kin Lau," she whispered. Feelings of concern for her aunt and the butler, Manfred, surfaced as most important, even as she fought within her heart against the other emotion, revenge.

Do not allow your emotions to dictate your actions, child.

"I hold the legacy." Kai Chen stared at her reflection in the mirror. Large emerald eyes, so vivid and striking, seemed almost dead of any emotion, but within her breast her heart raced frantically as she prepared herself mentally for the fight of her life. "I am Wing Chun."

A booming knock at the front door had Kai Chen running out of her bedroom, vaulting over the railing to somersault down to the first floor in front of the door in the foyer. The butler Manfred jumped back as though struck and yelled out in surprise as she landed beside him, grabbing the door handle.

"Find Suzette. You both need to leave immediately," Kai Chen announced firmly. The steely glint in her usually kind eyes caused Manfred to nod and dart up the stairs in haste, his old body moving faster than either of them would have considered.

The Tong or Triad would not knock, so she knew it was not them coming to delicately announce their arrival. Kai Chen would have to get rid of this visitor quickly. Flinging open the door she stared at Vaden. In his hands he held a dozen red roses. There was a tentative smile on his lips. Before she could shut the door in his face she noticed black figures darting down the sidewalk toward the house. Clutching his coat she pulled him inside and hastily slammed the door, even as several blades embedded themselves into the thick hard wood.

"What the-," Vaden yelled as Kai Chen pushed him toward the stairs.

"The Triad, Ji-Kin Lau, they are here. Protect my aunt and Manfred with your life," Kai Chen demanded in a fierce tone Vaden had never heard, desperation etched across her beautiful features.

"You cannot fight them all!"

"Shi de, I can. Go. Now!" she screamed, her eyes wild with fear. With relief, she watched as Vaden bolted up the staircase to find Suzette and Manfred. Kai Chen propelled herself through the house to the kitchen, where she grabbed every knife or blade she could find. Tucking them into her waistband and within the pockets and folds of her shirt, she knew the blades were not her first choice for use, but they were her only choice at the moment. Even as her mind wanted to consider why Vaden had thought he could come here with flowers to win her over she shoved the ridiculous idea aside.

Seeing a black figure outside the window, Kai Chen hid behind the door to the kitchen, watching as the door handle turned slowly and a Tong member stepped quietly inside. Lightning fast, Kai Chen captured his arm and used his forward momentum of entering the kitchen as leverage. Flipping him head over heels, face first onto the kitchen floor, she snapped his arm at the elbow, driving the knife he held in the same hand into his back. He had no chance to scream as she twisted the knife around and up into his chest cavity, killing him instantly, his distorted arm falling to the side as she removed the lethal blade. She tucked his bloody blade into the sleeve of her tunic.

Silently, she moved across the kitchen and into the hallway of the house as she heard several downstairs windows break. Peering around a corner to the foyer, Kai Chen noticed four black figures enter the area. With lightening speed she dispersed four knives from her waist into the necks of each Tong member. Their bloody gurgles told her she had made each mark as they fell to the floor, lifeless.

"You are very good, Kai Chen, but not good enough," Ji-Kin Lau's silky sounding voice echoed in the foyer. "First I will kill the worthless butler you have become so fond of, and then your sweet, dear aunt Suzette. But I will most enjoy killing your lover, Vaden LeBlanc. Perhaps he will be willing to fuck me for his life? He certainly did not hesitate to fuck Caroline Pennington."

Ji-Kin Lau's taunts filled the house, followed by her dark laughter.

Kai Chen understood Ji-Kin Lau must have gotten her information about everyone from the servant, Lee, who had been at Vaden's estate. He had been an informant for the Tong. And Ji-Kin Lau believed she could emotionally entangled Ka Chen with words.

Do not allow your emotions to dictate your actions, child. Remembering her grandmothers words, Kai Chen's green eyes flashed with a new brilliance.

"Silly, Kai Chen, did you really think running to America would stop me from exacting my revenge? You took my life when you took my face. You took my heart when you took Prince Tuan. Now, I will take the remainder of what you hold precious, before I take you to the depths of hell!"

Ji-Kin Lau's bitter words resounded throughout the house as two Tong members rounded the corner of the hallway where Kai Chen stood. Even as they threw their knives, Kai Chen dropped to the floor by splitting her legs wide and dropping her head to the floor, even as she whipped two more kitchen knives at the assailants. The blades rooted in their chests as they fell against each other before falling onto the floor.

Kai Chen fluidly returned to her feet as she grabbed a broom. Breaking off the end of the stick to use as a small staff she moved down the hallway toward the sitting room. Using one end of the stick she flashed it before the entrance to the room and was rewarded as several razor-edged coins embedded themselves into the wood.

"Ah, clever nun!" Ji-Kin Lau applauded, even as her voice moved away from the room.

Kai Chen darted into the sitting room, rounded the corner and entered the foyer where Ji-Kin Lau awaited her. The sounds of her aunt Suzette screaming, fierce grunts and glass breaking told Kai Chen that Tong members had found them upstairs. Her heart told her that Vaden would defend them to the death. There was nothing she could do for them. Her fate was to face Ji-Kin Lau. Even as Kai Chen kept her eyes trained on the deadly woman, Ji-Kin Lau ripped off her mask to reveal her hideously deformed face.

The puckered scar ran diagonally across the length of her face from eyebrow to chin, crossing her eyelid, nose and lips. As Ji-Kin Lau smiled, it further transformed her features into something bizarre and grotesque as the skin twisted at odd angles. Kai Chen watched as Ji-Kin Lau slowly began to move toward her. They silently circled each other in the large foyer. The sounds of footsteps above them did not distract Kai Chen as she focused solely on her deadly adversary.

A blinding fast movement from Ji-Kin Lau registered with Kai Chen as she moved just as quickly. Using her long, powerful legs Kai Chen flipped into the air, avoiding the knives that sailed below her. Landing in front of Ji-Kin Lau she immediately struck the woman several times in the face with rapid fists. Blood spurted from Ji-Kin Lau's mouth as she stumbled backward against a table.

Ji-Kin Lau released a blood-curdling scream as she propelled herself forward with a series of punches and kicks. Kai Chen blocked, parried, and redirected each strike before retaliating with her own aggressive assault. Both women employed wrists, elbows, forearms, knees, shins, and feet with a speed so blinding it was impossible to ascertain their motions. Kai Chen allowed her lifetime of training to take over, almost stepping out of herself as her body moved of its own accord. As she permitted her inner chi, or life energy, to take over Kai Chen lost all deliberation and allowed the spirit of Wing Chun to consume her. A dazzling energy seemed to filter throughout her as the essence of her martial art claimed every aspect of her.

Vaguely, Kai Chen heard Manfred and Vaden talking, while Suzette's gasps filled the room, even as she and Ji-Kin Lau moved across the room like whirling dervishes'. The power and intensity of the movements Kai Chen employed were driving Ji-Kin Lau backward toward the closed main front door of the house. Kai Chen could feel an immense supremacy and unearthly thunder resonate each time she struck Ji-Kin Lau. An intense power resonated within her as the tiny woman began to falter, to stumble, and to cry out as the sound of her bones snapped with each of Kai Chen's strikes. Ji-Kin Lau fell against the door as Kai Chen directed three straight fisted punches into the tiny woman's chest, splintering her sternum and driving the broken bones into her heart.

Stepping back, Kai Chen watched as bright red blood oozed from Ji-Kin Lau's slightly parted mouth. Her dark eyes began to glaze over as death claimed her, even as her body slid slowly along the length of the door until she fell to one side. The malevolent gleam in Ji-Kin Lau's eyes vanished, leaving the empty gaze of a woman who had allowed emotions to rule her actions, who had permitted evil to rule her life, and who had not been truly worthy of the gifts she had been given in this life.

"Forgive me," Kai Chen sighed aloud, her voice ringing with true sorrow and weariness. Her head hung low and her shoulders drooped as she clenched her fists, the only sign of the struggle within her aching heart. For long minutes she stood in that spot, eyes closed as she prayed to Buddha for direction and answers.

"Kai Chen," strong, familiar hands grasped her shoulders as she was pulled into a comforting embrace. Soon, Suzette and Manfred joined Vaden in the healing embrace as Kai Chen wept for those she had been forced to kill. Again. "You made a choice, Kai Chen."

"You had no choice this day, child," the Abbess maintained. "The decision was made for us when that evil woman entered our peaceful temple.

The words echoed in Kai Chen's mind as she recalled the day that fate had seen fit to send Ji-Kin Lau into the temple. A choice that day led to the path they were on today. It was Buddha's will.

☯

"Congratulations!"

A loud cheer resounded throughout the huge, glamorous ballroom as Vaden and Kay LeBlanc entered. Romantic music from live musicians filtered the room filled with ornate white and gold decorations as over five hundred guests rose to greet the newly married couple.

Kay's snow white gown of satin with a gossamer overlay fitted her lithe, slender form like a glove, enhancing every curve and showcasing her incredible figure. The scalloped bodice in front and back sported tiny lace pointed filigrees' twinkling with minute pearls and gems sewn into the material. Her small waist was enhanced by a flowing skirt with long train.

Her hair was twisted tightly behind her head with a tiara of diamonds glittering majestically. The men and women at their wedding reception stared at the daring, gorgeous wedding gown Kai Chen had designed for herself. Her flair for clothing was the talk of the town with all designers attempting to copy them for resale.

Vaden glanced down at his bride with love shining brightly in his blue eyes. It had taken him several days to finalize the massacre at Suzette Boussard-Minot's house with the police. They were more than happy to believe Vaden had single-handedly taken out several members of the Tong, believed to have been sent by Sebastian Madden. As investigation into Chinatown's Tong continued it was soon discovered that Sebastian had been dealing in opium trade and was now imprisoned.

Caroline Pennington's father had banished his daughter to London to conceal her pregnancy, and had paid his servants handsomely to keep the information confidential. Vaden felt immense relief in knowing the scheming vixen was nowhere near Kai Chen. After seeing Kai Chen almost effortlessly kill so many Tong members and Ji-Kin Lau, Vaden cringed at the thought of Caroline attempting to harass his new wife any further. Caroline did not have a clue what she would be up against.

Kai Chen sensed his gaze and glanced up, smiling at him, her eyes twinkling mischievously. Her striking green eyes held his as he swept her into his arms and kissed her soundly, wringing a great cheer from everyone in the room. A deep blush covered her cheeks as he escorted her across the floor to their table.

My wife, Vaden reflected with pride as he watched Kai Chen bewitch every person in the room with her beauty and charm. As they moved across the room she smiled and greeted everyone with a sincerity that spoke of her kind character. It had taken several days to convince Kai Chen that he had been duped by Sebastian Madden and Caroline Pennington. Finally, Suzette had interceded on his behalf by having Caroline Pennington's father explain his daughter's actions. Only then had Kai Chen accepted his marriage proposal.

"I cannot believe you are finally mine," Vaden whispered in Kai Chen's ear as their wedding reception continued.

"I cannot believe I said yes," she quipped then laughed at his outraged expression.

"Oh, you will pay for that later," Vaden promised as he pulled her gloved hand to his lips and pressed them against the white satin. Her laughter tinkled delicately, causing his eyes to darken with desire. "Missus. LeBlanc."

"I can hardly wait," Kai Chen said softly as her blush deepened.

"Do not fear. It will be magical our first time," he promised.

The remainder of the evening passed in a blur with an incredible meal of prime rib and roasted vegetables, a fantastic ten tier cake, champagne, and dancing. Vaden and Kai Chen hugged Suzette and Manfred as they beamed with happiness at the handsome couple who then made their escape from the reception. James Baxter and his father, Colonel Baxter, waved and threw rice with the multitudes of other guests as Vaden and Kai Chen climbed into their white carriage, drawn by six white horses.

"Finally! I have my wife to myself," Vaden groaned in mock weariness. Kai Chen's nervous laugh made him smile broadly. Gazing earnestly into her eyes, he asked with uncertainty, "Was the wedding and reception everything you hoped for?"

Kai Chen's eyes filled with tears as she smiled with joy. "I never wanted a wedding so big, but it is more than I could have ever dreamed, Vaden. I never thought to be married," she admitted sincerely.

"I am glad you enjoyed it. I wanted it to be special for you, Kai Chen. Hopefully, our future will be as special," he stated before placing a lingering kiss upon her lips.

As they reached LeBlanc Estate, Vaden assisted her from the carriage and with a flourish, opened the front door himself and carried her over the threshold. Kicking the door shut with his foot, he swiftly carried her up the wide staircase to his bedroom. Their bedroom. Placing her feet gently on the floor Vaden removed the exquisite tiara from her head and flung it on a nearby chair.

"Well, Kay LeBlanc, whatever shall I do with you now?"

Kai Chen nervously clutched her fingers together as she glanced about the enormous, masculine room. She could feel the heat in her cheeks as she fidgeted with her gloves. Vaden's strong hands helped her slide them off, and then cupped her face as he gazed into her emerald colored eyes.

"I love you, Kai Chen," he whispered against her lips before capturing them in a passionate kiss.

Kai Chen felt her body melt against his as the kiss deepened. Vaden's fingers removed the pins from her hair as the long tresses fell to her waist. Nimbly, his fingers unbuttoned the numerous tiny white buttons down the back of her wedding dress before sliding the material over her slim hips. Even as she felt all of the clothing fall away from her body, her own hands were divesting him of his jacket, vest, tie, and shirt. As her fingers moved to his pants, Kai Chen was suddenly swept up into his arms and placed gently upon the bed.

For several moments she gazed up at him, her green eyes dark and heavy lidded with passion. She observed his blue eyes visually caress her breasts with taut dark red nipples down to her flat stomach, and finally rest at the juncture of her thighs where her auburn curls covered the treasure he sought. The passion of his gaze was intense, but the love shining in his eyes filled her heart and allowed her to let go of her fear of the unknown, of her first time allowing Vaden to enter her body.

"You are the most beautiful woman I have ever seen, with my eyes and with my heart. I love you with all that I am and all that I will ever be," he declared almost breathlessly as he removed the remainder of his clothing.

Vaden's words were poignant, striking a chord of intense elation in Kai Chen's heart. Never had she thought to hear such words of love from a man in her life. Now, here was Vaden, the foolish American she had first met so many years ago, filling a void in her life she never thought imaginable. Kai Chen smiled with wonder as he moved over her, his face mere inches from hers as he stared into her eyes.

"I love you, Vaden," she returned in a husky voice before his lips captured hers.

Kai Chen felt his body move over hers as his hands and mouth stroked every inch of her, fully discovering her body. His tongue laved over a distended nipple before sucking greedily, causing her body to surge against his in anticipation. Vaden's large hands circled her slender waist before skimming down to her sinfully long, lean thighs. His groan of desire as he spread her legs made her heart skip a beat. Then she forgot about everything as his fingers lightly glided over her already wet folds, delving into her tight sheath. The feel of his lips replacing his hands wrought a whimper from her throat as her heart raced. A fine sheen coated her skin as his mouth moved over her musky entrance, his tongue flickering across the little nub until she felt her head whirling. She did not recognize her own scream as she climaxed, over and over, as he continued his merciless onslaught.

Finally, she felt him move, shifting his powerfully, muscular body between her thighs as his lips captured hers in a deep kiss. Ever so slowly, she felt the silky hardness of his sex slide against her wetness before he began to enter her. His large manhood filled her completely as he moved further inside her, stretching her tight virginal walls until he reached the fine barrier. Pausing for a moment, he allowed her body to become adjusted to his size, to the feel of him, as he lifted his head to gaze into her eyes. His massive frame shook slightly as he fought for control.

"My love, relax and let the magic happen," he soothed as he shoved further into her, breaking past her final barrier.

Kai Chen's slight wince of pain was forgotten as his lips met hers again. He moved further into her slowly until he was fully inside then slowly began to withdraw, only to surge into her again. She welcomed him with her kiss and body as they found the perfect rhythm, their bodies moving in unison. Her fingers dug into his back as her legs wrapped around his waist tightly. She thrust her pelvis against him, driving him even deeper into her. Within seconds she cried out again, her tight walls clenching around his swollen length, causing him to roar with his release.

Kai Chen's soft giggle moments later made him pause as he glanced at the impish expression on her face.

"What is so funny?" For the first time Vaden was uncertain. Was she laughing at him, at their lovemaking?

"I drank champagne and had sexual relations. I think I have now broken all of my vows," Kai Chen declared, her tone happy despite the fact those vows had meant so much to her at one time.

Vaden chuckled with relief at her words before kissing her deeply.

"I am sure Buddha will forgive you."

☯

1911
LeBlanc Estate

"We have a daughter!"

Kai Chen's weak, cheerful voice rang out as Vaden thundered into the bedroom where a physician and midwife hovered over his wife. His gaze traveled over Kai Chen's face, seeing her exhaustion, even though she tried to appear chipper. Her hair was still damp and her face pale, which was to be expected as she had only just given birth to their only child ten minutes ago.

Vaden sat carefully on the bed next to Kai Chen and kissed her cheek tenderly. He held out his arms for his daughter, holding the babe close as he counted every finger and toe, and fawned over her head of auburn hair and large green eyes.

"Thank you, Kai Chen, for our beautiful child," Vaden said to his wife earnestly as tears filled his eyes.

"It is Buddha's will," she said with a bittersweet smile. They had lost so many babes in the past ten years, five to be exact. It was as if they were not meant to have children as each would die very early in the pregnancy due to some unknown reason.

Vaden stared in awe at his daughter who returned the gaze with seemingly great seriousness. She was his new China doll, an exact replica of her mother. Already, she showed she would continue the Wing Chun legacy with her calm and peaceful nature. There was wisdom, a knowing in her gaze that captured his heart just as her mother had done so long ago.

"What shall we call her?"

"Suzette Ying LeBlanc." Kai Chen announced, wanting to remember the dear aunt who had been such a joy until her death four years ago, and her sweet mother.

☯

September 12, 1935
White Plains, New York
Suzette Ying LeBlanc marries Mengyao Fa Bo, their daughter Ng-Mui Bo.

April 22, 1963
White Plains, New York
Ng-Mui Bo marries Renshu Xin, their daughter Liu Chen Bo.

November 13, 1984
Liu Chen Bo marries John Smith, their daughters
Kay Chen Smith
Ng-Kin Smith
Yim Ying Smith

Always remember, Wing Chun is a salvation and a curse. The legacy must only go to a daughter who is pure of heart and truly worthy, even if she is not a daughter of your blood. If the secret of Wing Chun falls into the wrong hands, everything will change. Everything will change.

EPILOGUE

"The Art of War is self-explanatory."
— Sun Tzu, *The Art of War*

Kay Chen Smith closed the worn, leathered book as fresh tears streamed down her face. Her broken cries echoed in the silent training hall as she comprehended all that she had read; the sacrifices made by the women of her family, the strength and courage they had faced without ever wavering or faltering with their path in maintaining the promise of the Wing Chun legacy, and of a profound love between Vaden and Kai Chen. As though waking from a dream, Kay considered with new objectivity the now darkening Dein she had trained in all of her life. This was her destiny, her fate, her salvation and her curse.

Everything will change.

Nothing had changed except her, and yet, now everything had changed. Her heart and her mind now realized the import of her family legacy and of her personal responsibility. The importance of a truly loving relationship had been taught to her through Vaden and Kai Chen's story and of what true intimacy she should strive for in her own future relationship. Understanding the torrid sexual deviances of Prince Tuan, Ji-Kin Lau, Sebastian Madden, and Caroline Pennington, Kay Chen knew their path was never one she wished to follow. She now considered her earlier whining about friendship, dating, movies, and McDonald's as trivial and meaningless. Friends would come and go in her life but her martial art, her legacy of Wing Chun, would remain. Wiping away tears of sorrow for the tribulations her ancestors had faced, and of the great honor to carry this knowledge and skill from the great Buddhist nun, Ng Mui, Kay now viewed her life with fresh perspective.

"Daughter," a soft, melodic voice sounded from across the training hall.

Kay lifted her emerald gaze to see her mother standing with a sweet smile of knowing on her face. Without pause Kay launched herself across the room and threw herself into her mother's waiting arms. Her kind, patient, and lovable mother who had never raised her voice or hand to her. She had been blessed by Buddha to be Liu Chen's daughter, and she had taken it for granted her entire life. She was ashamed of who she had been for so long now that she understood the importance of Wing Chun, of the importance of legacy and family.

"Why didn't you tell me," Kay Chen wailed, once again weeping with regret in how she had treated her mother earlier that day in throwing the metal star at her during their training.

Liu Chen held her tightly for several seconds before declaring, "You had to discover the legacy for yourself in your own way. Ng Mui and Yim Wing Chun would have done the same thing in allowing you self-discovery. Only in discovering knowledge for yourself can you truly appreciate and learn that which Buddha wills for you."

"I am so sorry-," Kay Chen began as she dried her tears, but her mother stepped away with a smile and took the book from her hand. Liu Chen opened it and removed an old photo hidden in the binding. Handing it to Kay Chen they both peered intently at the image. It was of Kai Chen Boussard and Vaden LeBlanc on their wedding day. Kay Chen gasped as she stared at what appeared to be a picture of herself. She was the exact image of Kai Chen Boussard. Confusion and awe were transparent on her face as Liu Chen closed the book and smiled.

"Do not be sorry daughter for there was no injury. Come, dinner is waiting and your sisters will not leave you a thing to eat if you tarry," Liu Chen chuckled. "Eat, rest, and tomorrow is a new day for us all."

Kay Chen watched as her mother put the book within the confines of the elaborately decorated cabinet then replaced the rattan wall hanging with swift, fluid motions that she now truly noticed and understood for the first time. Her mother was amazing. Liu Chen was a graceful, potent warrior who she had never actually noticed or appreciated, until now. A huge grin broke out on Kay Chen's face and she almost laughed as she carefully held the delicate photo.

"What is so funny?" Liu Chen's smile lit up her beautiful Asian looking face, except for those uncanny green eyes that were a Chen trait from the Boussard line of the family.

"I was just thinking," Kay Chen said as they walked side by side from the Dein to go to the main house. "If my friends knew what you could do they would call you a 'bad ass'."

"Then we both are 'bad asses'. Yes?"

Both women laughed outright as they sprinted across the soft green lawn at amazing speed toward the main house where the knowledge that the Wing Chun legacy would continue in those who were pure of heart and worthy.

THE WING CHUN LEGACY CONTINUES...

Available in 2013

ETERNAL SPRINGTIME

Wing Chun Legacy

Kay Chen Smith is now twenty-five years old and the sole keeper of the Wing Chun legacy after the death of her parents. With her two younger sisters in college she is free to accept a pharmacist position for an international pharmaceutical company in China, the birth place of her martial arts legacy. Although she is fluent in Chinese and familiar with the culture, she finds herself in an alien world of high-tech business, sordid sexual tiers of prostitution, and modern warfare.

Even as Kay Chen finds odd discrepancies within the company, she finds the lure of her legacy calling to her from the temples in the southern provinces. As she embarks on the historical re-discovery of her family's past, she discovers that the past is not forgotten by the Elders of the Triad. In a whirlwind of violent events, Kay Chen is soon running for her life with help from the darkly mysterious John Hai, who is half Chinese-half American. The attraction between them is barely containable, but the man who claims to be a police officer is more than he appears. Kay Chen wonders if he is actually there to help her, or if he is searching for the legacy that she only holds.

August, 2012
Beijing, China

Kay Chen Smith gazed about the unfamiliar airport carefully, noting the exits, mass of people, security, and individuals from taxi services holding signs to greet their fare for travel. Excitement filled her as she contemplated her dual journey here to China. Not only did her job as a pharmacist for one of the world's leading pharmaceutical industries bring her here, but she was taking the opportunity to discover her family roots. She planned to go to Fukien Province, O-Mei and White Crane Temples, and to maybe even find the crossroads where Kai Chen Boussard had lived. Kay Chen would be here for the next six months and would have plenty of time for unearthing her ancestral past.

A smile curved her lips as she gazed at her reflection in the window of the huge airline terminal. Although it had been seven years since she had discovered her fate with the Wing Chun legacy, Kay Chen still held onto the photo of Kai Chen Boussard and Vaden LeBlanc taken on their wedding day. With maturity, Kay Chen was the spitting image of her great-grandmother who had died just weeks before she had been born. They were both tall and athletic; both had long dark auburn hair and the most vivid jade green eyes. If Kay Chen truly believed in Buddhism, she might just believe she was Kai Chen reincarnated. Although, why Kai Chen had not achieved true enlightenment in her last life, Kay Chen could not imagine. Perhaps only the great Buddhist nun, Ng-Mui, had achieved complete enlightenment?

"Really, Kay Chen? Reincarnation?" Her smirk brought a moment of shame as she realized she was making fun of the religion she had embraced her entire life. Sighing deeply, she exhaled and looked for a sign with her name. There would be a taxi service to take her to her hotel before she started work in one week. The free week would give her time to get acclimated to the semi-familiar Chinese culture, shop for clothes and toiletries, and to learn her way around Beijing.

Slowly, she walked along the parade of oriental men and women holding signs by the front of the terminals' exit. Seeing her name on a large red sign held by a short, thin Chinese man she walked toward him. As she neared him another Chinese man in the crowd bumped up against her right side, jarring her purse. With a quick lift of her right foot she tripped the man as they passed so close to each other, causing him to fall heavily to the floor. Swinging around swiftly, she planted her knee into his back and snatched her wallet from his hand.

"Give me a reason not to break your hand," she whispered in Chinese into his ear as she bent closer, her lips almost touching his jaw. She could see the sweat break out across his neck as she twisted his hand, her hard fingernail placed sharply on a pressure point on his wrist. He winced with pain and grimaced as he began to babble incoherently in Chinese.

"Is there a problem, Miss?" a man's voice from behind her asked in perfect English.

Glancing over her shoulder, Kay Chen saw a tall Chinese man. *That is uncommon*, she thought as she noted he was a good several inches taller than her five foot ten. He was extremely handsome with straight white teeth and hair almost to his shoulders, lending him a rakish appearance. He smiled at her, his eyes twinkling with merriment as he noticed her hold on the pickpocket's wrist.

"I believe he is leaving the airport terminal before the police are called, isn't that right?" Kay Chen's Chinese was clear, the dialect perfect from speaking the language her entire life.

Kay Chen released the smaller man on the floor who jumped to his feet, stared at her large green eyes for a moment and then sprinted out of the terminal as though hounds from hell pursued him. Chuckling to herself as she put her wallet back inside her purse, she turned to the man next to her and actually looked up to see his face. He had to be six foot six in height!

"Are you the official Chinese basketball reception committee?" Kay Chen quipped with humor as she arched a delicate eyebrow. She caught him staring into her vibrant green eyes. Their gazes locked. His eyes were chocolate brown, almost black, with incredibly long eye lashes for a man. For several seconds his gaze held hers as a lifetime seemed to pass between them. A sense of familiarity, an odd connection of oneness, held them in check with neither moving. Time seemed to stand still as Kay Chen felt almost compelled to walk toward him and press her body against his, inhale deeply of his unique masculine scent, and to press her full lips against his neck.

"No, but if it gets me your name I will have anyone you want here." He promised in English as he flashed a sexy grin. A dimple on his right cheek seemed to wink at her as she let her gaze travel over his crisp white shirt, snug blue jeans, and black loafers. The sound of his voice broke the hold between them and she actually took a step back. This was one gorgeous man, and he probably knew it.

Trouble, she immediately told herself. *Back away from the delicious, tempting hunk!*

Kay Chen laughed outright at his flirtatious manner before she gave him a flash of sparkling white teeth. With a flutter of her fingers to wave goodbye to the good-looking giant of a man, she then strutted over to her ride who waited for her patiently. The smaller man holding the sign with her name stared at her with an expression of amazement, having observed her fell the pickpocket and retrieve her wallet.

"Let's go," she announced in Chinese briskly as the little man immediately offered to take her only bag. Shaking her head in refusal she followed him toward the terminal exit.

As her purposeful, long strides propelled her toward the windows of the terminal she could see the reflection of the handsome, tall Chinese man behind her. Her gaze locked with his again as something unspoken passed between them. Confused by this feeling of being drawn to him, Kay Chen quickly moved outside and climbed into the waiting taxi. As her taxi driver pulled into traffic she turned to see the attractive man still staring at her, only now his expression was dark and menacing, causing a chill to race up her spine in warning. Somehow, Kay Chen had the feeling this trip was going to be more than she expected. She just needed to remember…

Always remember, Wing Chun is a salvation and a curse. The legacy must only go to a daughter who is pure of heart and truly worthy, even if she is not a daughter of your blood. If the secret of Wing Chun falls into the wrong hands, everything will change. Everything will change.

ABOUT THE AUTHOR

Lori Levesque's background in martial arts spans over 20 years studying Tae Kwon Do, Kenpo Karate, and Kali Stick Fighting, with a new love for Wing Chun. Occasionally, she assists training her youngest son for tournaments in Tae Kwon Do. Lori has a background as a registered nurse, serving in the U.S. Army Reserve and working in law enforcement for 10 years. Her interests include reading, movies, cooking, traveling, and football. Lori currently lives in Middletown, Ohio. You can contact Lori with questions or comments at her website: www.lorilevesque.com

2645901R00134

Printed in Great Britain
by Amazon.co.uk, Ltd.,
Marston Gate.

agony of Apostrophes

Sylvia Fielding

First Edition (electronic): September 2013

Second Edition (print): May 2017

ISBN 978-1-5272-0815-5

Published by Warrina Books

"Sylvia has produced a fresh and succinct way of mastering the use of the apostrophe. I particularly liked her many references to the everyday use of language. I thoroughly recommend it as an invaluable reference for all those involved in learning and teaching."

Patrick Larkin BA H Dip Ed
Assistant Principal
Former Chairman of Teachers' Association of Media Education

My thanks go to my family, friends and colleagues for their encouragement and support, and to all my website visitors whose apostrophe queries provided the basis for this book.

Contents

Introduction

This book answers the questions:

- Do I need an apostrophe in this?
- If so, why, and where does it go?

I've named this book "The Agony of Apostrophes" because I know that many people do agonise over where to put an apostrophe. In fact, nothing seems to cause us more trouble in English grammar than the apostrophe—and it's not even easy to spell.

On my website www.commasense.co.uk I invite people to email me with their apostrophe queries. Even though the rules are on there, it's become clear to me that people need to see lots of examples in order to find or work out the answer to their own particular problem. The content of this book is based on those queries and I have attempted to explain and show the correct use of the apostrophe in the many real situations that have been posed to me.

I was shocked to receive an email from a mother whose daughter's English homework had been incorrectly 'corrected' by her school teacher. The mother wrote to me for confirmation that what her daughter had written was, in fact, correct. The daughter had written, "the dog gave its owner the ball" but the teacher had corrected it to "the dog gave it's owner the ball", meaning: "the dog gave

it is owner the ball", which is clearly nonsense. The only time an apostrophe should be inserted in the word "its" is when it is short for "it is" or "it has". The daughter's version, "the dog gave its owner the ball" is correct because the word "its" (without an apostrophe) is the equivalent of "his, her, our, my, your, their"—"its" is the version that means belonging to, or associated with, a thing or person/animal of unspecified gender.

Of course, even a teacher of English could be forgiven for making a mistake as a one-off, but apparently this wasn't the only correction he had made. The daughter had also written, "buy your cucumbers and lettuces here", which the teacher had corrected to "buy your cucumber's and lettuce's here". The teacher had inserted apostrophes into what are straightforward plural nouns, that is, "cucumbers and lettuces", which the daughter had written correctly.

Fortunately, I've always been able to "do" apostrophes but, in the process of writing this book, I've come to realise that apostrophes are not that simple; so I won't pretend they are.

If we didn't have to bother with apostrophes, writing would be so much easier but, for me, it would take all the enjoyment out of writing. Personally, I love the challenge of using apostrophes to make sense of what I'm trying to convey to the reader.

To illustrate how the apostrophe clarifies meaning, take a look at the following statements:

These are my brothers
    these (people) are my brothers
These are my brother's
    these (things) belong to my brother
These are my brothers'
    these (things) belong to my brothers

In spoken language we can't see where the apostrophe is and, because we're usually face-to-face in conversation with someone, the meaning is clear in the context of what's being said. However, in written language the text can be ambiguous if the apostrophe is missing. In this sense, the apostrophe plays a useful and important role in making the meaning of written text clear.

There are several books containing rules on how to use the apostrophe, but my intention for this book is to communicate not only how to use it correctly and effectively, but also to create a reference book that is easy to use and which, hopefully, will become indispensable. How many times have you looked up a rule in a grammar book, or something in a dictionary, only to find that the example or guidance you're looking for isn't there and you're still none the wiser?

I've deliberately written this book with contractions (as in "I've" instead of "I have") to illustrate the broad use of the apostrophe, rather than the more formal way of keeping contractions in written text to a minimum.

And I've agonised over trying to come up with simple ways to explain where an apostrophe should go – I hope I've achieved this.

This is the second edition of my book in that it has an Appendix containing a sample of real apostrophe queries that have been emailed to me via my website since writing the first edition. The queries are in question and answer format, albeit with names changed where appropriate. I hope that other people's queries might provide the answers you may be looking for.

The first edition was in e-book format, but I soon realised that e-books do not work well as reference books. Finding the necessary information is nowhere near as easy as looking for answers in a physical book, which is why I decided to publish a paperback version.

If, after referring to this book, you still have unanswered questions or queries about how to use the apostrophe, feel free to email me at:

sfielding@commasense.co.uk

In this book, you will find the answers to questions such as:

- Why do I need an apostrophe?
- What are the rules for using apostrophes?
- When should I put an apostrophe in *its*?
- Do I need an apostrophe in *peoples*?
- Where does the apostrophe go in *childrens*?
- How do I make a word possessive?
- Should I put the "s" before or after my apostrophe?
- How do I treat words ending in "s"?
- Where do I put the apostrophe in someone's name?
- Should it be *Thomas's* car or *Thomas'* car?
- Do I need an apostrophe in *phone* or *pub*?
- Should *theirs* or *ours* have an apostrophe?
- Is it *your welcome* or *you're welcome*?
- Should it be *MOTs* or *MOT's*?
- Is it *potato's* or *potatoes*?
- Do abbreviations need an apostrophe?

So, why not begin by testing your knowledge of apostrophes using the quiz on the next page? Everything in the quiz, and more, is covered in the chapters of this book. There are 30 questions in total, and the answers can be found at the end of the book. (Note, you will need to jot down the numbers for your chosen answers.)

Introductory apostrophe quiz

1a) The peoples’ vote
1b) The people’s vote

2a) Is this mine or yours?
2b) Is this mine or your’s?

3a) The man, whose car I crashed into, is my neighbour
3b) The man, who’s car I crashed into, is my neighbour

4a) Jack is a friend of my mother
4b) Jack is a friend of my mother’s

5a) The boy’s were told the sweets were all their’s
5b) The boys were told the sweets were all theirs
5c) The boys were told the sweets were all their’s
5d) The boy’s were told the sweets were all theirs

6a) Two weeks notice
6b) Two weeks’ notice
6c) Two week’s notice

7a) The men's wives went with them on the trip
7b) The mens' wives went with them on the trip

8a) Where are the womens' toilets?
8b) Where are the women's toilets?

9a) Who told you its yours?
9b) Who told you it's yours?
9c) Who told you its your's?
9d) Who told you it's your's?

10a) Who's that man?
10b) Whose that man?

11a) Mr and Mrs Smith's house was burgled
11b) Mr and Mrs Smiths' house was burgled

12a) The Smiths' house is in darkness
12b) The Smith's house is in darkness

13a) MOTs carried out here
13b) MOT's carried out here

14a) Whose bag is this?
14b) Who's bag is this?

15a) Mind your P's and Q's
15b) Mind your Ps and Qs

16a) The salad contained lettuces and tomatoes
16b) The salad contained lettuce's and tomato's

17a) Which shoes? The red or the white one's?
17b) Which shoes? The red or the white ones?

18a) Your late!
18b) You're late!

19a) The dog has injured it's paw
19b) The dog has injured its paw

20a) Shall we go to the children's playground?
20b) Shall we go to the childrens' playground?

21a) I've been invited to Sue and Mark's wedding
21b) I've been invited to Sue's and Mark's wedding

22a) Don't forget your phone
22b) Don't forget your 'phone

23a) She was born in the '20s
23b) She was born in the 20's

24a) He was born in the 1920's
24b) He was born in the 1920s

25a) Look where you're going!
25b) Look where your going!

26a) The rain's stopped
26b) The rains stopped

27a) Policemen's helmets
27b) Policemens' helmets

28a) Tell me it's not going to rain
28b) Tell me its not going to rain

29a) The company has expanded its product portfolio
29b) The company has expanded it's product portfolio

30a) Women's shoes are next to the ladies' handbags
30b) Womens' shoes are next to the ladies' handbags

Please go to the **Answers to quizzes** chapter at the end of the book for the correct answers. There you will also find the relevant chapter references which will allow you to look up the rules or theory associated with each correct answer.

1 – Using the apostrophe to show possession

(How to show that something belongs to someone or something)

If you have trouble knowing where to put an apostrophe, you are certainly not alone. In fact, nothing seems to cause more trouble in English grammar than the apostrophe. But if you follow the rules in this and subsequent chapters, you should be able to solve almost any apostrophe problem that crops up.

The apostrophe is mainly used to show possession—ownership of something—for example, *the girl's school bag*, or *the old people's care home*.

The French language uses a more formal and long-winded way of showing possession, for example: *la mère de Marie* (the mother of Marie) or *le père de Jean* (the father of Jean). In the English language we rarely use this form; instead we would say *Marie's mother* and *Jean's father* although we mean *the mother of Marie* and *the father of Jean*. Likewise, we would not say *the school bag of the girl* or *the care home of the old people* as these phrases sound clumsy and too formal.

We also use the shortened form for phrases such as:

- two weeks' notice (notice of two weeks)
- one week's pay (pay of one week)
- one day's leave (leave of one day)

In the following phrases, the apostrophes have been deliberately omitted.

- The childs toys
- The students books
- The peoples vote
- The chickens eggs
- The childrens party

Written as they are, two of the above phrases are ambiguous – *the students books* could mean the books of one student or several students; similarly, *the chickens eggs* could be referring to one chicken or a few chickens, which is why we need an apostrophe to clarify the meaning. The other three phrases aren't ambiguous but they are incorrect without their apostrophes. So how do we work out where the apostrophes should go?

Below I will outline three different ways of working out where to put the apostrophe—each of the rules will work—it doesn't matter which you use, but you may wish to use all three to check that you've worked it out correctly.

The most commonly cited rule is to add **'s** to the end of singular words and also to plural words that do not end in an "s" (eg children, men, women, people). For plurals that end in an "s" (eg boys, ladies) just add an apostrophe to the end of the word after the "s".

However, here is an alternative rule that some may find useful:

To work out where the apostrophe should go, try changing the phrase or sentence around to its longer, more formal format containing the word "of". The apostrophe goes immediately after the last letter of the word or phrase that follows the word "of".

Here are the phrases written in their longer form and in their shorter form using the apostrophe correctly:

- The toys of **the child** = **the child**'s toys
- The books of **the students = the students**' books
- The vote of **the people = the people**'s vote
- The eggs of **the chicken = the chicken**'s eggs

- The party of **the children = the children**'s party

In the following examples, the rule works in the same way:

- Notice of **two weeks = two weeks'** notice
- Pay of **one week = one week's** pay
- Leave of **one day = one day's** leave
- The bag of **Cheryl = Cheryl's** bag
- The laptop of **Mike = Mike's** laptop

Yet another way of determining where the apostrophe should go is to ask the following question: *To whom or to what does it belong or refer?* The apostrophe then goes immediately after whatever word is the answer to that question.

Again, the apostrophes in the following phrases have been omitted.

1. The childs toys
2. The students books (*several students*)
3. The peoples vote
4. The chickens eggs (*one chicken*)
5. The childrens Christmas party

To determine where the apostrophes should go, the questions to ask are:

1. Who do the toys belong to? The answer is the **child** - the apostrophe goes immediately after the word "child" before the 's'. The correct statement is: The child's toys.
2. Who do the books belong to? The answer is the **students** - the apostrophe goes immediately after the word "students", after the 's'. The correct statement is: The students' books. (Note: if the book belonged to one student, the apostrophe would go after the word *student* and would be written: The student's books.)
3. Who does the vote belong to? The answer is the **people** - the apostrophe goes immediately after the word "people" before the "s". The correct statement is: The people's vote. (Note that *people* is already a plural word and to write *peoples'* would be incorrect.)
4. Who do the eggs belong to? The answer is the **chicken** - the apostrophe goes immediately after the word "chicken" before the 's'. The correct statement is: The chicken's eggs. (Note: if the eggs belonged to several chickens, the apostrophe would go after the word *chickens* and would be written: The chickens' eggs.)
5. Who does the Christmas party belong to? (Who is the Christmas party for?) The answer is the **children** - the apostrophe goes immediately after the word "children" before the 's'. The correct statement is: The children's Christmas party. (Note that *children* is already

a plural word and to write *childrens'* would be incorrect.)

2 – Contractions and abbreviations

(Using apostrophes with shortened words)

The apostrophe is also used to show that a letter, or letters, are missing from a word. A *contraction* is when two words have been contracted into one word, for example, *I've* (I have), *haven't* (have not), *isn't* (is not), *you'll* (you will *or* you shall), *it's* (it is). Contractions must have apostrophes to show where the missing letters are. An *abbreviation* is where a single word has been shortened, for example, pub, phone, demo – abbreviations do not need apostrophes.

Contractions

Where've you put the letter? *(Where have you put the letter?)*
Where's it gone? *(Where has it gone?)*
Where's Cindy? *(Where is Cindy?)*
What've you done? *(What have you done?)*
Who's there? *(Who is there?)*
Who's been a good boy? *(Who has been a good boy?)*
Note: don't confuse "who's" meaning "who is" with "whose" (see chapter 9)
Let's go *(Let us go)*
Why's that? *(Why is that?)*
You're welcome *(You are welcome)*
Note: a common mistake is to write "your welcome"

Don’t do that *(Do not do that)*
She’d prefer not to go *(She would prefer not to go)*
When I arrived, she’d gone *(When I arrived, she had gone)*
I’ll have to admit I’m sorry *(I will/shall have to admit I am sorry)*
We’ll definitely be there *(We will definitely be there)*
I’m hungry *(I am hungry)*
I didn’t see you there *(I did not see you there)*
Mandy’s off to Glastonbury *(Mandy is off to Glastonbury)*
Geoff isn’t coming *(Geoff is not coming)*
The alarm hasn’t gone off yet *(The alarm has not gone off yet)*
We’re almost there *(We are almost there)*
Why’s it important? *(Why is it important?)*
What’s that? *(What is that?)*
What’s he been doing? *(What has he been doing?)*
They’re also suffering *(They are also suffering)*
Note: don’t confuse "they’re" with "their" (see chapter 10)
9 o’clock *(9 of the clock—no longer in use in today’s English)*
Anywhere that’s blue on the map shows where we’ve been flooded
(Anywhere that is blue on the map shows where we have been flooded)

As you're studying science at school you'll know the answers
(As you are studying science at school you will know the answers)
Note: to write "As your studying science..." is incorrect
It's going to feel bitterly cold *(It is going to feel bitterly cold)*
It isn't the right address *(It is not the right address)*
Here's your bus *(Here is your bus)*
Most people who aren't scientists wouldn't understand
(Most people who are not scientists would not understand)
The sky's the limit *(The sky is the limit)*
My keys aren't there *(My keys are not there)*
He won't stop staring *(He will not stop staring)*
Note: "won't" is the abbreviated form of "will not"—strange as it seems; and "shan't is the abbreviated form of "shall not"
I shan't be coming with you *(I shall not be coming with you)*
I shouldn't think so *(I should not think so)*

Abbreviations

Where a word has simply been abbreviated (a clipped word), for example, *ad, advert, pub, demo, flu, phone*, it does not require an apostrophe and to insert one would be incorrect.

- She's got the flu.
- Are you going to the pub?
- Where's my phone?
- I love that advert (or, I love that ad).
- Would you like to see a demo of that?

However, apostrophes <u>are</u> needed in colloquial dialects (where the abbreviation is not a formally accepted word):

- Are you comin' with me or goin' with him?

And in terms such as:

- Fish 'n' chips
- Pick 'n' mix
- Born in '73
- The '90s; the '80s

Note: when referring to something that happened in, say, the 1920s this does not take an apostrophe but when abbreviating it to the '90s then it needs an apostrophe. There is no apostrophe needed before the "s", however.

3 – Its or It's?

(When to use *Its* and when to use *It's*)

Many of us are confused about whether to use *its* or *it's* and getting it wrong can be embarrassing both for the writer and the reader. But if you follow this simple rule, I guarantee you will never get it wrong again.

The only time you need an apostrophe in *its* is when it is short for *it is* or *it has*.

When being used in a possessive sense, for example, *the dog has lost **its** bone*, this should never have an apostrophe. If an apostrophe is inserted, the sentence is then saying, "The dog has lost *it is* (or *it has*) bone", which is clearly wrong. So, *its* without an apostrophe is always possessive and means belonging to something; it is the equivalent of *my, his, her, our, your and their,* when the gender is unknown or it is a 'thing', for example, *I need a new calculator – its keys keep sticking*.

Here's a paragraph showing the correct use of *its* and *it's*:

There's a lot of disagreement over whether it's wise to wash our hair every day. Some say that the hair on our heads should be washed as frequently as we take a bath or shower. Others say that shampoo, with its harsh chemicals, dries out the hair too much and that it's best to leave hair for several days between washes. Whether it's good for us or not to wash hair daily, it's been proven that hair will eventually cleanse itself through its own natural oils when left for long periods of time; its ability to self-clean has been well researched. It's a controversial subject but it's all down to personal preference in the end.

All the instances of *it's* in the above paragraph can be substituted either for *it is* or *it has*, that is, they are short for *it is* or *it has*. All the instances of *its* are possessive. Try substituting *it is* or *it has* in their places and the passage will not make sense. This is the test you can apply every time you use *its* or *it's.* If it has an apostrophe it can only mean *it is* or *it has.*

As a further example, the following is correct:

It's obvious that its mother has abandoned it (referring to a lost kitten, gender unknown).

Now try testing yourself on the use of *its* and *it’s* – which of the following is the correct version?

1. a) It's time to go!
   b) Its time to go!

2. a) The dog’s eaten its lunch
   b) The dog’s eaten it's lunch

3. a) Let's not forget that its only been a year
   b) Let's not forget that it's only been a year

4. a) Its my job to safeguard its location
   b) Its my job to safeguard it's location
   c) It's my job to safeguard it's location
   d) It's my job to safeguard its location

5. a) The project team achieved all of its deliverables
   b) The project team achieved all of it's deliverables

6. a) Unfortunately it's been taken out of my hands
   b) Unfortunately its been taken out of my hands

7. a) If its genuine, where’s its label?
   b) If it's genuine, where’s its label?
   c) If it's genuine, where’s it's label?
   d) If its genuine, where’s it's label?

8. a) It's already been useful; it's worth its weight in gold
   b) It's already been useful; its worth its weight in gold
   c) Its already been useful; it's worth it's weight in gold
   d) It's already been useful; it's worth it's weight in gold
   e) Its already been useful; its worth it's weight in gold
   f) Its already been useful; its worth its weight in gold

9. a) Poor baby—it's crying because it's dropped it's toy
   b) Poor baby—its crying because its dropped its toy
   c) Poor baby—it's crying because it's dropped its toy
   d) Poor baby—it's crying because its dropped it's toy
   e) Poor baby—its crying because it's dropped it's toy
   f) Poor baby—it's crying because its dropped its toy

Please go to the **Answers to Quizzes** chapter at the end of the book for the correct answers.

4 – Making plural words possessive

(How to use an apostrophe to show that something belongs to more than one thing or person)

This is also covered in chapter 1 but, as plurals can sometimes be trickier, this section contains examples of how to use the possessive apostrophe with plural nouns that end with an "s" and the few that do not end in an "s".

Here's a reminder of the rule: add ***'s*** to the end of plural words that do not end in an "s" (eg children, men, women, people), but for plurals that end in an "s" (which is the majority, eg ladies, friends) just add an apostrophe to the end of the word after the "s".

The apostrophe used correctly with plural words that do not end in "s":

- Men's fashion
- Children's books
- The children's playground
- People's preferences
- The people's choice
- The mice's cage
- Men's captain
- Men's hats
- Women's toilets (but ladies' toilets)

The apostrophe used correctly with plural words ending in "s":

- Babies' clothes
- Ladies' tennis tournament
- Ladies' fashions
- Seniors' captain
- Members' award evening
- The athletes' changing room
- The libraries' fate
- The twins' birthday

Note: it doesn't matter whether there are one or several *books* or *choices* or *preferences* or *tournaments*—it doesn't change the position of the apostrophe, ie

- children's books are over there
- my favourite children's book

Remember – if the plural ends in "s", put the apostrophe after it; if it doesn't end in "s", add an apostrophe and an "s" to the end of the word.

5 – Apostrophe mistakes

(Errors seen in print and on public display)

Chiselborough is one of the areas' most sought-after villages. X
Chiselborough is one of the area's most sought-after villages. √

[If we change the sentence around, it would be *Chiselborough is one of the most sought-after villages of the area*. There is only one area and the apostrophe goes immediately after the word area before the "s".]

... with it's new one piece stainless steel door... X
... with its new one piece stainless steel door... √

[The first phrase is saying, "with **it is** new one piece stainless steel door"; the same mistake can be seen in the examples below.]

The car it's self is in good condition for its age. X
The car itself is in good condition for its age. √

This car has just been through it's MOT. X
This car has just been through its MOT. √

Gone are the days where school's required women to take sewing classes. X
Gone are the days where schools required women to take sewing classes.√

[In the above, an apostrophe should never be inserted in a straight plural; this sentence is not possessive.]

Seen in an official letter from the Royal Mail:
Dear Sir/Madam, I am writing to ask if you require your post to be delivered on Saturday's. X
Dear Sir/Madam, I am writing to ask if you require your post to be delivered on Saturdays. √

[Again, straight plurals do not need an apostrophe.]

On a well-known insurance company's website:
Almost 25 year's experience in providing health insurance X
Almost 25 years' experience in providing health insurance √

[This is referring to 25 years of experience and is therefore possessive—the experience refers to 25 years, not 25 year; the apostrophe should go after the "s" of years.] Note: "company's website" is correct because there is only one company – "companies' website" would be incorrect.

Exclusively for the over 50's X
Exclusively for the over 50s √

[no apostrophe needed—this is just a straight plural]

On a courier's website:
Your item is automatically covered up to it's full value. X
Your item is automatically covered up to its full value. √

[The first sentence is saying: Your item is automatically covered up to **it is** full value; the same mistake is shown in the examples below.]

On an estate agent's website:
Marketed for sale with the benefit of it's own private entrance. X
Marketed for sale with the benefit of its own private entrance. √

Seen in large print on a banner outside a new housing estate:
"We could buy your home for it's market value." X
"We could buy your home for its market value." √

On a health website:
"Known for it's healing powers, aloe vera..." X
"Known for its healing powers, aloe vera..."√

On a mobile broadband comparison website:
It's good to see a provider that is not over egging what they are selling and is big on treating its customers' fairly. X
It's good to see a provider that is not over egging what they are selling and is big on treating its customers fairly. √

[They have used the apostrophe correctly in both instances of *its* and *it's* but have wrongly inserted an apostrophe in a straight plural.]

6 – Ordinary plurals

(When <u>not</u> to use an apostrophe)

Ordinary plurals (ie referring to more than one of something) should never have apostrophes. Inserting an apostrophe into words such as *tomatoes, potatoes, cucumbers and lettuces* is known, albeit disrespectfully, as the Greengrocer's Apostrophe. I suspect many of us have seen "tomato's and potato's or even "tomatoe's and potatoe's" outside a Greengrocer's shop, but this is always incorrect when referring to more than one of something. Do not use an apostrophe to make something into a plural. The following plurals are correct.

- One tomato; two tomatoes
- One potato; two potatoes
- One day; two days
- One baby; two babies
- One lady; two ladies
- One MOT; two MOTs
- One CD; two CDs
- One DVD; two DVDs

There is one exception to this rule, which is when you're writing, for instance, "Mind your p's and q's". If you were to write, "mind your ps and qs", this would be confusing for the reader, which is why it's necessary to insert an apostrophe to clarify the meaning. However, if you were to write "mind your Ps and Qs", using upper case, then apostrophes aren't needed.

While we're on the subject of plurals, how do we make proper names, for example surnames, into plurals?

> When a surname ends in an "s" simply add "es" to make it plural; when a surname does not end in an "s", simply add "s" to make it plural.

Mr and Mrs Thomas could be referred to as ***the Thomases***
Mr and Mrs Jones as ***the Joneses***
Mr and Mrs Lewis as ***the Lewises***
Mr and Mrs Smith as ***the Smiths***
Mr and Mrs Fielding as ***the Fieldings***
Mr and Mrs Dennis as ***the Dennises***
Mr and Mrs Phillips as ***the Phillipses***
Mr and Mrs Morris as ***the Morrises***

Again, do not add an apostrophe simply to make a name into a plural as in, for example, "I saw the Fielding's in town today"—this is incorrect—it should be written as "I saw the Fieldings in town today".

7 – Making names possessive

(How to use apostrophes with names)

Names do seem to cause a lot of problems; here are a few common surnames:

- Thomas
- Lewis
- Jones
- Smith
- Fielding
- Dennis
- Phillips
- Morris

Let's take the example of a house belonging to Mr Thomas, Lewis, etc; this is the correct way to write the phrases:

- Mr Thomas's house (the house of Mr Thomas)
- Mr Lewis's house (the house of Mr Lewis)
- Mr Jones's house (the house of Mr Jones)
- Mr Smith's house (the house of Mr Smith)
- Mr Fielding's house (the house of Mr Fielding)
- Mr Dennis's house (the house of Mr Dennis)
- Mr Phillips's house (the house of Mr Phillips)
- Mr Morris's house (the house of Mr Morris)

We simply add an ***'s*** to the name to show possession.

Add **'s** to singular words and to plural words that do not end in an "s". For plural words ending in "s" just add an apostrophe after the "s".

or

To determine where the apostrophe should go, change the phrase or sentence around to its longer, more formal format containing the word "of". The apostrophe goes immediately after the last letter of the word or phrase that follows the word "of".

So how do we write about a house belonging to the Thomases, the Lewises, etc? This is the correct way to write the phrases:

- The Thomases' house (the house of ***the Thomases***)
- The Lewises' house (the house of ***the Lewises***)
- The Joneses' house (the house of ***the Joneses***)
- The Smiths' house (the house of ***the Smiths***)
- The Fieldings' house (the house of ***the Fieldings***)

- The Dennises' house (the house of ***the Dennises***)
- The Phillipses' house (the house of ***the Phillipses***)
- The Morrises' house (the house of **the Morrises**)

However, when talking about a *household* we would simply use the family surname because the name in this instance is just describing the household (see chapter 8):

- The Thomas household
- The Lewis household
- The Jones household
- The Smith household
- The Fielding household
- The Dennis household
- The Phillips household
- The Brown household
- The Harris household
- The Morris household

While we're specifically looking at names, here are some more possessive examples – this time using first names:

- James's laptop (the laptop of James)
- St James's Square (the Square of St James)
- Marcus's address (the address of Marcus)
- Dennis's shirt (the shirt of Dennis)
- Chris's shoes (the shoes of Chris)

- Jess's children (the children of Jess)
- Charles's newspaper (the newspaper of Charles)
- Giles's sister (the sister of Giles)

There is one exception to adding ***'s*** to singular names, however (sorry, there's always an exception), and this is when the original name ends in an "iz" sound:

- Mercedes' trombone (girl's name Mercedes)
- The Mercedes' tyres
- Mrs Hodges' dog
- Mr Bridges' daughter

When talking about something belonging to a couple, for example *Jane and Simon*, the couple should be treated as if they were one entity with the apostrophe inserted after the last name.

- Jane and Simon's wedding
- Jack and Jill's pail of water
- Mum and Dad's anniversary
- Seb and Millie's parents
- Mr and Mrs Clark's daughter
- Mr and Mrs Evans's house

But, *Mr and Mrs Hodges' dog* and *Mr and Mrs Bridges' daughter* (see previous explanation above regarding names ending in an "iz" sound).

However, when the subject refers to two people or groups that are not linked and are separate, then an apostrophe would be needed in both:

- Where are the men's and women's clothing departments?
- Where are Sebastian's and Emilia's coats?

But what if we were talking about something belonging to me and my sister?

- My sister's and my views differed on the matter
- David's and her mother was always knitting

Admittedly, these last two sentences do sound odd, but they are correct. If writing these feels uncomfortable, use instead something like "Our views differed on the matter" and "their mother was always knitting" - provided of course that it's clear whom "our" and "their" are referring to.

8 – Possessive or adjective?

(Is it just a describing word—adjective—or does it need an apostrophe?)

(And words ending in "z")

So how should we treat words that end in "z", such as Heinz or Allianz?

If we were to talk about the customers of these organisations, it would be "Heinz's customers" and "Allianz's customers"—we simply add ***'s*** to make it possessive.

However, when we see 'Heinz Baked Beans' on a can, this doesn't in fact require an apostrophe because this is simply describing the type or brand of the baked beans. In the same way, I might describe myself as a Waitrose customer or a Tesco customer and, again, this does not need an apostrophe; I am simply describing the type or brand of customer that I am and, in these instances, the words *Waitrose* and *Tesco* are simply adjectives. If, however, we wanted to talk about the customers of Tesco or Waitrose then it would be Waitrose's customers and Tesco's customers. The difference is subtle. When something is merely an adjective, that is, describing something rather than belonging to or referring to something, then an apostrophe is not necessary.

Here are some examples:

Sports club
(describing the type of club, as in golf club and tennis club, for example)
Christmas lights
(describing the type of lights, rather than the lights of Christmas)
Library books
(describing the books, rather than books that belong to the library; if we were to write The Library's books, then this would mean the books belonging to the Library)
London Writers Group
(describing the type of group, ie a group in London for Writers; however it would not be incorrect to insert an apostrophe after "Writers" making it London Writers' Group which would then mean that it is a group of, or belonging to, the London writers)
Accounts department
(describing the department)
Pilates mat
(describing the type of mat used for Pilates)
Massed bands concert
(describing the type of concert)
Garden implements sale
(although this could be argued as a sale of garden implements, the apostrophe would not be wrong but it is also just describing the type of sale and therefore no apostrophe is necessary)

But what about something like *kids parties*? This is a slightly tricky one in that it could be argued that *kids* in this example could be an adjective describing the type of parties. If the word *kids* were substituted with, say, *childrens, womens, mens*, these clearly need an apostrophe as in *children's shoes, women's shoes or men's shoes*. The apostrophe could arguably be omitted in *kids parties*, but it may simply look as if someone has forgotten to put it in. My personal opinion is that *kids' parties* should be written with an apostrophe.

Here are examples both of when an apostrophe is needed and is not needed:

- The lawn was strewn with rose petals (describing the type of petals that were strewn over the lawn)
- The lawn was strewn with the rose's petals (meaning the lawn was strewn with petals belonging to a particular rose)
- The lawn was strewn with the roses' petals (meaning the lawn was strewn with the petals of several particular roses)
- Golf Superintendent's Newsletter
- Easter Newsletter

Lastly, company names are slightly tricky. Companies will often use apostrophes in their names according to their preference rather than according to any grammatical rule. We should therefore accept whichever convention is used or chosen by an organisation with regard to their trading names, for example, Waterstones, Barclays, Sainsbury's.

9 – Whose or Who's?

(When to use Whose and when to use Who's)

Who's means either *who is* or *who has* and should never be used in the following way:

"Who's coat is this?" Written in this way, it's actually saying, "Who is coat is this?" or "Who has coat is this?" which is nonsense. The correct way to write this is "Whose coat is this?" ***Whose*** is a word meaning "of which, of whom". A few examples are:

- Whose house is this?
- Whose coat is red?
- Whose keys are these?
- The man whose car I crashed into is suing me.
- The book whose pages are torn is not worth keeping.
- The petrol station whose lights are off is closed.

If we substitute *whose* with *who's* the above sentences would be translated as:

- Who is house is this?
- Who is coat is this?
- Who is keys are these?
- The man who is car I crashed into is suing me.

- The book who is pages are torn is not worth keeping
- The petrol station who is lights are off is closed.

These do not make sense at all and *who's* would be incorrect in the above. So, whenever you use *who's* in a phrase or sentence, remember that it is short for *who is* or *who has* and if the sentence or phrase does not make sense using the longer version of *who's* then you need *whose* instead.

Some examples of the use of "who's":

- Who's got the tickets? *(Who has got the tickets?)*
- Who's he? *(Who is he?)*
- Who's there? *(Who is there?)*
- The woman who's looking in the shop window is my aunt *(The woman who is looking...)*
- Who's who in the world of fashion? *(Who is who...)*

Now some correct examples using both forms:

- Who's the man whose children are misbehaving?
  Who is the man whose children are misbehaving?

- Who's the woman who's lost her purse?
  Who is the woman who has lost her purse?

- Who's the guy who's looking annoyed?
Who is the guy who is looking annoyed?

- Whose glasses are these? Who's lost their glasses?
Whose glasses are these? Who has lost their glasses?

- Who's the man whose children's names are Ben and Megan?
Who is the man whose children's names are Ben and Megan?

10 – Possessive adjectives & pronouns

(My, her, his, its, our, your, their, and mine, hers, his, its, ours, yours, theirs)

Possessive *adjectives* are words such as *my, her, his, its, our, your and their,* as in the following examples:

- My book
- Her car
- His coat
- Its owner
- Our house
- Your opinion
- Their fault

Possessive *pronouns* are what we would say in response to the question "Whose is this?" for example:

- Mine
- Hers
- His
- Its
- Ours
- Yours
- Theirs

None of the above should have an apostrophe but, unfortunately, we often see written *her's, our's, your's and their's,* but these are entirely incorrect.

And of course, as already mentioned in chapter 3, "it's" would also be wrong in this context.

11 – Examples with the apostrophe used correctly

(Lots of correct examples)

P = apostrophe used to denote possession
C = apostrophe used to denote missing letters (contraction)

This is our first full **year's** report as a Trust. (*P*)
It was a study on how to explore **one's** culture and the influences it has on routines
(ie the culture belonging to one) (*P*)
His **Master's** Voice (*P*)
The **Duke of Edinburgh's** role (*P*)
The **Prince of Wales's** visit (*P*)
My **sister-in-law's** birthday (*P*)
My **sisters-in-law's** wedding outfits were lovely (*P*)
(*Note: the plural of sister-in-law is sisters-in-law which is then treated, for example, like the word children, ie the children's outfits were lovely.)*
Maggie's pies (*P*)
Elvis's song (*P*)
It's just **people's** curiosity. (*C*, *P*)
Everyone's view is important to us. (*P*)
Something to suit **everyone's** taste. (*P*)
(Note that "everyone" is a singular word meaning "every one person")
Someone else's responsibility (*P*)

There's Annie **who's** a mother figure to them (*C*, *C*)
The **company's** mission statement (*P*)
A meeting of several finance **companies'** directors took place in London. (*P*)
A meeting of the finance **company's** directors took place in London (one company). (*P*)
The **child's** parents (*P*)
The **school's** reputation (*P*)
The child lost its way; **it's** easily done. (*C*)
The **men's** clothing shop (*P*)
The **men's** cars (*P*)
The **man's** children (*P*)
The **gentleman's** briefcase (*P*)
The **gentlemen's** bar (*P*)
Straight plurals **don't** have apostrophes. (*C*)
I am taking my **client's** instructions (one client). (*P*)
I am taking my **clients'** instructions (more than one client). (*P*)
The **boss's** office (*P*)
Mr **Cross's** salary (*P*)
Steve and Carol's party (*P*)
The **palace's** interior walls were covered with paintings. (*P*)
When **it's** gone, **it's** gone. (*C*, *C*)
Mrs **Ambrose's** dahlias (*P*)
Samuel **Pepys's** Diary (*P*)
A **joke's** a joke. (*C*)
Enough's enough. (*C*)
Whose are they? **They're** theirs. (*C*)

Who's the owner of these keys? (*C*)
Where's its label? (*C*)
Here's your book? **Where's** mine? **Where's** hers? (*C, C, C*)
The **ladies'** bags (*P*)
The **lady's** bags (*P*)
Buying this product helps save the **world's** forests. (*P*)
She was worried by her **father's** unhappiness. (*P*)
It's Angela's worst nightmare, **isn't** it? (*C, P, C*)
Jack has seven **years'** experience in design work. (*P*)
Fielding Consultancy **Limited's** accounts (*P*)
Tess's fear was apparent. (*P*)
Fernandes' restaurant (*the restaurant belonging to (Fernandes – names ending in an "iz" sound take an apostrophe but no extra "s"*) (*P*)
This **year's** calendar (*P*)
This **year's** events (*P*)
Past **years'** events (*P*) (*the events of past years*)
I need to give six **months'** notice. (*P*)
Sally's Gooseberry Jam (*P*)
Alice's Strawberry Jam (*P*)
The **boat's Simon's** [the boat's – (contraction of *boat is*) and Simon's – (possessive form of Simon, showing that the boat belongs to Simon) (*C, P*)
Young **People's** Services (*P*)
Thomas's room **isn't** at all tidy; **it's** a mess. (*P, C, C*)
This shop sells **children's** shoes. (*P*)

He is due to move up to Mrs **Morris's** class next year. (*P*)
Men's Captain (*P*)
Seniors' Captain (*P*)
Women's Captain (*P*)
Ladies' Captain (*P*)
Children's Captain (*P*)
Goat's meat (*P*)
Lamb's liver (*P*)
Susan's children's school is closing next year. (*P, P*)
It was his father **Bill's** car. (*P*)
The recipe is one of my mother **Anne's**. (*P*)
Jack is a friend of my **son's**. (*P*)
Millie was one of my daughter **Jane's** best friends. (*P*)
Mr and Mrs **James's daughter's dogs'** names are Tim and Sid (*P,P,P*)
Mr and Mrs **Fox's sons'** ages are 17 and 14 (*P,P*)
Tom's and Jerry's cartoon characters are brilliant (*P,P*)
Marion and Steve's house is a large extended bungalow (*P*)
She wrecked her husband **Alec's** car. (*P*)

The following are just as they are traditionally written:

- Mother's Day
- Father's Day
- Valentine's Day
- All Souls' Day

- St Patrick's Day
- April Fool's Day
- New Year's Day

And no apostrophe is needed in any of the following:

- CDs and DVDs (*not CD's and DVD's*)
- Hundreds of people
- The team played its best.
- Each of the divisions has its own recruitment policy.
- Everything is included in its plan.
- Please give me a demo to show me how the phone works.
- Shall we meet at the pub for lunch?
- One of our students fell ill on the morning of the exam.

12 – Explaining why the apostrophe is there

In this chapter I explain why the apostrophes are where they are in the correct examples that follow.

The film captures all the excitement of the young royals' nine-day tour.

The nine-day tour belongs to the young royals and, written in this way, *the young royals* needs an apostrophe to show that the nine-day tour belongs to them. The apostrophe is inserted after the "s" because there are two of them, that is, *royals* is a plural word. (See ch 1)

The film captures all the excitement of William and Kate's nine-day tour.

The nine-day tour belongs to William and Kate as a couple—they are treated as a single entity—which is why the apostrophe comes at the end of the couple's names. If there were several tours that William and Kate attended separately, then it would be written: "The film captures all the excitement of William's and Kate's tours". (See ch 7)

Michael's struggling to juggle his responsibilities.

In this example, the apostrophe is showing that there is a letter missing and two words have been contracted into one, ie *Michael is* struggling to juggle his responsibilities. (See ch 2)

Now it's time for the judges to vote.

Remember that an apostrophe in *its* means that it is either short for *it is* or *it has*. *Now it is time for the judges to vote*. (See ch 3)

It seems they're not being entirely honest.

The apostrophe here is showing that two words have been contracted into one and, if written in the longer form would be: *It seems they are not being entirely honest*. (See ch 2)

Within a few minutes' walk

This is saying: within a walk of a few minutes. When using the shortened form, minutes is then possessive and needs an apostrophe; the apostrophe goes after the "s" because *minutes* is a plural word. Other examples are: *in one day's time* or *in a few days' time*, ie time of one day or time of a few days. (See ch 1)

Fred is a friend of my father's

I apologise for this one, but this is a real anomaly and one that I don't understand the logic of myself. I would have expected that the correct way to write this would be *Fred is a friend of my father* but, having researched this extensively, it seems that this is the correct way to write it even though it appears to be a double negative. In its defence, we do say *Anne is a friend of mine* or *Stephen is a friend of his*, rather than *Anne is a friend of me* or *Stephen is a friend of him*. The way to avoid this is to say *Anne is my friend* and *Stephen is his friend*. But have you noticed the subtle difference in meaning? *Stephen is a friend of his* implies that Stephen is one of several of his friends, whereas *Stephen is his friend* does not imply the same meaning.

Consider this:

The recipe is one of my mother's, which is no doubt what we would say, but perhaps it is really a shortened way of saying, the recipe is one of my mother's recipes; this then makes sense.

Even though *Fred is a friend of my father's* is technically correct, it would appear that both *Fred is a friend of my father* and *Fred is a friend of my father's* are both accepted nowadays.

Appendix

(Actual apostrophe queries received and answers given since writing the first (e-book) edition of this book)

(Names have been changed where deemed appropriate.)

Q: *"All Year 11's are invited to a revision session". Please could you tell me whether year 11's has an apostrophe or not and the reasons why it does?*

A: This does not need an apostrophe because it is a straight plural. The only exception to this would be in a phrase such as, "Mind your p's and q's" because without the apostrophes it wouldn't make sense to the reader ie, "Mind your ps and qs". If you were to write, "Mind your Ps and Qs" then the meaning is clear and it should not have apostrophes. In your sentence, an apostrophe would be incorrect. The correct version is:
"All Year 11s are invited to a revision session."

Q: *When referring to multiple beneficiaries I understand that the singular "beneficiary" changes to "beneficiaries" but, if something belongs to those beneficiaries is an apostrophe required? For example "The best way to meet the beneficiaries needs..."*

A: The correct way to write this is "The best way to meet the beneficiaries' needs".

This is a shortened way of saying – "the needs of the beneficiaries". To make this plural word ie, beneficiaries, possessive you need to add just an apostrophe at the end because the word already ends in an "s". If the plural word did not end in an "s" eg, children, people, men, women, then these words would need an apostrophe in addition to an "s" to make them possessive ie, children's, people's, men's, women's. These words are treated as if they were singular words.

Q: *Parents views and childrens views?*

A: The plural of parent is parents and therefore the apostrophe goes after the "s" ie, parents' views – assuming that you are referring to the views of more than one parent. If, however, you are referring to the views of one parent, it would be parent's views, which normally would be preceded by "the" or "a".

The plural of child is children, without the "s", and therefore the apostrophe goes before the "s" ie, children's views.

So, when a plural ends in an "s", just add an apostrophe. When a plural does not end in an "s" ie, children, women, men, people, then you need to add an apostrophe and an "s" eg, women's, men's, people's.

Q: *I'm unsure of the apostrophe after the word girls in these sentences (the girls haven't done their homework) and (close the door of the girls cloakroom) is it girls'?*

A: In the first sentence – the girls haven't done their homework – the word "girls" is simply a plural and not possessive. It's the same as saying, for example, I haven't done my homework or they haven't done their homework. The word "girls" in this instance should not have an apostrophe.

In your second sentence – close the door of the girls cloakroom – "girls" in this instance is possessive and should have an apostrophe. It is the shortened way of saying, "close the door of the cloakroom of the girls. To make the word "girls" possessive, you should ask, "who does the cloakroom belong to?" The answer is "the girls"; the apostrophe goes immediately after the word that is the answer to that question ie, girls. If the cloakroom were referring to only one girl, then it would be "close the door of the girl's cloakroom".

Q: *(Writings difficult for some people) and (Buy your cucumber and lettuces here) - also whether they are omissions or possessions.*

A: "Writings difficult for some people" is a short way of saying "writing is difficult for some people". "Writings" is a contraction ie, where two words have been merged into one ie, "writing" and "is". Therefore, in the word "writings", the letter "i" is missing and it needs an apostrophe to show that a letter has been omitted. The correct way to write this is "writing's difficult for some people".

In the second sentence – buy your cucumber and lettuces here – the word lettuces is just a plural and is not possessive. Straight plurals ie, more than one of something, never have an apostrophe - an apostrophe should not be added to make something into a plural. The plural of lettuce is lettuces, and the plural of cucumber is cucumbers.

Q: *A current child care business operates under the name "A N Other Centre for Children". We are about to open a second premises and wish to change the business name to indicate the fact that there is more than one centre, i.e "A N Other Centres for Children", however there is some confusion as to whether an apostrophe is required after the s in centres or not.*

A: In this phrase, the word "Centres" is simply a plural and straight plurals do not need an apostrophe; in fact, to insert one would be incorrect. So, the correct way to write the name is: "A N Other Centres for Children" without an apostrophe. You would only need an apostrophe in the word "centres" if it were possessive.

Q: *learners development; the Academys behaviour policy - where do the apostrophes go for the words learners and academy?*

A: The first phrase depends on whether you are referring to just one or more than one learner. If you mean one learner, then the correct phrase is "learner's development", but if you mean more than one learner then it should be "learners' development". With a singular word, the apostrophe goes before the "s", and with a plural word it goes after the "s".

The second phrase is straightforward ie, "the Academy's behaviour policy" – the behaviour policy of the Academy. Again, as it is just one Academy then the apostrophe goes before the "s".

Q: *My order of preference is identical to Will's. I think this is correct, but does Will own his order of preference?*

A: Your sentence is really a short form of saying, "My order of preference is identical to Will's order of preference."

The clue to the answer to your question is in the "My order of preference" phrase, in that you own your order of preference simply denoted by the word "my". In the same way, Will owns his order of preference too and therefore the word Will's is possessive and is correct as you've written it.

Q: *Each party's commitments or each parties commitments? (there are 5 parties)*

A: The correct version is "Each party's commitments", even though there are 5 parties.

The word "each" is only used with one of something and in using the word "each" you are distinguishing between the commitments of the individual parties. Were you to say, for example, "the parties' commitments" (meaning the commitments of all the parties) then, as shown, the apostrophe would come after the "s" of "parties".

Q: *"...am I using correctly the apostrophe s in the following sentence?: 'supporting our communities' well being."*

A: If you are talking about more than one community, then your sentence is absolutely correct. However, if you were referring to just one community then the sentence would be "supporting our community's well-being".

Q: *Should it be:-*
(A) teacher's desk or
(B) teachers' desk

A: I am assuming the desk belongs to just one teacher. If this is correct, then it is (A) teacher's desk. If, however, the desk belongs to more than one teacher it would be (B) teachers' desk. The apostrophe comes before the "s" if you're referring to only one of something, and after the "s" when there's more than one.

Q: *Does this sentence need an apostrophe? "Time to order next years planner".*

A: This is really a shortened way of saying, "Time to order your planner for/of next year" and in the shortened form "next year" becomes possessive and therefore needs an apostrophe. As "next year" is singular, the apostrophe goes before the "s". The correct form is therefore "Time to order next year's planner".

Q: *Where to place the apostrophe in the following sentence? "A N Other won the viewers choice award."*

A: The award is the choice of the viewers, which means that the choice belongs to the viewers, making it possessive. Also, because there is more than one viewer, the apostrophe goes after the "s". The correct way to write this is: A N Other won the viewers' choice award.

Q: *Compiling a club Management Committee list. Mens Captain - where does apostrophe go? And do I need one for Ladies Captain?*

A: The correct way to write these is:

Men's Captain
Ladies' Captain

Regarding the men - ask yourself, who does the Captain belong or refer to? The answer is "the men" – the apostrophe goes immediately after whatever word is the answer to that question. Regarding the ladies - who does the Captain belong or refer to? The answer is "the ladies" – the apostrophe goes after whatever word is the answer to that question.

When a plural eg, "men" doesn't end in an "s", then you add an apostrophe followed by an "s". When a plural eg, "ladies" ends in an "s", you only need to add an apostrophe and no further "s".

Incidentally, were it to be women, instead of ladies, then it would be Women's Captain.

One more tip: try turning the phrase around to its longest form ie, Captain of the Men, Captain of the Ladies. Again the apostrophe goes after the word "Men" and after the word "Ladies".

Q: *Can you please advise me as to where the apostrophe (if any!) goes when I want to write 'merry christmas Olivers' meaning merry christmas to the Oliver's family! Is it just a plural?*

A: This is just a plural and "Merry Christmas Olivers" is entirely correct; there is no requirement for an apostrophe. I assume you are talking about the Olivers as a family, with the surname of Oliver. (Just as an aside – it would be "Merry Christmas to the Oliver family" rather than Oliver's family.)

Q: *What about when you are referring to parties. For example, the parties rights and conditions. Will it be the parties' rights and conditions?*

A: Yes, you are absolutely right – it would be "the parties' rights and conditions" because it's the rights and conditions of the parties.

Q: *I bought a cushion for friends stating "Christmas at the Kerr's" is this not correct?*

A: I will assume that the friends' surname is Kerr. The house belongs to the Kerrs (the plural of Kerr), which means it is the Kerrs' house.

When you say Christmas at the Kerrs' you are really saying Christmas at the Kerrs' house or home, but leaving off the word house/home. The correct way to write it is: Christmas at the Kerrs'.

Q: *Where does the apostrophe go in the following: Mens hat and Mans hat*

A: I think this one confuses many people, but ask yourself "who does the hat belong to?". The answers are:

men
man

The apostrophe goes immediately after whatever the answer to the question is; so it's men's hat and man's hat. Men, women and children are all treated in the same way ie, as if they were singular, rather than plural words, because they do not end in an "s". For example: men's shoes, women's clothing, children's books.

Answers to quizzes

Answers to introductory apostrophe quiz

1b) The people's vote
(Chs 1 and 4)

2a) Is this mine or yours?
(Ch 10)

3a) The man, whose car I crashed into, is my neighbour
(Ch 9)

4b) Jack is a friend of my mother's
(Ch 12)

5b) The boys were told the sweets were all theirs
(Chs 6 and 10)

6b) Two weeks' notice
(Ch 1)

7a) The men's wives went with them on the trip
(Chs 1 and 4)

8b) Where are the women's toilets?
(Chs 1 and 4)

9b) Who told you it's yours?
(Ch 3)

10a) Who's that man?
(Ch 9)

11a) Mr and Mrs Smith's house was burgled
(Ch 7)

12a) The Smiths' house is in darkness
(Ch 7)

13a) MOTs carried out here
(Chs 6 and 11)

14a) Whose bag is this?
(Ch 9)

15b) Mind your Ps and Qs
(Ch 6)

16a) The salad contained lettuces and tomatoes
(Ch 6)

17b) Which shoes? The red or the white ones?
(Ch 6)

18b) You're late!
(Ch 2)

19b) The dog has injured its paw
(Ch 3)

20a) Shall we go to the children's playground?
(Chs 1 and 4)

21a) I've been invited to Sue and Mark's wedding
(Chs 7 and 11)

22a) Don't forget your phone
(Ch 2)

23a) She was born in the '20s
(Ch 2)

24b) He was born in the 1920s
(Ch 2)

25a) Look where you're going!
(Ch 2)

26a) The rain's stopped
(Ch 2)

27a) Policemen's helmets
(Chs 1 and 4)

28a) Tell me it's not going to rain
(Ch 3)

29a) The company has expanded its product portfolio
(Ch 3)

30a) Women's shoes are next to the ladies' handbags
(Ch 4)

Answers to Its or It's quiz

1 a) It's time to go! *(It is time to go!)*

2 a) The dog's eaten its lunch

(The dog has eaten its lunch)

3 b) Let's not forget that it's only been a year

(Let us not forget that it has only been a year)

4 d) It's my job to safeguard its location

(It is my job to safeguard its location)

5 a) The project team achieved all of its deliverables

6 a) Unfortunately it's been taken out of my hands

(Unfortunately it has been taken out of my hands)

7 b) If it's genuine, where's its label?

(If it is genuine, where is its label?)

8 a) It's already been useful; it's worth its weight in gold

(It has already been useful; it is worth its weight in gold)

9 c) Poor baby - it's crying because it's dropped its teddy bear

(Poor baby – it is crying because it has dropped its teddy bear)

A final note

I sincerely hope that you find the answers to your apostrophe queries in this book – if not, please feel free to email your particular question to sfielding@commasense.co.uk and I will try to respond within a few hours. Then, once I've amassed another pile of queries, I'll write a third edition to update the contents of this book.

Glossary

Abbreviation
shortened form of a word, eg phone

Adjective
a word used to describe someone or something, eg small

Contraction
Where two words have been merged into one, eg can't, haven't

Plural
The form of the word meaning more than one, eg women, socks

Possessive
Is an adjective indicating possession as in "the possessive form of a word"

Singular
The form of the word meaning one of it, eg woman, sock

Bibliography

R L Trask, *The Penguin Guide to Punctuation*, Penguin Books, 1997

Lynne Truss, *Eats Shoots & Leaves*, Profile Books, 2003

Debra Hart May, *Proofreading Plain & Simple*, Career Press, 1997

E S C Weiner and Andrew Delahunty, *The Oxford Guide to English Usage*, Oxford University Press, 1994

Philip Gooden, *Who's Whose?* A & C Black Publishing Ltd, 2004

Caroline Taggart and J A Wines, *My Grammar and I*, Michael O'Mara Books Limited, 2011

Annette Lyon, *There, Their, They're,* Createspace, 2009

This book hopefully answers the apostrophe questions that you're unable to find the answers to elsewhere.

25437844R00052

Printed in Great Britain
by Amazon

Disney

Muziek

Disney
Educational Productions

RUBINSTEIN

COLOFON

TEKST BOEKJE Peter Smit
VORMGEVING Roel Siebrand

PRODUCTIE EN DISTRIBUTIE RUBINSTEIN PUBLISHING BV, AMSTERDAM ·

Het stokje van de dirigent

Als Mickey Mouse in **The Band Concert** het orkest leidt, heeft hij een stokje in zijn hand. Zo'n stokje heet 'dirigeerstokje'. Met dat stokje laat Mickey de muzikanten weten wanneer ze moeten beginnen en of ze luider, of juist zachter moeten spelen. Vroeger hadden orkestleiders geen stokje maar een staf, die ongeveer net zo groot was als de staf van Sinterklaas. Met zo'n staf gebeurde er een keer een ernstig ongeluk, dat de Franse componist en orkestleider Jean-Baptiste Lully het leven kostte. Toen een muzikant een fout maakte gaf Lully met zijn staf een harde klap op de vloer, ten teken dat het orkest moest stoppen. Helaas raakte hij zijn eigen voet en kreeg hij een lelijke wond. Die wond raakte ontstoken en een paar weken later stierf Lully aan bloedvergiftiging. De Franse koning Lodewijk de Veertiende was heel treurig om de dood van Jean-Baptiste Lully, die een goede vriend van hem was. Hij bepaalde dat de dirigeerstaf voortaan vervangen moest worden door iets kleiners, het dirigeerstokje. Dit gebeurde meer dan 300 jaar geleden, in 1687, en het stokje is nog steeds in gebruik.

Opdracht: ***een groot orkest bestaat uit tientallen muzikanten. Kun je een aantal instrumenten noemen die deze muzikanten bespelen?***

Klassieke muziek voor kinderen

Er is ook voor kinderen veel klassieke muziek geschreven. De bekendste drie van die muziekwerken zijn:

- *Peter en de Wolf*, van de Russische componist Sergej Prokovjev
- *De Tovenaarsleerling*, van de Franse componist Dukas
- *Het Carnaval der Dieren* van de Franse componist Saint-Saëns

De muziek van *De Tovenaarsleerling* werd beroemd door de tekenfilm die Walt Disney bij deze muziek maakte. Het verhaal is een oude legende over een tovenaarsleerling die alvast gaat toveren terwijl hij eigenlijk nog een heleboel moet leren. Dat gaat natuurlijk goed mis. In de tekenfilm is Mickey Mouse de tovenaarsleerling. Door zijn overmoed komt Mickey in allerlei gevaarlijke en spannende avonturen terecht. En door de muziek worden die avonturen nóg spannender! Gelukkig loopt het verhaal uiteindelijk goed af.

Opdracht: ***luister naar het laatste stukje van De Tovenaars-leerling van Dukas. Kun je aan de muziek horen dat het verhaal goed afloopt? En kun je vertellen hóe je dat hoort?***

Peter en de Wolf werd door Prokovjev geschreven omdat hij wilde dat kinderen wisten hoe de verschillende instrumenten apart klonken. Maar hij wilde daar ook een spannend verhaal bij vertellen. Prokovjev nam een oud Russisch volksverhaal, over een jongen die in zijn eentje het bos in gaat om een wolf te vangen. Als zijn grootvader merkt dat Peter weg is gaat hij hem zoeken, met de hulp van de andere jagers van het dorp. Prokovjev gaf elke persoon en elk dier een apart instrument. Peter wordt gespeeld door snaarinstrumenten, de wolf door blaasinstrumenten en de jagers door slaginstrumenten.

Opdracht: ***voorbeelden van snaarinstrumenten zijn een viool, een cello en een gitaar. Kun je een aantal blaasinstrumenten opnoemen?***

Het verhaal van *Het Carnaval der Dieren* is heel merkwaardig. De componist Camille Saint-Saëns was, net als Wolfgang Amadeus Mozart, een wonderkind dat al op zijn vierde concerten gaf. Toen Saint-Saëns al lang volwassen was, schreef hij speciaal voor zijn nichtje het *Carnaval der Dieren*. Het zijn korte stukjes over o.a. hanen en kippen, vissen, schildpadden, leeuwen, olifanten en kangoeroes. Ook over uitgestorven dieren (fossielen) schreef Saint Saëns een stukje muziek! Hij hield deze muziek geheim omdat hij bang was dat de mensen hem anders niet meer serieus zouden nemen. Pas na zijn dood werd de muziek voor het eerst voor publiek gespeeld en... het was meteen

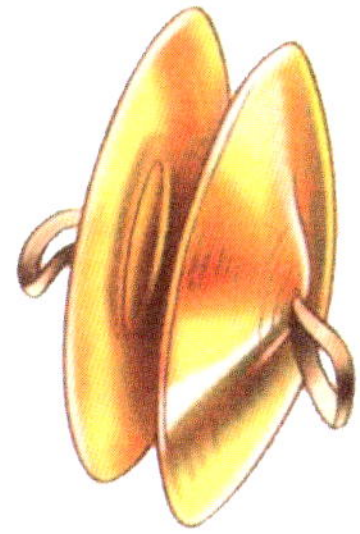

een groot succes! Tegenwoordig is het *Carnaval der Dieren* zelfs het meest bekende muziekstuk van Saint-Saëns.

Willem Tell, de held van Zwitserland

De *Ouverture Willem Tell* is geschreven door de operacomponist Gioacchino Rossini. Willem Tell was volgens het verhaal een Zwitserse boogschutter, die rond het jaar 1300 in opstand kwam tegen de wrede landvoogd Gessler. Deze landvoogd liet Willem Tell arresteren toen die weigerde om hem te groeten. Daarna bond de landvoogd de zoon van Willem Tell aan een paal en zette hij een appel op het hoofd van de jongen. Willem Tell moest vervolgens de appel met een pijl van het hoofd van zijn zoon schieten.
Toen dit lukte liet de landvoogd Willem Tell niet vrij, zoals hij eerder beloofd had. In plaats daarvan liet hij Willem Tell naar de gevangenis brengen, maar die wist onderweg te ontsnappen en begon een opstand om de landvoogd te verdrijven. Die opstand slaagde en Willem Tell werd de grote volksheld van Zwitserland.
Hoewel het niet zeker is of hij echt bestaan heeft zijn er veel boeken over Willem Tell geschreven. De Italiaanse componist Rossini las zo'n boek en besloot om van het verhaal een opera te maken. Het werd een 'opera buffa', wat 'vrolijke opera' betekent. En toen Walt Disney deze opera hoorde besloot hij om er een vrolijke tekenfilm van te maken!

Opdracht: ***bij welk bekend persoon zou jij muziek over zijn leven of avonturen willen maken? En voor welke soort muziek zou je dan kiezen (rap, pop, klassiek, jazz)?***

Maar niet voor Napoleon!

De beroemde Franse veldheer Napoleon inspireerde componist Ludwig van Beethoven voor het schrijven van zijn *Derde Symfonie*. Beethoven vond dat Napoleon in de landen die hij veroverde veel goede maatregelen invoerde. Maar toen Napoleon zichzelf tot keizer liet kronen was Beethoven heel teleurgesteld. Uit boosheid wilde hij de bladmuziek van zijn *Derde Symfonie* in het vuur gooien, maar dat werd verhinderd door zijn vrienden. Vervolgens droeg Beethoven de symfonie op aan 'Iemand die ooit een groot man was.'

Walt Disney, de held van de tekenfilm

Walt Disney was als kleine jongen al gek op tekenen. Zijn familie was heel arm, maar als hij eens een keer wat geld had kocht Walt meteen papier en potloden en tekende hij boerderijdieren en buurtkinderen na. Als Walt geen geld had, en dat was meestal, maakte hij met houtskool tekeningen op stukjes wc-papier! Na de lagere school nam Walt tekenlessen en ging hij voor een klein krantje spotprenten en stripverhalen tekenen. Hij ontmoette Ubbe Iwerks, een Nederlandse jongen die met zijn ouders naar Amerika was verhuisd. Ubbe wilde ook graag tekenaar worden en

ze besloten om samen tekenfilmpjes te maken. In het begin ging dat niet goed. Walt en Ubbe wilden het allemaal heel mooi doen, wat veel papier en inkt kostte zodat ze bijna niets met hun filmpjes verdienden.
Walt en Ubbe gingen twee keer failliet, maar telkens begonnen ze opnieuw. En in 1928, na tien jaar ploeteren, kregen ze dan toch succes. Ze maakten een paar tekenfilms met een figuurtje dat ze zelf hadden bedacht: Mickey Mouse.
Een jaar later was Mickey Mouse over de hele wereld beroemd en kochten miljoenen mensen kaartjes om de tekenfilms te zien. In 2008 wordt Mickey dus 80 jaar oud!

Edison, de uitvinder van de fonograaf

De bekendste uitvinding van Thomas Alva Edison was de fonograaf, het eerste apparaat waarmee je geluid kon opnemen en weer afspelen. Al een paar jaar na hij dit apparaat had uitgevonden werd de fonograaf overal gebruikt om muziek te laten horen. Artiesten gingen platen opnemen en hun fans kochten die platen met honderdduizenden. Vreemd genoeg had Edison, die zelf doof was, de fonograaf helemaal niet uitgevonden om er muziek mee op te nemen.
Het apparaat leek hem handig voor gebruik op kantoren en in rechtbanken. Met de fonograaf kon je de verhoren en de vergaderingen opnemen, zodat die dan later door een typist(e) konden worden uitgetikt.

Opdracht: ***na de fonograaf werden er verschillende andere systemen bedacht om muziek op te nemen en weer af te spelen. De laatste van die systemen is de MP3. Weet je nog een paar andere systemen die tussen 1900 en 2000 gebruikt werden om muziek mee af te spelen?***

Disney + Edison = Fantasia

Terwijl Walt Disney de tekenfilm steeds beter maakte, waren anderen bezig om de fonograaf van Edison te verbeteren. Er kwamen geluidsfilms in de bioscoop en toen dat geluid zo goed was dat je er klassieke muziek mee kon laten horen kreeg Walt Disney een idee. Hij wilde een tekenfilm maken waarin de nieuwste tekenfilmtechnieken en de nieuwste geluidstechniek te zien en te horen zouden zijn!

Deze experimentele tekenfilm heette *Fantasia* en verscheen voor het eerst in 1940. Bij muziek van componisten als Bach, Beethoven, Tsjaikovski, Dukas, Schubert, Stravinsky en Moussorgsky maakte de Disney-studio animaties met o.a. Mickey Mouse, dansende krokodillen, een berg die levend wordt en een optocht met lampionnen.

De film was een enorm succes en werd later nog 2x opnieuw uitgebracht. Een van de bekendste stukjes uit *Fantasia* is *De Tove-*

naarsleerling. Wie de leerling van de tovenaar is weet je al (Mickey Mouse), maar weet je ook hoe de tovenaar heet? Die heet Yen Sid, oftewel Disney achterstevoren!

Opdracht: ***weet je van de componisten die de in Fantasia gebruikte muziek maakten de voornamen te noemen?***

Dankzij de Eerste Wereldoorlog

Toen Walt Disney 17 jaar was ging hij in militaire dienst. In Europa was toen de Eerste Wereldoorlog aan de gang en Walt werd erheen gestuurd om mee te vechten. Toen hij een uur aan het front was werd het vrede en kon hij weer naar huis. Op de terugweg maakte Walt tekeningen van wat hij om zich heen zag en die tekeningen verkocht hij als souvenir aan andere soldaten. Het was de eerste keer dat Walt met tekenen geld verdiende en terug in Amerika besloot hij om tekenaar van beroep te worden.

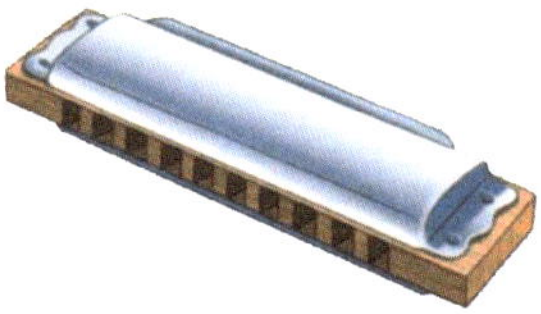

Een Franse pianist had minder geluk. Die raakte bij de gevechten zijn rechterhand kwijt. De Franse componist Maurice Ravel hoorde dit en vond het zó erg, dat hij meteen aan het werk ging. Hij componeerde een pianoconcert dat met de linkerhand gespeeld kon worden en noemde dit stuk dan ook: 'pianoconcert voor de linkerhand.' Het muziekstuk is nog steeds beroemd en staat op veel grammofoonplaten en cd's!

De compositie met de knal

De Russische componist Tsjaikovski schreef de *Ouverture 1812* uit vreugde over de overwinning van het Russische leger op Napoleon. Aan het slot van *Ouverture 1812* wordt een kanon afgevuurd. Bij uitvoeringen van dit muziekstuk in de openlucht wordt daarvoor wel eens een echt kanon gebruikt, maar dat gaat helaas ook wel eens mis. Zo vielen er in Canada veertig gewonden toen het kruit te vroeg ontplofte en een steekvlam het publiek in schoot...

Andere gebeurtenissen waar je een tekenfilm over zou kunnen maken:

- de Spaanse pianist Parejas Obregon wilde een zomerconcert geven, waarbij hij met zijn piano op een vlonder boven een rivier hing. Helaas schoot er meteen al bij het begin een kabel los, waardoor de piano, de pianist en de vlonder in het water vielen...
- de Engelse violist Peter Copper viel voorover toen hij een buiging voor het publiek maakte. Zelf mankeerde hij niets, maar zijn viool was doormidden. Die viool was een echte Stradivarius, die meer dan 400.000 Euro waard was...
- bij een concert in de Engelse stad York kwam halverwege de avond opeens een man in astronautenpak de zaal in die *Happy Birthday to You* begon te zingen. De man kwam van een felicitatiedienst en had zich in het huisnummer vergist...

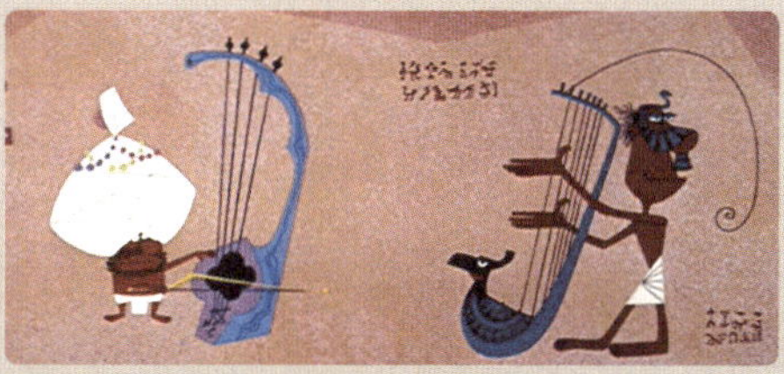

Mozart, het mega-wonderkind

Walt Disney begon al op zijn zesde jaar te tekenen, maar op die leeftijd was Wolfgang Amadeus Mozart al beroemd! Toen Mozart vier jaar was, kon hij al zo goed piano spelen dat mensen naar hem kwamen luisteren. En toen hij zes was, gaf hij een orgelconcert in de Duitse stad Wasserburg. Daarbij moest de kleine Mozart met zijn voeten op de pedalen van het orgel staan, omdat hij anders niet met zijn vingers bij de toetsen kon!

Toen Mozart negen was, schreef hij al zelf muziekstukken en had hij een Europese toernee door Frankrijk, Engeland, Duitsland en Nederland gemaakt. Mozart werd maar 35 jaar oud, maar bij zijn dood had hij meer muziekstukken geschreven dan componisten die meer dan tachtig werden, zoals Giuseppe Verdi, Richard Strauss en Igor Stravinsky!

Mozart en Beethoven

Mozart en Beethoven waren heel verschillende mensen. Mozart was altijd bezig met feestvieren en grappen uithalen, terwijl Beethoven juist altijd ernstig was en met iedereen ruzie maakte. Wel stierven zij allebei onder opvallende omstandigheden.

Mozart stierf terwijl hij het laatste stuk schreef van zijn beroemde

dodenmis, het Requiem. Toen Beethoven stierf klonk er opeens een zware donderslag, terwijl het verder helemaal niet onweerde.
Hun begrafenissen waren weer heel verschillend: bij Mozart waren er maar een paar mensen, bij Beethoven meer dan 30.000.

Roll over, Beethoven!

Over Mozart en Beethoven zijn later popsongs geschreven. De rock&roll-gitarist Chuck Berry had in 1956 een hit met *Roll over Beethoven* en de Oostenrijkse popmuzikant Falco had in de jaren '80 een hit met *Rock me, Amadeus*.
De Nederlandse popgroep Ekseption speelde in 1972 een stuk van Beethovens *Vijfde Symfonie*. Het werd een hit, maar veel Beethoven-liefhebbers werden er kwaad om. Toen een van hen zei: 'als Beethoven dit hoorde zou hij zich in zijn graf omdraaien' kreeg hij als antwoord: 'dan spelen we het nog een keer, dan ligt hij weer goed.'

Greensleeves, de hit van koning Hendrik

Vroeger werd de meeste muziek gemaakt in opdracht van koningen en andere edellieden. Er is ook een koning die zelf een bekend lied heeft gecomponeerd. Dat is de Engelse koning Hendrik de Achtste, die het lied *Greensleeves* schreef. Dit deed hij in het jaar 1530, toen hij verliefd werd op Anna Boleyn. Die liefde was snel afgelopen –

Anna Boleyn werd in 1536 in opdracht van Hendrik onthoofd – maar *Greensleeves* wordt nog steeds gespeeld. Het lied is door o.a. Rod Stewart, John Coltrane, Leonard Cohen, Enya en Jethro Tull op de plaat gezet.

Tekenfilmmuziek

Walt Disney is wereldberoemd geworden met zijn tekenfilms en zijn pretparken, maar hij heeft ook muziek gemaakt. Veel van de melodietjes die hij bedacht zijn in tekenfilms gebruikt. In Nederland zijn het geen hits geweest, maar in de Verenigde Staten hebben verschillende liedjes van Disney in de top tien gestaan. Wist je trouwens dat Walt Disney uit een familie van Franse ridders stamt? Oorspronkelijk heette die familie d'Isney en woonden ze in kastelen in Normandië. In het jaar 1066 trokken de Normandische ridders naar Engeland, waar ze een groot stuk land veroverden. Ze werden jammer genoeg geen koning. Anders zou de Mickey Mouse March door een andere Engelse koning zijn geschreven! Leuk om te weten is dat toen Walt Disney gevraagd werd om burgemeester van de stad Los Angeles te worden, hij als antwoord gaf: 'waarom zou ik burgemeester van Los Angeles worden als ik al koning ben van Disneyland?' Er zijn dus twee koningen die liedjes schrijven!

Aardappelmuziek

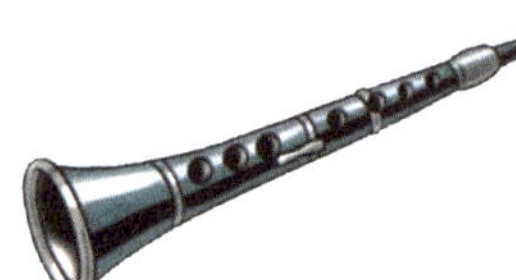

In de Amerikaanse stad New Orleans was het honderd jaar geleden mode om bij feesten een groepje jazzmuzikanten voor je huis heen en weer te laten lopen. Die jazzmuzikanten speelden dan op trompet of saxofoon en kregen daarvoor per persoon een of twee dollar.

Maar omdat veel mensen toen heel arm waren, liepen er ook wel eens mensen mee die helemaal niet konden spelen. Zo iemand heette een 'potato-man'. Potato is het Amerikaanse woord voor aardappel en als een potato-man een saxofoon te leen kreeg, werd daar eerst een aardappel in gestopt. Zo kon niemand horen dat de nepmuzikant eigenlijk geen noot kon spelen!

De Muzikant en de Oermensen

Toen de Duitse liederenschrijver Joachim Neumann succes kreeg vond hij zijn naam niet meer deftig genoeg. Hij liet zijn achternaam in 'Neander' veranderen en heette dus voortaan Joachim Neander. Hij stierf in het jaar 1680 en was toen zo beroemd dat de burgemeester besloot om een dal vlakbij het stadje voortaan 'Neanderthal' te noemen. Tweehonderd jaar later wist niemand meer wie Joachim Neander was, omdat zijn liederen uit de mode waren geraakt. Maar het naar hem genoemde dal werd wereldberoemd toen arbeiders daar de botten van een uitgestorven oermens vonden. Deze oermensen heten nu 'Neanderthalers', en zijn dus eigenlijk naar Joachim Neumann genoemd.